Also by Pierre Pevel:

The Cardinal's Blades

PIERRE PEVEL

THE ALCHEMIST IN THE SHADOWS

Translated by Tom Clegg

an imprint of **Prometheus Books**
Amherst, NY

Published 2011 by Pyr®, an imprint of Prometheus Books

Cover illustration © Jon Sullivan.

The right of Pierre Pevel to be identified as the author of this work and of Tom Clegg to be identified as the translator of this work has been asserted by them in accordance with the UK Copyright, Designs and Patents Act 1988.

Inquiries should be addressed to
Pyr
59 John Glenn Drive
Amherst, New York 14228–2119
VOICE: 716–691–0133
FAX: 716–691–0137
WWW.PYRSF.COM

15 14 13 12 11   5 4 3 2 1

Library of Congress Cataloging-in-Publication Data

Pevel, Pierre, 1968–
    The alchemist in the shadows / by Pierre Pevel.
        p. cm.
    Originally published: London : Gollancz, 2010.
    ISBN 978–1–61614–365–7 (pbk.)
    ISBN 978–1–61614–366–4 (e-book)
    1. Cardinals—France—Fiction. 2. Secret societies—France—Fiction. 3. Spies—Italy—Fiction. 4. Dragons—Fiction. I. Title.
PQ2716.E94A4313 2010
843'.92—dc22

                                                                            2010052052

Printed in the United States of America

This book is dedicated to Patrice Duvic,
who showed me the path

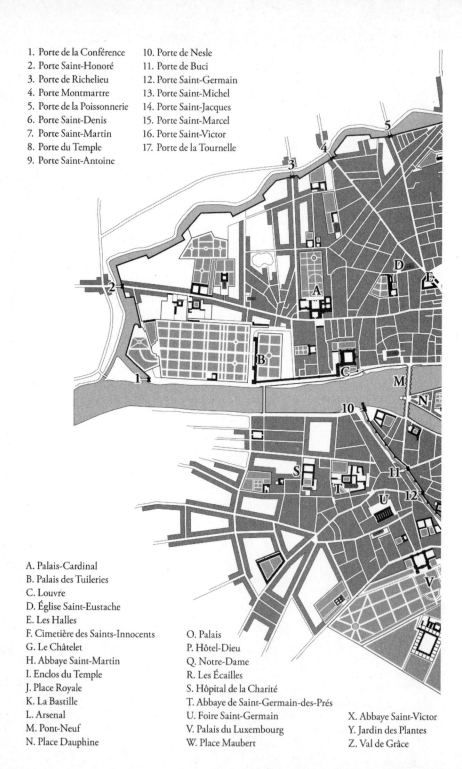

1. Porte de la Conférence
2. Porte Saint-Honoré
3. Porte de Richelieu
4. Porte Montmartre
5. Porte de la Poissonnerie
6. Porte Saint-Denis
7. Porte Saint-Martin
8. Porte du Temple
9. Porte Saint-Antoine
10. Porte de Nesle
11. Porte de Buci
12. Porte Saint-Germain
13. Porte Saint-Michel
14. Porte Saint-Jacques
15. Porte Saint-Marcel
16. Porte Saint-Victor
17. Porte de la Tournelle

A. Palais-Cardinal
B. Palais des Tuileries
C. Louvre
D. Église Saint-Eustache
E. Les Halles
F. Cimetière des Saints-Innocents
G. Le Châtelet
H. Abbaye Saint-Martin
I. Enclos du Temple
J. Place Royale
K. La Bastille
L. Arsenal
M. Pont-Neuf
N. Place Dauphine
O. Palais
P. Hôtel-Dieu
Q. Notre-Dame
R. Les Écailles
S. Hôpital de la Charité
T. Abbaye de Saint-Germain-des-Prés
U. Foire Saint-Germain
V. Palais du Luxembourg
W. Place Maubert
X. Abbaye Saint-Victor
Y. Jardin des Plantes
Z. Val de Grâce

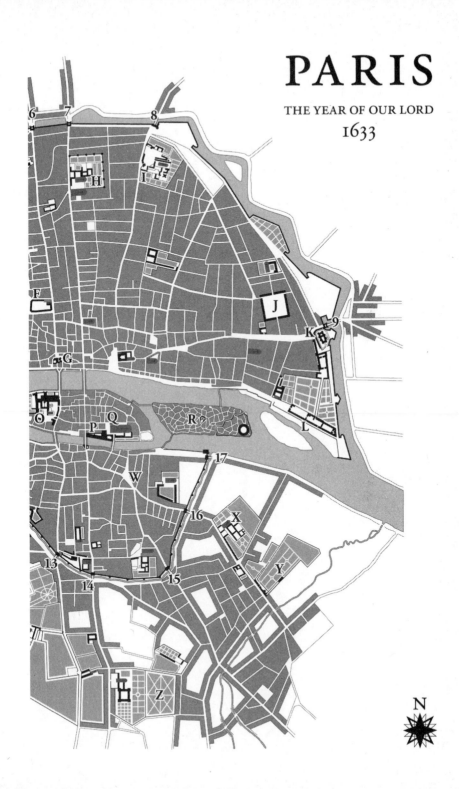

PARIS

THE YEAR OF OUR LORD

1633

N

PROLOGUE

JUNE 1633

It was that uncertain hour just before dawn, when the wind dies down and the mist begins to rise, the morning still a pale promise at the edge of night. A veil of dew already covered the countryside around the solitary manor, standing close to the border between Alsace and Lorraine. A great silence reigned beneath the long tattered clouds which lazed across a sky pricked with fading stars.

An elegant gentleman observed the manor from the edge of the nearby woods, watching the few lights that glowed within it. A mere shadow among the other shadows beneath the branches, he stood straight as a blade, his feet slightly spread, with his thumb tucked into his belt and one hand curled around the pommel of his sword. He was a tall handsome man. His name was François Reynault d'Ombreuse.

And today, in all likelihood, he would either kill a dragon or the dragon would kill him.

Behind the wall which protected the ruined manor and its outbuildings, mercenaries with tired, heavy eyes waited impatiently for the sun to rise. They leaned tiredly on their muskets or held up lanterns as they peered out into the lightening darkness, envying their sleeping comrades. They were soldiers of fortune, part of a band of thirty freebooters, who had fought and pillaged under various banners during the fifteen terrible years of war that had raged throughout the German principalities of the Holy Roman Empire. Now they had been hired to escort a quiet, pale-faced gentleman whose looks and manner impressed them more than they cared to admit. They knew nothing of him except that he paid well. As his entourage, they had crossed the Rhineland without ever pausing for long enough to unsaddle their horses, until they reached this manor. It had been abandoned for some time, but the thick outer wall and solid gate remained defensible. They had been camped here for two days now, at a safe distance from the roads and, most important, hidden from the Swedish and Imperial armies currently fighting for control of Upper and Lower Alsace. It seemed they would soon, secretly, cross into nearby Lorraine. Perhaps they would even visit France. But to what end? And why this halt?

François Reynault d'Ombreuse did not turn around when he heard someone come up behind him. He recognised the footstep of Ponssoy, a comrade-in-arms.

"They've even posted sentries out here, in this isolated place," Ponssoy said after counting the lanterns in the distance. "That's more than just cautious. . . ."

"Perhaps they know we're on their trail."

"How would they know that?"

Pursing his lips doubtfully, Reynault shrugged.

The two men served in the prestigious company of the Saint Georges Guards. They wore a half-cuirass for protection and were kitted out entirely in black: wide-brimmed black hats with black plumes, black cloth doublets and breeches, black gloves and boots made of tough leather, black belts and scabbards, and, last of all, black alchemical stones of shaped draconite which decorated the pommels of their rapiers. The sole exception to this martial mourning attire was the white silk sash tied about Reynault's waist, proclaiming his rank as an officer.

"It's almost time," Ponssoy finally said.

Reynault nodded and they turned away from the old manor, plunging back into the woods.

In a clearing, the twenty-five guards who formed Reynault's detachment prayed beneath the stars. They each placed one knee on the ground and one hand on the pommel of their sword, the other hand pressing their hat against their heart. They held a rapt silence, gathering their spirits before battle. They knew that they would not all live to see the sun set, but the prospect of such a sacrifice did not weigh heavily upon their souls.

Sœur Béatrice, also on her knees, faced the men. She belonged to the religious order they had sworn to serve, dedicated to defending France from the draconic menace. She was a Sister of Saint Georges, or a *Chatelaine*, as members of the order founded by Saint Marie de Chastel were commonly known. Tall, beautiful, and solemn, she was not yet thirty years of age. Although dressed in white, with a veil, her attire looked as much like a young horseman's as that of a nun. The heavy cloth of her immaculate robe concealed sturdy knee-boots and she had a leather belt cinched around her waist. She even carried a rapier at her side.

After a final amen the assembly stood and dispersed, just as Reynault and Ponssoy emerged from the trees. Ponssoy went over to join the guards, who wordlessly busied themselves with their final preparations: checking their weapons, helping one another with the straps of their breastplates, making sure the horses were correctly saddled, adjusting this, tightening that, taking all of the hundred precautions that prudence dictated but which also served to keep their minds occupied.

Meanwhile Reynault conferred with Sœur Béatrice. They had become well acquainted with one another over the past month, tracking the man now returning to France with the mercenaries he had recruited in the Holy Roman Empire. Their consultation was brief.

"He must not be allowed, at any cost, to regain his primal form," the Chatelaine emphasised. "Because if that happens—"

"If everything goes according to plan, he won't have time."

"Then . . . may the grace of God be with you, monsieur d'Ombreuse."

"And with you, sister."

A coughing fit woke the Alchemist.

Curled up on his straw mattress, he coughed until his lungs were raw. The fit was painful and it was some time before he could finally catch his breath and stretch out on his back, arms extended, his face glistening with sweat. The Alchemist—not his real name, but one by which certain people knew and feared him—felt worn out. His natural form was that of a dragon and his human body was causing him more and more suffering. He was struggling to keep the pain in check. He knew he was a monster, a monster whose flesh was tormented precisely because his true nature was rebelling against it. It was making regaining his primal form almost impossible for him. Each time it was an ordeal, a slow torture that threatened to kill him and whose aftermath left him feeling weaker still.

Outside, dawn was breaking.

The Alchemist sat up in bed, letting the blanket slip down his bony chest.

He was tall and thin, with an emaciated face of a morbid-looking pallor. His eyes were icy grey and his lips were vanishingly thin. He had slept in his clothes, in the room he had taken for his personal use when he and his mercenaries had installed themselves in this abandoned manor. They had already been encamped here for two days and nights, wasting precious time. Through his own fault. Or rather, the fault of the exhaustion and pain which prevented him from riding further. But he had recovered somewhat. Today they would resume their journey, tomorrow they would be in Lorraine, and soon after they would reach France where the Alchemist could pursue matters he had left neglected for far too long.

But right now . . .

Wracked by nausea he felt cold, then warm, and started to shiver.

The symptoms of deprivation.

For his apparent recovery was deceptive. He owed it entirely to the abuse of a certain liqueur, which caused him to burn with an evil fire that energised him even as it devoured him from within.

But wasn't the important thing to hold on and endure, whatever the price?

He turned on his side and, leaning on an elbow, stretched out a hand to a casket hidden near his boots, beneath an old rag. He opened it to reveal four large glass and metal flasks, each secured by leather straps. The first flask was already empty. The three others—one of which was already partly consumed—contained the precious liqueur distilled from henbane, a thick substance that resembled liquid gold.

As always, the first swallow was a delight.

The Alchemist let himself fall back onto the bed, a small smile on his lips. Eyes closed, he savoured the moment as much as he could. A warm, gentle feeling of well-being flowed into him, easing his suffering, lulling his soul. . . .

But loud cries suddenly broke the spell. The sentries outside had raised an alarm and their comrades were already responding to the threat. The Alchemist rose and went to the window, which was nothing more than a gaping hole that looked out over the manor courtyard and the surrounding countryside.

Horsemen. They were coming up the track leading to the manor at a gallop. Armed horsemen, led by a figure dressed in white.

The Alchemist immediately knew who he was dealing with. He also understood he was trapped in this manor, and it would not resist an assault for long.

He turned to the casket that lay next to the straw mattress.

Three flasks of golden henbane.

Enough to kill a man.

Enough to awaken a dragon.

The guards in black charged flat out, raising a cloud of dust that caught the first rays of the rising sun. The thunder of hooves made the ground shake. Reynault and Sœur Béatrice led the column. They rode side by side, their eyes fixed on the manor ahead, whose defence was being hurriedly organised. There were signs of movement, as hats and musket barrels appeared along the wall enclosing the courtyard. The Chatelaine unsheathed her sword and brandished the shining black blade, a blade made of draconite, high in the air.

The mercenaries shouldered their muskets and took aim. They knew their weapons had a range of one hundred and twenty paces and that it was best to let the enemy draw near before firing. So they waited.

The horsemen came on at a gallop, following the dusty track, three or four abreast. But what would they do when they arrived? They charged as if they saw an open gate before them. Yet both the heavy doors were closed tight and an old cart loaded with barrels full of earth had even been pushed behind them as reinforcement. Nevertheless, the guards came on at the same mad pace.

They were only two hundred paces away. At sixty, the mercenaries would start firing.

A hundred and fifty paces. The track ahead was a straight line. Her black sword still held aloft, the Chatelaine chanted an incantation in the draconic tongue.

A hundred paces. At any moment a hail of lead would mow down the front ranks of riders, felling both men and beasts whose bodies would in turn force those behind them to tumble.

Seventy-five. Sœur Béatrice was still chanting.

Sixty. The mercenaries were about to open fire. . . .

But at the very last second, the Chatelaine screamed a word full of power. Her blade shone with a sudden light and the twin doors of the manor gate shattered into splinters. The explosion was tremendous. It shook the walls, made the ground vibrate, and flung the cart and its barrels into the air. It killed, wounded, or stunned the mercenaries posted on either side of the gate and left the remaining defenders in shock, deafened by the blast and blinded by the cloud of dust.

The riders did not slow. They burst into the courtyard, firing their short muskets. Some of their enemies responded with their longer guns. Musket balls whizzed back and forth, striking their targets. One of them ricocheted off Reynault's breastplate. Another ripped off his hat. He dismounted, drew his sword and shouted curt orders to his troops. All around him, close-quarters combat broke out. Sœur Béatrice remained close by his side.

"WHERE?" he shouted over the din of yelling men and clashing weapons.

She seemed to search around and then pointed to the main building.

"THERE!" she cried.

"WITH ME!" Reynault commanded as he leapt forward.

He was immediately followed by Ponssoy and a few others who surrounded the Chatelaine. She knew how to fight, but it was her powers that could save them all as a last resort. Her survival was crucial.

Muskets appeared at the windows of the large manor house and began to blast away. One of the guards crumpled. Despite his loss, Reynault and the rest of his group nonetheless managed to reach the main entrance. It was barricaded shut—they would have to force their way inside. Someone found a beam to use as a battering ram and with each successive blow the twin doors shivered, then began to crack a little more every time. But they still held.

"Faster!" urged the Chatelaine, a fearful expression on her face. "Faster!"

The doors gave way at last. Reynault and his men rushed inside, charging straight into the mercenaries who greeted them with a murderous volley of musket fire. Several guards fell. Ponssoy was seriously injured and Reynault's thigh was pierced right through, although he paid the wound no heed. A furious melee broke out, in which even the Chatelaine took part. She and Reynault attempted to force a passage through the combatants, until she finally placed a hand on the lieutenant's shoulder.

He turned to her.

"Too late," she said in a quiet voice which he nonetheless heard perfectly clearly.

A dull rumble came from somewhere within the house. The stone floor slabs in the great manor hall began to tremble.

Reynault realised what was happening.

"RETREAT!" he shouted. "RETREAT! RETREAT!"

Carrying their wounded and fending off the mercenaries still pressing them, Reynault and his group hastily withdrew. The whole building was now vibrating, as if shaken by an earthquake. Its foundations began to sag. Tiles fell from the roof. The stones in the walls came loose.

Suddenly a whole section of the façade collapsed.

"Lord God, have mercy on us!" the sister murmured.

Around her, guards and mercenaries were locked in a confused mass, all of them speechless with terror.

A great black dragon emerged from the manor amid a cloud of plaster and a cascade of debris. Immense in size, it reared up and unfurled its leathery wings with a tremendous roar. A surge of power swept through the courtyard, a wave that churned the earth, toppling the men and causing the horses to bolt.

Only the Chatelaine, her white clothing flapping in the storm, managed to stay on her feet. Holding her black-bladed rapier in her right hand she spread her arms wide and began chanting again. The dragon seemed intrigued by the insignificant creature standing before it, somehow capable of summoning a power comparable to its own. It lowered its enormous head to peer at the sister, who continued her incantation without faltering. She chanted words in a language which found an echo in the dragon's brain—a brain dominated by brutal, primitive impulses, but not entirely devoid of intelligence.

Sœur Béatrice knew it was too late. She had failed. Now that the Alchemist had recovered his primal form there was nothing she could do to vanquish—or even restrain—the most powerful adversary she had ever encountered.

But there was one last card she could play.

Looking straight into the terrible depths of the dragon's eye, she gathered her remaining strength and plunged into the huge creature's tormented mind. The effort she had to make was both colossal and perilous. But after several false attempts, she finally found what she was searching for. The vision struck her soul like a fist.

For the space of one brief, yet seemingly eternal, moment the Chatelaine could *see*.

She saw the cataclysm threatening France, both her people and her throne, a cataclysm that would soon become a reality played out beneath ragged skies. It left her terrified, awed, and gasping, while the dragon—having been defeated in the very core of its being—screamed with rage before taking to the air and escaping with a few mighty beats of its wings.

LA DONNA

1

Beneath the dripping boughs of a forest which, on this dark night, was being buffeted by the wind and downpour of a violent storm, two young dragonnets were playing. They squabbled as they flew, heedless of the weather, chasing one another, spinning and fluttering in midair, improvising virtuoso acrobatics among the branches. The little reptiles were fighting over a small vole they had hunted down together, whose mauled remains were snatched from one mouth to the other in the course of their unruly game. They were brother and sister, both born from the same egg and thus perfectly similar, sharing the same golden eyes, the same scarlet-fringed black scales, the same grey belly, and the same slender, elegant profile.

And the same intelligence, too.

Growing tired of their play, the twins finally settled on a knotty root where they were sheltered from the worst of the rain. They shook themselves, and then folded up their leather wings. Pulling from either side, they tore the rodent in two and devoured it peacefully together. The darkness lay thick around them and, when the thunder ceased, the only sounds in the forest came from the rain, the wind, and the battered foliage. Yet something interrupted the dragonnets' meal. Something only they could perceive. Something that made them rear up sharply and captured their complete attention.

They remained frozen in place for an instant, like a pair of small onyx statues gleaming wet from the rain. They had to be sure they were not mistaken, that there was no danger of misinforming their mistress, and thus risk incurring her anger or, worse still, losing her affection. But there was no mistake. So they roused themselves and exchanged nervous growls before taking wing, the male vanishing into the shadows of the vast forest while his sister flew toward the source of their interest. She moved swiftly, weaving between the tree trunks and seeming to take pleasure in dodging them at the very last moment, only finally slowing when she recognised the sound of voices. She found herself a comfortable perch in the hollow of a tree . . .

. . . where she did not have very long to wait.

There were riders approaching.

* * *

There were three of them, following a muddy trail beneath the rivulets of rain-water cascading down through the forest canopy. Soaked to the skin, they plodded along in the haloes cast by the lanterns hanging from their saddles. These did not shed much light, but at least, between the flashes of lightning, allowed them to make out the puddles disturbed by their horses' heavy hooves.

Saint-Lucq led the way. Behind him, Captain Étienne-Louis de La Fargue endured the rain with perfect stoicism, as it spattered his aging, patriarchal features: pale eyes, handsome wrinkles, martial bearing, grim mouth, closely trimmed beard, and firm jaw. Tall and solidly built, he was wearing a sleeve-less vest over his doublet, which was made of leather thick enough to stop a musket ball fired from a distance, or even deflect a clumsy sword stroke. It was black, as were this old gentleman soldier's breeches, boots, gloves, and hat. As for the doublet, it was the same dark red as his baldric and the sash tied around his waist, knotted over his right hip.

Black and red . . .

They were, once again, the colours of the Cardinal's Blades, now they had been secretly recalled to service by Cardinal Richelieu.

"Are we even still in France?" Almades asked, with a trace of a Spanish accent.

Anibal Antonio Almades di Carlio, to give him his full name, rode slightly behind and to La Fargue's left, ready to draw level with a dig of his spurs and protect the flank that a right-handed cavalier would have difficulty defending. Thin and austere looking, he sported a fine greying mustache that he occasionally wiped dry—always thrice each time—with his thumb and index finger. He sat straight in the saddle, his waist snugly fitted into a red-slashed black leather doublet, and he was armed with a Toledo rapier whose guard consisted of a full hemispherical shell and two long straight quillons. Made of tarnished steel, this duelling sword offered no concessions to aes-thetic values whatsoever.

"I doubt it," La Fargue said to the Spanish fencing master. "What do you think, Saint-Lucq?" he enquired in turn, raising his voice against the din of the wind and the rain in the branches.

He knew the young man had heard him despite the distance between them. Saint-Lucq took the lead precisely because he heard—and saw—better than any common mortal.

Because he was no common mortal.

Saint-Lucq was a half-blood. The blood of dragons ran in his veins. With his slender, supple figure, smooth cheeks, and shoulder-length hair, his ancestry endowed him with enhanced senses, superior athletic abilities, and a personal charm that was both seductive and disturbing. He certainly had an allure, but there was also something dark emanating from him, with his silences, his long stares, his slow measured gestures, and his proud reserve. This darkness was heightened by the fact that he only wore black and, on him, the colour was associated more than ever with death. He only permitted two exceptions: the thin red feather in his hat and the lenses—also red—of the small round spectacles which hid his reptilian eyes. Otherwise everything, even the fine basket guard of his rapier, was black.

"We are in Spain," the half-blood declared without turning round.

They were five leagues from Amiens and had already reached the Spanish Netherlands, which began just beyond Picardy, comprising the ten Catholic provinces that had remained loyal to the Spanish Crown when the lands further north controlled by the Calvinists seceded to form the Dutch republic. The province of Artois, along with the towns of Arras, Cambrai, Lille, Brussels, Namur, and Antwerp, were thus all part of the territory of Spain, a power that was hostile to France and jealous in her exercise of full sovereignty. Spanish troops were garrisoned there and guarded the border, only a few days' march from Paris.

"This storm works in our favour," said La Fargue. "Without it our lights might be seen by a Spanish wyvern rider. They fly over this area every hour, when weather permits."

"So all we have to do is avoid the ordinary patrols," Almades observed wryly.

"Let's hope the person waiting for us had the same bright idea," the old captain replied in a more serious tone. "Or else we'll have come all this way for nothing."

Ahead of them, Saint-Lucq slowly turned his head to the left as his horse advanced at the same steady pace. He'd just spotted the dragonnet spying on them from the shadows, and he wanted to leave it in no doubt as to the fact. Intrigued at first, the young female craned her neck to peer out at him from her tree hollow. Keeping her golden eyes fixed on the half-blood as he passed, she tilted her head slowly to one side, then to the other. Could he really see her? Finally, when she was certain that the rider with the strange red spectacles was staring right back at her, she growled at him in hatred and fury before taking flight from her hiding place.

La Fargue and Almades both reacted to the sound of wings flapping swiftly through the forest and, thanks to a flash of lightning, they caught a brief glimpse of the small reptile as she sped away.

Saint-Lucq, expressionless, turned his gaze back to the trail ahead.

"We're almost there," he announced, just before the roll of thunder came.

The storm was still in full fury when the trail began to gradually slope upward and led the riders to the crown of a hill, where a large building could be seen emerging from the treetops, like an island in a sea of tossing boughs. It was a former inn which had been abandoned after being partially destroyed in a terrible fire. The windows were boarded up, the roof tiles rattled, and the inn's illegible sign swung wildly in the gusting wind and rain. An old wall surrounded the courtyard and a well. Only a few charred vestiges remained of the stables, evidently the starting point of the blaze.

The riders passed beneath a stone arch and crossed the courtyard, halting in front of the inn. They cast wary glances at their surroundings, and although they had extinguished their lanterns they still felt exposed out here in the open, beneath the turbulent sky. Remaining in their saddles, all three could see the wavering light coming from behind the boards nailed across a window on the upper floor.

"She's already here," La Fargue observed.

"I don't see her mount," Almades replied.

"Neither do I," added Saint-Lucq.

The old captain stepped down from the saddle into a mud puddle, and gave his orders: "Almades, with me. Saint-Lucq, keep watch out here."

The half-blood nodded and turned his horse around. Almades dismounted as La Fargue, always cautious, loosened his rapier in its scabbard. The weapon was well matched with its owner, being both solid and quite long: a Pappenheimer, named after the German general who had equipped his cavalry corps with it. La Fargue had put its qualities to the test—and had sometimes been tested by it himself—on battlefields in Germany and elsewhere. He appreciated its robust strength and long reach, as well as the guard with its multiple branches and the openwork shell that protected his hand.

The dark, cluttered ground floor of the inn smelled of old soot and wet wood. It was impossible to move without stepping over pieces of debris or making the floorboards creak alarmingly, as if they might give way at any moment. The wind whistled through the gaps between the planks that had been crudely nailed across the windows. A single lit candle had been placed on the lowest step of the staircase leading to the upper floor, the flame guttering in the draughts.

"Wait here," ordered La Fargue before climbing the stairs alone.

Obeying with some reluctance, Almades unsheathed his rapier and took up vigil below.

At the top of the stairway, the old gentleman found a long corridor with a second candle burning at the end, placed on the worm-eaten lintel of a half-opened door. Other doors—which led into the bedchambers—also lined this hallway. But the door at the end, in addition to being lit, was the only one which was not closed.

Since the way had been so kindly shown to him, La Fargue advanced toward the light. He trod carefully, however, keeping a cautious eye on each door as he passed, his hand resting on his sword. . . .

There were leaks in the ceiling, and in places, he could hear rain pattering in the attic, directly over his head. The roof must have split wide open, although neither he nor his men had noticed this when they arrived, but a section of it was invisible from the courtyard and could have been missing as far as they knew, not having made a point of inspecting it.

La Fargue stopped in front of the door indicated by the candle.

"Come in, monsieur," said a charming feminine voice.

A scraping could be heard through the racket of the storm, coming from just beneath the rafters. There was a peal of thunder at almost the same instant, but the sound did not escape the keen ears of the captain, who pondered for a moment, understood its meaning, and smiled to himself. And as if to confirm his suspicions, he then detected the clinking of a chain.

He entered.

This room had been spared by the fire, but not by the ravages of time. Dusty and decaying, it was lit by a dozen candles placed here and there. A large bed, of which only the frame and cabled columns remained, took up almost the entire space. At the rear was a door whose outer corner was bevelled to fit against the sloped ceiling just beneath the roof. Tattered curtains swayed before a window with broken panes. Planks had been nailed across it from within, but one of them had been ripped away recently. La Fargue understood why when he saw a dragonnet wend its way into the room from outside.

After shaking its dripping wings dry the small reptile leapt onto the wrist held out by a beautiful young woman who, turning to the old gentleman, greeted him in a friendly fashion.

"Welcome, monsieur de La Fargue."

She was perfectly poised and elegant, wearing a grey hunting outfit composed of a jacket that clasped her waist prettily and a heavy skirt that was hitched up on the right to allow her to ride in a saddle like a man. Her attire was completed by a pair of hose, a hat tilted coquettishly over one eye, and gloves that matched her fawn leather boots.

"Madame."

"You can't imagine, monsieur, my pleasure in meeting with you."

"Really?"

"Of course! Do you doubt it?"

"Yes. A little."

"And why is that?"

"Because my orders could be to arrest you and bring you to France to be tried. And in all likelihood, be convicted."

"Are those your orders, monsieur?"

La Fargue did not reply. Impassive, he simply waited.

He was nearly sixty years old, a more than respectable age in a century when anyone over forty was considered elderly. But if ordeals, battles, and grief had turned his hair white and left his eyes dull from lost illusions, time had not yet stripped him of his vigour and personal aura. Tall and wide-shouldered, with a proud, confident bearing, the old gentleman remained impressive both in his figure and in the strength that emanated from him— and he knew it. He deliberately resorted to silence rather than words to impose his will on others.

Standing before him, the young woman seemed small and fragile. She met his eyes for a moment, without blinking, and then, quite casually, pointed to a small table and two stools.

"I wager that you have not supped. You must be famished. Sit, please. You are my guest."

La Fargue took a stool and, as she busied herself with preparations, he was able to look more closely at this woman playing the role of hostess. She was a pale-skinned, red-headed beauty with delicate features, finely drawn lips, a charming smile, and dark, lively eyes. But the old gentleman was aware of the danger lurking behind this pretty face and innocent air. Others before him had learned that lesson to their bitter cost. The she-devil was cunning and had few scruples. And she was said to be a mercenary at heart.

With her dragonnet perched on her shoulder, she brought over a heavy wicker basket, removed the cloth covering it to dress the table, and arranged various victuals between the captain and herself, setting a porcelain plate, a fine-cut glass, and a knife with a mother-of-pearl handle before each of them.

"Would you pour the wine?" she proposed.

Readily enough, La Fargue took the bottle he saw poking from the basket, removed the wax stopper, and tipped the layer of oil that protected the wine from contact with the air out onto the floor.

"What should I call you?" he asked as he filled the glasses.

The young woman, who was amusing herself by feeding titbits to her dragonnet, paused and gave La Fargue a puzzled glance.

"I beg your pardon?"

"What is your name, madame?"

She shrugged and smiled as if he were jesting with her.

"Come now, monsieur. You know who I am."

"To be sure," allowed La Fargue. "But of all the names you have employed in the service of France, England, Spain, and the Pope, which do you prefer?"

She stared at him for a long moment and her eyes grew cold.

At last, she replied: "Alessandra. Alessandra di Santi."

She nodded with her chin at the glass which the old gentleman had not yet raised to his lips. "Aren't you drinking? The wine is from Beaune, and I believe it to be to your liking."

"Indeed."

"So?"

La Fargue gave a drawn-out sigh of restrained impatience.

"Madame, a short while ago you asked about my orders. Here they are: I am to hear you out and then report your words to His Eminence. So speak, madame. My men and I rode for ten hours, almost without a break, in order to meet you here, now. And I am anxious to leave again soon. Even in Artois, the Spanish climate does not suit my health. . . ."

And having said this, he lifted his glass and drained it in a single gulp.

Then he added: "I am listening, madame."

Thoughtful for a moment, Alessandra watched the old gentleman who was proving so immune to her charms. She knew he found her ravishing, yet her beauty inspired him with no need to please her in return. It was unusual in a man, and merited further study.

Outside the storm continued to rage. The intervals between lightning flashes and the resulting thunder seemed to be diminishing.

"I see that you have a poor opinion of me, monsieur de La Fargue," the young woman said in a provocative tone.

"My sentiment toward you is of no importance, madame."

"Come now, captain. What do you think of me? In all frankness."

La Fargue paused for a moment, aware that Alessandra was trying to control their conversation. Then he said: "I know that you are both intelligent and skillful, madame. But I also know that you are venal. And lacking in scruples."

"So you don't believe I am capable of loyalty. . . ."

"Only if you use the word in the plural form. Because your loyalties, madame, have been many in number. No doubt they still are, even if none of them will ever force you to act against your own interest."

"So in short, you don't believe me worthy of confidence."

"That's correct, madame."

"And what if I were to tell you that I have some knowledge of a plot?"

La Fargue raised an eyebrow.

"I would ask you whom this plot threatens, madame."

The pretty redhead smiled. She raised her glass to her charming lips, took a sip of wine, and then declared with utmost solemnity: "I have knowledge of a plot, monsieur. A plot that threatens the throne of France and whose scale goes beyond anything you can conceive."

The old captain gazed directly into Alessandra's eyes, which remained quite calm. She did not blink, not even when lightning struck so close that the inn shook.

"Do you have so much as a shred of proof to support your claim?" he asked.

"Obviously. However—"

"What?"

"However, I'm afraid I cannot proceed any further without some guarantees . . . from the cardinal."

"What do you want?"

"I demand His Eminence's protection."

La Fargue stared impassively at the young woman before rising to leave. "Goodbye, madame."

Alessandra leapt to her feet.

"Wait! Monsieur, wait!"

Was that a hint of fear in her eyes?

"I beseech you, monsieur. . . . Do not take leave in this manner. Grant me just one more moment. . . ."

La Fargue sighed.

"Is it truly necessary, madame, to inform you that the cardinal is as miserly in giving his protection as he is in giving his trust, that he only grants them to those who are deserving of them, or that you would need to provide much more than this if you wish to become one of their number? Come now, madame, think! Remember who you are! And ask yourself—"

At that moment a second dragonnet, identical to the first, entered by way of the missing plank at the window. Very nervous, it shook its wings and emitted a series of piercing cries intended for its mistress.

She listened to them, and then spoke quickly: "We must part now, captain. Riders are approaching along the same path by which you came. They shall be here soon, and it would be best if they did not find me."

"Who are these riders?"

"You shall make their acquaintance soon enough. They are one of the reasons that press me to demand the cardinal's protection."

"Abandon this foolish notion, madame. His Eminence will never—"

"Give him this."

She removed a thick sealed letter from her sleeve and held it out to La Fargue.

"What is this?"

"Take this letter to the cardinal, monsieur. It contains . . . it contains the shred of proof you just demanded. . . . When the cardinal opens it, he will see I am not inventing tales but that the throne of France is truly under threat."

They heard Almades call from below.

"Captain!"

La Fargue opened the chamber door a crack and saw the Spanish fencing master coming up the stairs at the far end of the corridor.

"Riders, captain."

"How many?"

"According to Saint-Lucq, at least five."

Behind La Fargue's back, the dragonnet uttered a brief hoarse cry. Already, whinnying could be heard outside.

"Seven," Alessandra informed them in a calm voice. "There are seven of them."

"Stay right here!" the old gentleman commanded over his shoulder.

He left the chamber, closing the door behind him, and entered a neighbouring room where Almades joined him. Through a gap between the planks in the window, they saw seven armed riders come charging into the courtyard.

"Where is Saint-Lucq?" asked La Fargue.

"Down below. He's the one who saw the riders coming."

"Damn it all!"

Leaving the Spaniard standing there, he returned to the chamber at the end of the corridor.

It was empty.

"*Merde!*"

But the little door at the rear was standing half open.

Behind it, some very steep stairs led to the attic. La Fargue climbed them and, pushing through a trap door, he rose up into the deafening fury of the storm. As he had guessed, a portion of the roof was missing leaving the attic open to the sky, directly exposed to the weather. And there he saw Alessandra, already in the saddle, struggling to force a wyvern to turn toward this exit. Its wings spread to keep its balance, the great reptile was resisting, digging its two clawed feet into the floor. It was frightened by the storm.

"THIS IS MADNESS!" the old gentleman shouted.

Keeping a firm grip on the reins that ran along the wyvern's neck to the bit in its mouth, the young woman smiled confidently at the captain.

"WORRY INSTEAD ABOUT THE PLOT AND PLEAD MY CASE WITH HIS EMINENCE! YOU MUST BELIEVE ME AND, IN TURN, THE CARDINAL MUST BELIEVE YOU. . . . BE PERSUASIVE! THE FUTURE OF FRANCE DEPENDS ON IT!"

"RENOUNCE THIS MATTER, MADAME!" La Fargue insisted, just before a blast of wind almost knocked him over.

Lightning was striking ever closer. Not far from the inn, a tree had burst into flame.

"INFORM THE CARDINAL. WE SHALL MEET AGAIN SOON, IN PARIS."

"WHERE? HOW?"

They could barely hear one another, even shouting at the top of their lungs.

"TOMORROW EVENING. DON'T WORRY. I KNOW HOW TO FIND YOU."

"MADAME!"

Alessandra's wyvern launched into the air and was already flying away into the storm, trailed by the fluttering silhouettes of the twin dragonnets.

La Fargue cursed, powerless to stop her. Then, remembering the riders, he went back down into the inn. Almades followed in his wake as he passed. They reached the ground floor and emerged into the courtyard that was now one immense, slippery mud puddle beneath the deluge of rain.

* * *

His back to the door, Saint-Lucq was facing seven horsemen who, forming an arc, had dismounted and drawn their swords. Clearly expecting trouble, they were dressed for combat, wearing wide hats, thick leather doublets, rough breeches, and riding boots.

Beyond that, they were not human.

They were dracs, La Fargue realised, as a flash of lightning gave him a glimpse of the nightmarish scaly, jowled faces beneath the dripping brims of their hats. Worse still, they were black dracs.

Dracs had been created long ago by the Ancestral Dragons to serve and fight for them. In time they had freed themselves from the tutelage of their creators, but they remained cruel, brutal beings who were rightly to be feared. Dracs enjoyed violence. They were stronger and tougher than men. And black dracs were even stronger and tougher than the ordinary kind.

"We're here, Saint-Lucq," said La Fargue from the doorway, moving forward.

Without turning round or looking away from the dracs, the half-blood took two steps to his right. The captain occupied his place while Almades covered their left. The trio had their swords in hand, but still waited before placing themselves *en garde*.

La Fargue noticed that the dracs stood in a pool of black mist that rose to their ankles and did not disperse.

Sorcery, he thought to himself.

"The woman!" the drac facing him snarled in a hoarse whistling voice. "We want the woman!"

He was the biggest and most muscular of the seven, which had no doubt earned him the right of command. His face was marked with bright yellow lines that followed the contours of certain facial scales to form complex, symmetrical patterns that La Fargue recognised.

"Impossible," he declared. "She is no longer here."

"Where is she?"

"Gone. She flew away."

"What?"

While La Fargue devoted his attention to the leader, Saint-Lucq and Almades were watching the six others. The dracs were tense and nervous, obviously making an effort to contain the desire for battle that consumed them. They were almost quivering, like starved dogs forbidden from throwing themselves upon a scrap of bloody meat. Only their fear of their chief held them back. They waited for the order, gesture, or pretext that would unleash them.

"She had a wyvern," La Fargue explained. "You brought the wrong mounts."

"Who are you?"

"Someone hunting the same game as you. But I arrived too late."

"You lie!"

Saint-Lucq had his eye on one drac—younger and more impetuous than the rest—who was struggling to control his aggressive impulses and twitched with each peal of thunder. The half-blood imagined the desire to hurt and to kill eating away at him like acid. The tiniest thing, probably, would suffice to . . .

"Do you really think so?" La Fargue replied to the drac leader. "Do you believe this woman only has one enemy?"

"Who do you serve?"

"That's none of your business. Even so, I could answer if you tell me who your master is. . . ."

The young drac who had attracted Saint-Lucq's attention could by now barely contain himself. His head was drawn in, his jaws were clenched, and he was breathing hard. His glance crossed that of the half-blood, who, with a thin smile on his lips, dipped his own head slightly to stare directly at him above his red spectacles.

"There are seven of us, old man," the drac leader observed. "And only three of you. We can kill you all."

"You can try, but you shall be the first to fall. And for what? For a woman who is long gone, if the storm hasn't already brought her wyvern down. . . ."

As if hypnotised, the young drac couldn't take his eyes off Saint-Lucq. He was filled with a boiling rage and the dracs on either side of him were aware of it. They didn't understand the cause but they, too, started to become agitated.

Then the half-blood supplied the final trigger: a discreet wink and a blown kiss.

The young drac screamed with rage and attacked.

Saint-Lucq easily dodged him, inflicting a nasty sword cut to the face as his opponent charged past. That could have been the signal all had been dreading or hoping for. La Fargue and Almades took a step back and placed themselves *en garde*, while the dracs were about to launch forward when their chief barked out an order that froze them in place: "SK'ERSH!"

For a few long seconds, no one dared to move. Bodies remained fixed in martial stances beneath the pitiless downpour. Only eyes shifted, looking left and right, watchful for the first threatening gesture.

"SK'ERSH!" the drac leader repeated in a lower tone.

Little by little, muscles relaxed and breathing resumed.

Blades were not replaced in their scabbards, but they were pointed back down at the sodden ground. His mouth bloody, the drac Saint-Lucq had wounded ruefully regained his place among his comrades.

Then their leader advanced slowly but resolutely toward La Fargue, who had to wave Almades back before he intervened. The black drac drew so close that they touched chests, allowing him to sniff at the captain's face from below.

He did so for some time, with a mix of avid hunger and animal curiosity.

La Fargue endured this examination without flinching.

Finally, the drac stepped back and promised: "We shall meet again, old man."

The dracs retreated in good order and soon vanished at a gallop into the night and the howling rain, taking their black mist with them.

"What now?" Saint-Lucq asked after a moment.

"We return to Paris," the captain of the Cardinal's Blades replied. "I don't know what's going on, but His Eminence must be warned without delay. The king's life may be in danger."

2

Cardinal Richelieu was preparing to take his leave with the other members of the Council when King Louis XIII called him back: "Cardinal."

"Yes, Sire?"

"Stay for a moment."

Lifting a red-gloved hand to his chest, Richelieu indicated his obedience with a silent nod and drew away from the door through which ministers and secretaries of state were departing. They passed one by one, without lingering or looking back, almost cringing as if they feared the sudden touch of an icy breath on the back of their necks.

Draughts were not uncommon in the Louvre, but in this warm month of June 1633 the only ones to be truly feared were the result of a royal cold spell. Such cold spells did not cause noses to drip, aggravate rheumatism, or force anyone to stay in bed, but they could provoke an illness serious enough to ruin destinies and finish careers. The members of the Council were well aware of this and were particularly wary of contagion. And they had all felt a distinctly wintry blast this morning when His Majesty had joined them with a brisk step and, upon sitting down and without greeting anyone present, curtly demanded that the order of the day be read.

The king held his Council every morning after breakfast and did not hesitate to summon its members again later in the day if the affairs of the realm warranted further attention. In this he followed the example of his father. But in contrast to Henri IV, who conducted his meetings so freely that they sometimes took place during strolls outside, Louis XIII—more reserved, more cautious, and more attached to proper etiquette—required formal deliberations, around a table and behind closed doors. At the Louvre, the Council met either in the chamber on the ground floor traditionally reserved for its use, or—as today—in the Book Room. This was no less formal a setting than the Council chamber but, as Richelieu had noticed, the king preferred its use whenever he was anxious to ensure the complete confidentiality of debates or foresaw the need for a discreet one-to-one conversation at the conclusion of the Council's session. Then he only needed to detain the person with whom he desired to speak for a few moments, and everything could be said in the time it took the other Council members to reappear in public.

The cardinal had therefore guessed that something was in the air when he arrived at the Louvre and was directed to the Book Room. The slight delay in His Majesty's arrival, and his manifest dissatisfaction during the meeting, had confirmed his suspicions and forced him to ponder. He was obliged to pay careful heed to the moods of the man who had raised him to the heights of power and glory, as the same man could just as easily precipitate his fall. No doubt Armand-Jean du Plessis, Cardinal Richelieu, deserved to exercise the immense responsibilities that Louis XIII conferred upon him. And no doubt he had demonstrated his exceptional abilities as a statesman over the past ten years since his recall to the Council and appointment as chief minister. But personal merits and services rendered counted for little without royal favour, and the cardinal could not afford to let the favour he enjoyed run cold. He had far too many enemies for that—ambitious rivals who were jealous of his influence and adversaries hostile to his policies alike—and all of them, in France and elsewhere, were eager to see his star wane.

To be sure, the king's esteem and affection for his chief minister were not likely to disappear overnight. As close as the Capitol might be to the Tarpeian Rock, Richelieu did not believe himself likely to fall victim to a royal whim. Nevertheless, Louis XIII was a grim, temperamental, and secretive monarch, who suffered from an inability to express his emotions and was often difficult to understand. The cardinal himself was often forced to make concessions to appease his authoritarian master, whose reactions could still surprise him on occasion. Taciturn by nature, the king would spend much time ruminating over his decisions, which he would then divulge suddenly and without explanation, or else explain badly. He was also rancorous in more private matters. Sensitive, he never forgave a slight completely and would nurse grudges that ripened, quietly and patiently, without the knowledge of those close to him. Then came the clumsy word, the indelicate gesture, the ingratitude, or some other small fault that finally proved too much for him to bear. When this occurred, Louis XIII gave way to cold angers which he expressed by way of stern reproaches, cruel humiliations, or even brutal punishments and disgraces.

It was one of these angers that the members of the Council sensed was imminent, and which—despite being great lords and high officials of the Crown for the most part—they had each dreaded they would bear the brunt of, right up until the moment when, to their immense relief, His Majesty had finally released them.

All in all, notwithstanding the king's awful mood, the Council meeting had proceeded almost as usual. Louis XIII had sat alone at the head of the long rectangular table around which the others had taken their places, ready to explain official business or read dispatches. Then the moment had arrived for debate and deliberations, during which each member had to defend or justify his advice. These deliberations were often fairly free discussions, which would become lively when views diverged, with the king insisting that all should express their convictions within his Council. This morning, however, no one really desired to stand out, to such a degree that Louis XIII soon became irritated and, wishing to have an opinion on a precise point, he questioned one secretary of state rather sharply. Muddling his papers in surprise, the man had stammered out a confused answer that the king had received with arctic coldness: he himself was afflicted with a slight stammer that he controlled by force of will. At that instant, all those present believed that the king's wrath would fall unjustly upon the poor man, but nothing ensued. After a long silence, a semblance of debate resumed and the king dismissed the Council an hour later.

But not before asking the cardinal to remain behind.

If Richelieu had only lent a distracted ear to the actual debates, he had been observing the proceedings closely, waiting to see which matter, when it was presented, would provoke a reaction—however restrained or disguised—from the king.

In vain.

Yet there was no lack of reasons for concern. There was the war being prepared against Lorraine, the hegemonic ambitions of Spain and its Court of Dragons, the intrigues of England, and the string of military successes by Sweden in its campaign within the Holy Roman Empire which risked upsetting the fragile balance of power in Europe. Within France's borders there were rumblings from the people due to the crushing weight of taxes, the Catholic party showed no signs of disarming, several Protestant towns were demanding the same privileges as La Rochelle, which the city had only obtained by victoriously withstanding a siege five years earlier, and plot after treasonous plot continued to be hatched, even in the very corridors of the Louvre. Finally, in Paris itself, churches were burning and there was an increasing threat of rioting against the Huguenots and the Jews, who were blamed for starting the fires.

But none of the foreign or domestic affairs that the Council had discussed appeared to be the cause of the rage Louis XIII was struggling so hard to contain. Since the king was very pious, could it be those reports, still confidential, indicating a disturbing revival of sorcerous activity in the capital? Did the king know something that his chief minister did not? The very idea was enough to worry the cardinal, who endeavoured to know everything in order to foresee everything and, if necessary, to prevent anything from happening.

The last Council member to leave was the marquis de Châteauneuf, Keeper of the Seals. Carrying with him the finely wrought casket containing the kingdom's seals which he never let out of his sight, he bade farewell to Richelieu with a respectful nod of the head.

A footman shut the doors behind him.

Agnès de Vaudreuil returned from her morning ride in the outskirts of Paris at around ten o'clock.

Travelling along rue du Chasse-Midi at a fast trot, she barely slowed when she reached the Croix-Rouge crossroads, despite the fact that it was very busy at this hour. The young baronne expected people to make way for her and make way they did, sometimes grumbling and more often railing after her. She followed rue des Saints-Pères as far as rue Saint-Dominique and—now in the heart of the faubourg Saint-Germain, a few streets away from the magnificent abbey which gave it its name—she turned into the very narrow rue Saint-Guillaume. Here she was finally forced to slow her horse to a walk to avoid bowling over some innocent passerby, street hawker, trader at his stall, goodwife haggling over the price of a chicken, or miserable beggar shaking his bowl.

People watched as she came to a halt before the Hôtel de l'Épervier. She had a wild, austere beauty that was striking to behold, with a slender figure, a proud bearing, a pale complexion, green eyes, full dark lips, and long black hair whose heavy curls inevitably escaped from her braid. But the observers were even more surprised by her thigh boots, black breeches, and the red leather corset she wore over a white shirt. It was a daring outfit, to say the least. And not content with publicly displaying herself in this manner, without even covering her head, she also wore a sword and rode her horse like a man. It was scandalous. . . .

Indifferent to the discreet commotion she was causing, Agnès swung down from her horse and into the noxious mud that covered the streets of Paris. She would have liked to spare her boots this indignity, but that meant ringing the bell and waiting for someone to come open up one of the great studded doors of the carriage gate. She preferred to push open the smaller, inset pedestrian door that was only locked at night and, leading her horse by the bridle, entered the paved courtyard where the iron-clad hooves clattered and echoed like musket shots.

Coming from the stable, André hurried to greet the baronne de Vaudreuil, respectfully taking the reins from her hands.

"You should have rung the bell, madame," said the stableman. "I would have opened for you."

There was a touch of both reproach and regret in his voice.

A very dark-haired man who was going prematurely bald on the top of his head, although sporting a tremendous mustache on his upper lip, he had the frustrated look of someone who was prevented from doing the right thing but had decided to bear with this in silence.

"It's quite all right, André. . . . Thank you."

While André took her tired, muddy horse to the stable, Agnès removed her gloves and looked at her surroundings with a resigned air.

She sighed.

The Hôtel de l'Épervier was a decidedly sinister place. Austere and uncomfortable, it was a vast residence with thick walls and narrow windows which had been built for a Huguenot gentleman after the Saint-Barthélemy massacre. Now it served as headquarters for the Cardinal's Blades, a clandestine elite unit commanded by Captain La Fargue under direct orders from Cardinal Richelieu. Agnès de Vaudreuil didn't like this mansion, where the nights seemed longer and darker than elsewhere. But she had no choice. Lacking lodgings of her own in Paris, she was obliged to live here, immediately available for the service of His Eminence. An order for an urgent mission could arrive at any time from the Palais-Cardinal.

Ballardieu, coming out onto the front steps of the main building, interrupted Agnès's train of thought. Massively built, with greying hair, he was a former soldier who had put on weight over the years thanks to his fondness for food and drink. His cheekbones were reddened by broken veins but his eye remained sharp and he was still capable of felling a mule with one blow of his fist.

"Where on earth have you been?" he demanded.

Restraining a smile, Agnès walked up to him.

Having raised her as best he could, dandled her on his knee, and taught her how to use her first rapier, he was always prepared to forgive Ballardieu's tendency to forget that she was a baronne and no longer eight years old. She knew he loved her, and that he was still awkward when it came to showing his affection. She also knew that he disliked it if she was absent for too long and fretted until she returned. As a child she had once disappeared for several days in troubled circumstances she no longer recalled, but it was an incident which had evidently marked Ballardieu for life.

"I went as far as Saint-Germain," she explained nonchalantly as she passed him and went into the front hall. "Any news from La Fargue?"

"No," replied the old man from the porch. "But it might interest you to hear that Marciac has returned."

She halted and turned round, now wearing a radiant smile.

Marciac had been sent off alone on a mission to La Rochelle three weeks earlier and had stopped sending news soon after. The Gascon's silence had been worrying her for several days now.

"Really?"

"God's truth!"

Marciac was bent over a basin of cold water, splashing his face and neck with both hands, when he heard a voice behind him: "Good morning, Nicolas."

He interrupted his ablutions, blindly grabbed a towel, then stood up and turned toward Agnès as he dried his cheeks. She stood on the threshold of his bedchamber, with her arms crossed, one shoulder leaning against the wall, eyes shining and a faint smile on her lips.

"Welcome home," she added.

"Thank you," Marciac replied.

He was still wearing the boots and breeches in which he had ridden, but he had stripped down to his shirt and rolled up his sleeves in order to wash. His doublet—an elegant bloodred garment cut from the same embroidered cloth as his breeches—lay on the bed next to an old leather travelling bag. His hat was hanging on the wall, along with his rapier in its scabbard and his baldric.

"How are you?" asked Agnès.

"Exhausted."

And as if to prove these words, he fell into an armchair, with the towel still around his neck and damp locks clinging to his brow. He did seem tired.

But delighted nonetheless.

"I was in such a hurry to get here," he explained, "that I barely slept three hours last night. And the sun! The dust . . . ! Lord, I'm dying of thirst!"

At that very moment, sweet, timid Naïs arrived from the kitchen bearing a platter, a jug of wine, and two glasses. Agnès had to step aside to let her pass. Seeing the servant girl, Marciac joyfully leapt to his feet.

"It's a miracle. Naïs, I adore you. Will you marry me? Do you have any idea how much I thought of you, during my exile?"

The young woman set down her platter, and eyes cast downward, asked: "Would you like me to make up the bed, monsieur?"

"How cruel! Asking me that, when I dream only of unmaking it with you. . . ."

Blushing, Naïs giggled, curtseyed, and quickly withdrew.

"Keep on singing, you handsome blackbird!" Agnès said mockingly. "You shall never pluck that fruit. . . ."

Marciac was indeed handsome, fair-headed, and full of charm. His hair was always in need of a comb, his cheeks could benefit from a razor, but he was endowed with a natural elegance that was perfectly suited to such neglect. He was more or less Gascon, more or less a gentleman, and more or less a physician. Above all, he was a formidable swordsman, an inveterate gambler, and an unrepentant seducer; a man who had lost count of his duels, his debts, and his conquests.

Shrugging his shoulders, he filled the glasses and handed one to Agnès. They clinked to mark their reunion.

Then Agnès perched on the window ledge while Marciac returned to his armchair. He would have offered his seat to any other woman, but the baronne de Vaudreuil did not expect such attentions from her brothers-in-arms.

"Now, tell me everything that's happened here," said the Gascon. "First off, who's the fellow who took my horse on my arrival? I go away for a few days, and there are new faces when I get back."

"That's our new groom, André. Formerly of the Picardy regiment, I believe."

"I suppose we've made quite sure that—"

"Yes," interrupted Agnès. "The man is quite trustworthy. He was a stableman at the Palais-Cardinal before he was . . . recommended to us."

"Good. . . . And what about the others?"

"Others?"

"La Fargue, Saint-Lucq, Leprat . . . You remember them? We all formed a band before I left. Damn! Have I been gone even longer than it seems?"

Since the jest was deserved and good-humoured, the young woman accepted it with good grace.

"Leprat is in Paris," she informed him, "but he tends to spend his mornings at monsieur de Tréville's house. As for Saint-Lucq and Almades, they are off on a mission with La Fargue. If all goes well, they should be back today."

Marciac merely cocked an inquisitive eyebrow at this news.

Agnès rose to close the chamber door, leaned against it for a moment, and then in a hushed tone said: "Lately, someone has been sending a few discreet signals to the cardinal. This individual claims to have very valuable information and proposed a meeting to discuss how this information might be—"

"Sold?"

"Negotiated."

"And His Eminence assigned La Fargue to meet this mysterious person."

"As a matter of urgency."

"My word, this individual must really be someone. Who are we talking about, exactly?"

"'La Donna.'"

"Ah . . . now I understand."

La Donna was the nickname given to an adventuress well known in all the courts of Europe. A clever schemer, a mercenary spy, and an expert seductress, she made her living from the secrets she discovered for her own benefit or on behalf of others. Beyond her beauty and intelligence, she was best characterised by her lack of scruples. She was venal, and her excellent services came at a high price. She always had several irons in the fire and was adept at playing them off against one another, making hers an exciting but highly dangerous existence. All those who became acquainted with this woman predicted a violent, premature death for her, but these same people did not hesitate to call upon her talents when needed. It was murmured that her ultimate loyalty lay with the pope. Others claimed she belonged to a secret society of dragons. All such surmises, however, overlooked her independent spirit and appetite for personal gain.

"But doesn't the cardinal have some grievance against her?" Marciac wondered aloud upon reflection. "Remember that business at Ratisbon . . . ?"

Agnès shrugged. Putting her hand on the doorknob, she said: "What do you want me to say? There are some cases in which a grievance might be more harmful to the one who nurtures it than to the one who causes it. . . . Well, I must go now."

Out of politeness, the Gascon rose from his chair. The young baronne was about to leave the room when, without warning, she went over and took him in her arms.

Not knowing the reason for this sudden display of emotion, Marciac let her embrace him.

"We were worried," she murmured in his ear. "Don't expect the others to tell you so, but you frightened us all. And if ever again you leave us for so long without sending news, I'll scratch your eyes out. Understood?"

"Understood, Agnès. Thank you."

She left him standing there, but from the stairs she called back: "Get some rest, but come down as soon as you're ready. I'm sure Ballardieu has planned a feast in your honour."

With a smile, the Gascon closed the door.

He remained thoughtful for a moment, then gave a huge yawn and turned longing eyes toward the bed.

A slender, nimble, forked tongue woke Arnaud de Laincourt by tickling his ear. The young man groaned, weakly pushing the scaly snout away, and turned over in his bed. But the dragonnet was stubborn.

It switched ears.

Come on, boy . . . You know him well enough by now to realise that he isn't going to leave you in peace. . . .

Giving up on sleep, Laincourt sighed heavily and opened his eyes.

"All right, Maréchal. All right. . . ."

Pushing back the sheet, he rose up on his elbows and gave the gaunt old dragonnet an unhappy look. Sitting there with its wings folded and its tail wrapped around its feet, the small reptile seemed to be waiting for something.

He's hungry.

Of course he's hungry, Laincourt replied without speaking. *He's always hungry. In fact, I'm starting to wonder how it is that he eats so much and yet remains so thin.*

Then out loud, he told Maréchal: "Do you know what a sorry sight you are?" The dragonnet tipped its head to the left. "Yes, you are. . . ."

Laincourt looked over at the big cage with bars as thick as fingers that sat in a corner of the room. It was standing open, as it was every morning, even though he had locked it before going to bed, as he did every evening.

He sighed again.

"Back in your cage!" the young man ordered, clapping his hands. "Go on! You know the rules! Into your cage!"

Don't be too hard on him. . . . When he was mine, he was never locked up.

Slowly, and with obvious reluctance, Maréchal turned around and waddled away. Then with a hop and a flap of his wings, he returned to his prison, closing the door with an insolent swipe of one clawed foot. As it clanged shut, the latch fell into place. The old dragonnet did not appear to be worried by this. Laincourt couldn't help smiling.

He was a thin brown-haired young man, with crystalline blue eyes. He was intelligent, cultivated, calm, and reserved. Some found him to be distant, as he was in some ways. Others judged his reserve to be a sign of arrogance. They were mistaken. The truth was that, while Laincourt looked down on no one, he simply didn't much care for his contemporaries, asking only that they leave him in peace and feeling no need to please them. He detested hollow platitudes, conventional opinions, and polite smiles. He disliked being forced into conversation. He preferred silence to small talk and solitude to futile company. When confronted with someone he found tiresome he smiled, nodded, said nothing, and excused himself as quickly as possible. For him, politeness consisted in saying "good day," "thank you," "goodbye," and enquiring only about the health of those he truly cared for.

As soon as he got out of bed and had pulled on his breeches, Laincourt went to close the window of his bedchamber. He had left it open to enjoy the night's cool breeze, but now it was letting in the heat as well as the stink and noise of Paris.

You've slept late again, boy.

So it seems.

That's a bad habit you've picked up since you've been idle and spent your nights reading.

Reading is not the same as being idle.

You are no longer employed.

I no longer have a master.

You will soon be in need of money.

Laincourt shrugged.

He lived on the second floor of a house in rue de la Ferronnerie, not far from the Saints-Innocents cemetery, between the neighbourhoods of Sainte-Opportune and Les Halles. Barely four metres wide, this street was very busy since it prolonged rue Saint-Honoré and crossed rue Saint-Denis at a right angle, thus linking two of the principal traffic routes in Paris. The flow of passersby, traders, horse riders, sedan chairs, carts, and coaches went by without interruption from morning till night.

Do you see him, boy?

Laincourt glanced out at the street.

At the entrance to a narrow passage between two houses, a gentleman dressed in a beige doublet was waiting, one hand holding his gloves and the other resting on the pommel of his sword. He was calm and did not appear to be hiding. On the contrary, Laincourt had the impression that he wished to be seen, and recalled having previously noticed his presence, here and there, in recent days.

Of course, he replied to the invisible presence.

I wonder who he is. And what he wants.

I couldn't care less.

A month ago, he would have cared.

A month ago, he would have immediately taken steps to have the man in the beige doublet followed, identified, and no doubt neutralised. But he no longer belonged to the Cardinal's Guards. At the end of a mission that had cost him his red cape and his rank as an ensign, he had turned the page on secrets, intrigues, lies, and betrayals in the service of His Eminence.

After washing with the remaining water in the pitcher, Laincourt dressed and found something in the pantry to calm Maréchal's hunger. Then he decided to go out and have a bite to eat himself. He would then visit his bookseller, Bertaud, in order to return two books for the price of one.

He had just put on his baldric and hung his sword from it when he saw that the old dragonnet had once again escaped from his cage and was now standing near the door, holding his collar and chain in his mouth. The young man promised himself that he would buy a padlock on his way to the bookseller but, being a good sport, he extended his fist to Maréchal.

"All right," he said. "I'll take you, too."

Outside in the street, the gentleman in the beige doublet had vanished.

The comte de Tréville, captain of the King's Musketeers, stood at his office window and sought to distract himself by looking out over the courtyard of his house on rue du Vieux-Colombier in the faubourg Saint-Germain. It provided a picturesque spectacle which he enjoyed, arousing nostalgia for the time when he was still a companion-in-arms to Henri IV. As usual, several dozen musketeers were to be found loitering on the cobbled courtyard strewn with fresh straw. Not all of them wore the cape—blue with a silver fleur-de-lis cross—as some were not on active duty. But all of them had their sword at their side and were ready for any opportunity to draw it. They walked or stood about, talking, laughing, playing dice or cards, demonstrating various fencing techniques, reading the gazettes together and commenting on the latest news, while keeping a watchful eye on the comings and goings on the great staircase and in the antechambers, which they also occupied.

"D'Artagnan!" Tréville suddenly called out in a loud voice.

Almost immediately, a door opened behind him. . . .

"Monsieur?"

"Tell me, d'Artagnan, isn't that the chevalier d'Orgueil I see near the stables?" Tréville asked without turning round.

The musketeer approached in order to peer over his captain's shoulder.

"It is indeed, monsieur."

"Ask him to come up, please."

"Monsieur, they're already queuing at your office door. . . ."

In fact, starting in the early hours of the morning, Tréville's days were marked by the unceasing flow of visitors he received at his mansion, when the king's service did not demand his presence elsewhere.

"I know, d'Artagnan, I know. . . . Tell my secretary to have them wait, will you?"

"As you command, monsieur."

"Thank you, lieutenant."

Alone once again, the captain of the Musketeers uttered a sigh and, regretfully turning away from the window, sat down at his desk. The sheets and ledgers piled there drew his tired glance. Useless paperwork. Tréville picked up a small box, opened it with a little key, and drew out an unsealed letter that he placed before him.

Then he waited.

"Come in!" he called, as soon as he heard a knock at the door.

A gentleman entered, wearing a crimson doublet with black buttons and slashes. He was tall, carried himself with impeccable posture, and advanced with a firm step. It was easy to see that he was—or had once been—a military officer. He was thirty-five to forty years of age, with sharp features and the confident gaze of someone who knows he has not faltered, and never will, in fulfilling his duties. He was armed with a rapier that had become famous. Entirely white, made of ivory, it had been carved from tip to pommel from a single dragon's tooth. He wore it on his right side, being left-handed.

Antoine Leprat, chevalier d'Orgueil and a former member of the King's Musketeers, removed his hat to salute the captain.

Tréville welcomed him with a smile.

"Good morning, Leprat. How are you?"

"Very well, monsieur. Thank you."

"And your thigh?"

"Completely healed, monsieur."

It was a somewhat excessive claim. But in the King's Musketeers men quickly acquired the habit of minimising the gravity of a wound and exaggerating the speed of their recovery, out of fear of being passed over when the next mission was assigned.

"But it was a rather nasty wound. . . ."

"It wasn't before I hit on the notion of jumping out of a window," Leprat replied with a smile.

"And what a strange notion that was. . . ."

"Indeed."

The two men, separated in age by more than fifteen years, exchanged an amused, knowing glance.

But Tréville's expression became clouded.

"Yesterday," he said, "I received a letter from your father." He pointed to the missive he had placed on the table before Leprat entered. "He is worried about you. He has become anxious since he heard that you left the Musketeers."

"My father the comte fears, above all else, that I will harm his reputation. By meeting an ignoble death while carrying out a clandestine mission, for example. I would be a source of pride to him if I died on the field of battle, wearing the cape of a true Musketeer, monsieur. But as far as posterity is concerned, there is nothing for him to gain if I serve under the orders of Captain La Fargue. . . . The comte's only concern is for the glory attached to his name," Leprat concluded.

"Perhaps he is also worried about the glory attached to yours. . . ."

The former musketeer smiled bitterly.

"If the comte were to hear my body had been found lying in the gutter, my death would bother him less than the state of the gutter."

Saddened, Tréville rose and returned to the window.

He remained there for a moment, hands behind his back, silent and troubled.

"All the same, chevalier, you will always be free to rejoin the Musketeers. As you know, you are only on leave of absence. Unlimited leave, to be sure, but a leave of absence nonetheless. Say the word, and I will reinstate you."

"Thank you, monsieur."

Tréville turned his back to the window and looked directly into Leprat's eyes.

"You know the esteem in which I hold Captain La Fargue. I have no wish to force you to choose between two loyalties. But you would also be serving the king by wearing the Musketeers' cape. So please keep yours, chevalier. And think on the matter. There will always be time and opportunity to change your mind."

Cardinal Richelieu emerged, extremely preoccupied, from his interview with Louis XIII. But he did not let his feelings show and decided to make an appearance in the Great Hall of the Louvre, where ministers and courtiers, officers and parasites, beautiful ladies and great lords were all gathered together. He seemed unruffled, smiled, engaged in conversation, and patiently endured the demands of his hangers-on, supplicants, and flatterers. To complete his pretence of normality, he envisaged paying a visit to the queen in her apartments. But was that a wise idea?

It was vital that he allay the suspicions of anyone who was already worried, or would soon be, over why the king—in an extremely ugly mood, moreover—had detained his chief minister at the end of the Council meeting. The decisions that Louis XIII had made and the irrevocable orders he had issued during their tête-à-tête could put the kingdom to fire and to the sword. When the moment came they would have to strike quickly, forcefully, and accurately—and without showing so much as an ounce of mercy. That moment was fast approaching. But until it came, the only way to avoid a fatal conflagration was to keep the king's plans an absolute secret. And a secret was best preserved when everyone remained unaware of its importance.

Hence the cardinal would try to behave as if nothing was amiss. Today he planned to attend all of his meetings and ensure that the number of messengers leaving the Palais-Cardinal did not significantly increase. To all appearances, he would keep to his ordinary routine.

Richelieu knew he was being watched.

His role as a statesman meant that even the least important of his visits—those he paid and the ones he received—were noticed, reported, and discussed. There was nothing extraordinary about this. He was a public figure, after all. But among those who took an interest in his activities there were some who harboured sinister projects. The cardinal had many enemies. First there were the enemies of the king, not all of whom were foreign. Then there were the enemies of his policies, including the Catholic party. And finally there were his personal enemies, who hated him because they envied his success or were jealous of his influence on Louis XIII, an influence that was greatly exaggerated but whose legend conveniently permitted the minister to be blamed for the faults and violent acts of his king.

There were two women to be found among Richelieu's most bitter personal opponents. The first was the queen mother, Marie de Médicis, Henrí IV's widow: humiliated and unable to forgive her son for preferring to entrust the conduct of the kingdom's affairs to the cardinal rather than to her, she continued to hatch schemes from her refuge in Brussels, and stoked the fires of every revolt that took place in France. The second woman was the beautiful, intelligent, urbane, and very dangerous duchesse de Chevreuse who, for the last fifteen years, had taken a hand in every plot, but was protected by her birth, her fortune, and her friendship with the queen, Anne d'Autriche.

These two women never disarmed, even if at times they were only accomplices of the cabals that were invented and led by other enemies of the cardinal. Enemies who might be Catholic or Protestant, Frenchmen or foreigners, humans or dragons, but who all had eyes and ears inside the Louvre, and none of whom could be allowed to get wind of what was now being set in motion.

Let us not give these people any cause for concern, Richelieu thought to himself.

And so he resolved, in the end, to go and present his respects to the queen.

Marciac awoke still dressed. He had barely found the strength to remove his boots before lying down and had immediately gone to sleep. Rising up on his elbows, he looked around his chamber with bleary eyes and yawned. Then he sat on the edge of the bed, stretched, yawned again, and scratched his neck while at the same time rubbing his belly, realising that he was famished

And thirsty. He was thirsty, too.

How long had he been asleep?

Not long enough to ease the stiffness after his swift and arduous ride from La Rochelle, in any case. By coach the journey took at least eight days. The Gascon, on horseback, had completed it in less than five, which could not be accomplished without some sore muscles. . . .

Grimacing, Marciac stood up and, with a heavy step, went to the window. It was open but the curtains were drawn shut. He spread them apart and then squinted, his eyes dazzled by the sun that was beginning to descend in the sky.

It was already the afternoon, then.

Still muzzy from sleep, the Gascon enjoyed the view for a moment. His bedchamber was on the second floor of the Hôtel de l'Épervier. Oriented toward the east, it offered a vantage point over the roofs of the Charité hospital in the foreground, and behind it the splendid abbey of Saint-Germain-des-Prés. With its abundant greenery, fresh air, and scattering of elegant buildings, the faubourg Saint-Germain was definitely a very pleasant neighbourhood.

The ringing of a bell tower succeeded in dragging Marciac out of his daydreaming and informed him of the time.

It was two o'clock.

He turned away from the window and went to wash, wetting and rubbing his blond locks over the basin. Finally feeling refreshed, he addressed a wink at his reflection in the small mirror hanging on the wall. He pulled on his boots, grabbed his hat and his baldric in case of an emergency, and went downstairs with his shirt hanging outside his breeches and his hair still damp.

One of the rare advantages of living in the Hôtel de l'Épervier was that the house was cool in summer. Otherwise it was a particularly sombre and austere place. On the ground floor, Marciac almost knocked down monsieur Guibot, who was standing at the bottom of the stairs. Small, thin, and scruffy-looking, the old concierge hobbled about with a wooden leg. He had bushy eyebrows and the bald top of his head was surrounded by a crown of long dirty blond hair. Guibot had served the Blades before they were disbanded and he had kept a jealous watch over their headquarters, which he inexplicably adored, until their return.

While Marciac barely avoided colliding with him in the front hall, the old man was busy clearing a path for two kitchen boys, dressed in pumps, white stockings, breeches, shirts, and aprons, who were arriving in the courtyard carrying a litter which held a large pâté in a circular pastry crust whose little chimney still steamed and filled the air with an appetising fragrance.

"Good afternoon, monsieur Marciac. . . . Make way, please. . . . Begging your pardon. . . . Watch the step, you two! And mind the door . . . ! There. . . . Gently, gently. . . . It's this way. . . ."

His mouth already watering, the Gascon followed the procession through the house and out into the garden.

The garden was in fact merely a square of nature which, left untended, had reverted to its wild state. The grass was high and brush had accumulated at the foot of the walls. A chestnut tree offered some welcome shade. At the rear, a little door opened onto a narrow alley. And right in the middle, beneath the tree, was an old wooden table that was never taken inside. It had gone white from weathering and some intrepid bindweeds climbed up its cabled legs.

Sitting at one end of this table on mismatched chairs, Leprat, Agnès, and Ballardieu were joking and laughing over glasses of wine, sometimes getting up to replenish their drinks from one of the bottles left to cool in a tub of water, or to scrounge a bite to eat from a plate. Absorbed in their amusement, they paid little attention to shy Naïs, who was busy setting out dishes on a tablecloth already loaded—in addition to the tableware—with cold meats, a roast goose, cheese, a pie, and a fat round loaf of bread. But the young servant girl always seemed to be forgetting something, forcing her to make further trips back and forth between the garden, the kitchen, the pantry, and the cellar. And each time, she scolded herself in a soft voice.

"Useless girl, do you have nothing but sawdust for brains?" she groused as she hurried past Marciac.

"Ah! At last!" cried Ballardieu when he saw who and what was arriving.

Then the old soldier spied Marciac and welcomed him with equal enthusiasm.

Space had to be made for the steaming pâté. Monsieur Guibot wanted to direct the manoeuvre, but Ballardieu, domineering, promptly took control of operations. The pâté left its litter undamaged and the two boys were sent off to the kitchen to have a drink before returning to their master, a pastry cook in rue des Saints-Pères.

"Slept well?" Leprat asked.

"Wonderfully," replied Marciac as he sat down.

"I'm glad to see you again, Marciac."

"I'm glad to be back. The captain hasn't returned?"

"Not yet. Nor have Saint-Lucq and Almades, of course."

"Here," said Agnès, passing a glass of wine to the Gascon. "Your health, Nicolas."

Marciac was touched by the gesture and he smiled.

"Thank you very much, baronne."

"You're welcome."

Naïs returned with a bowl of butter, which at first she didn't know where to put on the crowded table.

"Naïs," Ballardieu called to her. "Is there anything missing, would you say?"

The old soldier was no ogre, but his deep voice and red face caused the young servant girl to become flustered. She thought it was a trick question and hesitated, looking around the table several times with a panic-stricken look on her face.

"I—"

"Well, I say there's nothing missing," Ballardieu answered for her. "You can therefore come and sit down."

Naïs did not understand. Was she being invited to sit at the masters' table?

"I beg your pardon, monsieur?"

"Sit down, Naïs! And you too, monsieur Guibot. . . . Come on, hurry up! The pâté is growing cold."

The concierge did not need to be asked twice.

The servant girl, on the other hand, sought further advice. She looked to Leprat, who nodded in approval to her. That reassured her. Leprat was a gentleman, and moreover a former member of the King's Musketeers. And the baronne de Vaudreuil seemed not to care at all. So, if they saw no impediment to her sitting at the table . . . Her nervousness settling somewhat, she timidly placed one buttock on the edge of a rickety stool, praying that they would all forget she was present.

"And André?" Ballardieu persisted. "He should share in this feast, shouldn't he? Somebody should tell him to come. Guibot, go fetch him, would you?"

The concierge, who was already holding out a plate, grumbled under his breath but obeyed willingly enough. He went off on his wooden leg, avoiding the molehills.

Leprat passed a hunting dagger to Marciac.

"Go ahead," he said. "Do the honours."

The Gascon rose before the enormous *pâté en croûte* and looked around at the company seated at the table. Some of his best friends were here and had arranged this meal for him. He felt good, happy inside.

He was even in the mood to say a few words expressing his feelings.

Agnès guessed as much.

"Marciac," she said, "if the next thing you say isn't: 'Who wants this handsome slice?' I swear I shall make mincemeat out of you."

He burst out laughing and planted the blade in the golden crust.

The three riders arrived in Paris by the Montmartre gate.

Weariness from their travels had left them with drawn faces and great rings under their eyes. And they were all dirty and in need of a shave. They still wore the same clothing they had on when leaving Paris the previous day, having ridden more than forty leagues in under twenty-four hours to meet La Donna and then return as quickly as possible. Indeed, only the fear of killing their mounts had kept them from galloping the whole way back.

They soon parted ways.

While Saint-Lucq continued straight ahead down rue Montmartre, La Fargue and Almades took rue des Vieux-Augustins instead and then rue

Coquillière, before almost immediately turning left. At last, not far from the palace Cardinal Richelieu was having built for himself, they halted before a tavern in rue des Petits-Champs.

Its sign boasted an eagle daubed in scarlet paint.

The tavern's façade was set back from those of the other buildings on the same street, behind a mossy stone archway and a few feet of uneven paving. There were men occupying this space, glasses in hand, some of them standing around three barrels which served as a table, others leaning beside the tavern's wide-open windows conversing with those inside. Almost all of them were dressed as soldiers, wearing swords, striking dashing poses, and bearing scars that left no doubt as to their profession. Moreover, they addressed one another as much by rank as by name, and even the names were often a *nom de guerre*.

Having dismounted, La Fargue entrusted the reins of his horse to Almades and went inside.

The Red Eagle was one of the places in Paris most frequented by the musketeers serving His Eminence. Two companies of soldiers served the cardinal directly: the Guards on horseback and the musketeers on foot. The Guards wore the famous red cape. They were all gentlemen, protected His Eminence's person, and accompanied him everywhere. As for the musketeers, they were commoners. Ordinary soldiers, they only signed up for three years and carried out less prestigious duties. Still, they were excellent fighters and were bound together by a strong *esprit de corps*. The best of them could have joined the Guards if they had been of more noble birth.

From the threshold, La Fargue caught the eye of the person he knew to be the owner of the establishment, a tall redheaded man who was still relatively fit despite the incipient bulge of his belly. His name was Balmaire and he walked with a slight limp ever since a wound had forced this former cardinal's musketeer to hang up his sword. He wore an ample shirt, brown breeches, and had an apron tied around his waist. But instead of the usual white stockings and pumps he wore a pair of worn funnel-shaped boots, indicating that his role as tavern keeper did not define him entirely.

Recognising La Fargue, Balmaire addressed a silent salute to him from afar. The old captain responded in the same fashion and went across the taproom to a door giving onto a corridor and a narrow staircase. He climbed the stairs and, upon reaching the first landing, entered a dusty room with peeling walls, cluttered with some crates, old furniture, and chairs in need of repair.

Leaning forward, a tall, thin gentleman was gazing out the window at the street. The small, diamond-shaped panes of glass were filthy and had in places been replaced with pieces of carton, so that they blocked more light than they let through.

"You're late," said the comte de Rochefort without looking around. He stood up straight and slowly turned away from the window. He was close to fifty years of age. He had a haughty face with a pale complexion, dark eyes, and a penetrating gaze. There was a small scar decorating his temple, where he had been grazed by a pistol ball.

"I've come all the way from Artois," La Fargue retorted. "And you?"

The old captain waited, silent and impassive.

"I was about to leave," Rochefort lied.

"I need to see the cardinal."

"When?"

"As soon as possible. Today."

Rochefort nodded as if he were weighing up the pros and cons of this request.

It was said of Rochefort that he was His Eminence's damned soul. In fact, he was the henchman who took charge of the cardinal's dirty work and was therefore feared and hated. But he was perhaps Richelieu's most loyal servant and he was certainly the least scrupulous, a man who obeyed his master blindly and did not burden himself with moral considerations. Thus, while he would sometimes commit unspeakable acts when ordered to do so, he would only do so upon receiving the order.

"Did you meet with La Donna, captain?"

"Yes. Last night."

"And?"

"And now I need to see the cardinal."

The glances of the two men clashed for a moment, before Rochefort smiled joylessly and said: "We don't like one another at all, do we?"

"No."

La Fargue and Rochefort despised one another. Unfortunately the service of the cardinal forced them to work together once again, now that the Blades had reformed. The captain only took his orders from Richelieu. And he answered to him alone for his actions. But the comte was a necessary intermediary.

"I can't guarantee," Rochefort said, adjusting his baldric, "that the cardinal will receive you soon."

He donned his hat, preparing to depart.

"La Donna claims to know something of a plot against the king," La Fargue revealed.

Rochefort raised an eyebrow.

"Well, now . . ."

"And she is willing to reveal the details if certain of her demands are met."

"So La Donna is making demands. . . . What are they?"

"She asks for His Eminence's protection."

"Nothing else?" the cardinal's henchman said with amusement.

"What does it matter, if she's telling the truth?"

"No doubt, no doubt . . . but do you believe that she is?"

La Fargue shrugged.

"Who knows? But she gave me something that will perhaps help the cardinal form an opinion."

The old captain held out a stained and dog-eared letter that seemed to have got wet at some point. It was the letter La Donna had entrusted to him before fleeing into the storm on the back of her wyvern.

"This comes from La Donna?" Rochefort enquired.

"Yes."

He took the document and examined it with a casual air. Then he placed it in his pocket and walked to the door.

"I'm expected at the Palais-Cardinal," he declared from the threshold. "Then I will join His Eminence at the Louvre."

"Very well," replied La Fargue, who himself went over to glance out the window. "But time is running short. La Donna promised to make contact this evening and before I meet her again I need to know what the cardinal has decided with regard to her. Moreover, she is being pursued by a band of dracs who I'm sure will give her no respite. And if they find her before we do—"

"Dracs? What dracs?"

"Black dracs, Rochefort. Mercenaries. Judging by the markings on their leader's face, I would swear they are former soldiers from the Irskehn companies."

In the drakish tongue, Ir'Skehn meant black fire, and the Irskehns were cavalry companies levied by Spain and composed solely of black dracs. Although they were unreliable on a battlefield due to their inability to control their fury, these cavaliers had no equals when it came to marauding, harassing, and plundering. They were held responsible for several particularly horrible civilian massacres. The mere rumour of their arrival was enough to empty whole areas of the countryside.

Rochefort's eyes narrowed as he took this detail into account.

"And who else would privately hire Irskehns—" he started to say.

"—other than the Black Claw," La Fargue concluded for him.

Gripping the back of the chair and craning his neck, Maréchal was leaning far over his master's shoulder to observe the trictrac board. The old dragonnet was keeping a rapt eye upon the dice, which he loved to see roll across the flat surface. As for Laincourt, he sat unmoving with a blank gaze, his mind elsewhere.

"Come now, Arnaud! Are you going to play?"

The young man raised his head, forcing Maréchal to straighten up, and looked over at his opponent in bewildered surprise. Amused, the other man smiled at him, arms crossed, in a slightly mocking fashion but with an affectionate gleam in his eye. He was a bookseller called Jules Bertaud, about fifty years old. He'd known Laincourt for almost a year now, and already nurtured paternal feelings for him. They shared a taste for knowledge, for books, and more particularly, for treatises on draconic magic which were a discreet speciality of Bertaud's bookshop. Finally, they were both from Lorraine, which had helped to forge a bond between them.

"It is your turn, Arnaud . . ."

Once a week, Laincourt and Bertaud convened at the latter's establishment to talk and play trictrac. Since the weather was fine today, they had installed themselves in the pleasantly sunlit rear courtyard of the bookshop, which was located on rue Perdue in the neighbourhood surrounding Place Maubert, where booksellers and printers abounded.

"Oh yes . . ." said Laincourt, returning to the game. "It is my turn, to be sure. I need to roll, don't I?" he asked as he seized the dice cup.

His gesture immediately drew Maréchal's full attention.

"No," Bertaud replied impatiently. "You've already rolled—"

"Really?"

"Really!" called another voice.

In addition to the gaunt old dragonnet, the match had acquired another spectator: Daunois, a ruddy-faced man in his forties, with the physique of a stevedore and a rather sinister-looking face. In his case, however, appearances were deceiving. A printer by trade, Joseph Daunois possessed a fine wit that was intelligent, cultivated, and sometimes cruelly ironic. He and Bertaud were good friends who nonetheless could never resist trading barbed insults with one another.

The printer stood at the threshold of his workshop, and behind him one glimpsed workers busy with their tasks. But above all, one heard the creaking of the big hand presses and smelled the paper and fresh ink which rather effectively countered the city stinks that had worsened in the hot weather.

"Yes, really," Bertaud confirmed. "And you rolled a seven."

"Seven," repeated Laincourt.

"Yes, seven."

"Since he's telling you so!" interjected Daunois as he came over to join them.

His massive body cast a shadow over most of the small square table.

"Just give me a few moments to think," Laincourt begged, leaning over the trictrac board.

He said nothing, but it took him a few seconds to recall that his pieces were the white ones.

And to discover that he was in serious difficulty.

"That's right," the printer said jokingly. "Think it over. . . . We wouldn't want to you to make some hasty mistake—"

"You know," added Bertaud, "it's no good having me abandon my bookshop and customers to play with you if you take no interest in the game . . ."

The young man made to reply, but Daunois beat him to it, in a sarcastic tone: "Yes, because don't you know, Arnaud, that Bertaud's bookshop is positively packed? There's an impatient mob milling at the door and threatening to break through the windows. They're beating them away with sticks, riots are breaking out, and the city watch will soon be turning up to restore order. It's a right state of panic—"

The truth was that, even if Bertaud was not facing financial ruin, his shop was not well patronised.

"Have you already spoiled all the paper delivered to you this morning?" retorted the bookseller. "Don't you have some handsome inkblots to inspect? Some botched print you need to perfect? But perhaps I'm being a trifle unfair, seeing as in your shop, you press more fingers than pages. . . ."

He had risen as he spoke and, since he was rather small, did not make nearly as impressive a figure as Daunois standing before him. But he held himself firm and his gaze did not waver.

"Your witticisms only amuse yourself, bookseller!" replied Daunois, swelling his chest.

"And you, printer, bore everyone with your remarks!"

Their voices rose while Laincourt, not paying the slightest heed to their altercation, studied his pieces, wondering how to obtain as many points as possible. A trictrac board closely resembled that used for backgammon, with the same division into two sides and the same series of twenty-four black and white long triangles along which one moved the counters. But trictrac was a game with complex rules, where the aim was not simply to remove your counters as quickly as possible. Instead, players earned points as they progressed in order to accumulate a predetermined score.

Laincourt lent an ear to the discussion just as Daunois was growling: "Is that so? Is that so?"

"You heard me!"

"So how is it, then, that people say what they do?"

"And what, pray, are people saying?"

"Quite simply, that—"

"Papa?"

A pretty girl of sixteen, with dark hair and green eyes, had just opened the door leading to the room at the rear of the bookshop. The quarrel immediately ceased and its cause was forgotten.

"Good afternoon, Clotilde," said the printer with a kind smile.

"Good afternoon, monsieur. And good afternoon to you, monsieur de Laincourt."

"Good afternoon. How are you?"

"Very well, monsieur," the girl answered with a blush.

"Well, my girl?" queried Bertaud. "What is it?"

The bookseller's only daughter said in a faint voice: "There is someone in the shop, papa. A gentleman."

Bertaud, who had leaned down to listen to Clotilde, straightened up triumphantly.

"Excuse me," he said, his words directed so ostensibly at Laincourt that he could only be in fact aiming them at Daunois, "but I must attend to my business. Unlike some, I cannot spend all day idling about while others do my work for me."

Daunois, of course, could not let this pass by unanswered: "Allow me to bid you good day, Arnaud. I must return to my workshop, where there are some delicate operations awaiting that cannot be carried out without my supervision."

And thereupon, the printer and the bookseller, both draped in a theatrical air of dignity, turned on their heels and went their separate ways. Pretty Clotilde, however, did not follow her father back inside. She lingered for a moment within the frame of the doorway until, embarrassed when the eyes of the former Cardinal's Guard did not shift from the trictrac board, she finally withdrew. No doubt any man other than Laincourt would have perceived the sentiments she felt for him. But this young man, so skilled at detecting lies and dissembling in a thousand different clues, was unable to read the heart of a young girl in love.

Bertaud returned after a few minutes.

He sat back down, observing with pleasure that his opponent had finally made his move.

"So?" asked Laincourt. "This customer?"

"Bah! He only came in to browse. He didn't even know what he was looking for. . . ."

The young man nodded knowingly.

"Slender, elegant, with a blond mustache?" he guessed.

"Yes," the bookseller replied in astonishment. "But how——?"

"And wearing a beige doublet?"

"Precisely! Do you know him, then?"

"Slightly," said Laincourt, holding out the dice cup. "It's your turn, Jules. This game is certainly dragging on."

Upon leaving the Red Eagle, following his interview with Rochefort, La Fargue rejoined Almades and together they returned to the Hôtel de l'Épervier on their exhausted mounts.

They chose the shortest route, which is to say, they took the Pont Rouge. Thus named because of its coating of red lead paint, the wooden bridge had been built the previous year. Like the Pont Neuf, it allowed Parisians to cross the Seine directly, but there was a toll to be paid, making it less popular.

On the Left Bank, La Fargue and the Spaniard rode up rue de Beaune, through a neighbourhood that had only recently sprung up from the ground in the Pré-aux-Clercs, the former domain of Queen Marguerite de Navarre. Beyond it, they finally reached the faubourg Saint-Germain. Rue de la Sorbonne led them to the right-angled crossing with rue des Saints-Pères, which they followed alongside the façades of La Charité hospital before passing in front of Les Réformés cemetery and turning into the small rue Saint-Guillaume.

They arrived at their destination and, despite the questions about La Donna and the alleged plot against the king that still nagged at him, the old captain could only think of finding a bite to eat and then going to bed. He rang the bell at the entrance to the Hôtel de l'Épervier without dismounting, and waited for someone to open one of the great rectangular doors of the carriage gate. It was not monsieur Guibot but André, the new groom, who hurried over. Once inside the courtyard, La Fargue and Almades handed him the reins of their horses.

They found the others in the garden.

Agnès, Leprat, and Marciac were chatting away beneath the chestnut tree at one end of the old table, where the meal had not yet been cleared away. Looking happy and thick as thieves together, they sipped wine and conversed for the sole pleasure of enjoying one another's company. The heat was bearable out here in the garden. The air was fresher and a relaxed hush reigned which was only slightly disturbed by the regular snores from Ballardieu, asleep in an armchair.

The old soldier had drunk a fair amount of wine and he merely stirred in his sleep when the others greeted the new arrivals. He groaned and smacked his lips without opening his eyes as La Fargue and the Spanish fencing master sat down and took their ease, removing their hats and baldrics, downing a few glasses of wine, and attacking the remains of the repast.

While polishing off the last quarter of the *pâté en croûte*, the captain of the Blades recounted his meeting with La Donna. He reported what she had told him and what she was demanding in exchange for the information she claimed to possess. Then he described the confrontation with the dracs, without omitting any details. Almades, meanwhile, remained silent as usual, eating little, controlling his urges despite his hunger and thirst.

"Can we believe what this woman says?" Leprat wondered aloud. "Isn't she a schemer and a spy of the worst possible kind?"

"As far as scheming and espionage go," observed Marciac, "the worst possible kind is also the best. . . ."

"To be sure. But all the same . . . A plot against the king!"

"What is she like?" asked the young baronne de Vaudreuil. "They say she is very beautiful. Is she?"

"Yes," the captain answered. "She is."

"And what impression did she make on you?" Agnès persisted.

"I found her to be intelligent, determined, skillful—"

"—and dangerous?"

"Certainly."

"If we know anything about La Donna," Leprat commented, "it is that she only acts out of self-interest. So what does she gain from exposing this purported plot?"

"The cardinal's protection," Marciac reminded him.

"A protection that she must truly need," Agnès emphasised.

"True," agreed the Gascon. "You are thinking of the dracs—"

"Yes. La Donna is not only being hunted, but the pack chasing her is a ferocious one—"

"And snapping at her heels."

"Black dracs and an unnatural black mist," noted Leprat. "I don't know about you, but to me all this reeks of the Black Claw. . . ."

Marciac and Agnès both nodded.

Led by power-hungry dragons who would stop at nothing to achieve their ends, the Black Claw was a secret society which was particularly strong in Spain and her territories, including the Spanish Netherlands within whose borders La Donna had waited for La Fargue. Its most ancient, influential, and active lodge was to be found in Madrid. But although there were close links between it and the Court of Dragons, the Black Claw's goals were not always in accord with those of the Spanish Crown. Its ultimate aim, in fact, was to plunge Europe into a state of chaos that would permit the establishment of an absolute draconic reign—a reign that would spare no dynasty.

No human dynasty, that is.

"If La Donna is being pursued by the Black Claw," surmised the Gascon, "one can certainly understand her eagerness to find a powerful protector. . . . I would not like to be in her shoes—"

"And yet you are," Agnès said in an amused tone. "Do you suppose that the Black Claw has forgotten the defeat we recently inflicted upon its agents?"

"But in my case, I have you," Marciac responded. "Whereas La Donna has no one."

The young baronne smiled.

"But why would the Black Claw be after La Donna?" Leprat wanted to know.

"Perhaps"—Agnès started to suggest—"perhaps the Black Claw is the origin of the plot against the king. Perhaps La Donna somehow got wind of the secret, perhaps the Black Claw knows this, and now wants to silence her. . . ."

"All right," granted the former musketeer. "Or perhaps the Black Claw is seeking La Donna for some other reason, and she has concocted this tale in the hope that the cardinal will protect her, at least for a while. . . . What do you think, captain?"

In the heat of their discussion, Leprat, Marciac, and Agnès had forgotten the presence of La Fargue.

Turning their faces in unison, they saw Almades lifting an index finger to his lips in warning.

The captain was fast asleep in his chair.

Aubusson leaned back in his chair and considered the painting with a weary eye. It seemed to be resisting him today. Any further effort was useless. His mind was elsewhere and he could produce nothing worthwhile on the canvas.

"I might just as well go for a walk," he grumbled to himself as he put down his brushes and his palette.

Like all artists, he occasionally had black days and now had no trouble recognising the signs.

Nearly sixty years old, he had more than four decades of experience as a painter. Starting as an apprentice he had followed the ordinary course demanded by his guild. He rose to the rank of journeyman and finally—after completing a piece his peers judged to be of superior quality—that of master. Acquiring this title was essential for him to open his own studio. Aubusson could then accept commissions and earn a living from his work. He became one of the best portrait painters of his generation. Perhaps the very best of them, in fact. His renown had spread across borders and the courts of Europe vied for his services as he spent years roaming the roads of France, Germany, Italy, England, Spain, and even travelled as far as Hungary and Sweden. He reached the very height of his glory when Marie de Médicis, widow of Henri IV and mother of Louis XIII, had sent him to Madrid to produce a faithful likeness of the Infante Doña Ana Maria Mauricia, the future Anne d'Autriche, queen of France. It was said that even the Grand Turk himself had requested that Aubusson portray him.

These days, Aubusson no longer travelled.

Lacking a wife and children, he had retired to a charming country manor and was wealthy enough to take his rest following a career that had proved far more adventurous than he could have dreamed. He still painted, however. Landscapes mostly. But sometimes portraits when he chose to accept a commission. These tended to be rare now. Aubusson lived in such reclusion that many believed him dead or in exile, when in fact he resided only eight leagues northeast of Paris. His days passed peacefully near the village of Dammartin, with a couple of elderly domestic servants and a tall adolescent valet as his sole company.

This valet was grinding colours in a mortar when Aubusson decided to abandon his painting for the day.

"You will wash my brushes, Jeannot."

"Very good, master."

And thereupon, the artist left his studio, leaving its clutter, its golden light, and its intoxicating odours of paints behind.

Outside, the afternoon sun dazzled him as he crossed the courtyard. He hurried, the panels of his large sleeveless vest flapping against his thighs, his buckled shoes raising dust which then clung to his stockings, the hand shading his eyes pushing back the cloth cap on his head. He was quite tall. He had not gained weight as a result of age or retirement, and he remained a handsome man with a firm profile and a thick head of hair which was the same white as his carefully trimmed beard. Women were still attracted to him, although not nearly so many as in his prime. Back then, he had collected mistresses, sometimes selected among those whose portraits he painted at the expense of an overly trusting father or husband.

The big manor was silent.

In the front hall, at the bottom of the stairs, Aubusson washed his hands in a basin of clean water waiting for him. Then he took off his cap and the vest that he only wore when painting, exchanging them for a doublet hanging from the back of a chair. He had finished buttoning it when old Mère Trichet, who had heard him from the kitchen where she busied herself, brought him a glass of newly drawn wine, as she always did when he returned from the studio.

"Have you already finished for the day, monsieur?"

"My word . . . It seems to be one of those days when nothing goes right."

Mère Trichet—a woman in her fifties with a thick waist and a round face—nodded as Aubusson drained his glass and returned it to her.

"Thank you. Is the signora in her bedchamber?"

"No, monsieur. She is out at the back, with her monstrous beast. . . ."

The painter smiled but did not respond to this.

"I will sup alone this evening," he said as he left.

"Very good, monsieur."

Once out in the backyard where hens were pecking grain and a tired old hound was snoring, Aubusson went round the stable until he came to an enclosure. Here, beneath a sloping roof made of poorly joined planks, he found a chained wyvern asleep, its energy no doubt sapped by the heat. Crouched beside it, with her head bare and her long red hair sparkling in the sunshine, the beautiful Alessandra di Santi was stroking the great scaly head.

Leaning on the fence, Père Trichet was watching the scene with eyes squinted beneath the brim of his old battered hat, a lit clay pipe in his mouth. He was an elderly man, with a gnarly body hardened and worn from a life of labour. He spoke little, and when Aubusson joined him, he moved off with a visible shake of the head, his way of expressing utter disapproval of proceedings while washing his hands of the matter.

Even when domesticated and trained, wyverns remained carnivorous creatures powerful enough to tear off an arm with a single bite. And if one avoided approaching a horse from behind, one needed to take similar care with these winged reptiles, as placid and good-natured as they might seem. Elementary rules, known to all, or almost all—rules which La Donna evidently chose to ignore.

Standing up, she turned her back to the wyvern as she left the enclosure and, showing no fear of the beast behind her, said to the painter: "The poor thing is exhausted. I must say I've hardly spared her strength these past few days. . . ."

Smiling and serene, she wore a hunting outfit that looked delightful on her, very similar to the one she had worn the night before, in Artois, when she had met La Fargue.

"And you?" enquired Aubusson in a tone where concern outweighed reproach. "You promised me you would rest a while."

"I shall rest this evening," said Alessandra.

The painter helped her shut the gate to the enclosure.

"You must take good care of her," she added, looking over at the wyvern.

"I promise you I shall."

"She has truly earned it. Last night, for my sake, she faced a terrible storm and did not falter until she brought me here safely, despite—"

"I shall give up my own bed to her, if that will reassure you. . . . But am I permitted to have some care for you?"

The Italian spy did not respond, instead turning round to sweep the surrounding area with a slow scrutinising gaze.

"What is it?" asked Aubusson worriedly, in turn searching around them.

"I'm wondering where my little dragonnets, Scylla and Charybdis, might be."

"Bah! No doubt they're off hunting some poor field mouse, which they will deposit half-devoured in front of my door. . . ."

Taking Alessandra by the elbow, the painter led her toward a table placed in the shade provided by an arbour. They sat down and, once they were face-to-face, Aubusson gently squeezed the young woman's hands in his own and sought to capture her gaze.

"There's still time to abandon this course of action, you know that?"

Touched, La Donna gave him a smile full of tenderness. She felt troubled by this man so imbued with paternal instincts toward her. He was the only man she never made an effort to seduce.

"No," she said. "It's too late to turn back. And it has been too late for quite some time. . . . Besides, I've already made all my arrangements for this evening. The important thing is not to deviate from the plan. Remember, I shall no doubt be taken to La Renardière."

"I know. I'll scout out the domain tomorrow. And I shall return there during the night to make sure I will be able to find the path to the clearing, whatever happens."

"The domain is vast, but well guarded. Don't let them arrest you."

"If necessary, I shall say that I was out strolling and became lost. . . . But what if you're taken elsewhere?"

"Knowing the cardinal, that's highly unlikely."

"Nevertheless."

"Then I shall send you a warning by means of Scylla and Charybdis."

"And if you're someplace where you can't be reached?"

"For example?"

"Le Châtelet? Or the Bastille? Or in a cell at the château de Vincennes?"

Irritated, Alessandra stood up.

"You always take the blackest view of things!"

Aubusson rose to his feet as well.

"Your plan is too full of risks!" he exclaimed. "It will be a miracle if—"

He did not finish, feeling upset and embarrassed by his outburst.

With a smile and a knowing glance up at his face, the Italian adventuress indicated that she was not angry with him.

"You're forgetting one thing," she said.

"And what is that?"

"Even if they do not realise it, I shall have the Cardinal's Blades on my side."

The tavern was located in rue des Mauvais-Garçons, not far from the Saint-Jean cemetery. Like the surrounding neighbourhood, it was dark, filthy, smelly, and sinister. Although its dirt floor was not strewn with the same unhealthy muck that spattered the paving stones outside, the air stank of the smoke from pipes and the cheap yellow tallow candles, as well as the sweating, grimy bodies of its clientele. The One-Eyed Tarasque was a place where people came to drink themselves senseless, drowning their pain and sorrows in the sour wine. One such drunkard could be seen mumbling to himself in a corner. Not so long ago, a hurdy-gurdy player had performed his melancholy airs here in the evening. But he would be coming here no more.

Arnaud de Laincourt, however, still came.

He was sitting alone at a table upon which Maréchal, roaming as freely as his little chain would allow, was scratching at old wax incrustations in the wood. With a grey stoneware pitcher and a glass before him, the cardinal's former spy had a lost, distant expression on his face.

And a sad one.

Despite himself, he was thinking of all the sacrifices he had agreed to make in His Eminence's service, and the little thanks he had received in return. He was thinking back on all the years he had spent living amid lies, suspicion, betrayal, intrigue, and murder. He was thinking of that deceitful world where rest was never permitted, and which had little by little eaten away at his soul. He was thinking of all those who had lost their lives there. And in particular, of an old hurdy-gurdy player who had left nothing behind but a decrepit dragonnet.

Don't torment yourself on my account, boy.

Can't I at least shed a tear for you?

Of course you can. But I won't have you blaming yourself for my death. You know it wasn't your fault that I perished.

But I'm still alive. While you—

So what?

Laincourt looked at the empty stool in front of him.

It was the very same stool on which the hurdy-gurdy player used to take a seat during each of their clandestine meetings. The young man imagined that it was occupied once again. He had no trouble at all envisioning the old man, wearing his filthy rags and carrying his battered instrument on a strap around his neck. He was smiling, but his face was bruised and bloody. Laincourt could no longer remember him any other way than this, the way he had seen the hurdy-gurdy player for the very last time.

I've seen the man in the beige doublet again. The one who's been following me around these last few days and doesn't seem to care if he's seen. He was on the Pont Neuf. And I know he came by Bertaud's bookshop later. . . .

You can't avoid meeting him much longer.

Bah!

Just because you've finished with intrigues doesn't mean they've finished with you. The world doesn't work that way. . . . And besides, you were wrong.

Wrong?

Wrong to spurn the cardinal's offer.

The cardinal did not offer me anything.

Come now, boy! Do you think La Fargue would have proposed your joining his Blades without, at the very least, His Eminence's approval? . . . You should not have refused him.

Suddenly weary, Laincourt looked away.

To the others present in the tavern, he was just a young man whose dragonnet was patiently waiting for him to finish his drinking.

To travel from the Louvre to the Palais-Cardinal, all that was necessary was to take rue d'Autriche, then turn left on Saint-Honoré and follow to Richelieu's official residence.

A first obstacle, however, was posed in leaving the Louvre itself, which had been a medieval fortress before it became a palace. Its courtyard therefore had only one public exit: an archway so dark that one winter morning a gentleman had jostled King Henri IV there without even realising it. Twelve metres long, this archway led out to the east. It was the main access to the palace, the one used by royal processions, but also by a crowd of people who gathered before it from morning till night. Flanked by two old towers, it overlooked a nauseating ditch which could only be crossed by means of a narrow bridge defended by a massive fortified gate, known as the Bourbon gate.

Having left the Louvre through this gate, however, other obstacles still lay ahead. The gate opened onto rue d'Autriche, a lane running perpendicular to the Seine, between the École quay to the south and rue Saint-Honoré to the north. In Paris, the narrowness of the city's streets made the passage of traffic difficult everywhere. But the very modest rue d'Autriche was the place where all those seeking to enter the Louvre crossed paths with all those leaving the palace. To make matters worse, its pavement was always filled with coaches, since carriages were denied permission to enter the precincts of the palace, except in the case of certain grand personages, foreign dignitaries, or for reasons of health. Thus the resulting jams, collisions, and confusion were a permanent feature of rue d'Autriche, where people spent more time shuffling in place than advancing in the midst of a great din of shouts, insults, whinnying, hoofbeats, and creaking axles.

It was therefore with a certain amount of relief that, on the way to the Palais-Cardinal, it was finally possible to escape from rue d'Autriche and turn left onto rue Saint-Honoré. This street, although one of the longest in the capital since Paris had been extended westward, was not much wider than the others. Heavily frequented, it too had its share of daily traffic jams. But here at least, there was a more ordinary level of unruliness and bother. And here at least, travellers were no longer subjected to the stench from the stagnant waters in the ditches surrounding the Louvre.

Here at least, one could progress at a walking pace.

Bearing his magnificent coat-of-arms, Cardinal Richelieu's coach left the Louvre with the curtains drawn. It entered rue d'Autriche at a slow walk, moving toward rue Saint-Honoré where a horse escort would open the way for it until it arrived at the Palais-Cardinal.

The heavy curtains were intended to protect His Eminence from both the dust and public view. Nothing could be done, however, about the heat or the stink. Paris had been baking all day beneath a pitiless sun and the excrement and muck that covered its pavement had become a cracked crust from which escaped powerful, acrid, and unhealthy exhalations.

The cardinal held a handkerchief imbibed with vinegar to his nose and sat deep in thought, his face turned toward the window of the passenger door and the curtain that blocked it. Now that he had found refuge in his coach he was no longer obliged to put on an act for the ever-present spies at the Louvre. And although he remained in perfect control of his emotions, his severe expression and distant gaze betrayed the extent of his preoccupation. He considered the arrests he would have to order in conformity with the king's will, the interrogations that would then need to be conducted, and the truths that would emerge from them. Disturbing, embarrassing, scandalous truths. Truths that might very well compromise Queen Anne's honour and become a grave affair of State.

The queen, after all, was Spanish. . . .

The cardinal sighed and, almost as a means of distracting himself, asked: "Any news of Captain La Fargue?"

Then he slowly turned his head to look at the gentleman who had been sitting across from him, silent and still, ever since the coach first moved off.

"He returned today," replied the comte de Rochefort.

"Did you speak to him?"

"Yes, monseigneur. He asks to be received by Your Eminence as a matter of urgency."

"Impossible," Richelieu declared.

In order to confound any possible suspicions on the part of his adversaries, he had decided to maintain the pretence that today was an ordinary day, just like any other. He would, therefore, not receive the captain of his Blades. Not even discreetly, or secretly. For if someone happened to catch even a fleeting glimpse of La Fargue in the corridors of the Palais-Cardinal, the most astute observers would be sure to make a connection with the tête-à-tête which Louis XIII had so brusquely held with his chief minister that morning, after the meeting of the Council. A connection that had no basis in fact, as it happened. But it would be dangerous, nevertheless.

Rochefort did not insist.

"La Fargue met with La Donna last night," he said. "She claims to have knowledge of a plot threatening the throne of France. She offers to reveal it in return for—"

"How much?"

"She is not demanding money, monseigneur."

The cardinal quirked an eyebrow.

"Is La Donna no longer venal?"

"She demands your protection."

"My protection. Meaning that of France. . . . What does she fear? Or rather, who does she fear?"

"If one is to believe La Fargue, La Donna is being hunted by the Black Claw," Rochefort said dubiously.

"Ah," replied the cardinal, beginning to understand. "Naturally. That would explain a number of things," he added in a thoughtful tone. "Such as the lady's eagerness in seeking to contact me."

"She asked that this letter be delivered to you."

Richelieu looked at the letter held out to him, but at that instant the coach, which had previously been advancing very slowly along rue Saint-Honoré, came to a complete halt. Rochefort placed his hand on his rapier. Intrigued, the cardinal lifted the curtain of the coach door and called out: "Captain!"

The young Captain de La Houdinière drew up aside the coach on his horse.

"Monseigneur?"

"Why aren't we moving?"

"A tarasque, monseigneur."

Tarasques were enormous reptiles with hard shells. They had three pairs of very short legs. Heavy and slow, they possessed colossal strength and could easily knock over a wall by accident or pass right through a house without changing pace. As stupid as they were placid, they made excellent draught animals. They could also be readily harnessed to hoist machinery at building sites.

And there was no lack of building sites in the vicinity of the Palais-Cardinal.

"Do the best you can," said Richelieu before letting the curtain fall back into place.

But he had no illusions: there was simply no way of hurrying a tarasque when it crossed a street.

The cardinal considered the letter that Rochefort still held in his hand. Stained and dog-eared, it seemed to him thicker than a simple missive. No doubt there was something inside.

He did not touch it.

"Open it, please."

The comte undid the seal and unfolded the letter with a certain degree of apprehension. The threat of a possible attempt against Cardinal Richelieu's life was never far from his mind. And poisons existed—born of draconic alchemy—which, reduced to a very fine powder, could kill the first person who breathed them.

The letter from La Donna presented no such danger. On the other hand, what it actually contained prompted Rochefort to recoil in an instinctive, superstitious manner.

His reaction could not fail to interest the cardinal.

"Well, then?"

"Monseigneur, look . . ."

Richelieu lowered his eyes to peer at the object the other man was showing him, lying in the hollow of the unfolded letter. Still attached to the torn corner of a sheet of parchment, it was a seal in black wax stamped with the sign of the Grand Lodge of the Black Claw.

"Monseigneur . . . is that what I think it is?"

The cardinal took his time to examine it closely, and then nodded firmly.

"Most assuredly, Rochefort."

"But how could La Donna have obtained it?"

"That would be a very interesting question to put to her, wouldn't it?"

And as his coach started to move again, Richelieu turned back to the closed curtain of his coach door, as if absorbed by some spectacle that only he could perceive.

3

Rochefort came by the Hôtel de l'Épervier in the early evening. Upon entering the courtyard, he leapt from his saddle, threw his horse's reins to André, and dashed up the front steps of the mansion.

Inside, at the bottom of the great staircase, he came across Leprat, who, after La Fargue, was probably his least favourite of the Blades. To make matters worse, the former musketeer couldn't bear to see Rochefort walk into the house as if it were his own. He was not one of the Blades and never would be. Leprat therefore gave him a silent, icy welcome.

The cardinal's henchman, in a hurry, paid no heed to this.

"Where's La Fargue?" he demanded.

Leprat pointed toward the main hall on the ground floor, which the Blades had converted into a fencing room. It was a long, high-ceilinged chamber, decorated with gilt but now almost empty of furnishings, whose windows overlooked the garden. La Fargue was in discussion with Agnès and Marciac when Rochefort found him. Their conversation ended at once and all eyes converged on the intruder.

"We need to talk," Rochefort announced.

La Fargue considered him for a moment.

Then he nodded and with his chin indicated the door of an antechamber, toward which Rochefort briskly led the way. Once the door closed behind them, Agnès and Marciac, both looking intrigued, turned to Leprat who was watching from the threshold.

"La Donna?" guessed the young baronne.

Leprat shrugged, before glancing over his shoulder to see Saint-Lucq approaching.

Although he had returned from the mission at the same time as La Fargue and Almades, the half-blood had vanished and only now was making his reappearance. No one dreamt, however, of asking him where he had been or what he had been doing. Agnès noticed that his clothes—black and perfectly tailored, as usual—were clean and freshly pressed. They were certainly not the same ones he had been wearing on the journey to Artois with La Fargue. But his boots were somewhat dusty, suggesting that he had ridden along a dirt road since he had changed.

"Good evening," he said without addressing anyone in particular.

The others, preoccupied, answered him vaguely but their offhand greeting didn't offend him.

"Whose horse is that in the courtyard?" he asked.

"Rochefort's," answered Marciac. "He is in conference with the captain right now. He seemed to be in a hurry."

"What's it about?"

"La Donna, no doubt."

"I see."

The Gascon was seated at a small table, where there was some food, wine glasses, and bottles. Saint-Lucq joined him and, while he stood there and poured himself a drink, he asked: "And La Rochelle?"

Marciac pursed his lips and shrugged.

The half-blood drained his glass, peered at the Gascon through his red spectacles, nodded briefly, and went to sit in an alcove window that looked out onto the garden.

Marciac smiled.

It had been three weeks since they had seen one another. Three weeks during which Marciac, on his solo mission, could very well have been killed. But he knew that as far as welcomes were concerned, he could expect no more from Saint-Lucq.

The door of the antechamber opened and Rochefort, without glancing at anyone, departed as quickly as he had arrived. As for La Fargue, he took his time in emerging. He went over to the Blades and accepted the glass Leprat held out to him.

"So?" Agnès asked.

"So, La Donna has somehow managed to achieve her goal. I don't know why, but the cardinal is taking her very seriously. He believes this plot she claims to have discovered does in fact exist, and he charges us with unravelling the whole affair. . . ."

"And how are we to do that?" enquired Leprat.

"Obviously, first we need to find our lady spy again."

"Preferably before the dracs, who are also hunting for her," added Marciac.

"Yes. . . . The trouble is, we have no idea how to find her."

"Didn't she say she would make contact this evening, in Paris, captain?" recalled Agnès.

"Yes," La Fargue admitted.

"Then let's hope she doesn't delay too long before keeping her promise."

"And for now, captain?" Marciac wanted to know.

"For now," the old gentleman replied, "we wait."

"Ah—"

"What? Do you have other plans?"

"Yes. Two of them. And both have very beautiful eyes."

His dragonnet perched on his shoulder, Arnaud de Laincourt returned home from the One-Eyed Tarasque slightly drunk. He arrived at his house in rue de la Ferronnerie just as night was falling and found someone waiting outside for him. It was the man in the beige doublet who seemed to take great pleasure these past few days in dogging his footsteps without openly showing himself.

"Good evening, monsieur," said the gentleman.

"Good evening. You were waiting for me, I see."

"Indeed."

"In vain, I fear."

Without seeming to, Laincourt watched the darkening shadows around them carefully. Although there were still people travelling along rue de la Ferronnerie at this hour, it was never too early to carry out a well-executed ambush in Paris. Prudence was thus called for, until he knew exactly what the man in the beige doublet wanted from him. But the cardinal's former spy—for whom being alert to the slightest hint of danger was second nature—could detect no cause for alarm. And Maréchal, the old hurdy-gurdy player's dragonnet, remained placid.

"In vain? Could you not hear me out, before chasing me away?"

"I am not chasing you away, monsieur."

"Grant me just a few moments of your time. I only ask that you listen to me."

Laincourt was silent for a long while, examining the mysterious gentleman with an impassive eye. He was probably approaching forty years of age. Trim, fair-haired, with a well-kept mustache and royale beard, he was dressed elegantly but not ostentatiously. He had a frank and kindly demeanour, and his friendly eyes made no attempt to evade Laincourt's searching gaze.

"With your permission, it is time we had a certain conversation," the gentleman insisted.

A window opened above them. It was done discreetly, but not so quietly that Laincourt failed to hear it. No doubt it was monsieur Laborde, the ribbon seller who possessed a shop on the ground floor and resided on the first floor with his family, unless it was his wife, or both of them, pressed together and lending a curious ear to the proceedings below. Laborde was the principal lodger in the house. Enjoying the landlord's complete trust, he collected other lodgers' rent and made it his business to maintain the respectability of the entire house. When Laincourt was still an ensign in His Eminence's Guards, the ribbon maker had sought his good graces by fawning over him. But now the young man had returned his cape—and done so under such troubling circumstances that it had even started rumours—matters had changed.

Still hesitating over whether he should allow the gentleman a hearing, Laincourt wondered what advice the hurdy-gurdy player would have provided in such a situation.

I would advise you not to have this conversation on the front doorstep. Especially not with that fat Laborde eavesdropping. . . .

"Very well," the former spy decided. "Let's go inside."

"Thank you, monsieur."

Laincourt preceded the gentleman into a corridor that was both narrow and unlit, then led him up a staircase lacking both air and light. As they climbed, they kept a tight hold on the rickety banister, the former Cardinal's Guard cautioning the other man to be careful on the treacherous steps. Reaching the second floor, and allowing himself to be guided by habit, Laincourt found his door in the dark. He opened it with his key and left it wide open to assist the mysterious gentleman, who was still groping his way forward. A shadowy grey light filled the small apartment and outlined a faint, irregular patch of the landing.

Having arrived home, Laincourt remained faithful to certain routines. First of all he detached the leash from Maréchal's collar. Then he made the dragonnet enter his cage, before striking a flame to light a candle. Those tasks accomplished, he filled the small reptile's bowl with water, removed his hat, hung up his baldric, and only then turned his attention to the gentleman who, hat in hand, was looking about him.

Laincourt's apartments consisted of two badly ventilated rooms. Very modest and poorly furnished, devoid of any personal note, they were nevertheless clean and tidy—obviously the abode of a bachelor who had never let himself slide into sloth.

"Monsieur," said Laincourt, "I only have one chair to offer you. Take it, I shall use this stool."

"No need, monsieur. I shall not trouble you for long."

"As you wish."

"Permit me to introduce myself. I am the chevalier de Mirebeau and—"

"Just one thing, monsieur, before you continue."

"Yes?"

"Speak softly. If anyone were to bother to listen, they would hear everything through this wretched floor," indicated Laincourt, tapping his heel.

He imagined the Laborde couple below being showered with dust.

"I understand," the gentleman replied in a lower tone.

"So what is it you want, monsieur de Mirebeau? I have spotted you, here and there, for the past week."

"Forgive me, sir, but it has only been four days since I began observing you."

"Six days. During the first two, you were trying to hide."

Mirebeau admitted defeat: "That's right."

Laincourt didn't care if he was right or wrong.

"So? What do you want from me?"

"I have been charged with informing you, monsieur, that a certain party is surprised by the injustices that have been heaped upon you. This party is saddened to learn that you are alone and unemployed, and worries about your future."

"So, I have a guardian angel looking out for me. . . ."

"Your merits have not gone unnoticed, monsieur. Only a few weeks ago you wore the cape of His Eminence's Guards. You held the rank of ensign and you seemed destined for a lieutenancy. Without ever showing yourself to be unworthy of it, this cape was taken from you. Your name was then quietly cleared of any charges, but without the return of your cape, your rank or the honours that were your due. And then you were abandoned to your fate without further ado. . . ."

Laincourt studied the gentleman's eyes and tried to read the truth hidden within them. What did he know, exactly? Was he aware of the circumstances under which Laincourt had been arrested and then dismissed from the Cardinal's Guards? Did he know of the dangerous double role the spy had played with the Black Claw's agents? Of the sacrifices he had been forced to make to complete his mission successfully? Laincourt had accepted the assignment knowing the consequences full well. And he had been aware that it would require forsaking his rank and his uniform, because he was familiar with the rules of the game.

But in him Mirebeau only saw a loyal servant, dismissed out of ingratitude or negligence, whose legitimate ambitions had been shattered.

And, therefore, he had come to offer Laincourt a new master.

"You know how the world works. One cannot get very far or rise very high without a benevolent protector. The person I serve would very much like to count you as a friend. I said that your merits have not gone unnoticed. Your virtues are also known. As are your talents, which would finally be appreciated at their true value. Your Spanish is excellent, I believe. And you are perfectly familiar with Madrid. . . ."

Laincourt did not react to this. After all, it was no secret that he had spent two years at the Court of Dragons.

What he had actually been doing there, on the other hand . . .

"To be perfectly frank," he finally replied, "I don't believe I wish to offer my services to anyone. . . ."

Mirebeau's face took on a kindly expression.

"Would you like to think it over? I understand, and I shall not insist." He drew forth a note with a stamped seal from his sleeve. "But at least do me the favour of paying a visit to . . . to your guardian angel. Here. Go to rue Saint-Thomas-du-Louvre. Present yourself on the day and the hour of your choosing and show them this. You shall be received."

"All right," said Laincourt, taking the note.

"I bid you a good evening, monsieur."

The cardinal's former spy answered with a noncommittal smile, then watched the gentleman take his leave. He rose, went to the window, and soon saw Mirebeau come out into rue de la Ferronnerie and follow it east toward the Saint-Honoré neighbourhood. Without even thinking about it, Laincourt invoked the presence of the hurdy-gurdy player who approached to look over his shoulder.

You're not going to examine the seal on the letter, boy?

I don't need to see it to know at whose door I would be knocking.

No, of course not. There are only two noteworthy dwellings on rue Saint-Thomas-du-Louvre, after all.

Laincourt nodded as, with narrowed eyes, he continued to watch Mirebeau walking away into the distance.

One of them is the mansion of the marquise de Rambouillet. It's said she hosts a literary salon of the highest quality in her home.

True. But the other is the Hôtel de Chevreuse, and I rather think that is where your guardian angel is hoping to see you. . . .

* * *

That night at the Hôtel de l'Épervier there reigned an atmosphere similar to the eve of battle. The Blades, assembled in the fencing room, found ways to quietly kill time in the candlelight. Leprat and Marciac played dice on a corner of the table. Ballardieu was balancing slowly back and forth on a tilted chair facing one of the windows, watching the night sky while he drank a glass of wine. Agnès was leafing through a treatise on fencing. Lying on a bench with his eyes shut, one knee bent, and his hands gathered on his chest, Saint-Lucq might have been asleep. And Almades was sharpening his rapier, giving it three long strokes with the whetstone before turning the blade over.

Three strokes along one edge . . .

. . . three strokes along the other.

Three strokes along one edge . . .

Naïs and monsieur Guibot had gone to their beds. Only the Blades remained, along with André who was guarding the saddled horses in the stables, and La Fargue who had retired to his office.

. . . three strokes along the other.

Three strokes along one edge . . .

All of them were booted and armed, ready to spring into action as soon as their captain gave the word for their departure. They only needed to seize their hats, jump into their saddles, and spur their mounts with their heels. Within the hour, they could be anywhere in Paris. Patiently, they awaited the order.

. . . three strokes along the other.

How would La Donna make her presence known? And, above all, when? Midnight was approaching. The Blades had been waiting all evening for a message or a signal. The beautiful spy knew she was being hunted. She would have to be extremely careful. Would she use some indirect means to reestablish contact? But in that case, which one? The dragonnets? Yes, one of the twin dragonnets to which she seemed so attached could deliver a message. Here at the Hôtel de l'Épervier. Or at the Palais-Cardinal. Or even at the Louvre.

Three strokes along one edge . . .

. . . three strokes along the other.

"You win," Leprat said to Marciac after a last unlucky roll of the dice.

"Another game?"

"No, thank you."

The musketeer stood up.

"As you like," the Gascon said. "But you'll need to make up for lost ground eventually. Don't forget, you already owe me Piedmont and the duchy of Cleves."

It was a game between the two of them. It started one day when, neither of them having even a sou in their pocket, they divided Europe up equitably between them and started betting with their territories. Whether they had subsequently come into funds or not, they had continued to play for these imaginary stakes ever since, keeping a careful account of their losses and gains.

Three strokes along one edge . . .

. . . three strokes along the other.

"Never fear, I won't forget," said Leprat. "No more than I shall forget winning the bishopric of Munster from you."

Giving Marciac an amused smile, he went to knock on La Fargue's half-open door.

La Fargue had arranged for his personal use a small private office that communicated with the fencing room by a door and with the upper floors by means of a tiny spiral staircase, hidden behind a moveable wooden panel. Here he received visitors, meditated, and wrote reports to His Eminence. But he rarely shut the door.

This evening, like the Blades, he too waited in a silence measured out by the long, regular strokes of Almades's whetstone. Booted and armed, he was leaning back in his armchair with his crossed ankles up on his worktable. Pensive, he played with a small pendant that he normally wore around his neck, winding the chain around his index finger—first in one direction, then the other. It was a worn, scratched, tarnished piece of jewellery which had a cover to protect the miniature portrait within. That of a woman La Fargue had loved long ago, but which also resembled closely the daughter they had produced together.

Grown into a young woman, that daughter had recently made a reappearance in his life. She had been in danger and he had been forced to take steps to protect her, putting her beyond the reach of both the Black Claw and Cardinal Richelieu's agents. But it had meant he was separated from her once again. He did not even know where she was now, as prudence dictated. But at least his mind was at rest, knowing there was nowhere his daughter would be safer than in the hands into which he had entrusted her.

La Fargue lifted his head and closed his fist over the pendant when he heard Leprat knock at his door.

"Yes?"

The musketeer entered.

"I'm afraid nothing is going to happen this evening," he said.

"So am I."

"It will soon strike midnight."

"I know."

"Should I order the horses unsaddled?"

"Let's give La Donna another hour to manifest herself."

"Very well."

At that same instant, Almades ceased sharpening his rapier. Leprat turned and saw André arriving, a letter in his hand.

"Where's the captain?" asked the groom.

The Spaniard pointed in the direction of the small private office. André crossed the fencing room, watched attentively by the whole company, as La Fargue and his lieutenant walked out to meet him. Agnès, Marciac, and Ballardieu rose to their feet. Almades sheathed his blade, now sharp as a razor. Saint-Lucq remained stretched out on the bench, but had turned on his side, his head propped up by one elbow.

"Captain," said André, "a rider just delivered this."

"Thank you," replied La Fargue, taking the letter from him.

The seal was Cardinal Richelieu's. The old captain split it open and unfolded the letter amid a deep silence.

Everyone waited.

La Fargue read the contents, and then announced: "La Donna presented herself at the Palais-Cardinal an hour ago."

The others looked at him without understanding.

"She came to offer herself up as a prisoner," he explained with a faint, ambiguous smile. "And when you think about it, it's a clever move on her part. . . ."

4

I t was not the most well known of the sixteen gates of Paris. It was not the most frequented, or the best defended. And once night fell, and the thick doors between the two massive towers were closed, it became a dark, silent edifice whose sinister calm would—ordinarily—go undisturbed until the following morning.

The dracs arrived shortly after midnight, their mounts walking in the black ground-hugging mist that accompanied them.

There were eight in all.

Seven vigorous black dracs and one other drac with pale scales, the colour of dirty bone. The black dracs were riding calm, powerful warhorses. Wearing gloves and boots, they were dressed like hired swordsmen. Wide leather belts were cinched around their waists and they had solid rapiers at their sides.

The other drac was unarmed. But he carried a large carved staff hung with various small fetishes: tiny bones, teeth, feathers, old scales. Dressed in stinking, filthy rags encrusted with what looked like dried blood, he rode bareback on a giant salamander whose belly grazed the black mist and whose slow, steady step set the pace for the whole group. The drac was very old. He was missing some teeth and his back was bent. His yellow eyes, however, gleamed with a lively spark. And a particularly virulent and baleful aura emanated from him.

The dracs drew to a halt on the narrow stone bridge that crossed over the fetid ditch before the gates. They waited, as the mist beneath them stretched out dark tendrils that snaked their way beneath the city gate in order to accomplish their task on the far side. The task did not take long. The tendrils immediately withdrew.

The old drac raised his staff in one gnarly hand, tipped with jagged yellow claws, and pointed it at the door.

He mumbled a few words in the drakish tongue.

The sound of scraping and several dull thuds could be heard inside.

And then the heavy doors opened, while the portcullis lifted with a clanking noise.

The archway, long and empty, was only lit by two sputtering torches.

The dracs passed through it slowly, without sparing a glance for the dying pikeman who staggered out of the guards' lodge and stretched out an arm, trying to cry for help before he collapsed. He died, his body convulsing, retching up a black bile that ran from his mouth, nostrils, and eyelids.

The dracs emerged from the gate and melted, one by one, into the shadowy streets of Paris.

LA RENARDIÈRE

1

Alessandra di Santi, also known as La Donna, had been awake since dawn. She rose carefully from her bed, trying not to disturb the two dragonnets still curled up asleep. Silently she went to sit by the window, half naked, with an old Italian song on her lips, methodically combing her hair. She was pale and beautiful, caressed by the dawn sunlight that warmed her long red tresses.

The young woman had a view of the garden and the entire domain of La Renardière—the name of the small castle where she had dwelt for the past five days—from her bedchamber. It was a hunting lodge, quite similar to the one which had just been finished for the king in Versailles. It comprised a central pavilion with two wings framing a courtyard, and to the front, beyond a dry moat crossed by a stone bridge, stood a forecourt flanked by the servants' quarters. Although in truth it lacked for nothing, La Renardière only provided the basic comforts. But the place was both discreet and peaceful, only an hour's ride from Paris, a short remove from the road to Meudon, and practically invisible behind some dense woodland.

In short, it was a perfect retreat.

Having combed her hair, Alessandra shook a little bell to warn the chambermaid—who had been graciously put at her disposal, along with an elegant wardrobe—that she wished to wash and dress. The clear tinkling sound attracted first Scylla, the female of the pair of black dragonnets, and then her brother Charybdis, who followed close behind. The twins vied playfully for their mistress's affections. They jostled one another, craning their necks for a caress and rubbing their snouts against La Donna's throat and cheeks. She laughed, pretending to repel the small reptiles' assaults and gently scolding them for being such impudent little devils. An involuntary swipe of a claw scratched Alessandra's shoulder, but the wound closed almost immediately and the single drop of blood that had welled up slid down her perfectly healed skin.

The chambermaid's knock at the door interrupted their frolics.

She had been at La Renardière for five days. Five days of being taken, each morning, to Paris to be interrogated. Five days of being treated with a mixture of courtesy, wariness, and resentment.

"This is your room, madame. And this is your key. At night please avoid leaning too far from your window. Someone might fire a musket at you by mistake."

When she had presented herself at his door and made herself his prisoner, the beautiful spy had placed the cardinal in an extremely delicate position. The Parlement of Paris—which was the kingdom's most important court of justice—had recently convicted her in absentia on several charges of corruption, blackmail, and theft. And, for the most part, they were quite right in doing so. But Richelieu did not want her to be punished for these crimes: first, because the pope was unlikely to allow her to be executed; second, because she was in a position to reveal State secrets which no one in Europe wished to see divulged; and third, most crucially, because she claimed to have knowledge of a plot against Louis XIII and was demanding, before she would say more, that her life and liberty be guaranteed. But the Parlement was jealous of its authority and if it learned the truth, it would call for La Donna's immediate arrest. Once that happened, whatever was subsequently decided, the legal and political complications would accumulate—and as for the plot against His Majesty, they would be forced to wait until it was set in motion to discover its nature and scope. . . .

Happily, the members of Parlement could not be displeased by things of which they remained ignorant. It was thus in greatest secrecy that Alessandra spent her mornings with a magistrate at Le Châtelet, where she was asked questions which she answered graciously, while always endeavouring not to say too much. She stayed at La Renardière the rest of the time, protected by musketeers. There were a dozen of them, who patrolled the grounds and occupied a small wooden pavilion in the woods by the entrance to the hunting lodge's grounds. But the young Italian woman was not fooled: the musketeers were there to keep a watch on her as much as they were to protect her, just as the domestic servants in the residence were there to spy on her as much as to serve her. All of them were Richelieu's people, as was the gentleman who acted as her bodyguard.

That one was a Cardinal's Blade.

Seated at her dressing table, Alessandra was finishing arranging her hair and attire to her satisfaction when there was a knock at the door.

"Come in, monsieur!"

It was Leprat. Freshly shaven, wearing boots, breeches, gloves, and a doublet, he was dressed in red, black, and grey. His spurs jingling at each step, he entered the room with his hat in hand and his sword at his side.

"Good morning, monsieur le chevalier," La Donna greeted him, her eyes on the mirror which the chambermaid slowly moved around her. "Did you sleep well outside my door?"

"No, madame."

The young woman pretended to be concerned. She turned theatrically in her seat and placed a hand to her throat.

"Did you sleep poorly, monsieur? Are you feeling ill?"

"No, madame."

Alessandra went from worry to pouting anger, still play-acting.

"Then you must have slept elsewhere. That's very poor on your part. You abandoned me and I could have been assassinated. I'm very upset with you. I was happier when I thought you were ill. . . ."

Leprat smiled.

"I was at your door, madame. But I didn't sleep. And I feel quite well."

"Well, thank goodness on both counts! I am doubly reassured."

Returning her attention to her toilette, La Donna continued to inspect her reflection in the mirror.

"Madame, would you be so good as to make haste. Your breakfast is served, and monsieur de La Houdinière will no doubt arrive soon."

Irritated, La Donna snatched the mirror from the chambermaid's hands.

"Monsieur de La Houdinière shall have to wait," she said. "And in Paris, inside that depressing Châtelet where he insists on receiving me, monsieur de Laffemas can also wait. And, if necessary, the cardinal can wait too!"

"Madame. If you please . . ."

Alessandra caught Leprat's eye in the mirror.

She smiled at him, adjusted a curl of hair for form's sake, returned the mirror to the servant, and then rose to turn toward the former musketeer. She looked ravishing, in a snugly fitting but otherwise fairly plain brown-and-cream dress which nevertheless enhanced her pale skin, her red hair, and her pretty bosom. She seemed to be waiting for a compliment, but Leprat limited himself to a brief nod of approval.

The beautiful Italian woman had to satisfy herself with that and accepted the arm offered to her before passing into the antechamber.

Kh'Shak, the huge black drac, hesitated for a moment before opening the door and descending the stairs with a cautious step, almost on tiptoe, holding the scabbard of his rapier to keep it from knocking into anything.

The cellar was silent and warm, stingily lit by fat yellow candles whose flames gave off acrid wisps of smoke. The place reeked, filled with strong odours that would turn a human stomach but which were pleasant to drakish nostrils: the smell of blood, offal, and meat both fresh and spoiled.

The old pale-scaled drac was sitting cross-legged on the dirt floor. He was wearing the dirty, smelly rags that were his sole clothing, and his ceremonial staff—the big carved stick with its feathers, bones, scales, teeth, and coloured beads—was resting across his meagre thighs. Eyes shut, he sat completely still, hardly breathing at all. The gutted body of a small white goat lay before him. Other remains were rotting here and there, mutilated and half devoured.

Halting at the bottom of the steps Kh'Shak hesitated again, as if afraid to enter the cellar completely and set foot on the spattered, blood-soaked floor where he knew awful rituals had been carried out. Yet he was by no means a coward. His courage and fierceness had earned him his position as chief.

But when it came to magic . . .

"Saaskir . . ." he ventured in a hoarse voice.

Saaskir. A drakish word meaning both priest and sorcerer, two notions that were blurred together in the dracs' tribal culture.

"Yes, Kh'Shak?" answered the old drac. "What is it?"

The black drac cleared his throat. Still unmoving, his eyes still closed, the other had his back toward him.

"Have you found her, saaskir?"

"No, my son," said the sorcerer in the calm, patient tone that one usually employed with small children. "I haven't found her yet. La Donna has concealed herself behind seven veils. I rip one away each night, and soon, she will be revealed in full nudity beneath the Eye of the Night Dragon. Then I shall see and, after me, you will be the first to know. . . ."

"Thank you, saaskir."

Kh'Shak was about to turn away, still troubled, when the old drac called out to him: "You're worried, aren't you?"

The great black drac wondered how he should reply. He opted for the truth.

"Yes, saaskir."

"That's good. You are a chief. It is your role to worry about things others do not care about, to think of things which others forget, to see what others ignore. . . . But as the days pass, your warriors are growing restless, and you're afraid you won't be able to restrain them for much longer."

Was the saaskir casting doubt on his authority? Kh'Shak's blood began to boil.

"My warriors fear me and respect me! They shall obey!"

The old drac sorcerer gave a faint smile that the other could not see.

"Of course, of course . . . So, all is well?"

"Yes," Kh'Shak was obliged to concur. "All is well."

A silence ensued, during which the black drac did not know what to do. Finally, the old sorcerer's sugary voice came again: "Now, Kh'Shak, you must leave me. I need to rest."

La Donna was finishing her cup of chocolate while a servant cleared away the remains of her breakfast. Sitting in an armchair, she eyed Leprat, who was looking out of a window. He was watching the track that emerged from the woods and then ran in a straight line, crossing the forecourt between the servants' quarters to the bridge over the dry moat.

Antoine Leprat, chevalier d'Orgueil.

One of Captain La Fargue's Blades, therefore. And a former member of the King's Musketeers, it would seem. Calm, reserved, courteous, and watchful. Probably incorruptible. In a word: irreproachable. Tall, dark-haired, and grim-eyed. Attractive, to those who liked mature men whose faces had been marked by the years, and by their ordeals. He had a brutal side to him. This Leprat knew how to fight and had no fear of violence. His muscular body was doubtless covered with scars.

Alessandra di Santi's glance must have been too intense in the silence, because Leprat felt it and turned to her. She did not make the mistake of suddenly averting her eyes, which would have been a tacit admission of a guilty sentiment.

Instead, cleverly, she chose to conceal the motive of her interest.

"Where did you acquire that strange sword, chevalier?"

As always, Leprat had his white rapier at his side, a single piece of ivory carved, from tip to pommel, out of an Ancestral Dragon's tooth. It was an extraordinary, formidable weapon, lighter and yet more resilient than even the best Toledo blade.

"It was entrusted to me."

"By whom? Under what circumstances?"

The former musketeer smiled and turned his head back to the window without answering. His eyes drifted toward the tree line.

"Come now, monsieur," the beautiful spy insisted. "We've shared this roof and most of our waking hours for several days and I still know almost nothing about you."

"Just as I know almost nothing about you. No doubt it's best that way."

Alessandra rose and walked slowly up to Leprat, approaching him from behind as he continued to gaze outside.

"But I only desire that you know me better, monsieur le chevalier. Ask me questions, and I'll answer them. . . ."

"I leave the task of questioning you to monsieur de Laffemas."

"Would a little chocolate soften you? There's some left."

Turning from the window, Leprat suddenly found himself in close proximity to La Donna. She had drawn so near they were almost touching. Shorter than him, she looked up at him over the rim of the cup, which she held against her moist half-opened lips.

Her eyes were smiling.

"Do you like chocolate, monsieur le chevalier?"

"I . . . I don't know."

"You've never tasted it?"

"No."

Not widely known previously in France, chocolate now enjoyed some slight notoriety since Queen Anne d'Autriche, who had acquired a taste for it during her childhood in Spain, asked that it be served to her in the Louvre. Still reserved for the rich elite, chocolate was, curiously enough, sold by apothecaries.

"It's delicious," murmured Alessandra. With both hands she raised her cup to Leprat's mouth. "Here, try some."

Their glances met, hers seductive, his troubled.

For an instant that slowly stretched between them, the former musketeer almost gave in to temptation . . .

. . . but the chambermaid—knocking and then immediately entering the room—broke the spell. She brought La Donna's gloves, cloak, and hat. Having surprised Leprat, who quickly drew back, she acted as if she had seen nothing.

"Bah!" said Alessandra, shrugging and turning away. "It's gone cold now, in any case. . . ."

Leprat found La Renardière's maître d'hôtel already on the front porch, waiting as usual.

"Monsieur."

"Good morning, Danvert."

Together they watched a coach pass over the dry moat and enter the courtyard. Twelve cavaliers escorted the vehicle, all of them Cardinal's Guards armed with swords and short muskets, although they did not wear the cape. Monsieur de La Houdinière rode at their head. He was the company's new captain and the successor to sieur de Saint-Georges, who had died a month earlier under circumstances which were so infamous that they remained secret, to the satisfaction of all concerned.

The coach drew to a halt at the bottom of the steps. La Houdinière leapt down from his saddle and went over to Leprat. They shook hands like men who held one another in esteem but who could not permit themselves to fraternise—for the first belonged to His Eminence's Guards, while the second remained, even if he had momentarily hung up his cape, a member of His Majesty's Musketeers. There was a traditional rivalry between these two corps, and a lively one: it was a rare fortnight which passed without a guard and a musketeer engaging in a duel for one reason or another.

La Houdinière and Leprat, however, were on good terms.

Their acquaintance had begun when they fought together the previous year, when Louis XIII had marched on Nancy for the second time—and before he had to for a third—at the head of his army to persuade Duke Charles IV of Lorraine to show better sentiments toward the king of France. On the eighteenth of June, a cavalry regiment from Lorraine had been holding one of the crossings over the Meuse river, close to the small town of Saint-Mihiel and not far from the king's quarters. Hostilities had not really commenced yet—in fact, Charles IV was continuing to parley—but Louis XIII was determined to strike a lightning blow as a demonstration of force. A unit of elite soldiers drawn from the Navarre regiment, the gendarmerie, the light cavalry, the King's Musketeers, and the Cardinal's Guards had therefore been placed under the comte d'Allais's command. La Houdinière—who was then still a lieutenant—and Leprat had been among this elite. Surprised, trapped in their trenches, and soon stricken by panic, Lorraine's forces had suffered a terrible defeat. It had been a massacre which few had survived.

Later the two men's paths had often crossed, but they had not worked closely together again until now. They shared the responsibility of guarding La Donna, Leprat here at La Renardière and La Houdinière during her daily journeys to Le Châtelet, where the spy was interrogated. They thus met twice a day, when the one relieved the other.

"Is everything all right?" asked La Houdinière.

"Yes," replied Leprat. "Any orders from the Palais-Cardinal?"

"None."

And that was everything that needed to be said.

Wearing her cloak and hood, Alessandra soon made her appearance, smiling and unruffled. Ever a gentleman, La Houdinière opened the coach door for her and lent her his hand as she climbed into the passenger compartment. Then he remounted his horse and, after a final salute to Leprat, gave the signal to depart.

The former musketeer stood for a moment watching the coach and its escort move off. He was tired but could not rest just yet.

He turned to Danvert, the maître d'hôtel, who was waiting patiently.

"Let's go," he said, returning inside. "We have much to do."

The old woman was sitting in a peaceful, sunny garden in one of the numerous convents in the faubourg Saint-Jacques.

She spent the better part of her days here, when the heat was bearable, reading and biding her time in an armchair that was brought out from her bedchamber for her. Otherwise she shared the ordinary life of the nuns, punctuated by prayers and meals. She was not obliged to do so, but it suited the character she had invented for herself, that of a rich, pious widow, weary of the world and desiring to pass the last years of her life in retreat from it. Within the convent she was known as madame de Chantegrelle. Only a month earlier, however, she had been the vivacious vicomtesse de Malicorne and, thanks to magic, had looked less than twenty years old—an age which was scarcely more deceptive than the one her present appearance suggested. For her true age was a number of years which stretched far beyond the ordinary span. Ordinary for human kind, that is.

But she was a dragon.

The so-called madame de Chantegrelle lifted her eyes from her book and sighed as she considered both the garden and the life that was hers at present. She had loved being the vicomtesse de Malicorne. She'd possessed youth, beauty, wealth, and power. All of Paris had courted her and vied for her favours. What a shame to have been forced to abandon that role! Officially, the vicomtesse had perished in a fire that had left nothing of her but a charred, unrecognisable corpse—in point of fact, that of some wretched woman taken from the gutter. It was a tragic loss but an almost banal event in Paris, where fire was the cause of many fatal accidents. . . .

The truth was, the ritual intended to mark her triumph had instead brought about her ruin. Anyone but her would not have survived the ordeal, no doubt. But that did not assuage her regrets. And it did nothing to diminish the desire for revenge that burned inside her. If not for Cardinal

Richelieu, if not for Captain La Fargue and his cursed Blades, today she would have been at the head of the first Black Claw lodge ever founded in France. . . .

The sound of a light footstep on the gravel garden path drew madame de Chantegrelle's attention. A nun approached her and, after making sure she wasn't asleep, whispered a few words in her ear. The old woman nodded before turning her head to look at her announced visitor, who stood a short distance away beneath a stone arch covered with climbing roses in flower. A fleeting expression of surprise and fear passed across her face, but she greeted her visitor with a polite smile and extended a hand to be kissed.

The man was dressed as a gentleman, in grey and black, with a sword at his side. He might have been fifty or fifty-five years of age. He was an intimidating figure: tall, rather thin, and hieratic in bearing. He had an emaciated oval face with strangely smooth skin, as if it had been stretched a little too tight over the ridges of his face, and a morbid, sickly pallor. His icy grey eyes crinkled up whenever he coughed—with a dry, brief, guttural sound—into the handkerchief which he dabbed at his fine, livid lips.

Like the woman he now joined, he was a dragon. He had borne many names, some of which she had learned. But the one he preferred was a *nom de guerre*: the *Alchimiste des Ombres*, the Alchemist of the Shadows. Where had it originated, exactly? She didn't know. In any case, it was by this pseudonym— or sometimes merely by a sign featuring an "A" and an "O" intertwined— that the Black Claw designated one of its best independent agents.

A novice having brought him a chair, the Alchemist sat down with a nod—not so much in thanks but rather in acknowledgement of the chair being placed at his disposal, as a matter of course.

"I have known of your setbacks for some time, madame. But I have only now had the opportunity to pay you a visit. Please forgive me."

"My 'setbacks,'" noted the old woman. "How kindly put—"

"I will add, in my defence, that it was hardly easy to find you."

"What can I say? Madame de Chantegrelle is far more discreet than the vicomtesse de Malicorne. And who would concern themselves with a dying old lady living out her final days in a convent, surrounded by sisters whose affection for her was ensured by bequeathing to them what remains of her fortune?"

The Alchemist gave one of his rare smiles, which barely lifted the corners of his thin lips. Like all dragons, he was amused by human religions and the shortcomings of their representatives. His race had no other form of worship than that of ancestors, no other divinities than the Ancestral Dragons whose existence, even in times immemorial, was not subject to doubt.

"Do you lack money, madame?"

"No, thank you. But I am touched by your concern, although it does seem to me that your visit cannot be one of pure courtesy."

"Madame, I—"

"No, monsieur. Don't defend yourself on this subject; you would only be lying, after all . . ." She sighed. "I am indeed most ungrateful in reproaching you. Since . . . since my setbacks, visitors have been rare. The Black Claw is quick to forget anyone who can no longer serve it. I do not regret that—I'm happy to still be alive. I imagine I owe it to my birth, to my rank. And perhaps because they believe I've been rendered harmless once and for all—"

"I wager that they are mistaken on that point."

"Do you really think so?"

The former vicomtesse looked at the Alchemist.

"Yes," he said, returning her gaze without wavering.

It meant nothing, she knew that.

Nevertheless, she chose to believe that he was sincere.

"I just need to rest, hence my self-imposed retreat here. And then one day, when I have recovered some semblance of my past power—"

She broke off, eyes shining and lost in the distance.

The Alchemist waited for her to return from her dreams of restored glory. But perhaps those dreams had carried her too far away. After a moment, he heard her murmuring, as she nodded her head vaguely: "Yes . . . Some rest . . . I only need some rest. . . ."

The inn, a little way from Vincennes on the road to Champagne, was full of soldiers going to join their regiment at Châlons-sur-Marne. Swords, daggers, and pistols lay on all the tables; muskets and halberds leant against the walls. The noisy, mixed-up, indistinct, but warlike conversations reverberated around the common room where a golden light poured in through the windows. Mocking sallies were thrown above heads wreathed in pipe smoke. Other jests answered them and loud laughter erupted.

Captain La Fargue entered and, from the inn's threshold, where his impressive silhouette was outlined against daylight and blocked the exit, he surveyed the assembly with a slow glance. Eyes narrowed, he did not find the person he was looking for, while ignoring the curious looks that were being warily cast in his direction. Anyone but him would no doubt have drawn some remark that would have started a fight. But none of the soldiers present were stupid enough or drunk enough to pick a quarrel with a man like La Fargue.

A rare kind of man, intimidating and dangerous.

Entering in turn, Almades approached the captain from behind and said in his ear: "Round the back."

La Fargue nodded and, accompanied by the Spaniard, went out into the sunny back yard. There he found the comte de Rochefort, who was playing skittles with a group of gentlemen.

Seeing who had arrived, the cardinal's henchman took his time to aim, launched the ball, and managed a fairly good throw. Satisfied, he rubbed his hands together while his playing companions congratulated him. He thanked them, excused himself, finally nodded to the captain of the Blades, and went to recover his doublet, which he had removed in order to play more comfortably. Putting it back on, he invited La Fargue to sit with him at a small table beneath a tree. There was a glass and a jug placed upon it. Rochefort drank from the glass and La Fargue, provocatively, from the jug.

"Please, help yourself," said the cardinal's man ironically.

The old gentleman soldier gazed at him steadily. And for good measure, without blinking, he wiped his mouth with the back of his hand and smacked his lips.

"How very elegant . . ."

"What do you want, Rochefort? I have better things to do than watch you play skittles."

The comte nodded vaguely. He glanced distractedly at their surroundings, and then took a deep breath as he collected his thoughts. Finally, in an almost casual tone, he asked: "What do you make of La Donna?"

La Fargue sighed and leaned back in his chair.

"My opinion of her has not changed," he replied in a weary voice. "I believe we cannot trust the woman. But I also believe she has come to us with a story that forces us to give her allegations serious consideration. For even if it were the duchesse de Chevreuse herself claiming to denounce a plot against the king . . ." At these words, Rochefort raised an eyebrow, but the captain was not deterred. "Even if La Donna were La Chevreuse, I say, we would have to lend her an attentive ear."

"The cardinal is of the same mind as you. Moreover, there is this . . ."

Rochefort discreetly pushed something across the table to La Fargue, an object which looked very much like a jewel case made of precious wood. The captain took it, opened it, and saw a black wax seal inside, still attached to the torn corner of a sheet of parchment.

"That was in the packet La Donna gave you, not long ago, to deliver to His Eminence. Do you know what it is?"

La Fargue sat up in his chair.

"Yes. This is a Black Seal. Each of them contains a drop of dragon's blood, used by the Black Claw to seal its most precious documents. . . ." He returned the case, and Rochefort pocketed it immediately. "So the Black Claw is a player in this game."

"In one fashion or another, yes."

"What does La Donna say on this matter?"

The cardinal's man grimaced.

"Not much . . . neither on this matter nor, indeed, on any other. According to Laffemas she has no equal when it comes to answering a question without saying anything. . . ."

For several days now, the beautiful Alessandra di Santi had been transported in secret to a room in Le Châtelet and interrogated, also in the greatest secrecy, all morning. Monsieur de Laffemas conducted these sessions. Beginning his career as an advocate in Parlement, then a master of petitions, he had since been appointed a state councillor. He enjoyed the confidence and esteem of Richelieu, to whom he owed a great deal. Now, at the age of fifty, he was the lieutenant of civil affairs at Le Châtelet, that is to say, one of the two magistrates—the other being the lieutenant of criminal affairs—who worked as deputies to the provost of Paris. An honest, rigorous, and devoted man, Isaac de Laffemas was in charge of State prosecutions and therefore the object of enduring hatred due to his role in the great trials ordered by the cardinal.

Thinking about the man's difficulties with La Donna, La Fargue couldn't prevent himself from letting a smile show. Rochefort saw it and also smiled, adding: "To top it all, without a doubt, is the fact that Laffemas always comes out feeling quite pleased with himself. It is only when he reads the minutes of his interrogation that he realises how, every time, La Donna has not answered the question, or only very partially, or she has merely repeated information she has already given him, and which wasn't worth very much to begin with. She mixes truth and falsehood, all the while cleverly wielding allusion, innuendo, digression, hollow phrases, and misleading revelations. She knows how to play at being naïve, foolish, forgetful, and charming by turn. Poor Laffemas is losing his wits as well as his sleep over her. And yet, he still returns each morning determined not to let her get the best of him—"

Rochefort was interrupted by the skittles players, applauding an able bowler.

"Very well," said La Fargue. "La Donna is leading Laffemas around by the nose. But it's only fair. . . . After all, she promised to tell us what she knows of this plot on the condition that she is protected. That means a pardon, without which she will always be persecuted in France. In accordance with the sentences passed by the Parlement, her proper place, right now, is in prison. She knows this full well and, unless she is subjected to torture, she will remain silent on the essential question until she receives her guarantees."

"The cardinal is not in a position to offer her such guarantees right now. And time is running out. Not simply because we believe the date of execution of the plot against His Majesty is fast approaching. But also because each day that goes by increases the chances that La Donna's presence will be discovered. And when it reaches the ears of the members of the Parlement—"

"The king can annul a ruling by the Parlement, in his Council. He has that power."

"Certainly. But will he want to use it?"

La Fargue raised an astonished eyebrow.

"Do you mean to say that His Majesty does not know what is going on?"

Rochefort ignored the question.

"Whenever the king annuls a ruling it's always a very unpopular decision. The Parlement protests loudly, everyone gets stirred up, and there are inevitably a few brave souls ready to stoke the people's anger and cry tyranny. . . . And kings dislike it when there are rumblings among the people. Especially on the eve of a war."

"Lorraine."

"Yes, Lorraine. . . . You see, La Fargue, to succeed without making too many waves, these sorts of affairs have to be carefully arranged. Public opinion has to be prepared, some loyalties have to be bought in advance, favourable pamphlets have to be written, suitable rumours propagated . . . It's much easier than you probably think, but it demands care, money and, above all, time. And time is what we lack most. . . ."

La Fargue was starting to take full stock of the problem: a spy who would or could not talk, a plot threatening the king looming on the horizon, and an hourglass whose sands were already funnelling downward.

After a brief moment of reflection, he asked: "What are His Eminence's orders?"

* * *

Holding the door, Leprat waited patiently while Danvert gave Alessandra di Santi's bedchamber a final but thorough glance.

This had been their routine since La Donna came to stay at La Renardière. Each morning, as soon as the coach which took her to Le Châtelet departed, they visited her apartments. Leprat supervised, although his presence was not truly necessary. The domestic servants the cardinal had so graciously assigned to serve the lady spy knew their business. They did not content themselves with observing her every deed and gesture and making daily reports. They also inspected her bedchamber and antechamber with a fine-tooth comb, under the maître d'hôtel's keen eye, and he—rather than Leprat—directed their search and ensured that nothing was overlooked.

Danvert was alert and gave precise orders, but otherwise said little. He was about fifty years old. With his trim figure, grey hair, and the naturally hale complexion of Mediterranean folk, he had devoted his life to providing perfect service. He was gifted with all the qualities of the best maîtres d'hôtel, whose duty was to ensure the smooth running of a household and to manage the domestic staff. That is to say, he was discreet, intelligent, honest, attentive, and foresighted. But he also had a flaw that was very common in his profession: a type of arrogance inspired by the sense—often well founded—of being indispensable.

In practice, he was the true master of La Renardière. Assisted by a staff which was at his beck and call, he kept the premises in readiness to welcome any guest on short notice, even in the middle of the night, to stay for any length of time from a few hours to days or even weeks on end. He was aware of the exceptional nature of the guests the cardinal received here. It seemed he was never surprised by anything, did not ask to know any more than was necessary, and performed his duties with zeal without ever becoming emotional about his work. Leprat quickly took his measure and came to rely on him, in the same way that a good officer would rely on an experienced sergeant. It was a decision that the former musketeer was not given cause to regret, and on which he congratulated himself the first time he witnessed the servants' systematic search of La Donna's apartments: Danvert clearly knew what he was doing.

"A problem?" asked Leprat when the maître d'hôtel hesitated.

Only the two of them remained in Alessandra's antechamber.

Danvert was chewing on his lower lip, a certain sign of perplexity. He did not answer, and, acting on an impulse, he went over to the cage where

Alessandra's dragonnets were cooped up. One of the twins—no doubt the male, Charybdis—growled at him when he checked the padlock securing the little door.

That done, the maître d'hôtel finally decided to leave and, in passing, gave Leprat an apologetic look for making him wait. But the Blade gave him a reassuring glance in return.

"It would be simpler if we knew what we were looking for, wouldn't it?"

"Indeed, monsieur. We can never be too careful."

Leprat closed the door, turned the key twice in the lock, and the two men walked away.

"I'm going to get some sleep," announced the former musketeer, stifling a yawn. "Wake me if you need me."

"Very good, monsieur."

The dragonnets waited for the voices and the sound of footsteps to fade away in the distance.

Once calm was restored to the deserted bedchamber, Scylla's eyes sparkled and the padlock opened with a click. Charybdis immediately pushed the little door open with a clawed foot. The twins escaped from their cage and swooped up the chimney flue. They emerged into the sunlight in a puff of soot that went unnoticed below and which—even had it been seen—would have had no clear cause. For although they were not invisible the two dragonnets had become translucent, looking as if they were made of a very pure water that barely disturbed the passage of light.

After some joyful and expert aerial acrobatics, Scylla called her brother back to their duties and they sped off toward Paris together.

2

At the Hôtel de l'Épervier, they were waiting for La Fargue.

The Blades were gathered in the garden, in the shade of the chestnut tree, around the weather-bleached old table whose legs were tangled in the tall weeds. Agnès and Marciac were playing draughts while Ballardieu watched the game, sucking on his unlit clay pipe. Saint-Lucq, sitting casually nearby, as impassive as ever behind his red spectacles, juggled with a dagger. And Almades, leaning back against the tree trunk with his arms crossed, simply waited. Leprat was missing, and for good reason: he had orders not to leave La Renardière where La Donna was due to return early in the afternoon, under close guard. Glasses of wine and a bowl of juicy fruit attracted buzzing insects to the table, standing in the dappled sunlight which filtered through the chestnut tree's leaves.

La Fargue finally arrived. He took a seat—turning a chair until its back was against the table, and straddling it—and they all listened to his words closely.

"Here's what it's all about," he began. "You know that since she gave herself up La Donna has been interrogated in secret at Le Châtelet every morning, by the Paris provost's lieutenant for civil affairs."

"Monsieur de Laffemas," Agnès noted.

"Laffemas, yes. He is both honest and tenacious. He can be difficult at times, but he's hardly the monster that some people claim. In any case, he's smart and not easily fooled. In short, he seemed to be the perfect man to worm information out of La Donna—"

"But?" Marciac interrupted.

"But La Donna is causing problems. Without her smile ever faltering, she deceives, lies, and evades him. Days have passed without her saying very much about what she has done or learned since she began her career as a spy."

"And concerning the plot?" asked Saint-Lucq.

"On that subject," the old gentleman answered, "she hasn't even pretended to respond. She simply repeats, over and over, that the cardinal knows the price of that information. Laffemas has tried to learn a little more with indirect questions and falsely innocent allusions to the matter, but in vain. So far, La Donna has always seen straight through Laffemas's game and she's played her own cards marvellously."

"She's a crafty bitch," the half-blood said. "But then, no one succeeds in her line of work by being an imbecile—"

"Or ugly," added Marciac. "Is she as beautiful as they say? Could I relieve Leprat? He must be getting bored out there, all alone at La Renardière—"

Agnès gave a ringing laugh, and Saint-Lucq smiled at the crudeness of this manoeuvre.

"Out of the question," said La Fargue with absolute seriousness.

"But—"

"I said no."

"All right!"

The Gascon shrugged his shoulders and, sulking a little, poured himself a glass of wine. The young baronne de Vaudreuil gave him a sympathetic pat on the back.

Then she declared: "On this point at least, La Donna has never been mysterious: she has always said that she will reveal the details of the plot against the king in exchange for the cardinal's protection. But she's still waiting to receive that protection. How can we reproach her for remaining silent on the subject? What could she possibly hope to gain by speaking before she obtains her guarantees? She's not an idiot—"

"But that's where the shoe pinches," said La Fargue.

"How's that?" asked Ballardieu in his loud voice, frowning.

"The cardinal cannot give La Donna his protection while she's considered to be a criminal, which is what she will continue to be until she's acquitted of the crimes she's been convicted of. Or until the king pardons her."

"But we're taking about La Donna!" Agnès exclaimed. "Clearing the name of the adventuress would require a rehabilitation trial that would be a parody of justice!"

"And for that same reason, the king cannot pardon her with the stroke of a quill without risking a scandal," La Fargue acknowledged. "In short, La Donna is asking for something she knows is impossible—"

"Let's not forget . . ." added Almades in a flat tone which nonetheless drew everyone's attention, "Let's not forget that time is against La Donna as well as us—"

"What?" said the Gascon, astonished.

"Let us suppose that there is in truth a plot against the king. A plot about which she has some vital intelligence. What will happen if the plotters make their move while La Donna is still at His Eminence's mercy?"

Agnès understood.

"The cardinal will be merciless."

"And La Donna will be lucky if this adventure doesn't end in a noose," concluded Marciac.

The Spanish fencing master nodded.

"So what game is she playing at?" the baronne de Vaudreuil wondered.

"That is precisely what the cardinal wants us to discover," declared La Fargue with enough authority to retake control of the debate and nip any further idle speculation in the bud.

The others all turned back to him and waited for him to continue.

"Let's start by finding those black dracs who are hunting La Donna. They know more about her than we do, and if we could learn why they are tracking her . . . Besides the cardinal would be pleased to hear they have been prevented from doing any further mischief."

"How do we find them?" enquired Saint-Lucq.

"They are somewhere in Paris. They arrived five days ago."

This piece of news aroused surprise. Then Ballardieu, who read the gazettes avidly, recalled that the previous week the guards at one of the Paris gates had been found dead without any clues as to who had killed them. The authorities had quickly removed the bodies. Was there a connection between the dracs' arrival in the capital and the deaths of these unfortunate men?

"Yes," La Fargue asserted. "One of the guards survived a few days in a delirious state. He spoke of dracs and of a 'creeping black death.' The cardinal's master of magic thinks it's the same black mist that accompanies our dracs. . . . By the way, Agnès and Marciac, you will be seeing him this afternoon."

"The master of magic?" asked the Gascon.

"The cardinal believes he can be useful to us."

"Good," said Agnès.

The old captain then turned to Saint-Lucq: "As for you—"

"I know," replied the half-blood. "If the dracs have been in Paris for five days without being spotted, there is only one place they can be. . . . Do you have any special instructions?"

"No. Find them, that's all. And don't get yourself killed. . . . For my part, I will be meeting a man Rochefort claims knows La Donna well, who might be able to help us pin her down."

"Who?" Marciac asked distractedly, observing bitterly that the bottle of wine was empty.

"Do you remember Laincourt?"

"The man Richelieu wanted us to recruit last month? The one who refused?"

Listening to the Gascon, one might wonder which crime, in his eyes, weighed more heavily against the former Cardinal's Guard: having almost become a member of the Blades out of favouritism, or having declined the offer?

"The very same."

Marciac pulled a face.

"He saved my life at risk of his own," Agnès said in a conciliatory tone.

"So what?" the Gascon retorted in perfectly bad faith. "We save each other's lives all the time and we don't make a song and dance out of it—"

The captain clapped his hands and stood: "Get going!" he cried. "Into your saddles!" And then, in an almost paternal manner, he added: "And watch out for yourselves."

The group of people in the service of any great personage formed his "household." Thus one might speak of the king's household, or those of the queen, the duc d'Orléans, and the marquis de Châteauneuf. As social customs required that everyone lived in a manner befitting their birth and rank, some households could have as many as two thousand servants all of whom had to be paid, fed, dressed, lodged, and looked after as needed. This applied especially to the king's household, but also to that of Cardinal Richelieu. And it cost fortunes.

Numerous, prestigious, and particularly onerous to maintain, the cardinal's household was commensurate in size with the rank of the public figure it served. It was composed of a military household and a civil household. Devoted to the protection of His Eminence, the military household comprised a company of horse guards, a company of musketeers, and a third unit of gendarmes, which was generally deployed in military campaigns. In practice, the right to maintain a military household amounted to possessing a small private army. It was thus a privilege the king rarely granted. But the numerous plots aimed at Richelieu had made it necessary in his case, as well as a mark of the trust which Louis XIII accorded his chief minister.

The cardinal's civil household encompassed all those who were not men of war. In addition to the multitude of domestic servants, kitchen boys, and stable hands, along with other minor employees occupied with necessary but largely anonymous tasks, it included: a high almoner and master of the chamber who filled the role of general superintendent and thus controlled the household's purse strings; a confessor; three auxiliary almoners; secretaries; squires and gentlemen servants, all well-born, the first looking after the cardinal's horses and teams, the second accompanying him about his duties or carrying out delicate missions on his behalf; five valets who commanded the lackeys in livery; a maître d'hôtel who reigned over the ordinary staff and dealt with suppliers; a bursar; three chefs, each assisted by his own cooks; four wine stewards; a bread steward; two coachmen and four postillions; a mule driver; and porters.

To which list, one could add a physician, an apothecary, and two surgeons. Plus one master of magic.

Every great household had to have one. Of course as the practice of draconic magic was against the law, masters of magic were not themselves magicians. Or, at least, they weren't supposed to be. But their knowledge of dragons and associated arcana was much sought after in order to detect and thwart any possible threats. Some of them called themselves astrologers or seers; others were doctors or philosophers; some were even men of the Church. Many were simply charlatans or incompetents. However, for a select few scholars, draconic magic was an object of serious study which required a reasoned approach.

The cardinal's master of magic was named Pierre Teyssier. He possessed a brilliant and original mind and although Richelieu rarely called on his services he did finance Teyssier's research and publications, in his capacity as a patron and friend of the sciences.

Teyssier lived in rue des Enfants-Rouges, and he was expecting a visit from the Cardinal's Blades.

Agnès and Marciac, accompanied by Ballardieu, decided to go to rue des Enfants-Rouges on horseback and thus spare their boots from contact with the foul Parisian muck, which—in addition to being sticky and smelly—was corrosive and ruined even the best leathers. They would also be able to breathe more easily, with their heads above the crowds in the streets which would soon become oppressive in this heat. Indeed, they made a detour in order to take the Pont Neuf across the Seine, more to benefit from the breeze from the river than from the lively street entertainers performing there. This bridge, unlike others in the city, was not lined with houses, making it possible to enjoy the open air, as well as the unique view of the capital's river banks.

Having travelled along the quays, however, they were finally forced to return to the stuffy, noisy, and polluted atmosphere of the city's streets. With Ballardieu bringing up the rear, the three Blades crossed the narrow, populous Place de Grève, in front of the Hôtel de Ville, without even glancing at the bodies rotting on the gallows. Next they took rue des Coquilles and rue Barre-du-Bec, tiny medieval alleys where passersby were tightly squeezed, then rue Sainte-Avoye and rue du Temple, until they reached their destination.

Located in the northeast of the capital, rue des Enfants-Rouges was named after the hospital of the same name, a hospice for orphans whose little inmates were dressed in red. The neighbourhood was peaceful, still dotted with cultivated fields and dominated by the hulking donjon that rose in the Enclos du Temple. Surrounded by a crenelated wall, this former residence of the Templar knights now belonged to the Order of the Chatelaine Sisters. Marciac pointed out the house La Fargue had described to them before they left the Hôtel de l'Épervier.

"This one," he said.

He and Agnès dismounted, knocked at the door, introduced themselves to the old manservant who came to open up, and followed him inside. Ballardieu was left with the horses. There was a stall selling refreshment further up the street and the former soldier, with his eyes shining and his mouth dry, cheerfully envisaged a long wait.

"Don't get drunk," the young baronne warned him before they parted.

Ballardieu made his promise and went off, leading the mounts by the bridle.

The cool air inside the magic master's dwelling was pleasant.

As they waited in an antechamber Marciac removed his brown felt hat and wiped his brow. Agnès envied the comfortable casualness of his attire; she, too, would have liked to go about with her shirt collar wide open and her doublet unbuttoned, although in honesty she had little cause for complaint. True, the thick leather corset that cinched her waist was a little heavy, but her riding outfit—with breeches and boots—was far more practical than the starched dresses that polite society would have normally imposed on her given her gender and rank. Polite society which the baronne Agnès Anne Marie de Vaudreuil blithely chose to ignore.

"What?" asked the Gascon, noticing her watching him out of the corner of her eye.

"Nothing," she said at first. Then she added impishly, "That's a pretty doublet."

They were standing side by side, looking straight ahead, in an antechamber which was almost devoid of furnishings.

"Are you mocking me?" asked Marciac warily.

He feigned nonchalance, if not indifference, toward his clothing, but was in fact quite careful of the image that he presented and even fastidious in his own fashion.

"No!" Agnès protested, hiding a smile.

"Then, thank you," he retorted, without looking at her.

The doublet in question was a crimson garment that Marciac had not been seen wearing before his long, solitary mission to La Rochelle. The cloth was of quality and the cut elegant. It must have been expensive, yet all of the Blades knew full well that the Gascon chased after two things in life: money and skirts. And he was only ever lacking for money.

"A gift?" Agnès persisted.

"No."

"I deduce, then, that you have funds. Did the cards smile on you?"

The Gascon shrugged and said modestly: "Yes they did, rather . . ."

"In La Rochelle?" the baronne asked with some surprise.

La Rochelle had been the Protestant capital of France since the failed siege in 1628 and the withdrawal of the royal armies. Agnès genuinely doubted that gambling dens abounded there, so Marciac was either lying to her or he was hiding something, but she was not given the occasion to ferret out the truth. Someone was coming.

They had expected to see the manservant who had asked them to wait. Instead a young man entered, barely twenty years of age. Perhaps less. He looked like some student from the Sorbonne, with wrinkled clothes, a badly buttoned waistcoat, short but tangled blond hair, a joyful almost impudent air, and his hands still damp, as if he had just finished drying himself with a towel after a wash.

One of the master's pupils, no doubt.

"My apologies for keeping you waiting," he said. "I know your visit was announced, but . . ."

He did not complete his sentence, but smiled and looked at the visitors.

After a moment of hesitation, Marciac explained: "We're here to meet with His Eminence's master of magic."

"Yes, of course," the young man replied, still smiling.

And as he stood before them in expectant silence, realisation dawned upon the two Blades and they glanced at one another in astonishment.

It was Agnès who guessed first.

"I beg your pardon, monsieur, but would you be—"

"Pierre Teyssier, at your service, madame. How can I be of use to you?"

Laincourt pushed the door open and entered the cool dim interior of the small esoteric bookshop with pleasure. Removing his hat, he mopped at his brow with a handkerchief, only to see Bertaud—after begging another customer to excuse him—come hurrying over.

The bookseller seemed anxious.

"There's someone here, waiting to see you," he said in a low voice.

"And who would that be?"

Rather than answer, the bookseller instead pointed with his chin at a nook inside the shop. The cardinal's former spy looked over calmly, at the very moment when La Fargue put a book he had been glancing through back on a shelf.

The two men stared at one another without either showing any particular emotion.

Then, not taking his eyes off the old captain, Laincourt said over his shoulder: "Don't worry, Bertaud. The gentleman and I are already acquainted."

Turning away from the window, the Alchemist went over to his desk.

He had changed his clothes since his morning visit to the former vicomtesse de Malicorne. He still wore black, but now his attire was that of a member of the bourgeoisie rather than a gentleman. Here, at home, he was a scholar, a master of magic known as Mauduit.

He sat in his armchair with a sigh of mixed relief and discomfort. Maintaining this cursed human appearance was becoming more and more taxing, both physically and emotionally. It caused him fleshly pain, to be sure. But more, he found it an intolerable humiliation that he, a dragon, was forced to wear the outward rags of such an ignoble race.

Stretching a hand toward an elegant liqueur service stowed in a case, he poured himself a small glass of a thick yellow fluid that shimmered like liquid gold. It was golden henbane. Or more precisely, the liqueur distilled from golden henbane, a plant whose cultivation, trade, and consumption were strictly forbidden in France, as it was almost everywhere in Europe, but which permitted the preparation of various potions and brews that were highly prized by sorcerers. For common mortals, however, it was a powerful drug. Particularly sought after by members of high society in search of thrills, it was sold under the cloak at premium prices.

There was a knock at the door.

The so-called Mauduit closed the liqueur case, sat up straight, and hid his glass before bidding his visitor to enter. But the man who appeared already knew his secrets. He was a hired swordsman with an olive complexion and sharp features. Booted and gloved, his sword at his side, his clothes and hat were made of black leather. A patch—also of black leather, with silver studs—hid his left eye but failed to conceal the smear of ranse that spread around it, across his cheekbone, his temple, and the arch of his eyebrow.

The Alchemist relaxed, recovered his glass, and pointed to the case as the visitor dropped himself into an armchair.

"Do you want some?"

"No," replied the one-eyed man, who had a strong Spanish accent.

Eyes closed, the Alchemist slowly drank the liqueur and enjoyed every drop. The dragons took great delight in golden henbane. It was not only delicious to their palate but, more important, it helped them reclaim their fundamental nature. It was often necessary. If the primeval dragons of long ago had struggled to assume and preserve a human appearance, how many now, among the last-born of their race, were not even capable of maintaining an intermediate draconic form? The Alchemist would have been ashamed to admit it, but the metamorphoses were becoming more and more difficult for him, too. The latest transformation, in Alsace, had proved particularly painful. It had almost killed him. Without the golden henbane it was possible he would not have succeeded at all. And without it, his present sufferings would have been unbearable.

"Really, you're sure?" insisted the Alchemist, pouring himself another dose. "It's excellent."

This time the ranse victim contented himself with a curt shake of the head.

He called himself Savelda and, like the Alchemist, he served the Black Claw. He was the henchman of the masters of the secret society. Or, rather, a trusted lieutenant. The one the elders of the Grand Lodge sent when the matter was important, the one who carried out their orders without ever questioning them.

"Well?" asked Savelda. "Your visit to see la Malicorne?"

"She is a spent force."

"I told you so."

"I had to be sure. . . . In any event, we can expect no help from her. It's a shame. I'm convinced that our projects would have appealed to her. She would have loved to take part in them. . . ."

"No doubt."

The Alchemist waved his hand, as if to dismiss an affair that was definitely closed.

"Where are you with your recruitment?" he enquired.

"Progressing. But finding reliable men at such short notice isn't easy."

"What can I say? The men I brought back from Germany all perished in

Alsace, so do the best you can." The Alchemist clenched a fist and his eyes blazed. "Those cursed Chatelaines!" he hissed between his teeth. "They very nearly had me. If I had failed to assume my primal form . . ."

He rose and, shaking his head, went over to the window.

"Speaking of which . . ." said Savelda after a moment. "Our masters are becoming alarmed. The Grand Lodge still supports your plan, but the fact that you encountered the Chatelaines on your route has them worried.

"I'm touched by our masters' concern for my well-being. . . ."

The one-eyed man ignored his irony.

"What could the Chatelaines know?" he asked.

"Nothing. Those bitches don't know anything."

"Nevertheless . . ."

The Alchemist spun round and stared into Savelda's eyes.

"They've always been after me," he asserted. "Should we have hoped that they would just conveniently give up on the eve of our venture? They recently tried to capture me, just as they've tried in the past and as they shall try again in the future. And that's all."

"Very well. But let's be twice as prudent, all the same."

"I am never lacking in prudence, or in determination. So apply yourself to reassuring our masters of the Grand Lodge and remind them that it is only a matter of days now before the destiny of France takes a . . . different turn."

The Ile Notre-Dame—later known as the Ile Saint-Louis—for a long period had remained in a wild state. Until fairly recently there had been no bridges permitting access to the island, either from the quays along the Seine or from Ile de la Cité, so it was rarely visited except by anglers or, on sunny days, by amorous couples whose rowing boats rocked gently among the tall rushes and beneath the weeping willows' drooping branches. Occasionally, it was the scene of murders. The first dracs settled there during the reign of Henri IV. They built scattered huts for themselves on its banks which soon grew into a village. The king allowed this, against his ministers' advice. He knew that the dracs posed a problem for Western societies that would not be resolved on its own, and he realised that the capital's gates could not shut them out, any more than could the borders of his kingdom. Finally, he understood that dracs and men were forced to coexist now that the dracs had freed themselves from the millennial tutelage of the dragons. But Henri IV was also aware of the danger these creatures, with their ferocious, violent nature, represented. So he let them establish themselves on this marshy island, in order to live there by themselves and be contained as far as possible. And when the canons of Notre-Dame protested, the king responded by purchasing their island, to do with it as he saw fit.

Under the aegis of Henri IV, the drac village prospered. By 1633, it had been transformed into a neighbourhood built entirely of wood, whose damp lanes, dark alleys, lopsided houses, and shacks built on stilts covered the entire island, which Parisians had renamed as Ile Notre-Dame-des-Écailles, or Our Lady of the Scales. As for the neighbourhood itself, it was nicknamed Les Écailles with a mixture of scorn and fear. Although the king's authority still prevailed there, Les Écailles did not form part of the commune of Paris. It was a faubourg in the very heart of the capital, exempt from municipal taxes and visits from the city watch. During the day, the presence of humans was more or less tolerated, although it was understood that anyone who ventured onto the island did so at their own risk. At night, on the other hand . . .

Between dusk and dawn Les Écailles revealed its true character, that is to say: it was both bewitching and deadly. For at night the neighbourhood became the theatre of a life animated by the primitive energy that heated the blood in the dracs' temples and dug into their bellies. Once night fell, fires were lit; fiery red braziers glowed on street corners; torches sputtered outside tavern doors. Along the winding alleys, dracs jostled one another at almost every step due to their dense numbers. The night air was filled with heady scents. Faint melodies met and became intertwined. Brawls broke out: sudden, violent, and always bloody. Warlike chants rose from smoke-filled cellars. Tribal drums beat and their disturbing rhythms sometimes carried across the Seine to disrupt the sleep of ordinary Parisians. On the island, even the dreams of humans were unwelcome.

Here a human being was a stranger, an intruder, an enemy.

Prey.

But a half-blood?

Night was falling when Saint-Lucq crossed, alone, over the small southern branch of the Seine by one of the three rickety wooden bridges which had been built to link Ile Notre-Dame-des-Écailles to the capital. Four grey dracs were killing time around a big fire. They saw his solitary silhouette arriving and supposed that providence had supplied them with a cheap way to entertain themselves. One of the dracs, urging the others to watch him perform, strutted forth to meet Saint-Lucq and deliberately planted himself in his path with an evil grin on his lips.

The half-blood did not slow down or veer aside by even an inch.

But he halted just before bumping into the drac who surpassed him in terms of height, weight, and strength.

And he waited.

The drac, who until then had been exchanging nods and winks with his companions at a distance behind him, suddenly looked perplexed. This wasn't going as planned. The man should have tried to avoid him while he, by taking successive sidesteps, would have cut off any attempt to advance. And this cruel little game would have continued until his victim became exasperated, fled, or tried to force his way past.

But instead . . .

Because the brim of his hat hid his eyes, Saint-Lucq slowly lifted his head until the grey drac's scaly features were reflected in the scarlet lenses of his round spectacles. The drac's gaze became lost in them, while the half-blood stood there unmoving.

He waited, expressionless, for the reptilian to smell, detect, discern in him the blood of a superior race, a blood that would make the drac's primordial instincts scream out in fear and respect.

As finally happened.

Frightened and ashamed, unable to bear the dumbfounded looks on his comrades' faces, the drac stepped aside, letting Saint-Lucq continue on his way, and then fled down the nearest alley.

The other three members of the band were speechless for a moment. What had happened? Who was this man in black, calmly walking at a steady pace, and now disappearing around a corner to penetrate further into Les Écailles?

After a brief consultation, they resolved to follow him.

And kill him.

The nightmares had stayed at a distance for some time, but tonight the whole baying pack had returned to haunt Agnès's sleep. Awakening with a start, her throat and brow damp with sweat, she knew she would not be able to fall asleep again immediately in the warm night air. She therefore got up and, feeling a slight pang of hunger, decided to find herself something to eat. She would no doubt locate something to nibble in the kitchen, as she waited for sleep to return or for dawn to break. In any event, it was pointless to remain in her bed, surrounded by shadows and at the mercy of her regrets.

Without paying much heed to convention, the young baronne de Vaudreuil dressed in a summary fashion and, barefoot, silently descended the shadowy main staircase. All of the denizens of the Hôtel de l'Épervier were fast asleep . . .

. . . except for one person, already in the kitchen.

It was La Fargue.

Sitting alone in the candlelight, his hat and his Pappenheimer placed beside him, the old gentleman was polishing off a substantial snack.

Upon seeing who had joined him, he smiled and greeted her softly: "But who have we here? Are you hungry, baronne?"

Agnès cast a longing eye over the appetising victuals on the table.

She yawned.

"Well, yes, as a matter of fact . . ."

"Then sit down," La Fargue invited her, pointing to the place opposite him.

She took a seat, watching the gentleman cut a piece of bread, butter it, and then spread a thick slice of pâté upon it.

"Here," he said.

Agnès bit deeply into the tartine, and her mouth was still full when La Fargue, handing her a glass of red wine, asked: "So? This master of magic?"

She had to swallow with the help of a sip of wine before answering.

"Frankly, the man seemed very young and a trifle . . . whimsical."

The old captain smiled faintly.

"Sieur Teyssier often gives people that impression."

"Are you acquainted with him, then?"

"Well enough to know that he is extremely learned. Besides, His Eminence is not in the habit of surrounding himself with mediocrities."

Still dubious, the baronne de Vaudreuil shrugged and continued to devour her tartine.

"He spoke of the men the dracs killed when they entered Paris that night," she declared. "According to him, the poor wretches all died of the ranse."

The ranse was a terrible disease said to be transmitted to humans by dragons and which, in its final stages, corrupted the soul as much as the body. The process, however, was usually a slow one. Those who fell victim to the disease could live with it for years.

"They succumbed in just a few minutes?" La Fargue queried in astonishment.

Agnès nodded, unable to reply, once again having her mouth full.

She gulped, and added: "Teyssier had one of their hearts in a jar. It was a black, revolting thing that could have come from the carcass of some old man who'd suffered from the disease for years. But in fact, it belonged to a halberdier on guard that night. The man was not even thirty. . . ."

La Fargue grimaced.

"The dracs have a sorcerer," he said.

"That was Teyssier's opinion. . . . Is there any more pâté?"

Agnès had finished her tartine and, with a hungry look, was examining the rest of the food on the table.

"I'll take care of that. Tell me what else Teyssier had to say."

And while the old gentleman prepared a second tartine for her, Agnès explained: "Teyssier believes that the dracs have a sorcerer with them, and it's thanks to him they can follow La Donna's trace. He believes they will find her sooner or later, unless they abandon their hunt—"

"—or they are stopped."

"Yes—not too much butter, please—in all likelihood, if the sorcerer were eliminated, La Donna would no longer be in any great danger."

"Couldn't another sorcerer take over?"

"That's what I asked. But Teyssier affirms that it is not quite so simple. A bond has to be formed between the sorcerer and his prey, and such bonds are not easily woven."

La Fargue nodded his head gravely and mulled things over while Agnès started on her second tartine. She respected his silence by chewing as quietly as possible.

"La Donna is hoping that we will rid her of this sorcerer." La Fargue said.

"Who knows? It's a risky wager, if their trap is gradually closing about her as time passes. As Teyssier puts it, it's a little like a net that the sorcerer tightens each day. Or rather, each night, because drakish sorcery is a nocturnal thing. . . ."

"But La Donna was all alone, up until these last few days. Now she has at least twelve musketeers to accompany her wherever she goes. And that's not counting Leprat, who is worth six men alone. I think that, as far as her personal safety is concerned, her situation has improved."

"So she invented a plot against the king to force us to protect her?"

"No, because she will have to offer a full account soon of what she has already affirmed. But I wager that she has played the card of this plot to her sole advantage. . . . I shall go and talk to her tomorrow."

"And Arnaud de Laincourt? Wasn't he supposed to assist us in this affair? Weren't you supposed to meet him today?"

"According to Rochefort, he knows La Donna well and he could be useful to us. But he refused to give me an answer, even though I saw his eye light up with a strange spark when I mentioned La Donna—"

"I think he would make a fine recruit."

"Perhaps."

"And the cardinal thinks so, too. . . ."

"True. But I am the sole judge of who does or does not wear this ring."

La Fargue tapped the steel signet ring he wore on his finger, a ring which all the Blades possessed. Agnès de Vaudreuil carried hers beneath her shirt, hanging on a chain around her neck.

Her hunger satiated, she stifled another yawn and stretched.

"Captain, with your permission I'm going to retire to my apartments and try to get some sleep in the few hours of cool night air that remain."

"Of course. It's very late."

The young woman rose.

"And thank you for the tartines," she said with a smile.

A smile that La Fargue returned in a paternal fashion.

"But now that I think of it . . ." he suddenly recalled. "Where did Marciac get to?"

"He went to gamble at La Souvange's mansion. And I believe he intended to visit Gabrielle tomorrow."

"Ah . . . ! Good night, Agnès."

"Until tomorrow, captain."

At home, in his bed, Arnaud de Laincourt was trying to read by candlelight. But he was finding it impossible to concentrate. He finally gave up, turned his book over on his chest, laced his fingers together behind his neck, and uttered a long sigh.

Then, from the shadows which he haunted, the memory of the hurdy-gurdy player said: *You're thinking about the offer from the duchesse de Chevreuse.*

Yes.

The House of Chevreuse is one of the greatest households in France. Under its protection, there is no glory or honour that a man such as you cannot hope to attain after a few years. . . . But I sense your trouble: for someone who has served the cardinal so well, joining the duchesse and her party would be almost like going over to the enemy. And then there is La Fargue, isn't there?

Indeed.

What exactly did he want today?

He wanted my help in a delicate matter involving La Donna.

That sounds rather like the cardinal, calling you back to his service for a time.

No doubt . . .

There was a silence.

Then, just before Laincourt drove him from his thoughts, the hurdy-gurdy player told him: *You will have to make a choice, boy. . . . And don't take too long about it, or others will do the choosing for you.*

Of the three grey dracs who had followed Saint-Lucq since his arrival on Ile Notre-Dame-aux-Écailles, two were lying dead in the mud, now darkened by their blood, at the end of an alley where they had thought they could easily put paid to their victim—who was armed, to be sure, but also alone and visibly unaware of the danger he was in. As for the third drac, he was currently being held at bay by the point of a rapier that was nicking his larynx, and struggling to comprehend how the human could have surprised and then overcome them. All three dracs had entered the alley with swords in their fists, their senses searching the shadows and the silence, and suddenly death had struck twice.

In the nocturnal darkness, with two small red disks in the place of eyes, Saint-Lucq was no more than a silhouette brandishing his rapier—a rapier which did not so much as tremble as it caught a small sliver of the pale moonlight.

"First, you will listen," he said in a calm voice, "and then you will think. And finally, you will speak. . . . Don't speak until you have thought, and above all, don't speak until you have listened carefully. Do you understand? You may answer."

"Yes," replied the drac.

"Perfect. This is the moment when you listen. Seven black dracs. Mercenaries. They have been in Paris for five days now, and in those five days no one has seen them. That can only mean one thing: that they have been hiding in Les Écailles for the past five days. I want to find them and I'm counting on you to lead me to them. A mere piece of information or two shall satisfy me. That, and nothing less. . . . Have you understood what I just said?"

The drac, still immobilised by the point of the sword threatening to pierce his throat, nodded.

"Good," said Saint-Lucq. "Now, this is the moment when you think. . . ."

At La Renardière, Alessandra saw the sun rise and knew it was approaching the hour when the chambermaid would knock at her door. The young Italian woman's pallor betrayed her anxious state. Seated in an armchair before her window, with a shawl wrapped around her shoulders and Scylla in her lap, she stared blankly out at the scenery and started whenever she spied signs of movement in the sky.

Charybdis had still not come home.

The two dragonnets had been slipping out of the manor each morning for four days now, and flying to Paris to accomplish a mission whose importance they scarcely understood but whose urgency they nevertheless felt. They returned each afternoon, before their mistress was brought back to La Renardière and her apartment was once again visited.

The previous day, however, Scylla had been alone in the cage when Alessandra returned.

The adventuress was immediately worried, but she had to deal with her most pressing concern first, making sure no one noticed the absence of the male dragonnet. Luckily, Charybdis and Scylla were twins. By leaving their cage open and letting the female come and go freely, all Alessandra had to do was to call "Charybdis" from time to time in order to convince others that both little reptiles were present, if never together in the same room.

Finally they had all left her alone and La Donna, from her window, had scanned the skies all night, tormented by the long wait. In vain. Dawn had come, and now morning. La Renardière began to stir and Alessandra would soon have to show herself, to endure the hypocritical chatter and attentions of her chambermaid, to put on a brave face with Leprat, and then let herself be taken by coach to see that miserable Laffemas, in his no less depressing Châtelet. . . .

Assuming that Charybdis's disappearance wasn't noticed by someone first, would Alessandra be able to maintain the illusion of normality for so long?

She doubted it.

Charybdis and Scylla were far more than pets to her. She adored them and regarded them as her allies, partners whose faithful services she readily employed.

Too readily perhaps.

If anything had happened to Charybdis she would never forgive herself, although she knew she'd had no choice but to use her dragonnets to locate her pursuers' hiding place within Paris. It was in fact the second part of her plan. First, deliver herself up to the cardinal, be held at La Renardière, draw the dracs to Paris, and force them to establish a base in the only area within a radius of ten leagues where no one would notice them: Ile Notre-Dame-des-Écailles. Thus the prey would corner the hunters—concluding the first part of her scheme. Next, discover their lair before they discovered hers. And finally, having achieved all that, carry out the third and last part of a plan that had been carefully thought out in advance. . . .

There was a knock at the door.

Surprised, Alessandra leapt to her feet, at a loss for a moment before she recovered her wits. She shut Scylla in the cage, threw the shawl over it, and barely had time to slide beneath the bed sheets before the chambermaid came in. It was a typical technique used by domestic servants who were overly curious, either professionally or as a personal vice: knock, open the door, catch sight of something by surprise, and, if necessary, excuse themselves, lie, and pretend to have heard permission to enter.

"Get out!" cried Alessandra, feigning to still be half asleep.

"But, madame—"

"I said, get out!"

"But it's already late, madame!"

"You pest! Leave at once or I shall beat you!"

The chambermaid was in full retreat when La Donna's slipper hit the door.

How much time did I gain? La Donna wondered. *Probably less than an hour. The chambermaid will knock at my door once more, and then it will be Leprat. And I won't be able frighten him away by throwing slippers. . . .*

Despondent, Alessandra got up and walked to the window, taking care to remain far enough away so as not to be seen from the garden. Wasn't she supposed to be keeping to her bed out of laziness? Eyes narrowed, she peered up at a sky that was now clear blue . . .

. . . and held her breath when she saw Charybdis.

He was coming back to her.

His flight was erratic, to be sure. But it was her little dragonnet approaching with a great deal of valiant if clumsy flapping of his wings, no doubt too tired to maintain the spell that made his body translucent. Alessandra was unconcerned by that, however. Right now, all that mattered to her was that Charybdis was still alive and, throwing caution to the winds, she opened the window to gather the dragonnet in her arms.

He took refuge there, trembling, exhausted, with a slight wound on his flank, but quite alive.

Moreover, he had succeeded in his mission.

"Yes?" Guibot enquired, opening the pedestrian door within the great carriage gate by a few inches.

"Captain La Fargue, please."

"Are you expected, monsieur?"

"I believe so. I am Arnaud de Laincourt."

The little old man, to whom the name meant nothing, nevertheless stepped back to allow him entry. Then, having carefully closed the door behind him, he hurriedly hobbled on his wooden leg to precede the visitor into Hôtel de l'Épervier's courtyard. It was about one o'clock in the afternoon. The sun shone in a cloudless sky and its white heat crushed everything beneath it.

"Might I trouble you to repeat your name, monsieur?"

"Laincourt."

"This way, monsieur."

La Fargue received Laincourt in the saddlery, a small room which could only be entered by crossing the stable. He isolated himself there on occasion to work leather with sure, precise gestures, the movements of a conscientious artisan that fully occupied his attention, sometimes for hours on end. Today, sitting on a stool before the workbench, he was restitching the seams of an old saddle bag. Without raising his eyes from his task, he asked: "Do you work with your hands?"

"No," replied Laincourt.

"Why not?"

"I don't have the skill."

"Every man should know how to do something with his hands."

"No doubt."

"Good artisans know what pace they should work at if they want to do things well. It requires patience and humility. It teaches you about time. . . ."

In response to this, the young man held his tongue and waited. He didn't understand the meaning of this preamble and when in doubt he always preferred not to express an opinion.

"There!" La Fargue declared, having assured himself of the solidity of his final stitch.

Rising, he called out: "ANDRÉ!"

The groom, whom Laincourt had seen in the stable upon arriving, appeared in the doorway.

"Captain?"

"Here's something that could still be useful," said the old gentleman, tossing him the repaired bag.

André caught it, nodded, and went away.

La Fargue filled a glass with wine from a bottle that was waiting in a

bucket of cool water and offered it to Laincourt. It was quite warm in the saddlery. The sun beat down on the roof and the nearby heat of the horses in the
stable did not help matters. The two men toasted, Laincourt lifting his glass
and La Fargue raising the half-full bottle.

"If you are here," said the captain, taking a swig from the bottle, "that
means you have come to a decision. . . ."

"Yes. I've decided to help you to the extent that I can. But I should like
to make it clear that I shall not commit myself to more than that. I want your
assurance that no matter what secrets are revealed to me from this moment
on, my freedom will be returned to me as soon as I demand it."

"You have my word on it."

"Thank you. So, what do you expect from me, monsieur?"

"Follow me."

Snatching up his baldric and his hat as he passed, La Fargue led Laincourt
out of the stable. They crossed the mansion's paved courtyard and passed
through the main building to the garden in the rear, where they sat down at
the old table beneath the chestnut tree. Sweet Naïs brought them more to
drink and a plate of cold meats, and discreetly left them in peace.

La Fargue recounted the whole business that occupied the Blades at
present, from the rendezvous in Artois to their current situation, including
the plot which La Donna claimed to have information about and the resistance she was offering to the questions Laffemas put to her.

"La Donna is in the cardinal's power?" Laincourt exclaimed. "And has
been for nearly a week?"

"Yes."

"Where is she being held? In which prison?"

"She has been given lodging at La Renardière."

"Under close guard, I hope."

The old gentleman nodded.

"A dozen of the cardinal's musketeers protect the domain. And my lieutenant is lodged under the same roof as La Donna."

"You can be sure she is doing her utmost to seduce him."

"Leprat is not a man to let himself fall under some beauty's spell."

Laincourt did not respond to this. He took a sip of wine and then, after
contemplating the weed-choked garden with his quiet gaze, said: "I still
don't know what you expect of me."

La Fargue paused before saying: "The cardinal thinks very highly of you,
monsieur. And he maintains there is no one in France who knows La Donna

better than you. I should therefore like to have your opinion concerning this affair, now that you know the nature of it and all the details.

The young man allowed himself a few instants of reflection before replying.

"One thing is for certain: La Donna is lying."

"Why?"

"Because she always lies. And when she isn't lying, she's concealing something. And if she isn't lying or concealing something, it's because she's busy deceiving you."

"Do you think she is lying about the plot?" asked La Fargue.

"You do realise that this plot comes at exactly the right moment to provide her with protection, just when the Black Claw is, in all likelihood, trying to hunt her down."

"Nevertheless—"

"Yes, of course. Nevertheless, you cannot afford to be deaf to La Donna's claims. The risks and the stakes are too great."

"Precisely."

"I can tell you two things. The first is that if this plot exists, La Donna has only evoked it because doing so serves her own interests. The second is that if she is giving monsieur de Laffemas so much trouble, it is because time is presently on her side. No doubt she is waiting for some event to happen. What might that be? I don't know. And we shall probably only find out once it's too late to do anything about it."

La Fargue remained silent and thoughtful for a long time, his gaze distant. His meditation, however, was interrupted by Almades, who approached, after clearing his throat in warning, and handed him a note.

"This was just delivered," said the Spaniard before returning from whence he came.

Laincourt watched the old gentleman read the missive before shaking his head in a fashion that expressed both amusement and admiration, a small smile on his lips.

Finally La Fargue asked: "If you were to meet La Donna, if you had the occasion to speak with her alone, would you be able to disentangle the true from the false in all that she might tell you?"

The cardinal's former spy shrugged his shoulders and pursed his lips.

"Frankly, I don't know . . ." he admitted. "Why?"

La Fargue handed him the note.

"Because today she has asked to speak with you."

* * *

Delivered with the back of the hand, the slap struck him with full force, reopening the wound on his cheek and provoking general hilarity. Ni'Akt fell over backward, spilling the meagre contents of his mess kit on the ground, which caused even more laughter. But he immediately got back up and, his eyes shining with fury, he stood before the one who had struck him and was now taking cruel enjoyment from the situation.

They were dracs—more, black dracs—and this was how dracs behaved, as Ni'Akt knew all too well. He was the youngest of the band. It was normal for him to be subjected to taunts and humiliations from the more senior members, until another took his place. But since that famous night in Artois when he had tried to attack that cursed half-blood, he had become a veritable punching bag who was spared nothing. In fact, his comrades did not reproach him so much for stepping out of line as for the fact that he had been beaten, wounded, and then ridiculed. Dracs did not tolerate weaklings. And the ones taking it out on Ni'Akt, moreover, were feeling bored.

They had been cooped up in the rickety, rotting shack deep in the heart of Ile Notre-Dame-des-Écailles for almost a week now. In the cellar their saaskir, their sorcerer-priest, was performing the necessary rituals to find the woman they had orders to kill. But for the time being they had nothing to do. Their chief, Kh'Shak, had forbidden them to even leave the shack. Under these conditions, tormenting Ni'Akt was welcome entertainment for his five companions.

Simmering with anger, his temples buzzing and his eye aflame, Ni'Akt struggled to restrain himself. Ta'Aresh had struck him while he'd been trying to find an out-of-the-way corner where he could eat in peace what little the others had deigned to leave him. Ta'Aresh, the biggest and strongest of their number, after Kh'Shak. Ta'Aresh who looked down on him and defied him to defend himself.

Ni'Akt hesitated.

The dracs' violent customs allowed him to fight back, just as they generally permitted the use of force to resolve even the slightest problems or differences within the group. However, Ni'Akt did not have the right to fail. If he struck Ta'Aresh, the latter could only save face by killing him. It would force a fight to the death. . . .

The young drac preferred to beat a retreat, which only earned him more scornful laughter.

But he had a plan.

This morning, at dawn, he had overheard Kh'Shak conferring with the saaskir after returning from a discreet nocturnal sortie. The chief had learned that a half-blood was looking for them, asking lots of questions and leaving bodies behind him. Evidently, venturing into Les Écailles did not frighten him. In fact, he seemed to arouse a peculiar fear in the dracs he encountered. . . .

Like Kh'Shak, who was growing worried, Ni'Akt was convinced this half-blood was the same one they had met on the night when they had almost caught up with La Donna: he had the same black clothing, the same scarlet feather on his hat, and, above all, the same round spectacles with red lenses.

To the young drac it seemed as if destiny was offering him a chance to wash away the affront he had received. This evening he would sneak out and, if luck smiled upon him, he would find the half-blood.

And then he would kill him, bring back his head, and drop it into Ta'Aresh's lap.

La Donna's carriage was about to take her back to La Renardière when La Fargue and Laincourt, followed by Almades, arrived in the Grand Châtelet's courtyard at a slow trot.

Le Châtelet was a sombre fortified edifice which had originally been built to defend the Pont au Change, but had since been rendered useless for military purposes following the enlargement of Paris and the construction of new city ramparts by King Philippe Auguste in the twelfth century. Massive, sinister, and somewhat deteriorated, Le Châtelet stood on the Right Bank, its main façade looking out over rue Saint-Denis. At present the seat of the law courts under the jurisdiction of the provost of Paris, it possessed several round towers and a large square pavilion, a sort of keep which housed a prison. The sole entrance was an archway flanked by two turrets. Fairly long but narrow, it opened onto a small, foul-smelling courtyard where visitors were immediately struck by the full misery of the place.

From his saddle, monsieur de La Houdinière, captain of the Cardinal's Guards, had already raised his arm to give the departure signal to the coach and its escort. He froze on seeing La Fargue and frowned when he recognised Laincourt, having been his direct superior until the young man had left the company of His Eminence's horse guards. La Houdinière had only been a lieutenant then, and he had not delved into the circumstances behind Laincourt's dismissal. All he knew was that those circumstances were murky.

"You're returning to La Renardière already?" La Fargue observed in surprise as he approached at a walk.

Almades and Laincourt remained behind.

"Yes!" replied La Houdinière. "Monsieur de Laffemas chose to cut short his interview today as he deemed it to be entirely unfruitful. La Donna's latest whim, it seems, has exhausted his patience."

"A whim which I believe I know," said the old gentleman, looking at the coach where a pretty hand had discreetly lifted the window curtain.

The note he had received at the Hôtel de l'Épervier had come directly from Laffemas. La Houdinière, no doubt, did not know its contents.

"Would you allow Laincourt to have a conversation with La Donna, right here?" asked La Fargue.

The other man thought for a moment and then shrugged.

"All right."

He gave the necessary orders, and Laincourt, after a nod from the captain of the Blades, dismounted. He walked across the uneven paving of Le Châtelet's courtyard and, under the gaze of his former brothers-in-arms, climbed aboard the vehicle. No one heard what was said within, behind the richly padded walls and the thick drawn curtains. But less than half an hour later the coach and its escort moved off, taking La Donna back to La Renardière, while La Fargue, Laincourt, and Almades proceeded to leave Paris by the Saint-Martin gate.

Taking the road to Senlis, then the one leading to Soissons, the three riders passed Roissy and continued at a gallop to Dammartin. There, they needed to ask for directions. The first goodwife they came across in the village square was able to assist them. Everyone living in the area knew the manor belonging to the famous painter, Aubusson.

"Where did you meet La Donna?" La Fargue asked Laincourt as they followed the track that had been indicated to them.

Keeping a watchful eye all about, Almades brought up the rear in silence.

"During my stay in Madrid," Laincourt replied. "She was already busy there, hatching schemes."

"Were you adversaries or allies?"

The young man smiled.

"Frankly I still don't know, to this day. But I would probably not be far wrong to say that La Donna had no true ally but herself, as is always the way with her. . . ."

"You seem to be very wary of her."

"As if she were a salamander on live coals."

"But she must, for her part, hold you in some esteem. Laffemas has interrogated her for days, practically in vain, and here she is suddenly confiding in you."

"Don't be fooled, monsieur. I count for nothing in this whole affair. If La Donna spoke to me it is merely because she had already decided to speak, to me or to someone else, in the fullness of time."

"Then why did she ask for you?"

"Someone constrained by force or a threat to reveal a secret will often offer a final resistance by demanding the right to choose the person they shall finally speak to. It's a way of not surrendering completely, of maintaining some semblance of freedom and control."

La Fargue nodded.

"And La Donna, according to you, was playing out such a scene."

"Yes."

"But why?"

"So that it would seem like she was finally giving in. So that we would be less suspicious of her impromptu revelations. And so that we would not wonder why she chooses to speak now, when in fact that is the only question which should interest monsieur de Laffemas."

"Why now."

"Precisely. Why now."

The old captain raised his eyes toward the manor whose red-tiled roofs could be seen behind the trees that crowned the hill.

They were getting closer.

"And this Aubusson. Do you know who he is or why La Donna is sending us to him?"

"He is a painter," said Laincourt, drawing on his recollections. "A portrait artist who, some years ago, was quite renowned. At present he seems to have retired from the world. . . . But I do not know what bonds unite him to Aless—to La Donna. I imagine they met at a princely court somewhere in Europe, when Aubusson still travelled abroad."

"Perhaps she was his mistress," La Fargue suggested slyly.

"Perhaps," said Laincourt impassively.

"And perhaps she still is," added the old gentleman, watching the other out of the corner of his eye. "I have heard that she sometimes uses such means to further her ends."

"We're almost there now."

* * *

120

Aubusson was reading when his valet came to warn him that three riders were coming up the road leading to the manor. Visitors were rare in these parts. Understanding what was going on, the painter thanked the boy, put his book down, and went to his room to find the thick leather folder that Alessandra had placed in his care the week before. "You'll know the moment has arrived when a certain Captain La Fargue comes seeking these papers," she had told him. "You won't have any trouble recognising him. A white-haired gentleman, but still big, strong, and full of authority. His visit will be the signal."

From the window of his chamber on the upper floor, Aubusson watched the riders enter the courtyard at a walk, and immediately spotted La Fargue.

Aubusson called back his valet: "Jeannot!"

"Yes?"

"When the oldest of those three riders tells you his name is La Fargue, I want you to give this to him."

The boy took the folder, but hesitated.

"The matter has already been settled and he won't ask you any questions," the painter reassured him.

Jeannot scurried away. He ran down the stairs, crossed the front hall with his heels clattering on the flagstones, burst out onto the front porch, and went with a quick step to meet the visitors.

Without seeking to conceal himself, Aubusson watched the scene from his wide-open window. After exchanging a few words the valet gave the leather folder to La Fargue. The latter untied the ribbon that held it shut, cast a glance at the documents it contained, and, without expression, closed it once more.

After which, he lifted his eyes to look up at the painter, as if in search of confirmation.

Is that all? he seemed to be asking.

Aubusson gave him a slow, grave nod, to which the old gentleman responded with a brief salute before giving his companions the signal to depart.

The portrait artist watched the riders head off into the distance at a fast trot and waited for his valet to rejoin him.

"Monsieur?"

"Go to the village and ask the master at the staging post for two saddled horses."

"Two, monsieur?"

"Yes, two. And don't tarry on the way . . ."

The boy scampered off again.

. . . because it's happening tonight, Aubusson added to himself.

"And now?" Laincourt asked, in loud voice in order to be heard over the beating hooves.

"Here," replied La Fargue. And without slowing their pace, he handed over the leather folder they had obtained from Aubusson.

The cardinal's former agent hastened to slip it inside his doublet.

"What am I supposed to do with it?" he asked.

"You must take it to rue des Enfants-Rouges, to sieur Teyssier. He is the—"

"—master of magic for His Eminence, I know. But why?"

"So that he can study these documents and determine their authenticity. I will be content with his first impression. Wait until he communicates that to you, and then come and find me at the Hôtel de l'Épervier. Almades and I are going there directly, in case there is news waiting for me there."

"News from La Donna?"

"Among others, yes."

"Can you tell me what these documents are, that I'm carrying?"

"If they are in truth what they seem to be, they were stolen from the Black Claw. As for their content, I cannot say. The text appears to be in draconic. . . ."

Saint-Lucq tottered backward, leaning against a scabby wall and, eyes closed, waited to recover his breath and his calm. Strength and lucidity returned to him. His heart ceased to beat so furiously. He inhaled deeply and reopened his eyes.

The body at his feet lay in a spreading puddle of black blood. The fight had taken place in a deserted alley in Les Écailles. It did not seem to have drawn anyone's attention, which was a good thing. But someone could turn up at any moment. Night was falling, which meant that Les Écailles would soon be swarming with creatures the half-blood would rather not have to face, especially not with drac blood on his hands.

Saint-Lucq resheathed his rapier. Then, crouching, he pushed his red spectacles up onto the bridge of his nose and turned over the body to examine it.

A drac, then.

A black drac. Young. One whose cheek bore a nasty wound that the half-blood abruptly recognised: it was the hired blade he had provoked and wounded that night during the storm, in Artois. Saint-Lucq supposed the young drac had spotted him and been unable to resist the temptation to take immediate revenge. Had he warned his comrades? Probably not. If he had, the half-blood would not have confronted a single impulsive adversary in a hurry to finish him off, but instead a whole group of determined, well-organised mercenaries.

Saint-Lucq stood up again.

He looked around, sniffing at the damp air, and was suddenly convinced that he was close to his goal. It wouldn't be long now before he found the lair of the dracs on La Donna's trail.

Upon their return to Paris, La Fargue and Almades left Laincourt at the entrance of rue des Enfants-Rouges and continued down rue du Temple. They took the Pont au Change, crossed the Ile de la Cité, and then the small arm of the Seine by way of the Pont Saint-Michel. On the Left Bank, they passed through the Buci gate as they returned to the faubourg Saint-Germain and, finally, rue Saint-Guillaume and the Hôtel de l'Épervier. They entrusted their horses to André, and La Fargue immediately summoned his troops. Only Leprat and Saint-Lucq were missing, the former on duty at La Renardière and the latter busy searching Ile Notre-Dame-des-Écailles. So it was therefore Agnès, Marciac, and Ballardieu who joined Almades and their captain in the main hall on the ground floor—their converted fencing room. They all found a seat wherever they could.

La Fargue began by asking if they had received any news from La Renardière, the Palais-Cardinal, the Louvre, or even Le Châtelet. And when they replied no, he proceeded to recount the events of the afternoon. After— and even during—this recital, he had to answer questions about Aubusson, Laincourt, La Donna, and above all, the famous documents they had received from the painter. This took a good hour.

"So," Marciac summed up, "having revealed the existence of a plot against the king, La Donna spends almost a week dancing this strange *pas de deux* with monsieur de Laffemas until, one fine morning, she suddenly declares that she will speak to none but Laincourt and, without further ado, sends him to the one person who can provide proofs of her claims."

"That's right."

"Am I the only one to find this rather astonishing?"

No one knew how to reply to this, except Ballardieu, who muttered: "I find this Italian woman very capricious. I say a good spanking would probably suffice to bring her back to sweet reason. The cardinal has coddled her, if you want my opinion."

The others glanced at one another, thinking there was a certain amount of good sense in the old soldier's words. Marciac, however, was the only one to really imagine the spanking.

"But that's not the most important thing," said Agnès. "After all, if La Donna has found some personal advantage in this affair then so much the better, since without it she would have kept the information to herself or else sold it to the highest bidder. What does matter, on the other hand, is the plot itself. Our first duty is to protect the king, the queen, and the cardinal. Not to guess at the secret motives of a foreign spy."

"Agreed," said the Gascon. "So what about these papers found at the painter's home, this Aubusson? Do they even attest to the existence of a plot?"

La Fargue shrugged.

"How can we know? I can only say that if these documents are authentic, their value is immense."

"Documents belonging to the Black Claw," Almades reminded them.

"Yes. They will reveal their secrets once they've been translated. It's only a matter of time."

"To be sure. But isn't time precisely what we lack?" Agnès emphasised.

A silence followed, finally interrupted by monsieur Guibot, who knocked, opened the door, and announced Laincourt. The latter was promptly invited to enter. Looking grave, he distributed courteous nods all round, gratified Agnès with a more pronounced salute, and then gave La Fargue a questioning glance.

"Speak," said the Blades' captain.

"I have just come from His Eminence's master of magic. He cannot yet attest to this formally, but the authenticity of the papers he has studied appears to be borne out. According to him, they are quite definitely Black Claw documents, and may even emanate from the Grand Lodge itself—"

The Black Claw had many lodges throughout Europe, France excepted. The Grand Lodge was that of Madrid. Historically, it was the first to be founded, and it remained the most important and influential of them all.

"—and they have much to do with a certain Alchemist," Laincourt concluded.

This last revelation had the effect of a thunderbolt in a clear sky. All those present were dumbstruck, as if seized by a superstitious awe. Then, slowly, eyes turned to La Fargue.

His face had turned frighteningly pale.

"What name did you just say?" he asked faintly.

Not understanding the commotion he had just provoked, Laincourt hesitated.

"The Alchemist. . . . Why?"

"You say these papers of the Black Claw relate to him. What else?"

"That was all Teyssier said on the subject."

"Could La Donna have dealings with the Alchemist?"

"Who knows?"

La Fargue rose from his chair with a determined air.

"Almades," he said. "Ask André to saddle two horses. You and I are leaving for La Renardière at once."

"Captain . . ." Agnès objected. "It will be the black of night by the time you arrive. . . ."

But the old gentleman appeared not to hear her.

"Monsieur de Laincourt," he asked, "could you be ours until morning?"

When the young man nodded, he went on to say: "In that case, I want you to return to sieur Teyssier and oblige him, if necessary, to spend all night studying the documents we entrusted to his care. Make sure he knows how important this is. If you wish, Agnès or Marciac will accompany you."

And turning to those two, he added: "But I want at least one of you to remain here, to wait for news from either of our two parties. Is that understood?"

Less than a quarter of an hour later, after La Fargue and Almades departed into the dusk, it was decided that Agnès would go with Laincourt to see the cardinal's master of magic.

"It's up to you to guard the fort," she said to Marciac.

Embarrassed, the latter rubbed a hand over his stubbled cheeks and, drawing the young baronne aside, out of earshot of the others, he murmured to her: "I have to go somewhere, Agnès."

"What? Now?"

"Yes."

"Where?"

"I can't tell you that."

"Nicolas . . ." Agnès sighed.

"I swear to you it doesn't involve a woman. Or a card game."

"So what is it then? Or rather, who?"

"I would tell you if I could. . . ." Then in a more breezy tone, as if they had already reached an accord, he said: "Listen, I promise I won't be long. And anyway, Ballardieu will be here. It's not as if I'm abandoning the place to the enemy, is it?"

And after dropping a quick kiss on the young woman's brow, he left her there, making a discreet exit from the mansion through the rear garden. Agnès stood for a moment with a troubled expression on her face, before pulling herself together and quickly dashing up the main staircase to her bedchamber.

Now armed and booted, a leather cord securing the heavy plait of her black hair, Agnès joined Laincourt in the stable, where he was helping André and Ballardieu saddle two more horses.

"We need to make haste," she said. "The Paris gates will be closing soon. Need a hand?"

Although its ramshackle walls and muddy ditches were very poor defences indeed, Paris was a fortified city and its gates were closed during the night. The Hôtel de l'Épervier, being located in the faubourg Saint-Germain, lay outside the city's walls, whereas His Eminence's master of magic lived within. To be sure, the Blades all possessed passes signed by Richelieu himself, but persuading the city watch to open up was both a tiresome business and an enormous waste of time.

Laincourt did not answer. He continued to busy himself with the horses as if he had not heard Agnès, and then, with a stony expression, he asked: "Will you tell me what this is all about?"

The young baronne de Vaudreuil exchanged an embarrassed look with Ballardieu. Then she told herself that the cardinal's former agent no doubt deserved to know the heart of the matter. She sighed and with a resigned air, waved to André and Ballardieu that they should leave.

And once she and Laincourt were alone in the stable she said: "Go ahead, ask your questions. I will answer if I have the right to do so."

He had just finished saddling his mount. After tightening a last strap, he stood up and caught the baronne's gaze.

"What happened, just now?" he wanted to know. "Why did La Fargue react the way he did when he heard me speak the Alchemist's name? And why did the rest of you, at that same moment, seem so worried?"

Agnès wondered where she should start.

"What do you know of the Alchemist, monsieur?"

Laincourt pursed his lips.

"I know what is said about him."

"Which is?"

"Which is that he is the oldest, the craftiest, and the most formidable of the Black Claw's agents. The very best of them, in fact. But this name—the Alchemist—is all anyone knows of him, and it is, no doubt, a *nom de guerre*. No one knows what he looks like, his age, or even his true gender. He is supposed to have been involved, to a greater or lesser degree, in every important plot and bloody revolt that has taken place. Yet, even if we can detect his presence everywhere, no one has ever caught sight of him anywhere—"

"—to the point that some people doubt his very existence," Agnès finished for him. "Yes, I've heard all that before. . . . But are you one of these sceptics, Arnaud? If you are, then I urge you to revise your opinion. Because the Alchemist, to our great misfortune, does indeed exist. He was even on the verge of being captured, once. By us, by the Blades, acting on La Fargue's initiative."

Laincourt frowned.

"I didn't know that," he confessed.

The young woman's face darkened.

"It was five years ago," she said.

Night had fallen upon Ile Notre-Dame-des-Écailles when Kh'Shak, returning after an hour's absence, entered a miserable back yard and found his soldiers standing in front of the shack where they had been hiding these past few days. Ready for an expedition, the black dracs were heavily armed and struggling to contain their impatience. Kh'Shak was surprised. He had given no orders to prepare for a sortie before he left in search of Ni'Akt, the youngest member of his unit. Since they had been in Paris, Ni'Akt had suffered more than his fair share of humiliation and insults from his elders and Kh'Shak had feared for a moment that he'd deserted. But guided by rumours, he had quickly found his dead body—already stripped of its possessions—lying in a fresh pool of blood. And then he had come right back.

Kh'Shak walked right through his men without looking at them.

He went into the shack and descended the rotting stairs to the damp cellar filled with its appetising odour of rotting meat. Gutted animal carcasses littered the dirt floor and there were yellow candles burning that produced much smoke in addition to their dim light.

Kh'Shak had expected to find his saaskir cross-legged on the ground in the middle of the room. But the old pale-scaled drac was sitting on a keg, gnawing a haunch of raw, spoiled meat with what remained of his yellowed teeth, finally at the end of his long fast.

"Ni'Akt is dead," announced the hulking black drac. "He went out despite my orders and was killed. I think the half-blood murdered him."

The other drac nodded but continued to eat.

"That means he will find us soon," added Kh'Shak. "He is very close now."

"It doesn't matter," said the sorcerer. "The one we are searching for has finally revealed herself to the Eye of the Night Dragon. I know where she is hiding and I shall lead you there by thought."

"At last!"

"Did you believe the task was easy?"

"No, but—"

The old drac lifted a thin clawed hand in an appeasing gesture.

"Rejoin your men, Kh'Shak. Find your horses and leave without further delay. If you act quickly and well, La Donna will be dead this very night."

3

That night, at La Renardière, Alessandra di Santi was reading when she heard riders approaching at a gallop. As her bedchamber only offered a view of the garden paths and the great tree-lined park, she went into the antechamber and, parting the curtains slightly, caught a glimpse of La Fargue and Almades as they jumped down from their saddles and climbed the front steps where they were met by Leprat.

She smiled, withdrew from the window, adjusted her red curls as she passed in front of a mirror, told herself that the soft yellow light of the candles decidedly suited her, and, back in her room, returned to her armchair and her book.

The chambermaid soon admitted La Fargue, and lifting her eyes to his, La Donna greeted him with a dazzling smile.

"Good evening, captain. To what do I owe the pleasure of this visit?"

The old gentleman closed the door without replying, turned the key twice in the lock, looked briefly out the window, drew the curtains, and then, looking grave and almost menacing, came to stand before the beautiful lady spy.

"Ah!" she said, putting her book down. "So this is not a social visit. . . ."

"Enough play, madame."

Serene, Alessandra rose under the pretext of pouring herself a glass of liqueur from a bottle placed on the side table. If she remained seated, she would be permitting La Fargue to dominate her with his massive figure and hold sway over her, something which she detested.

"And what game do you think I am playing, monsieur?"

"I still don't know the rules or the object. But I can affirm that it ends here and now. I am not monsieur de Laffemas, madame. I am a soldier. If you persist in playing games, our conversation will take a most discourteous turn."

"Are you threatening me monsieur?"

"Yes."

"And you are a man who is willing to transform your threats into action. . . ."

This time, the captain of the Blades was silent.

La Donna met his stare without blinking, returned to her armchair, and invited La Fargue to sit facing her, to which he consented after removing his baldric and his sword.

"It's about the Alchemist, isn't it?" Alessandra guessed.

The old gentleman raised an eyebrow. What exactly did she know about the blows the Alchemist had struck against the Blades?

"Rest assured," she said as if reading his thoughts, "I don't know the details of what transpired a few years ago at La Rochelle. I only know the bare essence. But perhaps that is already too much for your taste?"

La Fargue gave La Donna an expressionless stare.

"Do you know the nature of the documents that you arranged to have handed over to us today?"

Alessandra shrugged with an air of annoyance.

"Obviously."

"Is the Alchemist part of the plot against the king that you claim to have information about?"

"Of the plot against the *throne*," she corrected. "And yes, the Alchemist is the principal instigator. The duchesse de Chevreuse is also a participant—"

La Fargue greeted this revelation without much surprise, but he hadn't heard the worst yet.

"—as is the queen," the adventuress finished.

The old captain was visibly shaken.

"You mean the queen mother, of course. . . ."

Alessandra rose from her chair, going over to the large cage and teasing one of her dragonnets by sliding an index finger between the bars.

"It's true, of course, that the queen you speak of is also implicated," said the beautiful Italian woman in a lighthearted tone. "Isn't she always? But I was thinking of the other, of the reigning queen. . . ."

"Of Anne d'Autriche."

"Yes."

La Fargue now rose in turn, pacing back and forth in front of the fireplace, and finally asked: "These documents from the Black Claw, how did you come by them?"

"I stole them."

"From whom?"

"By God! From one of its members! And as you can imagine, although I don't know how they learned it was me, they are most displeased about it!"

"Why?"

Sincerely puzzled, Alessandra looked at the old gentleman.

"I beg your pardon?"

"Why did you steal these documents from the Black Claw?"

"Ah . . . !" she said, finally understanding. "Would you believe me if I told you that I dislike the Black Claw as much as you do and that, when possible, I apply myself to doing them harm?"

He approached her.

"No," he replied. "I would not believe it."

She smiled and resisted the temptation to step back.

"So, why?" La Fargue insisted.

"Because I received the order to do so."

He came closer still.

Now they were practically touching and Alessandra had to tilt her head to see the black look on her interrogator's face.

"Who was it, who gave this order?" he demanded in a grave, menacing tone.

"It came from our masters, of course, captain."

"I serve the king of France and Cardinal Richelieu. Do you claim to do the same, madame?"

The young woman did not blink.

"I claim nothing of the sort, monsieur. Do you really want me, here and now, to name those I am thinking of, and know that you are too?"

La Donna and the old captain both remained silent for a moment, face-to-face, he trying to probe her soul and she opposing him with the calmness of an indomitable will. They did not move, glaring at one another, barely breathing.

And someone knocked at the door.

"Captain!" called Leprat.

La Fargue hurried to open up.

"What is it?"

"The sentries in the park no longer answer to the calls," replied Leprat. "And the valet I sent to alert the other musketeers posted at the entrance to the domain has not returned."

Marciac had been waiting in front of the massive Saint-Eustache church for a few moments when Rochefort finally arrived. The cardinal's henchman was accompanied by two other gentlemen, whom he asked to wait behind. Then he walked up to the forecourt alone and, not seeing the Gascon, slowly spun around, searching the darkness.

"Since when do you bring company to our meetings?" Marciac asked him, emerging from the shadows.

"Since it pleases me to do so."

"It's contrary to our accords."

"They are far enough off that they cannot hear you or see you. And don't speak to me of accords that you have been the first to betray."

"Does the cardinal have any reason to complain about the success of my mission in La Rochelle?"

"No. But he still recalls that, not so long ago, you refrained from saying anything about a certain person of interest to us."

Marciac knew that Rochefort was referring to the hidden daughter of La Fargue, who had been found and protected a month earlier by the Blades. To ensure her security, the Gascon had even entrusted her to the care of the only woman he had ever loved. Gabrielle, who happened to keep a certain establishment—the Little Frogs, in rue Grenouillère—where amiable young women practised the profession of satisfying the desires of generous men.

"I didn't know who she was and, therefore, was unaware of the interest that she might hold for you," Marciac defended himself.

"And where is she, at present?"

"I have no idea."

"But there was a time when she was hiding in Paris, wasn't there?"

"Yes," the Gascon admitted reluctantly.

"And where was she?"

"It doesn't matter."

Rochefort displayed a sinister smile.

"I have the notion that this girl was in a house that was quite ill-suited to someone of her sex and her age. And since you are not offering me any information, it's possible that I might have to start knocking down doors and asking questions in rue Grenouillère. . . ."

Marciac's blood started to boil. His face turned red and, with a sudden move, he seized Rochefort by the collar, lifted him up on the tip of his toes, and forced him back several steps until he thumped into the church door.

"Don't you dare go near Gabrielle!" he spat. "Don't threaten her! Don't even look at her. Forget you even know of her or, as God is my witness, I'll kill you."

Livid, his lips twitching, Rochefort replied in a toneless voice: "Release me, Marciac. Remember we have spectators who won't keep their distance for long if you cause trouble. . . ."

The Gascon had indeed forgotten about the gentlemen who were waiting at the corner of rue du Four. In the darkness of night they would have difficulty seeing what was happening. But from their attitude, he could see that they were starting to worry.

"Will they do me an evil turn?" Marciac asked mockingly.

"It will be enough that they recognise you."

The Gascon thought about it and then reluctantly released his grip on Rochefort.

"Don't go near Gabrielle," he warned again, jabbing a menacing finger. "Ever."

And he was so wrapped up in his anger that he did not see the blow coming that caused him to topple backward.

"And you," hissed Rochefort, "don't ever lay a hand on me again. Don't forget who I am, don't forget who I serve, and above all, don't forget what you are."

Upon which, the cardinal's henchman turned on his heels and calmly walked away, rubbing his fist.

"Damn!" La Fargue swore.

Leprat had just informed him that, in all likelihood, La Renardière was being attacked.

Without sparing La Donna a glance, he left his lieutenant by the door and went to look out of the window. The garden looked deserted despite the fact that musketeers were supposed to be patrolling there. Further off, the park was a great rectangular lake of blackness, surrounded by trees as far as the eye could see. A crescent moon and some stars dispensed a paltry bluish glow over the scene.

The Blades' captain cursed under his breath.

If the enemy had overcome the sentries without a fight, by now they could be anywhere within the domain.

"It's the dracs," announced Alessandra. "They've found me."

At that instant, a silhouette—with a round back and taking large strides—crossed a garden path and vanished again into the shadows. A hired blade, clearly. But a drac? A man? La Fargue couldn't say. But his instinct told him La Donna was right.

"Stay right here," he ordered her in a tone that brooked no argument.

Snatching up his rapier in its scabbard, he buckled on his baldric as he left the room with a determined step, Leprat following in his wake.

"The chambermaid?" he asked the former musketeer.

"I am here, monsieur."

The woman in the service of La Donna was standing in a corner of the antechamber, near the cot on which she normally slept. Worried, almost frightened, she did not dare to move.

"Go and join your mistress next door," La Fargue commanded her. "Do you have the key?"

"Yes," replied the woman showing him her bunch.

"Then lock yourselves in." Leprat said in turn. "And don't open the door for anyone except the captain or myself. Is that clear?"

"Yes, monsieur."

The two men did not wait to see if they were obeyed.

They hurried down the great stairway to join Almades on the ground floor where, as a security measure, he had already extinguished most of the torches. Only a few candles remained lit here and there.

"Well?" La Fargue asked in the large front hall filled with shadows and echoes.

"They are still not showing themselves," said the Spaniard, standing slightly back from the window through which he kept watch on the courtyard. "But I've seen some wisps of that black mist—"

"So it is the dracs."

"They've come to capture La Donna," said Leprat.

"Yes. Or to kill her."

The old captain also took up a position at a window from which he tried to take stock of the situation. The hunting lodge consisted of a small central pavilion and two wings enclosing its courtyard. The whole building was surrounded by a dry moat crossed by a stone bridge, a bridge which, unfortunately, they were too late to defend. The servant quarters lay beyond the moat, on either side of a long forecourt that stretched along the axis of the path leading to the woods.

La Fargue spared a thought for the servants housed in the outbuildings. Were any of them still alive?

"All of the windows within a man's reach are solidly barred," Leprat indicated. "And only the main pavilion, where we are now, is occupied. Elsewhere, the doors are locked and the rooms are empty."

Of the three of them, he was the only one who knew the place well.

"In fact," replied La Fargue, "right here in this front hall is where we stand the best chance of defending ourselves, isn't it?"

"Yes. And from here we can guard the main stairs."

"There are others. There are service stairs. And the hidden ones."

"To be sure, but the dracs won't know where to find them. Whereas this one . . ."

In French châteaux the main staircase was always found near the entrance of the central pavilion, of which it formed the backbone.

"Then let's barricade ourselves," decided the captain of the Blades, already pushing a bench into place. "God only knows when the dracs will make their assault."

Shots were suddenly fired, and the windowpanes by the main door shattered. The horses that La Fargue and Almades had left outside whinnied. Almost immediately, the three men heard a dull thud from above, the sound of a body falling heavily.

"Hold them back!" exclaimed La Fargue as he rushed to the staircase.

Already, other shots resounded and more musket balls came crashing into the walls.

The captain of the Blades climbed the steps two at a time, crossed the antechamber in La Donna's apartments, and ran into a locked door.

He swore, striking his fist against the panel, calling: "OPEN UP! IT'S LA FARGUE!"

Receiving no response, he moved back a pace, lifted a knee, and sent his foot crashing against the door. It shook on its hinges without giving way. He swore even louder, took a running start, and threw himself forward shoulder-first. The wood split, the lock broke, and the door flew open as if it had been hit by a battering ram. La Fargue stumbled into the bed chamber. But he managed to keep his balance and unsheathed his sword by reflex when he saw what awaited him inside.

The chambermaid was lying unconscious on the floor, next to the scattered keys from her bunch. At the rear of the room a wall tapestry was folded back, caught in a door that had been shut too quickly. But above all, there was a black drac who had just entered by the wide-open window.

From the yellow patterns decorating his facial scales, La Fargue identified him as the chief of the drac mercenaries who had been sent after La Donna by the Black Claw. As for Kh'Shak, he recognised the old gentleman soldier who had barred his way in Artois with surprise and pleasure.

The captain of the Guards immediately placed himself *en garde*.

His opponent smiled and, instead of a sword, brandished a pistol.

"I promised you we would meet again, old man," he said taking aim.

The very same moment the shot rang out, the entire building was rocked by an explosion.

On the ground floor, the main door had just been blown into pieces, destroyed by the explosion of a black powder charge. Thick smoke invaded the front hall and, dazed, Leprat and Almades painfully picked themselves up from the floor, coughing amid the last bits of debris that were raining down.

His ears ringing, Leprat thought he could hear drakish war cries. Tottering on his feet, he had just realised that he'd managed to keep hold of his pistol when he saw a silhouette outlined in the gaping frame of the doorway. He took a very approximate aim and missed his target by a fraction. The drac rushed him. Still shaken by the explosion, he was late in comprehending what was happening. And he was only starting to draw his rapier when the drac struck.

Too slow to react, the musketeer saw his death rushing toward him . . .

. . . when he heard another loud blast.

Leprat quickly recovered his wits upon seeing the drac's head burst. His face spattered with black blood, he turned to see Danvert armed with a smoking arquebus. Other dracs were pushing their way into the building and Almades had already engaged two of them.

His white rapier clenched in his fist, Leprat dashed forward to lend him a hand.

Kh'Shak had aimed for the head and had scored a hit. But his arm had wavered at the last moment due to the explosion, so that the pistol ball had merely cut deeply into La Fargue's brow as it skidded over the bone, rather than penetrating his brain.

His hat torn away, the Blades' captain reeled. His vision was blurred and his ears rang as blood dripped down into his eyes. He thought he was going to collapse yet, somehow, he remained standing. But the floor seemed to be swaying beneath his feet.

Kh'Shak, still brandishing his smoking pistol, struggled to understand how his adversary could still be alive and on his feet, face bloodied, after receiving a ball in the middle of his forehead. Then he pulled himself together, threw his pistol away, and drew his sword as he marched toward La Fargue.

The latter, half stunned, saw the drac coming as if through a veil. He parried as best he could one, two, three successive attacks with the wild gestures of a drunken man, and attempted a riposte that the other easily countered.

The drac started to play a cruel game with him.

"You're no longer up to this, old man."

He lunged, bypassing La Fargue's uncertain parry, and plunged the point of his blade into the captain's right shoulder. The old gentleman moaned as he retreated, bringing his hand up to the wound. The keen pain aroused him somewhat from his torpor. But the floor continued to move beneath him and his buzzing temples continued to deafen him.

"You should have hung up your sword long ago."

Another lunge and this time La Fargue felt two inches of steel penetrate his left thigh. His leg faltered beneath his weight and almost gave way beneath him. He only just succeeded in remaining on his feet. Still retreating, he wiped a sleeve across a brow that was sticky with blood and sweat. He blinked several times. And with an immense effort of will he managed to focus on the blurred silhouette that was tormenting him.

"It's too late for regrets now, old man. Goodbye," said Kh'Shak, as he prepared to deliver the fatal stroke to his exhausted opponent.

But it was La Fargue who attacked.

Dropping his sword and roaring like a savage beast, he rushed at the drac, grappling with him and shoving him backward. Wide, massive, and solid, the captain of the Blades was a force of nature despite his age. And as strong and vigorous as he was, the huge drac was unable to halt the old gentleman's momentum. Benefiting from the element of surprise, the man was also powered by an overwhelming rage born of desperation. Kh'Shak felt himself being lifted off the floor. And he realised too late that La Fargue was propelling them both toward the open window.

"You old fool. You're going to—"

His teeth red with blood, La Fargue wore an evil smile of triumph and rancour as they toppled together into empty space.

With Charybdis flying ahead and Scylla right behind him, Alessandra moved away as quickly as possible from La Renardière and into the surrounding forest. After stunning her chambermaid and stealing the key to the small hidden door, she had descended a damp, narrow stairway. Then, taking advantage of the confusion that reigned at the hunting lodge, she had discreetly made her escape.

Scylla gave a raucous cry: they had arrived.

And, indeed, La Donna soon saw the clearing ahead of her where Aubusson, her friend and accomplice, was waiting with two horses he had hired that day from the master of the staging post at Dammartin.

They exchanged a long embrace.

"At last!" said the painter. "You did it!"

"Not yet."

"What? You're free, aren't you?"

"I shall never be entirely free as long as that sorcerer lives."

"Don't tell me you intend to—"

"Don't worry, just return home. The cardinal's men will soon be asking you numerous, pressing questions."

"No. I'll come with you."

"Don't. You've done enough already. We'll meet again soon, my friend."

And hitching up her skirt to reveal the breeches and boots she had donned before leaving her apartments at La Renardière, she mounted a horse and dug her heels into its flanks.

"Captain! Captain!"

La Fargue slowly regained consciousness. The last thing he remembered was the sound of the drac's ribs cracking as they hit the ground.

Moaning, the old gentleman discovered innumerable pains as he sat up to see Leprat descending into the moat.

"Captain! Are you all right?"

"I'll live. And him?"

He leaned on one elbow and pointed to the drac stretched out beside him.

"Dead," replied the musketeer.

"Good. And the others?"

"Also dead. But there were only five of them. Six, with this one."

"So there's one still missing. That's too bad. . . . And La Donna?" La Fargue asked as Leprat helped him to his feet.

"She's nowhere to be found."

At the home of the cardinal's master of magic, Agnès and Laincourt were drowsily waiting in an antechamber, one on a bench and the other in a chair, when the sound of a door being flung open roused them.

It was Teyssier, coming in search of them.

His face looked drawn, there were rings under his eyes, and his hair was dishevelled. His fingers were ink-stained and in his hand he held dog-eared sheets of paper, covered with cramped writing and many crossings-out. Unshaven, he had spent the entire night studying the documents La Donna had stolen from the Black Claw.

"I need you to escort me to the Palais-Cardinal," he said in an urgent voice. "I must see the cardinal as soon as he wakes."

Laincourt turned to the window.

The night was just starting to grow pale.

Dawn was breaking over Paris and the Ile Notre-Dame-des-Écailles.

Down in the cellar that stank of rotting remains, his ritual staff across his thighs, the old drac was crouched in a meditative posture. He did not make the slightest gesture and kept his eyes closed when he heard steps behind him.

"I've been waiting for you," he said in the drakish tongue.

"Pray to your gods one last time," replied La Donna, unsheathing a dagger.

The sorcerer stood up and faced her.

Dressed in a sturdy leather hunting outfit, she was alone. She had preferred not to bring her two small companions out of fear of being recognised at the gates of Paris. A pretty young redheaded woman with two dragonnets would not go unnoticed, and she had excellent reasons to believe that all of the cardinal's informers—although they might not know why—had received instructions to keep a lookout for her. Besides, even without Scylla and Charybdis, returning to Paris was imprudent on her part.

But Alessandra di Santi knew there was still an act to be played out in this story, before she disappeared for good.

The old drac gave her his toothless smile.

"What is it, sorcerer? Do you think I will hesitate to stab you if you stare at me? Then you do not know me. . . ."

La Donna, however, was about to fall victim to her pride.

Too sure of herself, she did not see the danger coiled in the shadowy corners of the cellar, which was already creeping out to surround her. Silent and deadly, tendrils of black mist snaked toward her, licking her boots, winding around her ankles.

"Your little dragonnets, they would have sensed it—" said the drac.

"Sensed it? Sensed what?"

"This—"

The sorcerer's eyes sparkled. His fists clenched around his staff and he suddenly brandished it in the air. Instantly, the tongues of black mist rushed to attack the young woman, like a vine suddenly wrapping itself around a column. They seized her and pinned her arms against her body. Incapable of making the slightest movement, she felt herself lifted from the floor.

"I understood too late," said the old drac. "I realised too late that you had stopped running. I saw, too late, that you were only hiding for long enough to discover my lair. . . . Indeed, how did you manage that? Your cursed little dragonnets, no doubt. . . ."

He shook his staff and rattled the talismans—little bones, scales, beads, claws—that hung from it. La Donna stiffened, her body paralysed. She tried to speak, but could only manage a hiccup. Like a vice, the wisps of mist were now crushing her chest. She was starting to lack for air.

"But it wasn't enough for you to draw my warriors into a trap. Even once you were rid of them, you knew your flight would never be complete as long as I held within me that small shred of your soul which I stole from you. You needed to kill me. And that's why I was waiting for you."

The sorcerer shook his staff again. Alessandra gave a jolt. Her eyes round with fear, she felt the black mist running fine, agile fingers over her throat toward her face, her lips, and her nostrils.

If this horror reached inside her . . .

"Dying of the sudden ranse is extremely painful, did you know that?"

La Donna gathered her last strength to tear herself away from the mist that threatened to invade her nose, her mouth, her throat, and her entire being. In vain. She gave a long painful moan in supplication. Tears welled up at the corners of her eyes.

The worst thing was that she and the sorcerer were not alone in the cellar. La Donna had seen someone slowly emerge from the shadows behind the drac's back. But why didn't he act? Why wouldn't he help her? Was he content to watch her die? Why? What had she done to deserve such indifference?

Do something. . . . For pity's sake do some—

She was losing consciousness when the mist suddenly relaxed its embrace. The young woman collapsed on the dirt floor and, through a veil, saw the sorcerer frozen in shock, a blade pointing at his chest. Then the blade disappeared with a sound of steel clawing at scales and bone, and the old drac fell down dead. First to his knees. And then on his belly.

The black mist dissipated.

Coughing and spluttering but quickly regaining her wits, La Donna dragged herself backward away from the body and the pool of blood spreading beneath it.

"Wh . . . What were you waiting for?" she finally asked, between two great gulps of air.

"I was waiting to hear the full story," replied Saint-Lucq.

"You bastard."

"You're welcome."

The half-blood crouched to wipe his blade on the sorcerer's filthy, stinking rags. Then he stood up, resheathed his sword, and, from behind his red spectacles, watched La Donna struggle to her feet, one hand seeking support from the wall.

"You'd better hurry, madame," he said in a voice that betrayed no emotion. "As perhaps you would like to rest for a little while, before your next appointment with monsieur de Laffemas at Le Châtelet."

Rue Saint-Thomas-du-Louvre was located in a neighbourhood that stretched from the palace of the Louvre in the east to that of the Tuileries in the west, and between rue Saint-Honoré to the north and the Grande Galerie to this south. This old neighbourhood had undergone various upheavals over the centuries, to the point of now finding itself curiously embedded in the royal precinct, after the Grande Galerie—also known as "Gallery on the shore"—was built to link the Louvre to the Tuileries along the bank of the Seine. But whatever its changed circumstances, it had kept its medieval appearance. Dirty, cramped, and populous, it offered an unfortunate contrast with the royal buildings that surrounded it on three sides.

Running north from the quays, rue Saint-Thomas-du-Louvre ended at rue Saint-Honoré, opposite the Palais-Cardinal. It took its name from a twelfth-century church dedicated to Saint Thomas of Canterbury, and had acquired a certain notoriety due to the two adjoining mansions of Rambouillet and Chevreuse. The first was the Parisian residence of the marquise de Rambouillet, who hosted a famous literary salon there. The second belonged to the duchesse de Chevreuse, whose reputation as a lover, schemer, and woman of the world needed no further embellishment.

This evening, the duchesse was receiving guests.

Torches burned at the monument gates of her mansion, lighting up the street in the gathering dusk. Other torches illuminated the courtyard. The guests were already arriving in coaches, in sedan chairs, on horseback. But also on foot, escorted by lackeys who carried lights and who, once they reached their destination, helped their masters change their shoes or even their stockings. Groups were forming at both ends of rue Saint-Thomas. And people were almost jostling one another before the mansion itself. They conversed gaily, already pleasantly anticipating the excellent evening they would be spending. The jesting of men and the laughter of women rose from the scene, disturbing the night's nascent tranquillity.

In the courtyard, the chairs hindered the carriages as they made the turn to deliver their occupants to the front porch. Made nervous by the agitation, the horses held by their bits whinnied and threatened to rear up between their traces. Lackeys and coachmen did their best to prevent any mishaps. For their masters, it was a question of making the most noteworthy appearance thanks to the splendour of their team and the magnificence of their attire.

There was, however, one guest who—although he came unaccompanied by any servant and descended from a simple hired chair—inspired a certain amount of awe. Thin and pallid, with icy grey eyes and bloodless lips, he was dressed in the austere black robes of a scholar and did not exchange glances with anyone.

"Who is that?" some of those present asked in hushed voices.

"That's Mauduit."

"Who?"

"Mauduit. Madame de Chevreuse's new master of magic!"

"The one they say is a sorcerer?"

Mauduit.

That was how he was known here. But he had borne and still bore many other names.

And, to a few people only, he was known as the Alchemist of the Shadows.

THE CHEVREUSE AFFAIR

1

The meeting took place at nightfall, on the road to Saint-Germain-en-Laye, in a hostelry whose old sign depicted a hart's head in yellow, flaking paint. The establishment had seen better days. Once a thriving business, it had suffered since a bridge had been built at Chatou to replace the ferry—which had previously been the only means of crossing the Seine in these parts. Although the bridge did not change the itinerary of those travelling back and forth between Paris and Saint-Germain, it did save time and make the stop at the Golden Hart less necessary.

The riders arrived at dusk.

There were four of them, all wearing great dark cloaks, wide felt hats, riding boots, and carrying swords at their side. One of them was Cardinal Richelieu, riding incognito between two of his most loyal gentlemen and following the new captain of his Guards, monsieur de La Houdinière. On this expedition, however, the latter was not wearing the prestigious scarlet cape with its distinctive cross and white braid beneath his cloak. He dismounted in the courtyard, knocked on the door according to the agreed code—three times, once, then three times again—and looked around him as he waited for a response.

A wyvern screamed in the distance. Perhaps a wild one, although they were rarely found in France except in the most out-of-the-way corners of the kingdom. More likely a trained wyvern, being ridden by a royal messenger or a scout from one of the regiments assembling around Paris before setting off for Champagne, in preparation for the forthcoming campaign against Lorraine.

Someone, at last, opened the door a crack.

It was Cupois, the hosteller, who presented an anxious face with a sallow complexion, topped by a crown of red hair.

"Is everything ready?" La Houdinière demanded.

"Yes, milord."

The hosteller had no idea who he was addressing, although he was sure he was dealing with a great lord involved in some dangerous intrigue. That, of course, worried him. But the lure of gold proved stronger than his misgivings when La Houdinière—without saying who he was or whom he served—had come by shortly before noon to inspect the place, giving strict instructions and leaving a handsome sum in advance. Cupois only knew that the Golden Hart had been chosen for a meeting that was at least confidential, if not clandestine, in nature.

"There are some gentlemen already waiting for you," he said. "They are upstairs in the largest of my rooms, where, according to your orders, I have placed a table and chairs."

La Houdinière entered, examined the common room which was plunged into half-light, and listened closely to the silence that reigned within the hostelry.

"Did they have the password?" he asked, to set his own mind at rest.

"Of course," replied the hosteller, peeking outdoors. "Without it, I would not have allowed them to enter."

The captain of the Cardinal's Guards could not refrain from smiling at the notion of Cupois trying to prevent La Fargue from entering anywhere.

"Good," he said. "Go join your wife in your chamber and don't come back out."

"I prepared a light meal and I—"

"No need. Go to your bed, monsieur Cupois."

His tone was courteous, but firm.

"They're coming," said Almades, interrupting a conversation between La Fargue and Laincourt.

Standing at the window, but at a discreet distance, he kept watch on the surroundings of the Golden Hart. Laconic as always, he added: "Four riders. One of them comes in advance as a scout. I cannot make out his face."

"Rochefort," surmised the captain of the Blades. "Or La Houdinière."

"La Houdinière. He has just dismounted," said the Spanish fencing master.

Laincourt joined him to take a look outside.

"The cardinal is waiting on his horse," he reported. "The other two are gentlemen from his entourage. I have met them before at the Palais-Cardinal—"

"So, no sign of Rochefort," La Fargue concluded.

As usual he was wearing a sleeveless black leather vest over a doublet of the same red as the sash that was tied about his waist, with his Pappenheimer at his side. His close-cropped white beard was neatly trimmed, but his face was drawn, betraying the strain of the recent fight at La Renardière and his desperate fall from the window. Although he tried not to let anything show, he still experienced some pain when he moved.

"No," confirmed Laincourt. "No sign of Rochefort."

"We serve the same master, he and I. And yet I must confess I always feel more at ease when I know where he is and what he is doing. He is a little like a ferocious dog. I do not like to imagine him roaming about freely in the garden. . . ."

Arnaud de Laincourt nodded and then turned his head toward Saint-Lucq when the latter said: "Perhaps Rochefort is too busy with La Donna. . . ."

The half-blood was lying stretched out on the bed away from the others, in the shadows. Remaining perfectly still, hat over his eyes and fingers crossed on his chest, he had appeared to be napping until now. With Laincourt and Almades to accompany La Fargue, his presence here was useless and he knew it. But the cardinal had specifically asked that he came. He did not know why.

At the mention of the Italian lady spy, La Fargue pursed his lips doubtfully.

The Blades had been without news of Alessandra since Saint-Lucq had laid hands on her once again. They only knew that she had since been incarcerated in the Bastille and later transferred elsewhere. If monsieur de Laffemas was still interrogating her, he was no longer doing so at Le Châtelet.

"You can be certain," said Laincourt in a grave voice, "that La Donna has not spent more than two or three nights in a gaol cell. And if the cardinal is keeping you in the dark as to where she is being detained, it may be because she is no longer being detained anywhere."

Saint-Lucq sat up suddenly and pivoted to perch on the edge of the bed.

"Are you saying that she is now free?" he asked in surprise, pushing his red spectacles up to the bridge of his nose.

"I'm saying I would not be too surprised to learn that she was. . . ."

"And how the devil—?"

Laincourt admitted his ignorance with a shrug. But then he added: "La Donna never plays a card without having another one up her sleeve. By returning to Paris after her escape from La Renardière, thanks to the drac attack, she knew she risked being recaptured. And no doubt she made some arrangements to protect herself in this event."

La Fargue and Saint-Lucq exchanged a look while the cardinal's former spy remained deep in his own thoughts. As for Almades, he continued to keep his silent vigil upon the courtyard.

"They're coming inside," he announced.

Then he looked out at the horizon where clouds darker than night were massing. He saw the first flickers of lightning from the storm which was now looming over Paris.

Leaning from a third-storey window, Marciac twisted himself around in order to expose his face to the welcome rain which, after a prolonged heat spell, was now pouring down upon the capital. Eyes closed, he smiled and breathed in deeply. The blowing wind and rumblings of thunder did not bother him in the least.

"Great God, that feels good!" he exclaimed. "Sometimes there's nothing better than a storm. . . ."

"A powerful thought," retorted Agnès, hauling him back inside by the collar. "Now, if you could just avoid revealing yourself to the whole world . . ."

She closed the window.

"No need to worry on that account," said the Gascon wiping his face with a hand. "The hosteller swore to me our man would not be back till midnight."

He was soaked, dishevelled, and delighted.

"And how does he know that, your hosteller?" asked the baronne de Vaudreuil.

Marciac shrugged blithely.

"I didn't think to ask," he confessed. "But he seemed particularly sure of himself on this point."

Agnès rolled her eyes and shook her head. She was dressed like a horseman, as usual—boots, breeches, white shirt, cinched red leather corset—and had tied her thick black hair back into a long plait. At her side hung a rapier whose handsome elegance had often reserved deadly surprises for her enemies.

The thunder rolled above them, causing the windowpanes to rattle and the whole building's frame to creak. They were in the attic.

"There's Ballardieu too," insisted the Gascon. "He's watching from the street below, isn't he?"

The young woman was forced to agree: "Yes. Ballardieu is keeping an eye on things below. . . . But let's complete our task here and return to the mansion as quickly as possible, all right? In fact, we should already have finished by now."

"Very good, madame la baronne."

Pretending not to see Marciac's mocking bow, Agnès slowly swept her candleholder from side to side before her, surveying the bedchamber into which they had discreetly introduced themselves after bribing the owner. The room was rather shabby, as was the rest of the establishment, a very modest hostelry in the faubourg Saint-Jacques. It contained a bed, a chest, a table, and a stool. Its legitimate occupant had also left behind a large leather bag.

Each of them holding a light, Agnès and Marciac got to work without conferring or hindering one another. Their mission consisted of verifying one of the few, rare pieces of intelligence that La Donna had provided to monsieur de Laffemas. According to her, an emissary of the queen mother—a certain Guéret—was in Paris to hand sensitive documents over to the duchesse de Chevreuse. Based on the spy's information, the Blades thought they could unmask this Guéret, but first they had to confirm his identity.

"What are we searching for, exactly?" asked the Gascon, kneeling before the clothing chest he had just opened.

There was more rumbling from the storm outside and the sound of the rain spattering down on the tiles of the roof resounded in the chamber. Already, drops were falling from a crack in the ceiling.

"Letters," answered Agnès. "Papers. Anything that proves we have located the right person. But without taking or disturbing anything. The man must not have the slightest reason to suspect that we have our eye on him. . . ."

"Oh dear!" said Marciac in a strangely toneless voice, "I'm afraid that particular cat is already out of the sack."

Busy examining the contents of the leather bag, the young woman had only been lending him a distracted ear.

"Pardon?" she said, after a moment.

Raising her head, she saw the Gascon leap in pursuit of someone in the corridor. The chamber's legitimate occupant, no doubt. Whoever he was, they had not heard him coming over the sound of the storm and, for a few heartbeats, Marciac and the man had stared at one another in mutual disbelief . . .

. . . just before a clap of thunder broke the spell and precipitated the chase.

Recovering from her surprise, Agnès cursed, climbed over the bed, and dashed out of the room in pursuit of the two men.

Having entrusted his cloak and hat to La Houdinière, Cardinal Richelieu— in high boots, breeches, and a doublet made of grey cloth—removed his gloves and announced: "I must be at the château de Saint-Germain within the hour, where I will be joining the king and his court. So let us be brief, monsieur de La Fargue. My escort is waiting for me in the woods a quarter league from here."

Almades and Saint-Lucq having gone downstairs to join the two gentlemen belonging to His Eminence's suite, only four men—the cardinal, La Fargue, La Houdinière, and Laincourt—remained on the upper floor of the Golden Hart, in a strangely quiet and desolate room that smelled of old wood and dust. A few candles placed here and there made the shadows dance and hollowed the faces of those present. Richelieu looked even more emaciated than usual and his glance seemed more penetrating.

"What news of this plot that La Donna claimed to denounce?" the chief minister asked. "Is there any evidence of it, according to you? And if so, what can you tell me about it at present?"

La Fargue cleared his throat before replying.

"If there is one point on which La Donna has never wavered, monseigneur, it is this one. There is a plot, and it threatens the French throne."

"And what is its nature?"

"We still don't know. But we believe that the Black Claw is behind it."

The cardinal gathered his fingers into a steeple before his thin lips.

"The Black Claw, you say?"

"Yes, monseigneur."

"With the complicity of other parties?"

"Yes. That of the duchesse de Chevreuse. And of the queen, monseigneur."

Having said his piece, La Fargue fell silent.

A hush settled around the table as Richelieu stared at him for a long moment. Laincourt tried to remain as impassive as the captain of the Blades, but the effort cost him and he detected signs of a similar struggle going on within La Houdinière.

However indirectly, La Fargue had just accused the queen of treason.

"Do you have proof of this claim?" the cardinal finally enquired. "Not proofs concerning these complicities, but of the plot itself?"

"Not as such, monseigneur. Only the documents delivered to us by La Donna which attest to—"

"Those documents do not attest to much, captain," Richelieu interrupted in a severe tone of voice. "Teyssier has given me a preliminary translation to read. The documents are incomplete and very vague, even supposing that they are authentic."

"La Donna can testify to that. Let her be interrogated."

"Impossible."

"Impossible, monseigneur? What do you mean?"

"The woman is no longer in our power," said the cardinal in a voice that was too calm not to be worrying. "After she escaped from you, during the few hours of liberty she enjoyed before being recaptured, she managed to communicate her situation to certain individuals who are very well disposed toward her. . . ."

As Richelieu spoke, La Fargue recalled Laincourt's prediction and, out of the corner of his eye, he watched for a reaction from the younger man. He was not the sort to say "I told you so," implicitly or not. But nevertheless it appeared he had foretold matters correctly and, according to the cardinal, on the very day that Saint-Lucq had retaken La Donna into custody, an emissary from the pope had demanded an audience with His Eminence to discuss the case of the beautiful lady spy.

"The threat was scarcely veiled," said Richelieu. "She was to be liberated at once, or else accused and presented to her judges. That is to say: the very members of the Parlement who would have insisted on asking questions and expressing loud protests concerning La Donna for reasons of which you are already aware. Therefore, since it was not in the interests of the king to allow a scandal, and since the support of His Holiness could be useful to the kingdom in the near future . . ."

La Fargue nodded with a sombre face. France was merely waiting for a pretext to invade Lorraine, a Catholic bastion at the very gates of the Holy Roman Empire, which was itself being torn apart by war.

"But all this matters little in the end," the cardinal pursued. "Madame de Chevreuse is part of this plot, you say? Very well, there will soon be no worries on that score. In fact, I can tell you that the duchesse will shortly be placed under arrest, and for proven motives."

"Which are, monseigneur?"

"Treason," indicated Richelieu, with a gesture of his hand to indicate that he would say no more on this subject. "Others, just as prestigious as La Chevreuse by their birth, rank, or fortune, will be similarly inconvenienced. Special trials will be held. Sentences will be pronounced. And heads will roll."

La Fargue frowned. He feared he was beginning to understand where all this was leading.

"Are you ordering me to give up this mission, monseigneur?"

"Nothing can be allowed to compromise the success of the matter I have just mentioned."

"But, monseigneur—"

"It is an affair of State, captain."

"And a plot against the king is not?"

"It is a shadowy plot, at best."

"A plot of which the Alchemist himself is the mastermind!" exploded La Fargue.

Silence fell, heavy as an executioner's ax.

La Fargue had raised his voice and, despite being willing to pardon the old gentleman many things, the cardinal had frozen, his eyes suddenly blazing with anger. Laincourt held his breath and saw the captain of the Blades, embarrassed, inhale deeply.

"I . . . I humbly beseech Your Eminence to forgive my outburst."

Richelieu paused until his gaze grew more peaceful and then he finally said: "The Alchemist, yes, of course. . . . That name must bring some very bad memories to mind, captain. . . ."

"Indeed."

"I therefore understand your . . . lapse. And I forgive it."

"Monseigneur, said La Fargue in a more composed voice, "thwarting this plot is above all a matter of protecting the king. But it is perhaps also a means of inflicting a terrible blow against the Black Claw by killing or capturing the Alchemist."

"And it also risks compromising the fruits of some long, patient investigations into some of the most eminent personages in the kingdom. All this may yet fail if you disturb the duchesse or her accomplices with your operations."

"It is a question of neutralising the Alchemist, monseigneur. A similar opportunity may not present itself for a long time to come."

"I am well aware of that. But you are hunting with hounds and have only just set off in your pursuit, whereas I have been laying my snares for some time now. Although you and I are not hunting exactly the same prey, you could very well end up frightening mine by tracking yours. And, to top it all, you may only be hunting a shadow."

La Fargue was silent. What other argument could he make? Richelieu knew all the facts, all that was at stake, all the risks, all the secret realities which would lead him to take, alone, a decision that would no doubt have heavy consequences.

The cardinal granted himself another moment of reflection and then said: "Very well, captain. Since the life of the king may depend on it, endeavour to foil this plot that threatens him. It may, possibly, lead you to the Alchemist, who is an enemy of France. If it does, you must neutralise him. . . ."

The captain of the Blades wanted to thank him, but Richelieu raised his index finger to signal that he had not finished yet.

"However, I am aware that this enemy of France is also your own since the tragic events at La Rochelle. Do not let that obscure your judgement. Be prudent and discreet. Forbid yourself the slightest false step. Do not act lightly, and above all, do not commit some mistake that might irretrievably wreck the trials we are now preparing. . . ."

La Fargue nodded. The cardinal, however, continued: "That being said, I set two further conditions. The first is that you keep me informed of your projects, and of your successes as well as your failures."

"Certainly, monseigneur."

"The second is that you transfer Saint-Lucq to my service."

Although it left La Fargue unperturbed, this request—which was in fact an order—surprised Laincourt. But it confirmed in his mind the half-blood's unique status within the Blades. Did he really belong to them? The others seemed to consider him one of their best. However, where they willingly expressed their pride at serving under La Fargue, Saint-Lucq set himself apart and adopted the pose of an exceptional mercenary who remained with the Blades by choice but who could leave tomorrow. Moreover, Laincourt knew that when the Blades had been disbanded, Saint-Lucq was the only member the cardinal had continued to employ on secret missions. That could not be insignificant.

"All of the Blades serve at Your Eminence's discretion, monseigneur," said La Fargue.

"Good," replied Richelieu, rising and accepting La Houdinière's aid in donning his cloak. "I'm relying on you, La Fargue. But you should know that you don't have much time. The duchesse de Chevreuse will be hosting a great ball at Dampierre. The morning after this ball she shall be placed under arrest, as will all those who are implicated in her schemes, throughout France. The king desires this, so that her fall immediately follows her moment of triumph."

The cardinal paused here, thinking to himself that this decision corresponded well with the character, at times cruel and devious, of Louis XIII. Calmly, he put on his gloves.

"One last thing, captain. The king is very attached to the success of this . . . Chevreuse affair. He has been following its slow development closely for several months now and is growing impatient. He will not tolerate seeing the duchesse escape from the arm of his justice, even if it were to occur in the course of protecting His Majesty from a plot. . . ."

Before putting on his hat, Richelieu fixed La Fargue with his steely gaze and added: "Do you understand me, captain? And are you fully aware how ungrateful kings can be?"

"*Merde!*" Marciac snarled, seeing the runaway jump from one roof to another across an alleyway.

Not knowing whether Agnès was following him closely or not, he did not slow down, took the same leap in turn, and, in the dark and the wet, landed as best he could on the other side.

He swore again as he almost lost his balance.

"*Merde!*"

And then he resumed the pursuit under the pouring rain . . .

. . . hoping mightily that he was in fact chasing Guéret, the agent that the queen mother had sent to the duchesse de Chevreuse. Provided La Donna hadn't lied. Provided they had not been mistaken about the room at the inn or its occupant. Nothing was certain. On discovering two strangers searching his belongings the other man, to be sure, had not raised a hue and cry but had instead immediately taken to his heels. And now he was still fleeing as if he had the Devil on his trail, over rain-slicked rooftops in the middle of a stormy night, at the risk of breaking his neck. Frankly it was not the behaviour of a man with a clear conscience. Nevertheless. If this fellow was not Guéret, then Marciac was making a huge mistake. . . .

Out of breath, soaked to the skin, his face spattered by volleys of fat, stinging raindrops, he slowed down for an instant and sought to catch a glimpse of his fugitive. He spotted his silhouette thanks to a flash of lightning. The foolhardy man had not weakened. He continued running and appeared to be taking a giant leap over a major obstacle. Feeling anger grow within him, the Gascon resumed the chase and discovered, by almost falling into it, the nature of the obstacle in question. He managed to halt himself at the last minute on the verge of empty space. This time, it was not a matter of crossing a narrow alley. Or even a street. He looked down into the shadowy well of a small courtyard.

"*Merde de merde!*" exclaimed Marciac furiously.

Going around would mean letting the other man escape. But so would waiting here for much longer.

The Gascon hesitated. He backed up a few steps, all the while cursing himself, his contrary fate, and imbeciles who scarpered over roofs during a deluge in the middle of the night. He took a deep breath and cursed some more.

And launched himself into thin air.

Windmilling his arms and kicking his legs, Marciac's leap was not a beauteous thing to behold. But it propelled him across five metres of cavernous darkness to land on the ridge of a sloping roof.

After that, things took a turn for the worse.

The roof was not only sloped but also streaming with water, that is to say, it was extremely slippery. And most of its tiles were just waiting to be dislodged.

Like a high wire artist in a gale, Marciac teetered, waving his arms, shifting from one leg to the other. . . .

"Oh, *merde* . . ."

He fell onto his arse and slid down the slope, faster and faster, preceded by a cascade of tiles which came loose beneath his heels.

"*Merde-merde-merde-merde-merde-merde-merde* . . ."

And then there was only empty space.

"*MEEEEEEEEEEERDE!*"

Some worm-eaten planks slowed his fall with a crash, a thick layer of straw then cushioned it further, and finally a hard bump on the floor of a stable brought matters to a conclusion. Marciac felt pain, swore in his usual manner, and still very angry, rolled over on his side, grimacing.

Which he probably would not have done if he had known he was about to put his nose in a pile of . . .

"*Merde.*"

Agnès's heart leapt in her chest when she saw Marciac fall.

"NICOLAS!"

She too jumped across the small courtyard, landed with more aplomb than the Gascon, and cautiously succeeded in reaching the edge of the roof.

"NICOLAS!" she called out in an anxious voice. "NICOLAS!"

"I'm down here."

"ANYTHING BROKEN?"

"Don't think so, no."

"HOW ARE YOU?"

Displaying a definite sign of good health, Marciac's boiling temper rose to the surface.

"ADMIRABLY WELL!" he shouted sarcastically. "NO GASCON HAS EVER SPENT A BETTER EVENING! SO HOW ABOUT GOING AFTER THAT OTHER ACROBAT, HMM?"

Reassured, Agnès withdrew from the edge of the roof and stood up. Beneath the storm and making use of the flashes of lightning she scanned the rooftops around her, but did not see the runaway and finally picked a direction at random. She doubted she would ever be able to catch him. Even if she knew which way to go, the man now had too great a lead.

A little further on, coming around an enormous chimney, Agnès found herself looking out over a wide crossroads. The person she was looking for was not visible on any of the surrounding rooftops.

It was the end of the chase.

Regretfully, she was about to turn back when her glance fell onto the street below.

And there, dimly lit by one of the big lanterns that were left burning all night in a few scattered places in the capital, she saw the man lying unmoving on the pavement five storeys down, surrounded by a dark puddle riddled by the falling raindrops.

They rode at a walk, through the night, along the road toward Paris and the storm. La Fargue and Laincourt went ahead. Almades followed, quiet and attentive. The old gentleman had not said a word since they had left the Golden Hart shortly after the cardinal's departure with his escort and Saint-Lucq. He seemed absorbed in his thoughts and Laincourt chose to respect his silence. Besides, he was fairly preoccupied himself.

Around them, the darkness seemed immense and the storm rumbled in the distance like the anger of some ancient god.

"It was at La Rochelle," La Fargue said suddenly, without taking his eyes off the path ahead. "Five years ago, during the siege of 1628. We were there, some of the Blades and I, the others being busy in Lorraine. We had infiltrated the besieged town in order to carry out the kind of missions that you might expect. . . ."

"Captain, I—"

"No, Laincourt. It's important that you understand. And I know you are the sort of man who can keep a secret. So don't interrupt me, will you?"

"Very well."

"Thank you. . . . For the most part, it was a matter of collecting intelligence and, by night, taking it back to our own lines. The cardinal was thus kept informed of the state of La Rochelle's defences, of the imminence and scale of relief from the English, of the true severity of the food shortages caused by the blockade, of the shifting opinion among the population and the difficulties encountered by the town's leaders. We also carried out, on occasion, acts of sabotage. And, more rarely, we eliminated traitors and foreign agents."

La Fargue turned to Laincourt and asked him: "But you already know all that, don't you?"

"Yes."

Nodding to himself, the captain of the Blades shifted his position in the saddle slightly to ease the pain in his back.

"We were doing what we do best. Meanwhile, the siege was turning in favour of the royal armies after the cardinal ordered a dike built to prevent ships reaching or leaving the port. . . . Then one evening, when I secretly met with Rochefort, he told me the Alchemist was in La Rochelle. Why was he there? My new mission was precisely to learn this and, if possible, to seize him. I endeavoured to do so with zeal because the Alchemist's renown, as well as the mystery surrounding him, was already immense. He was an enemy of France and his arrival in La Rochelle had to be significant: something important was afoot. . . ."

La Fargue paused in his recital of the tale and, holding back a grimace, rotated an aching shoulder. After his fall into the moat at La Renardière, Marciac—who had once almost become a doctor—examined him and determined that nothing was broken. But the captain of the Blades, as solid and tough as he was despite his age, was not indestructible and had increasing difficulty recovering from the physical ordeals he inflicted upon himself in the line of duty.

"I soon learned that the Alchemist was supposed to attend a meeting. With whom, I did not know. But I knew where and when, so I prepared an ambush. And in doing so, I walked straight into the trap that the Alchemist had set for us."

La Fargue's glance was lost in memory for a moment.

He resumed his account: "I am convinced, now, that the Alchemist's mission was in fact to unmask us and remove us as an effective unit in the conflict."

"Were you under suspicion?"

"No. But the blows we struck against La Rochelle's forces would have indicated that a clandestine enemy unit was operating within the town walls. . . ."

"So the Alchemist arranged for the cardinal's men to learn he was in La Rochelle, is that it? So that you would be informed in turn and make every effort to capture him."

"Yes, that's my belief. Aware of his own value, he made himself the bait to flush us out, which he managed without difficulty. A simple, effective plan. A brilliant plan. Often, the real trick consists in making your opponent believe he's calling the tune. . . ." The old gentleman slowly shook his head, as if the years had suddenly caught up with him. "It was a disaster. One of us, Bretteville, perished during the ambush. And another, Louveciennes—"

"—betrayed you and fled. Today he lives in Spain, as the wealthy comte de Pontevedra."

The captain of the Blades nodded gravely before adding: "That same night, the dike gave way. Soon English supplies and relief forces arrived in La Rochelle by sea. The king realised that he could no longer win by force of arms alone, not without beggaring the kingdom, and he commanded the cardinal to open negotiations. Richelieu disavowed us to avoid having to justify our activities during the siege; he affirmed that we were acting without orders and that he was not even aware of our existence. For the Blades, it meant disgrace. And soon the end, since the cardinal dismissed us from his service."

"Until recently."

"Yes. Until recently."

La Fargue fell silent.

Laincourt followed suit, but one question continued to haunt him. A question he did not dare to ask, but which the captain of the Blades was able to guess: "Ask it."

"I beg your pardon, captain?"

"Your question. Go ahead, ask it."

The young man hesitated, and then: "How can we ever know for sure?" he heard himself wonder aloud. "How can we know if you're pursuing this mission to avenge yourself upon the Alchemist or not? How can we know if you prefer seeking justice for yourself to serving the king and France?"

Behind them, Almades pricked up an ear.

La Fargue smiled sadly.

"You can't," he replied.

In the faubourg Saint-Jacques, Agnès was making her way back toward the hostelry under the continuing downpour, through deserted streets sporadically lit by flashes of lightning. The young baronne, soaked and furious, walked briskly, a curl of hair dangling in front of one eye.

She soon met up with Marciac and Ballardieu. They were going in the same direction, the old soldier supporting the limping Gascon.

Ballardieu lowered his eyes upon seeing Agnès.

"Well?" she asked, directing her words at Marciac.

"Sprained ankle. Very painful . . . And the other man? Did you lose him?"

"Dead."

"You killed—?"

"No! He fell and broke his skull."

"So we have a problem."

"As you say."

The young woman turned to Ballardieu and told him in a frosty tone where he could find the body. Then she ordered: "Dump it in the Seine. But strip it first and make sure it's unrecognisable. And keep all the clothing."

"Yes, Agnès."

The old soldier went about his tasks without further ado.

Taking his place, Agnès propped Marciac up and slowly, because the Gascon was heavy and could only hobble, they made their way back to the inn.

"He may not be to blame," said Marciac.

Agnès knew he was referring to Ballardieu and replied: "He should have warned us the man was coming. That was his job. And I'm convinced he's been drinking. . . ."

The Gascon could find nothing to say in response to this.

But after a few more metres in the rain, he said: "La Fargue isn't going to be happy, is he?"

"Not in the least bit."

They had just lost the only lead likely to take them to the duchesse de Chevreuse, to the Alchemist, and to the plot against the king.

2

The rain continued after the storm and did not cease until dawn. Paris woke fresh and reinvigorated. To say that the capital was clean would have been an exaggeration; it would have required a deluge of biblical proportions to carry away the filth accumulated on its streets and to remove the foul muck clinging to its pavements. But the worst had been washed away and Parisians, upon rising from their beds, were grateful to have finally been relieved of the dust and stink of recent days. It even seemed that the cocks crowed more valiantly and the bells rang more clearly this morning, while the city glistened beneath the sun's first rays.

"Dead," repeated La Fargue in a tone which did not bode well. "Guéret . . . is dead."

The garden still being soaked, they had gathered in the large fencing room inside the Hôtel de l'Épervier. The atmosphere was tense. Even those Blades who were not involved in the previous evening's fiasco were keeping their heads down. Only Almades, who had stationed himself slightly apart from the others to guard the door, seemed completely aloof.

"Yes, captain," Agnès confirmed.

She, Marciac, and Ballardieu had not had time to change from the night before. Their clothing had dried on their backs and left them looking bedraggled, not to mention their tousled hair, weary faces, and obvious chagrin. Ballardieu in particular wore a hangdog look.

"How?" La Fargue demanded.

"Guéret surprised us while we were in his room," Marciac explained.

He was sitting down with one bare foot resting on a stool.

"And killing him seemed like a good idea to you?"

"No!" the Gascon defended himself. "He fled over the rooftops. We pursued him and, unfortunately, he broke his skull in a fall."

"Unfortunately. That's one way of putting it. . . . And how was it that Guéret managed to surprise you? Was no one keeping watch?"

Agnès and Marciac exchanged an embarrassed glance. Ballardieu kept his eyes fixed on the floor in front of him.

"Yes," said the old soldier. "I was."

"And you didn't see the man coming back. . . ."

"It was a dark night," the Gascon interjected. "And with the rain, the storm—"

"—and the wine, am I wrong?" La Fargue continued relentlessly.

"No," confessed Ballardieu. "I just went off for a moment to buy a bottle and—"

The Blades' captain thundered at him: "YOU BLOODY OLD TOSS-POT! HAVE YOU ANY IDEA WHAT YOUR FOOLISHNESS HAS COST US?"

Ballardieu kept his mouth shut. There was an oppressive silence in the room.

After a moment, La Fargue rose and went to a window. It opened onto the wet garden, where the chestnut tree's leaves were shedding their final drops upon the old table. Hands behind his back, he took the time to regain his calm. Then, still facing the garden, he said in a quieter voice: "Any witnesses?"

"None," replied Agnès. "And the innkeeper will hold his tongue."

"The body?"

"Thrown, naked and unrecognisable, into the Seine. With the waters still high from the storm, he'll never be found."

"His belongings?"

"His baggage and the clothes he was wearing are all here."

From over his shoulder, La Fargue glanced at the table the young woman was pointing to. On it were placed the small travelling chest, the big leather bag, and Guéret's still-damp clothing. Papers found in the false bottom of the chest were also spread out.

Leprat was already inspecting them in silence.

"There are sealed letters, a map of Lorraine and another of Champagne, false passports, promissory notes . . ." he finally announced. "Add to that French, Spanish, and Lorraine currency, and you have everything one might expect to find in the possession of a spy who, according to marks on this map, came from Lorraine and passed through Champagne to reach Paris."

"And the letters?" asked Marciac, craning his neck to see from his armchair.

"There are three of them, all addressed to the duchesse de Chevreuse. The first comes from Charles IV, the second is from his brother, the cardinal of Lorraine, and the third is from the Spanish ambassador to Lorraine. I did not think it appropriate for me to open them."

Nancy was the capital of the duchy de Lorraine, of which Charles IV was the sovereign. Located on the border of the Holy Roman Empire and defended by one of the most formidable fortresses in Europe, Lorraine was a rich territory much coveted by France. Relations between Louis XIII and his "dear cousin" Charles were, moreover, execrable, the duke seeming to do everything in his power to exasperate the king and defy his authority. Twice now, royal armies had marched on Nancy to compel Charles to respect the treaties he had signed. And twice the duke had made promises that he failed to keep. Thus his palace continued to welcome dissenters, plotters, and other adversaries of Louis XIII. Banished for a time from France, the duchesse de Chevreuse had been one of their number.

"And that's everything?" asked Agnès.

"My word," replied Leprat in surprise, "it doesn't seem such a bad haul to me. . . ."

Even La Fargue looked at the young baronne with puzzlement.

Was she joking?

"To be sure," she explained, "these passports, maps, and letters are by no means worthless. But Guéret was sent to the duchesse de Chevreuse by the queen mother, wasn't he?"

She looked at them all intently, as if they were missing something obvious. And it was the captain of the Blades who was the first to see what she was driving at.

"In all this," he said, pointing at the documents cluttering the table, "there is nothing from the queen mother addressed to La Chevreuse. . . ."

"Exactly. The queen mother is not going to dispatch one of her agents merely to collect a few letters in Lorraine and deliver them to the duchesse, is she . . . ? Are you sure you haven't missed anything, Antoine?"

Leprat considered the dead spy's belongings displayed before him.

"I believe so, yes."

"What about the clothes our man was wearing last night?" suggested Marciac.

Agnès came to the musketeer's assistance and together they found a leather envelope concealed in the lining of Guéret's doublet. As it was closed with a strip of sealed cloth, they hesitated and looked to La Fargue for permission to proceed. He nodded gravely and they broke the wax seal.

The envelope contained a letter along with several handwritten sheets that Agnès perused, showing signs of a growing astonishment.

"It's a pamphlet," she said. "It's about the queen, her failure to give birth to an heir, and the king's supposed intention to repudiate her on those grounds. The author claims that the king has already communicated with

Rome on this matter and that he will soon be in a position to choose a new wife. . . ."

All those listening gaped in disbelief.

After eighteen years of marriage Queen Anne d'Autriche was still childless. She had had several miscarriages and, for some time now, had suffered from the disaffection and indifference of her husband. Indeed, Louis XIII only rarely visited her bed. Nevertheless, the repudiation of the queen would provoke an outcry in the kingdom and a possible scandal at the royal court. But above all, it would constitute a *casus belli* with Madrid, Anne being the king of Spain's sister.

"Do you think there's any truth in it?" asked Agnès.

"Who knows?" replied La Fargue. "But if people believe it, what does it matter?"

"This text was no doubt meant to be printed secretly in Paris," noted Leprat. "And then spread like wildfire."

"In order to provoke unrest?" asked Marciac.

"Or to cause a big enough upset in Europe to embarrass the king and oblige him to renounce any such project. . . ."

"And so that's it? La Donna's plot against the king?" the baronne de Vaudreuil exclaimed incredulously. "Tell me another one!"

"No," La Fargue intervened. "There's something else going on. But whether its content is true or pure invention and calumny, this pamphlet is by no means innocent. I believe we have laid our hands on the package the queen mother was seeking to have delivered to the duchesse de Chevreuse."

"And the letter probably contains special instructions to go with it."

"Shall I open it?" asked the musketeer, holding up the missive that accompanied the manuscript.

"Yes," ordered La Fargue.

There was, in an iron cabinet somewhere within the Palais-Cardinal, a whole collection of stolen or counterfeit seals, including that of the queen mother. Her seal could be replaced if necessary.

Leprat split the seal and unfolded the letter.

"We have a problem," he said immediately. "This is all in code."

When he arrived at the Hôtel de l'Épervier, Arnaud de Laincourt saw a sedan chair leaving with Marciac as its passenger, escorted by Ballardieu. The spectacle astonished the former spy, who moved aside and bemusedly acknowledged the Gascon's wave.

"I'm going to rest my wounds at Les Petites Grenouilles," Marciac announced. "Come and visit me there when you have a moment. I'm sure you'll receive a fine welcome!"

Laincourt watched without saying a word as the chair passed through the door and then spotted La Fargue walking briskly toward the stable, where Almades was holding two saddled horses by their bridles.

"Monsieur!" he called.

The captain of the Blades halted.

"Yes, Laincourt?"

"Could you grant me a minute?"

"It will be a short one. I have to take some documents we found in Guéret's possession to the Palais-Cardinal."

"You captured him?"

La Fargue reflected that he would probably save time if he fully briefed Laincourt right away.

"Follow me," he said, signalling to Almades that he should wait there.

They entered the main building by the closest door, which was that of the kitchen. The two men sat down and, having asked Naïs to leave them, the old gentleman recounted the most recent events to Laincourt. The latter listened very attentively, occasionally nodding and taking mental note of every detail.

"One thing is for certain," he said when the captain concluded, "this pamphlet does indeed smack of the queen mother."

Banished from the kingdom and exiled in Brussels, Marie de Médicis, widow of Henri IV and mother of Louis XIII, was an embittered old woman still brooding over the way her eldest son had brutally evicted her from power and replaced her with Richelieu. She schemed, dreamed of revenge, and placed all her hopes in her other son, Gaston d'Orléans, also known as "Monsieur," who she hoped to one day see ascend to the French throne.

"You're right," the captain of the Blades acknowledged.

"And this encrypted letter, could you show it to me, please?"

"Might you be able to decipher it?"

"Possibly. I used to be one of the cardinal's code secretaries."

Laincourt took the letter that La Fargue held out to him and ran his eyes over it rapidly. The text consisted of a single block—without punctuation or breaks in the lines—made up of symbols that were mostly borrowed from alchemy.

The cardinal's former spy smiled faintly.

"It's a very simple cipher. Each symbol stands for a letter, and that's about all there is to it."

"You can tell all this with just a glance?" asked La Fargue, giving the young man a measuring look.

But Laincourt was already absorbed in deciphering the text.

"Perhaps certain symbols stand for frequently used words. Or certain persons. But there's nothing more complicated than that. . . . And see how this sign occurs so frequently? No doubt it's an 'a' or 'e,' if the text is in French. And you see this one, it's doubled several times suggesting that it's a consonant, an 'r' or 's' or 't,' for example. . . ."

His eyes shining, Laincourt displayed an excitement that was unusual for this young man, ordinarily so thoughtful and reserved.

"Just a moment," he said.

And, without waiting, he rose, went over to the chimney mantelpiece, snatched up a small notebook that Naïs used for her shopping, tore off a page, returned to his seat, and with a lead pencil began to transcribe the coded letter. His eyes danced from one sheet to another while his hand wrote nimbly, as if possessed of a life of its own. With pinched lips and clenched jaws, his face betrayed his intense concentration.

"This will be easier than I dared to hope," he said.

"Why is that?"

"Because I already know this cipher."

La Fargue was discovering that Laincourt had hidden talents which could be highly useful to the Blades. A few minutes went by in a tense silence, broken only by the scratching of pencil on paper.

"And there you have it!" the young man declared, pushing both the letter and his transcription toward La Fargue. "You may have trouble reading my writing, but at least you won't be late in arriving at the Palais-Cardinal."

He was almost out of breath, but displayed no pride or even satisfaction in his work.

Smiling, the captain of the Blades sat back in his chair and considered Laincourt with the admiring and amused gaze of someone who has just been fooled by an amazing feat of magic.

"You asked if I could spare you a little of my time," he said after a moment. "For what reason?"

"I have a way to get close to La Chevreuse."

"How?"

The young man then explained how the chevalier de Mirebeau had approached him with his offer, and a note that would give him entry to the Hôtel de Chevreuse.

"And you propose to make use of this note," concluded La Fargue.

"Yes."

The old gentleman thought for a moment, weighing the pros and cons.

"All right," he said at last. "But you must be very careful."

"Understood."

"Keep your eyes and ears open, but in a natural fashion. Remember the cardinal's orders: we must not, at any price, risk arousing the duchesse's suspicions. Don't listen at doors, peer through keyholes, or ask any indiscreet questions."

"Very well."

"And above all, be very wary of the duchesse de Chevreuse. You wouldn't be the first person that she has led astray. . . ."

La Fargue had just rejoined Almades, who was patiently waiting for him in the courtyard with their two horses, when a coach entered by the carriage gate which Guibot, hobbling on his wooden leg, had hastened to open.

"Who is that?" asked the Blades' captain. "Did you hear the name announced through the hatch?"

"No," admitted the Spanish fencing master. "But it's rare to see monsieur Guibot hurry like that."

Drawn by a smart team of horses, the vehicle halted in front of them and they understood the reason for their concierge's alacrity upon seeing the marquis d'Aubremont emerge from the cabin. A man of honour and duty, he bore one of the most prestigious and respected names in France. He was also the last friend La Fargue possessed in this world. Like the captain, he was about sixty years old with grey hair, a dignified air, and precise mannerisms. He and La Fargue exchanged a warm greeting. They hadn't seen one another since the marquis had buried his eldest son.

"My friend," said La Fargue, whose eyes sparkled with a contained joy. "If you know the pleasure that I—"

"Thank you, my friend, thank you. . . . I too am very happy to see you again."

They had once been part of an inseparable trio: La Fargue, d'Aubremont, and Louveciennes. Companions and brothers-in-arms, they fought together during the civil and religious wars that had ravaged the kingdom, and then helped the "man from Béarn" take the French throne and become King Henri IV. Upon the death of his father, d'Aubremont had been called away by the family obligations that came with bearing a great and noble name. Twenty years later, however, the first of his sons, who had until then been a member of the King's Musketeers, was to follow Leprat and join the Blades. Endowed with an adventurous and rebellious spirit, the young man had grown distant from his father and adopted the name of a small holding belonging to his mother, that of Bretteville. And it was only after recruiting him that La Fargue learned that he was the eldest son of his old friend.

"Pardon my arrival in this fashion," said d'Aubremont. "But I could not set down in a letter what I am about to tell you. . . ."

"What is it?" asked the captain of Blades in a worried tone.

"Could we speak inside, please?"

Exhausted after a particularly active and sleepless night, Agnès went upstairs to lie down in her bedchamber. She slipped between the fresh sheets with a shiver of delight and, already drowsy, vaguely heard the sound of a coach entering the courtyard. Then she closed her eyes and it seemed to her that she had just dozed off when there was a knock at her door.

"Madame . . . Madame!"

It was Naïs, whose voice reached her from the corridor, through the fog of her interrupted sleep.

Agnès muttered something into her pillow that very fortunately was transmuted into an indistinct groan, as her words were hardly polite and certainly unworthy of a baronne de Vaudreuil.

"Madame . . . Madame . . . You must come, madame . . ."

"Let me sleep, Naïs."

"You were sleeping?"

"Yes, by God!"

Timid Naïs must have hesitated, for there ensued a moment of silence during which Agnès nourished the hope of having prevailed.

"But monsieur de La Fargue is asking for you, madame! He's waiting for you. And he's not alone."

"Is he with the king of France?"

"Uhh . . . no."

"The pope?"

"No."

"The Great Turk?"

"Not him, either, but—"

"Then I'm going back to sleep."

Agnès turned over, hugged her pillow, gave a long sigh of contentment, and let a faint smile appear on her lips as she once again abandoned herself to slumber.

But she heard Naïs announce in a small voice: "He's with the marquis d'Aubremont, madame."

La Fargue and d'Aubremont were in the captain's private office. Having finished tying back her heavy black mane of hair with a leather cord as she dashed down the stairs, Agnès hurried to join them. She granted herself a pause in front of the door, however, to briefly check her appearance and catch her breath. Then she knocked, entered, greeted the marquis with whom she was already acquainted, sat down at La Fargue's invitation, and waited.

With a small nod of his head, the captain indicated to his friend that he could speak freely.

"Madame, I have come here today seeking advice and assistance from monsieur de La Fargue, who, after listening to me, thought that you might be able to help."

"But of course, monsieur."

Agnès had the deepest respect for this honest and upright gentleman, a father whom fate had struck all the more cruelly since his son had been killed before they had the chance to effect a reconciliation. Like all the Blades, she felt somewhat beholden to him because of this.

"It's about my son . . ."

Agnès was surprised. Did the marquis mean Bretteville?"

"My younger son, I should say. François, the chevalier d'Ombreuse."

"Isn't he serving with the Black Guards?"

"Indeed, madame."

The Black Guards were one of the kingdom's most prestigious light cavalry companies. The king financed them from his own private purse, although they did not belong to his military household, and he appointed their officers. These handpicked gentlemen served the Sisters of Saint Georges, the famous Chatelaines. They formed the military guard for these nuns whose mysterious rituals, over the past two centuries, had been successful in defending France and her throne against the dragons. In their black uniforms, they protected the Sisters, escorted them, and, occasionally, carried out perilous missions on their behalf.

"Here's how matters stand," continued d'Aubremont. "My son has disappeared and I do not know whether he is alive or dead."

The young baronne de Vaudreuil addressed a concerned glance at La

Fargue, who told her: "Three weeks ago, the chevalier left on an expedition along with a few men from his company. It seems he was supposed to make his way to Alsace, with a possible detour into the Rhineland."

Alsace not being French territory, Agnès thought the expedition must have been either an escort mission or a covert military operation. But even without that, the region was filled with dangers. War was raging there. Imperial and Swedish troops were contending for control of the cities while mercenary bands pillaged the countryside.

"François could not reveal more than that," the marquis explained. "Knowing that he was bound to secrecy, I did not ask any questions. Indeed, he probably told me more than he ought to have done. . . . But it was precisely because of this that I suspected it was an important matter and one which was causing him great concern. And I understood just how accurate my suspicions were when I learned that, on the eve of his departure, François spent a long while praying at his brother's tomb. . . ."

Visibly overcome by emotion, d'Aubremont fell silent.

"Since then," said La Fargue, taking up the account from his friend, "the chevalier has not sent any news. And as for the enquiries that the marquis has recently made of the Sisters of Saint Georges, they have yielded no results. He has received no answers. Or very evasive ones."

"It's always the same closed doors, the same silences, and the same lies," said d'Aubremont in a voice vibrant with contained anger. "Because I know they are lying. Or at least hiding something from me. . . . But don't I have the right to know what has become of François?"

Agnès gazed deeply into the eyes of this old gentleman who had already lost one son and now feared for the life of the second.

"Yes," she said. "You have the right."

"Of course," the captain of the Blades pointed out, "it would be fruitless to call on the cardinal . . ."

". . . since the Mother Superior General of the Chatelaines is his cousin," the young baronne concluded for him.

"And as for speaking directly to the king . . ."

"As a last recourse only!" decreed the marquis. "Kings are to be served, not solicited. Besides, what would I say to him?"

There was a moment of silence.

Agnès turned to La Fargue, who, without pressuring her to do anything, waited for her to come to a decision.

"Monsieur," she said to the marquis, "I can promise you nothing. But since my novitiate I have kept up several acquaintances among the Sisters of Saint Georges. I will go see them and perhaps I can obtain the answers you are seeking."

D'Aubremont gave her a smile of sincere gratitude.

"Thank you, madame."

"However, do not harbour any great hopes for I do not—"

"It would be enough to know that my son is still alive, madame. Just so long as he is still alive. . . ."

Immediately after the marquis d'Aubremont took his leave, Agnès ordered a horse to be saddled for her. She would have to make haste indeed in order to reach her destination before nightfall. La Fargue joined her in the stable while André finished preparing Vaillante, the fiery young baronne's favourite mare.

"I know how much this costs you, Agnès."

They stood side by side, watching the groom busying himself with her mount.

The young woman nodded lightly.

"I know what it costs you to resume contact under these circumstances with the White Ladies," La Fargue continued. "And I wanted to thank you."

Because they dressed entirely in white, "White Ladies" was one of the nicknames given to the Sisters of Saint Georges. They were also known as the "Chatelaines," after their founder, Saint Marie de Chastel.

"No need to thank me, captain."

"Of course, the marquis cannot know how great a favour you are doing him, but—"

"The Blades owe him this service at least, don't you think?"

"True."

Out in the courtyard, one of the horses Almades still held by the bridle snorted.

"I must go to the Palais-Cardinal," La Fargue said. "Have a safe journey, Agnès."

"Thank you, captain. I'll be back tomorrow."

The duchesse de Chevreuse had been born Marie de Rohan-Montbazon.

In 1617, at the age of fifteen, she married Charles de Luynes, the marquis d'Albert. Twenty-two years older than her, at the time Luynes enjoyed the king's favours and accumulated responsibilities, wealth, and honours, despite his mediocre intelligence. Soon appointed superintendent of the queen's household herself, the young, beautiful, and joyful marquise de Luynes knew how to please Anne d'Autriche, who was already growing bored with life at the French court. A sincere friendship grew up between them, but the king began to turn away from his wife and he deemed that Marie had a bad influence upon her. It was true that the superintendent was by no means unsociable and willingly partook in the pleasures of life. And while her husband was promoted to duc and then supreme commander of the royal armies, she became the mistress of the youngest son of the duc de Guise, Claude de Lorraine, prince de Joinville and duc de Chevreuse. Luynes died in 1622, during the course of a military campaign in the south of France against the Huguenots when Marie was twenty years old. Exposed to the hostility of Louis XIII, she nevertheless continued her duties with respect to the queen. But one evening, while she led her friend on a run through the halls of the Louvre as a game, Anne d'Autriche fell and, three days later, she suffered a miscarriage. This tragic loss provoked the king's wrath. He blamed Marie, pronounced the young widow's disgrace, and banished her from the royal court.

Defying social conventions, Marie married the duc de Chevreuse barely four months after Luynes's death. Louis XIII was opposed to their union. But the duc's loyalty, his glorious military record, and his blood ties with the House of Lorraine persuaded the king to forgive him and, shortly after, to allow the duchesse to rejoin the queen's entourage. From that position, she then embarked on one of the most notorious careers as a schemer—and as a lover—in the history of France. In the space of only a few years she pushed the queen into the arms of the duke of Buckingham and very nearly succeeded in causing a great scandal. She opposed the marriage of the king's brother, Gaston, to mademoiselle de Montpensier. She took part in a plot against the cardinal that was barely foiled and was implicated in another against the king himself. Her life was saved only by her status as a foreign princess. Condemned to retire to her country holdings, she fled to Lorraine and, without giving up any of her other pleasures, she continued to involve herself in conspiracies. After the siege of La Rochelle, England negotiated a peace treaty with France and interceded on behalf of the duchesse. She thus returned to France after a year in exile, surrounded by a certain diabolical aura, thirty years old but not ready to settle down. But she was either lucky enough or smart enough not to take part in the revolt that started in the summer of 1632 in Languedoc, which ended with the victory of the royal troops and a death sentence for the duc de Montmorency.

In Paris, the duchesse de Chevreuse lived in a magnificent mansion on rue Saint-Thomas-du-Louvre, between the Louvre and the Tuileries. Remodelled for her by one of the most celebrated architects of the day, this splendid dwelling was composed of a central building flanked by two square pavilions, from which two wings extended to frame the courtyard. The latter was closed off by a third, lower wing, which contained a monumental gate decorated with pilasters and sculptures. The lateral wings contained the facilities that were indispensable to the life of any great household: kitchens, offices, servants' quarters, stables, and coach houses. As for the central building, it housed the private apartments and the halls, a string of grand rooms that were used only on social occasions. To the rear, a terrace overlooked an exquisite garden.

The Hôtel de Chevreuse was a veritable palace where the duchesse gave superb parties which tended to take a licentious turn. It was also a den of intrigue into which Arnaud de Laincourt, on this very afternoon, was determined to enter.

"Come in, monsieur! Come in!" called out madame de Chevreuse in a light-hearted tone.

Laincourt hesitated for a brief instant, then doffed his felt hat and crossed the threshold of the doorway that had been opened for him.

The room into which he had been admitted was part of the duchesse's private apartments. The furniture, the parquet floor, the wood panelling, the draperies, the gilt work, the painted ceilings, the ornaments, and the framed canvases were all in the best possible taste and evidence of an extraordinary luxury. The air in the room was perfumed. As for the atmosphere, it was feverish. The chambermaids and wardrobe mistresses were engaged in whirling ballet with the duchesse at its centre. Sitting before a mirror that was held out for her, she had her back turned to the door and was giving precise instructions whose results she immediately verified in her reflection. It was a question of adding a hint of rouge here, a pinch of powder there; of arranging a few stray locks that did not fall perfectly; of bringing another necklace and, upon further thought, changing the earrings which simply wouldn't do.

Believing himself forgotten, Laincourt was seeking a discreet means of recalling his presence to mind when madame de Chevreuse, her back still turned, said: "You must forgive me, monsieur, for receiving you so poorly."

"Madame, if my visit is ill timed—"

"Not at all, monsieur! Not at all . . . ! Stay."

Laincourt thus remained, and waited.

Now the great matter was the perfect tilt of the duchesse's hat, the finishing touch to a ritual whose importance the young man could only guess at and which he witnessed with a certain degree of embarrassment.

"You were spoken of very highly to me, monsieur."

"I was?"

"Does the idea displease you?"

"Not at all, madame. But since I do not know who holds me in such good esteem as to speak—"

"Well then, first of all there is the duc. But it is true that my husband looks favourably upon any who come from Lorraine as he does. You are from Lorraine, are you not, monsieur?"

"In fact, I—"

"Yes, yes . . . However, it is monsieur de Châteauneuf above all who praises your merits. . . ."

Charles de l'Aubespine, the marquis de Châteauneuf, was the kingdom's Keeper of the Seals, the highest-ranking figure in the State after the king and Cardinal Richelieu.

"Monsieur de Châteauneuf is one of my most excellent friends. Did you know that?"

With these words, and after a final glance in the mirror, the duchesse rose and turned to Laincourt. He was immediately struck by her beauty, her tawny hair, her milky complexion, the flawless oval of her face, the sparkle of her eyes, and the perfection of her carmine mouth. She had, moreover, an air of joyful boldness that was a provocation to the senses.

"But I must take my leave," she said as if in regret. "It has already been half an hour since the queen sent word that she wished to see me at the Louvre. . . ." She extended her hand to be kissed. "Come back this evening, monsieur. Or rather, no, come back tomorrow. That's it, tomorrow. At the same time. You will, won't you?"

Laincourt would have liked to reply, but she had already left him standing there.

She disappeared through a door, abandoning the young man in a cloud of powder and perfume, exposed to the somewhat mocking gazes of the chambermaids. . . .

Upon his return from the Palais-Cardinal, La Fargue found Leprat exercising alone in the fencing room. The musketeer was practising lunges in particular in order to limber up the thigh which had been wounded a month earlier and still remained a little stiff. Wearing boots, breeches, and a shirt, he was sweating and did not spare his efforts, sometimes pressing an imaginary attack, then stepping back into position and beginning the exercise all over again.

He broke off when he saw his captain enter.

"I need to speak with you, Antoine."

"Of course."

"In my office, please."

Still catching his breath, Leprat nodded, resheathed his white rapier, and grabbed a towel to wipe the sweat from his face and the back of his neck while La Fargue went into his private office. He joined the old gentleman there as he finished putting on his doublet and, with his brow still damp, he asked: "What is it, captain?"

"Sit down."

The musketeer obeyed and waited. Behind his desk, La Fargue appeared to be choosing his words, before he asked: "How is your thigh?"

"It still causes me an occasional jolt of pain, but that's all."

"That fight with the dracs was a bit of an ordeal, wasn't it?" the captain said, only half-jokingly.

"That it was," agreed Leprat.

A silence fell, and stretched . . .

Until finally, the captain of the Blades announced gravely: "I have a mission for you, Antoine. A particularly dangerous mission that you will be free to refuse once I have laid it all out for you. I would understand in that case. Everyone would understand. . . ."

More intrigued than worried, the musketeer gazed back with narrowed eyes.

"But first of all, read this," said La Fargue, holding out a handwritten sheet.

"What is it?"

"The transcription of the encoded letter we found on Guéret's body."

Leprat frowned as he struggled to read Laincourt's handwriting.

The letter began with salutations addressed by Marie de Médicis to madame de Chevreuse. Then, in a pompous style, the queen mother assured the duchesse of her friendship and wished her success in all her endeavours, including "certain affairs with respect to Lorraine." She expressed a desire to be of assistance to her "very dear friend" and, to that end, was placing at her disposal a French gentleman of no fortune, but "a devoted, capable man who will know how to render you great services." This man was in fact the bearer of the letter, Guéret, of whom the queen mother provided a fairly precise physical description. She explained that the man was being sent first to Lorraine and then to Paris, where he would wait every evening at the Bronze Glaive, wearing a opaline ring on his finger, as had already been agreed. The queen mother went on to describe the precarious state of her finances, of which she did not complain for her own sake, but for those who had followed her into exile. And finally, she concluded with the usual polite formulas.

"Well?" asked La Fargue. "What do you make of it?"

Leprat pursed his lips.

"This missive hardly deserved to be enciphered."

"To be sure. But what does it tell us about Guéret?"

The musketeer reflected and, looking for clues, ran his eyes over the letter once again.

"First, that he is an agent of the queen mother as we suspected," he said. "And second . . . Second, the duchesse de Chevreuse does not know him since the queen mother had to describe him."

"Very true."

Leprat, then, understood: "The portrait of this Guéret could in fact be my very own. . . ."

"Yes, it could."

His chest and feet bare, Marciac lifted the curtain slightly to look down at the street without being seen. Behind him, in the bedchamber, Gabrielle had dressed again and was finishing arranging her hair by the rumpled bed. After an afternoon of passionate lovemaking and tender complicity she would soon have to take her leave of the Gascon. She was the owner and manager of Les Petites Grenouilles, an establishment whose young and comely boarders made their livings from an essentially nocturnal activity. Their first customers would be arriving soon.

"What are you watching for?" she asked as she placed a last pin in her strawberry-blonde hair.

Although she was beautiful, the attraction she exercised over him owed less to her beauty than to her natural elegance. She could seem cold and haughty, especially when anger lit up her royal-blue eyes and a glacial mask slipped over her features. But Marciac knew her doubts, her fears, and her weak points. Because she was both the only woman he truly loved and the only one he did not feel obliged to seduce. Even Agnès still had to repel his amorous assaults upon occasion.

"Hmm?" he muttered distractedly.

"I asked, what are you watching out for?" said Gabrielle.

"Nothing."

His mind was visibly elsewhere and she knew he was lying.

In truth, she even knew what he was observing. Or rather whom. What surprised her, on the other hand, was how little time it took to arouse Marciac's suspicions. He must have been aware of something as soon as he arrived, because they had barely left the bed since then.

She wanted him to think of something else.

"How long have you been back in Paris?"

"A few days."

"You could have paid me a visit sooner, rather than waiting until you were injured."

Marciac had a bandaged ankle. It was still painful, but no longer prevented him from standing. If he didn't put too much weight on it and granted himself a good night's rest, he could be walking almost normally the following day. And there would be no trace of it at all the day after that.

"Sorry," he said. "I've had no free time."

Gabrielle rose. With a sly smile on her lips, she approached the Gascon and embraced him tenderly from behind, placing her chin upon his shoulder.

"Liar," she murmured in his ear. "You were seen at La Sovange's mansion."

Madame de Sovange maintained, on rue de l'Arbalète in the faubourg Saint-Jacques, a rather famous gambling house.

Now it was Marciac's turn to want a change in the subject of conversation.

"Do you know this individual, standing over there beneath the sign with the head of a dog? The one with the leather hat?"

She barely glanced at the man he was referring to.

"I've never seen him before," she said, drawing away from the Gascon.

And then she added from the doorway: "Get dressed and come say hello to the little frogs. They won't stop asking after you until you do."

"I will."

Gabrielle departed, leaving Marciac convinced that she was holding something back concerning the man in the leather hat. Peeking out at the street again, he saw the man exchange some words with a newcomer, then walk away, leaving the other man standing there.

That dispelled any doubts the Gascon might still be harbouring.

A man who stood hanging around all afternoon in the same place might be an idler or even some sort of mischief-maker. But when he was relieved at his post in the early evening, then he had to be a lookout.

Alone in his bedchamber, leaning over the basin, Leprat lifted his face dripping with cool water and observed himself in the mirror. He was bare to the waist but already wore the breeches and boots of another man who was at this very instant floating dead in the Seine. The rest of his attire—a hat, a shirt, a doublet whose lining had been resewn, and a steel sword in its scabbard— waited upon the bed.

Leprat gave his reflection a hard stare.

He had accepted the mission La Fargue had proposed to him, that is to say, infiltrating madame de Chevreuse's clandestine schemes by passing himself off as Guéret, the agent the queen mother had sent to the duchesse from Brussels. Since he was ignorant of almost everything about the person he was supposed to replace, it was a risky business. Guéret was a French gentleman of no fortune, that much was certain. And no doubt he had followed the queen mother when, removed from power and humiliated, she had chosen to leave the kingdom. But aside from that?

Leprat, in fact, could only rely on a certain physical resemblance with the man whose identity he was trying to usurp. A resemblance which, furthermore, would not fool anyone who had met Guéret. And the musketeer knew that he would probably die under torture if he was unmasked. . . .

Bah . . . he told himself philosophically, as he bent once again to splash water on his face . . . *if no one kills you today, you know what will kill you tomorrow.* . . .

Upon his back, the ranse spread in a broad violet rash with a rough surface. The disease was progressing. It would one day take his life and was already weakening him, as witnessed by the wound to his thigh that was taking longer than it should to completely heal.

How much time do you have left? Leprat wondered. *And more, how much longer can you keep it a secret?*

He stood up straight and smiled sadly at his image in the mirror.

This secret that is eating away at you . . .

The expression had never been so apt.

Agnès arrived in the early evening. The abbey was located in a peaceful corner of the countryside, far from any heavily travelled roads, and was surrounded by the fields, woodland, and farms from which it derived its revenues. From the vantage point of her saddle, the young baronne took her time observing the handsome buildings and the white, veiled silhouettes moving about behind the enclosing walls. The memories of her novitiate with the Sisters of Saint Georges came back vividly to her. Then she gently nudged her horse forward with her heels as bells rang out in the dusk, calling the Sisters to prayer.

She was soon admitted to wait in the cloister where she stood alone, exposed to the curious glances and whispers from the passing nuns. She knew from experience how small a world an abbey was and how fast news travelled there. No doubt her name was circulating and it was already being murmured that she had asked to meet the mother superior. Did they remember her here? Perhaps. In any case, everyone would be wondering about the motive behind her visit. . . .

Feeling quite satisfied with the effect that both her presence and her armed horseman's outfit were having, in particular on the young novices who were jostling one another to spy on her from behind some columns, Agnès forced herself to remain patient and impassive. The severe sound of a throat being cleared, however, was enough to remind the adolescent girls of their duties, before the mother superior's arrival dispersed them entirely.

About sixty years in age, Mère Emmanuelle de Cernay was an energetic woman with strong features and a frank gaze. Accompanied by two nuns who walked behind her, she gratified Agnès with a tender smile, hugged her, and kissed her on both cheeks. The young woman responded with similar warmth to these displays of affection.

"Marie-Agnès! It's been so long since we have seen you. . . . And your last letter dates from over a month ago!"

"The Blades have been reformed, mother."

"Really? Since when?"

"Since about a month ago, in fact."

"I didn't know. . . . Are you still under the command of that old gentleman?"

"Captain La Fargue, yes."

"And are you happy?"

"My word . . ." replied Agnès with a somewhat guilty smile.

"Then that's all right, that's all right. . . . Just don't find yourself on the receiving end of a sword stroke that will make you regret not having taken the veil!"

"It would have to be a very nasty sword stroke, indeed, mother. . . ."

The abbess took Agnès by the arm and they walked together beneath the gallery of the cloister. Shaking her head resignedly, the old woman said: "Intrigue. Racing about on horseback. Sword play. . . . You have always loved all that, Marie-Agnès. . . ."

"And the boys. You're forgetting the boys, mother superior."

The abbess chuckled.

"Yes. And the boys. . . . Did you know that the ivy on the north wall is still called 'Agnès's ivy' by some of the older nuns?"

"I didn't climb it that often."

"Let's say rather that you weren't caught every time you climbed it. . . ."

Still talking in this relaxed manner, they left the cloister for a garden at the entrance to which the mother superior asked the two nuns trailing them to wait behind. And once she and Agnès had moved out of earshot, she confided: "One of those two is spying on me. I don't know which one. But what can I do? The Mother Superior General continues to be suspicious of me, after all these years. . . ."

Mère Emmanuelle had previously been the head of the Sisters of Saint Georges. But following some dark dealings, she had been ousted in favour of the current Superior General, who happened to be part of the Richelieu family. Since then, the order had become a more or less blatant instrument of the cardinal's policies, to the great displeasure of Rome. The concordat of Bologna, however, had granted the king the right to appoint the recipients of the Church's major benefices in France, including the abbesses and abbots of the religious orders.

"But what can I do for you, Marie-Agnès? I imagine that you have not come to tell me that you wish to complete your novitiate. . . ."

The young baronne smiled as she thought of how very close she had come to taking the veil, then she spoke of the fears of the marquis d'Aubremont, his approach to the Blades, and the promise she had made to him.

The mother superior thought for a moment.

"An expedition to Alsace, you say . . . ? Yes, I think I did hear something about that. Its goal, I believe, was the destruction of a powerful dragon. And as is proper in such cases, a louve was leading the hunt."

Among the Chatelaines, there existed a small number of exceptional sisters who, thanks to a papal dispensation, were allowed to wield magic as well as the sword to fight the draconic menace. They were nicknamed the *louves*, or she-wolves, because their headquarters were located in the Château de Saint-Loup, not far from Poitiers. But also, and above all, because they were solitary and merciless huntresses. If Agnès had come close to pronouncing her own vows, it had been with the sole intention of becoming a louve herself.

"But I don't know the details of this affair," Mère Emmanuelle was saying. "And, in particular, I don't know what success the expedition had. . . . But if you like, I can make enquiries and let you know what I discover."

"Thank you, mother superior."

"Nevertheless . . . Nevertheless, be very careful, Marie-Agnès. It won't take the Superior General long to learn of the reasons for your visit, and I doubt she will take a kind view of your becoming mixed up in the order's business. . . ."

In the office of magic at the splendid Hôtel de Chevreuse, in rue Saint-Thomas-du-Louvre, the man bent forward to examine the painted portrait the duchesse was showing him. Tall, thin, and pale, he appeared to be about fifty-five years in age. He was wearing the black robes of a scholar and a cloth beret, also black in colour, with a turned-up, crenelated edge.

"Do you see, master?" asked madame de Chevreuse.

He was her master of magic and exercised an insidious but immense influence over her. She believed he was called Mauduit, was of Italian origin, and had spent long years studying and practising the occult arts abroad. In truth, he was a dragon as well as an agent of the Black Claw.

While he studied the portrait by candlelight, the duchesse poured two glasses of a golden liqueur with a heady aroma. When he heard the clink of crystal and smelled the odour of henbane the Alchemist's nostrils flared and a gleam of longing briefly lit up his steely grey eyes, while the tip of a rosy tongue licked at his lips. But he retained control of himself, succeeded in masking a desire that was becoming a need, and, with a steady hand, accepted —casually, without taking his eyes off the canvas—the glass held out to him. He dipped his bloodless lips in the liqueur and contained the shiver of pleasure that obliged him to shut his eyes.

"You will soon have to find me some more of this delicious henbane from Lorraine," said madame de Chevreuse.

"Certainly, madame."

"Will you tell me, someday, who your supplier is?"

"Madame, whatever would become of a master of magic who gave away his secrets?"

She smiled, rose, and took several paces about the room as she gazed incuriously at the books of magic and various alchemical and esoteric objects that were on display.

Then she asked: "So? What do you think of my find? I can assure you that this portrait is most faithful."

The Alchemist pursed his lips.

"Precisely, madame. This young woman is far too pretty. She won't fool anyone."

The duchesse was expecting this reaction and had prepared a visual effect. Smiling, she showed him a small piece of carton shaped like a theatre mask, which she placed upon the portrait.

"And now, master?"

The master of magic looked again at the painting and could not prevent a start of surprise.

"Admirable . . . !" he admitted. Then a shadow of doubt passed over his face. "But her size? Her figure?"

"They are a perfect match in every respect," madame de Chevreuse reassured him.

"As is her hair. . . . And where is this marvel hiding?"

"She has been staying here, in my home, for several days now. I will present her to you during the course of a dinner I am hosting."

"But will she be capable of—"

"I will answer for her."

"On condition that she accepts."

"How can one refuse a queen?"

The Alchemist gave one of his rare smiles, which always seemed cruel.

"Yes, of course . . ." he said. "But it will still require some scheming on your part to place your protégée in the queen's entourage. How do you hope to accomplish that?"

"Through the marquis," replied the duchesse with a hint of annoyance. "Or through my husband the duc. We'll see."

"Time is running short, madame. If all is not ready in time for your great ball at Dampierre . . ."

"I know it all too well, monsieur. All too well. . . . Now, a little more henbane?"

Leprat had already been waiting for an hour. With an ordinary sword at his side, he was wearing Guéret's clothing and jewellery, including a ring adorned with a handsome opaline stone that he had slipped on his left ring finger. He had of course put away his ivory rapier and the Blades' steel signet ring, along with anything that might compromise his false identity. He hoped it would suffice. For although he had no doubt that the duchesse de Chevreuse was not personally acquainted with Guéret, this was perhaps not the case for all those who surrounded her and served her.

Once again, he gazed about the tavern's taproom. Sitting at the end of a table, he did not conceal the opaline on his ring finger but nor did he flash it about, to avoid trouble. While the Bronze Glaive was no cutthroats' den, it was not the most reputable of places. Located outside the faubourg Saint-Jacques, less than a quarter of an hour's walk from the inn where Guéret had been lodging, the establishment was exempt from the taxes and regulations that applied in Paris. Wine was cheaper here and they continued serving it after curfew every evening of the week, until midnight.

Every evening of the week, that is, except the previous evening, when the owner, having gone to Tours to bury a dead relative, had closed the tavern. Leprat had discovered this by listening to a conversation between two regulars. It explained, at least, why Guéret had returned to the inn earlier than expected and surprised Agnès and Marciac in his bedchamber. This extraordinary closure had indirectly killed him.

The difference between life and death often depends on the tiniest things, Leprat mused.

Absentmindedly toying with the opaline that served as his recognition sign, he did not react when a gentleman sat down next to him and asked without giving him a look: "Did you have a safe journey from Flanders?"

"I've come from Lorraine."

"Did you take pains to ensure you were not followed?"

"From Nancy?"

"The cardinal has eyes and ears everywhere."

Leprat glanced at the stranger. He was slender and fair-haired, with a well-trimmed mustache and royale beard. He was elegantly but unobtrusively dressed in a beige doublet. And he had a friendly air.

The musketeer lowered his eyes to the gentleman's hands, who let him catch a glimpse of an opaline ring on his own index finger before he said: "Wait a little while and then meet me around the back."

He immediately rose and went out, after paying for the glass of wine which he had not touched.

Leprat imitated him five minutes later.

In the dark night, he had difficulty finding the narrow arched passageway that led to the rear of the tavern. He could not see a thing and was unfamiliar with the place. His instinct, moreover, told him that something was amiss. Had he already been unmasked? He thought for an instant about giving up, turning around, and returning to the Hôtel de l'Épervier.

Despite everything, he decided to continue.

And was knocked unconscious the moment he set foot in the rear courtyard.

* * *

Each house in Paris had a sign. The shops and taverns had them, of course. But so did the dwellings, which was how one told them apart in lieu of numbers. These signs served to designate the addresses of both commercial establishments and private individuals: rue Saint-Martin, where the sign of the Red Cock hangs, for example. This only applied, however, to premises belonging to commoners. Private mansions, still reserved solely to the aristocracy under Louis XIII, did not have signs. Instead they took the names of their owners, often decorated with prestigious coats-of-arms on their pediment, and that was address enough: Hôtel de Châteauneuf, rue Coquillière. Or even: Hôtel de Chevreuse, Paris.

Parisian streets were thus graced with innumerable signs in multi-coloured wood that added to the capital's renown and gave it, when the weather was fine, a festive air. The subjects of these signs were varied—saints, kings of France, and other sacred or profane characters; tools, weapons, and utensils; trees, fruits, and flowers; animals and other imaginary creatures—but showed no evidence, on the whole, of any real artistic vision or profound taste for the picturesque. For every Horse Wielding a Pickaxe or Gloved Wyvern, how many Tin Plates and Golden Lions? The most curious thing, however, was the fact that the signs for shops never evoked anything related to the nature of their business. There were no boots for cobblers or anvils for blacksmiths. Only taverns were required to distinguish themselves with a sheaf: a handful of knotted hay or twigs.

If signs served a useful purpose and brightened up an otherwise sordid urban setting, they nevertheless represented a certain hazard to the public due to the tendency of shopkeepers to give them excessive dimensions for the purposes of publicity. The ironwork that supported them often extended out a *toise*, or a measure of about two metres, into the street. Considering the width of an ordinary street in Paris, that meant signs often hung in the middle of the pavement. Added to the usual stalls and awnings, these ornaments thus hindered traffic and aggravated the crush in the most commercial streets, which were also the most heavily frequented. There were more than three hundred signs in the neighbourhood of Les Halles, and almost as many on rue Saint-Denis alone. Coaches were constantly knocking them down. Riders on horseback had to duck to avoid them. And even pedestrians often bashed their skulls on these gaudily painted wooden panels.

Usually due to distraction.

But not always.

"Hup!"

Turning round, the man saw a monkey's head diving toward him, received a blow from the sign in the middle of his brow, and keeled over backward, while the suspended panel continued its forward motion before reversing at the height of its swing.

Marciac caught it and stopped its movement.

Then he gave a calm, satisfied look at the man lying unconscious in the street at his feet, his arms spread out in a cross.

This scene took place in rue Grenouillère at the crack of dawn where, as in the rest of Paris, the neighbourhood was just beginning to wake.

Marciac returned to Les Petites Grenouilles on tiptoe. The house was still sleeping at this hour of the morning, since the last customers, as usual, had taken their leave late during the previous night. This suited the Gascon perfectly, as he was counting on regaining the warmth of Gabrielle's bed without her being aware he had ever left. But as he was about to take the stairs, holding his boots in his hand, he heard a voice say: "So? How is that ankle?"

He froze, grimacing as he closed his eyelids tightly, then reopened one eye and turned his head to look through a wide-open door. He saw Gabrielle sitting alone at the kitchen table. Her face was in profile and she held her head stiffly upright as she ate, staring straight ahead of her. She had a large shawl around her shoulders and was wearing only a nightshirt, without having done anything about her hair or appearance.

She was beautiful, nevertheless.

The Gascon resolved to join her. He hated explanations and reproaches, but this time would not be able to escape making the former or receiving the latter. Reluctantly, he fell into a chair.

"My ankle is much better," he said. "Thank you."

Then he waited for the tongue-lashing to start.

"Where were you?" Gabrielle finally asked.

"Out."

"In order to exchange a few words with Fortain, I imagine."

Marciac frowned.

"Fortain?"

"The man who was watching the house. He was no longer there when I woke up. But you have reappeared. Whereas he—"

"Then you know."

"That there are five or six men who have been discreetly watching the house these past few days? Yes, I know. The fact is, you see, I'm neither totally blind nor a complete idiot. Even the girls know something is up. The only one who hasn't realised is poor old Thibault."

Thibault, the porter at Les Petites Grenouilles, was a man of absolute devotion but limited intelligence.

Marciac nodded.

"All right," he allowed. "But do you know who these men work for?"

"Yes. For Rochefort."

Astonished, the Gascon studied Gabrielle's expressionless face. She still hadn't accorded him the slightest glance.

"And how do you know that Rochefort is behind all this?"

"I recognised two of his men. Including Fortain."

"Why didn't you say anything to me?"

"I might ask you the same question. In my case, it was because I was afraid you would only make matters worse by getting mixed up in this. A strange idea, that, wasn't it?"

Embarrassed, Marciac did not at first find a reply, but then he said: "I had to know, Gabrielle. I had to make sure that—"

"That Rochefort was watching my house? Very well. Rochefort is watching my house. So what? He can discover nothing he doesn't already know. But now that you've attacked one of his men, what will happen? Do you believe he'll let that go unanswered?"

"I'll speak to him."

"And why would he listen to you, since he has no love for the Blades and only takes orders from the cardinal? He won't be able to resist the temptation of reaching you through me. For if you've guessed that Rochefort has become interested in me, you must know it's because of your captain's hidden daughter. Isn't it? Of course, I didn't know that when I took her in and I don't know where she is now, but what does that matter?"

Gabrielle rose, abandoning the plate of fruit and cheese which she had barely touched. She had, in fact, mostly been digging her fingertips into a quarter loaf of white bread.

She wrapped the shawl around her shoulders more tightly, walked toward the door, halted, turned around, and looked at Marciac closely.

At last, she said: "I'm going to ask you one thing, Nicolas."

"Yes?"

"You knew. Even before you got rid of Fortain you knew that—"

He interrupted her: "Fortain is alive. And quite well. I am not an assassin, Gabrielle. I only dragged him off to get the truth out of him."

She had no trouble believing him.

"But even before that, you knew he was one of Rochefort's men, didn't you? And you knew why Les Petites Grenouilles was being watched. . . ."

Marciac thought for a moment.

But however much it might cost him, he hated lying to Gabrielle.

"Yes," he recognised, "I knew."

"So it wasn't even a question of making sure . . . Merely of sending a message to Rochefort. So that he would understand that you and the Blades would not stand back with your arms crossed if he bothered La Fargue's daughter."

"La Fargue's daughter or you, Gabrielle. La Fargue's daughter or you."

She looked at him. He was sincere.

"Yes," said Gabrielle. "And do you believe you have done well to protect me, today?"

She left the kitchen, went to the staircase, and from there told Marciac: "I love you, Nicolas. But I would prefer it if you did not sleep here tonight."

She returned alone to her bedchamber.

Leprat woke up with a severe headache and a devilish thirst. He was lying in his breeches, stockings, and shirt, stretched out on a made-up bed in a chamber he had never seen before. He didn't know how he came to be here, but he was sure of one thing: he had left Paris. The air smelled fresh.

The musketeer sat up and, as he rubbed his skull and the handsome bump where he had been struck, he considered his surroundings. His boots were neatly awaiting him by the door. His doublet hung from the back of a chair. His hat was placed upon a table and his sword hung in its scabbard from one of the bedposts. The room was modest but clean and quiet, plunged into an agreeable shade by the curtains that obscured the window.

As he stood, Leprat noticed that the pockets of his breeches had been turned inside out and he concluded that his boots had probably been removed to make sure he was not concealing anything inside them. That made him think of his doublet and he hastened to feel the lining. It was empty and he saw that it had been carefully unsewn. The people who had knocked him out and brought him here had stolen all the secret documents he was supposed to deliver personally to the duchesse de Chevreuse. His career as the queen mother's agent had not got off to a very good start.

Except, despite what the nasty blow to his head seemed to portend, he was neither dead nor a prisoner. If he had been unmasked, he would not have woken here in this manner. Indeed, he would perhaps not have woken at all.

A cow lowed outside.

Leprat went to part the curtains and was dazzled for a moment by the flood of light that suddenly poured into the room. Then he gradually began to make out a pleasant rural landscape, but one which failed to evoke any particular memories in him. He still didn't know where he was, except that he was looking at a corner of the countryside from the upper storey of a house located at the entrance to a village or small town. And if his day's growth of beard was not lying, he had not slept more than a night and was therefore still in France, probably not far from Paris.

But apart from that . . .

Determined to find out more, Leprat dressed and put on his baldric, finding Guéret's steel sword to be much heavier than his ivory rapier, and then left the room. He descended some stairs and emerged into a charming, sunlit garden where he found, eating at a small table beneath a canopy, the man in the beige doublet who had approached him in the Bronze Glaive.

The gentleman rose as soon as he caught sight of Leprat and welcomed him with an open smile.

"Monsieur de Guéret! How are you feeling? Did you sleep well?"

"Fairly well, yes," replied Leprat, who still did not know what tack he should adopt in these circumstances.

"I'm delighted to hear that. Join me, please." The gentleman pointed to an empty chair at his table and sat back down. "I've just returned from Paris and finally found time to eat. Will you share this late breakfast with me?"

"Certainly."

"I am the chevalier de Mirebeau and you are here in my home."

"Your home, which is to say . . . ?"

"In Ivry. Paris is little more than a league from here."

Leprat sat down at the table and discovered he possessed a healthy appetite.

"Bertrand!" called the gentleman. "Bertrand!"

A stooped and rather dreary-looking lackey appeared in the doorway.

"Yes, monsieur?"

"A glass for monsieur de Guéret."

"Very good, monsieur."

And tearing a leg from a chicken, Mirebeau said: "I imagine you have many questions. I don't know if I can answer all of them just yet, but I owe you an apology for the nasty trick we played on you last night. I can only hope that Rauvin did not strike you too hard. . . ."

"Rauvin?"

"You will meet him soon. The man has a tendency to be . . . zealous about his work. And he has an excessive, indeed, almost unnatural, sense of wariness. . . . In short, it's down to him that you were knocked out—"

"Knocked out and searched."

"You realise we needed to assure ourselves that you were in fact who you claimed to be. As for the documents you were carrying, have no fear. I delivered them to the person for whom they were intended."

"My orders were to place them personally in madame de Chevreuse's hands."

Mirebeau smiled.

"Unfortunately, it is impossible for you to meet the duchesse immediately. But these papers needed to be delivered to her as soon as possible, didn't they . . . ? Also, there was an encoded letter inside your doublet. Do you know of its nature?"

"Not exactly, no."

"The queen mother invites the duchesse to take you into her service."

"That much, yes, I did know. And have already accepted in advance."

"Perfect! In that case, the duchesse's desire is for us to form a team. Does that pose an inconvenience to you?"

"Perhaps."

"Really?" said the gentleman in surprise. "Why is that?"

Leprat looked directly into Mirebeau's eyes.

"If I was ordered to place the documents in the duchesse's own hands, it was not merely to ensure that they arrived at their proper destination but also to satisfy myself that no one was trying to trick me. I do not know you, monsieur. I do not know if you are in the service of madame de Chevreuse. I do not even know if you have ever met her. In fact, for all I do know, you could very well be in the service of Cardinal Richelieu. . . . On the other hand, if the duchesse were to receive me . . ."

Still maintaining a smiling, friendly demeanour, the man in the beige doublet nodded calmly and then said: "I applaud your prudence, monsieur. And I understand your concerns. . . . However, considering your position, your only option is the following: to place your trust in me during the time it takes to prove yourself. . . ."

"Or?"

"Or you can choose to leave."

"Which is not likely to please Rauvin, is it?"

"Probably not."

Agnès returned to the Hôtel de l'Épervier at the same time as Marciac. She was on horseback. He was on foot and still limped a little, carrying a bundle of his belongings on one shoulder.

"Already recovered?" she asked.

"Already cast out," he corrected.

She nodded, the tumultuous relationship between the Gascon and Gabrielle having long ceased to surprise anyone who knew them both.

"And you, Agnès? Where do you return from?"

The young baronne de Vaudreuil jumped down from her saddle while Guibot opened up one of the doors of the carriage gate and she apprised Marciac of her approach to the former Mother Superior General of the Sisters of Saint Georges. Then, once inside the courtyard, she entrusted the reins of her horse to André and asked the old porter with the wooden leg: "Is the captain here?"

"No, madame. He was called to the Palais-Cardinal. And this letter arrived for you this morning."

It was now almost noon.

Agnès took the missive, recognised the seal of the Order the White Ladies printed on the red wax, opened it, and read.

"Bad news?" enquired Marciac.

"This letter is from the Superior General of the Chatelaines. It expresses her wish to see me this afternoon, which amounts to the same thing as a summons."

"Like that? All of a sudden?"

"Yes, in a manner of speaking."

"Will you go?"

"I don't have a choice in the matter. But I should have liked to speak with La Fargue before going."

"You will have to content yourself with talking to me," said Marciac, taking Agnès by the elbow. "Come, we'll have dinner and then I will accompany you to the Enclos."

Laincourt had made an effort with his appearance before presenting himself for the second time at the Hôtel de Chevreuse. He had donned his most elegant doublet, found a matching pair of gloves, carefully polished his boots, and stuck a new feather in his hat. His meeting the previous day with the duchesse had made a deep impression on him. She was not only breathtakingly beautiful, but her elegance, poise, and nonchalant manner had disarmed him. She moved with the most natural ease in extraordinarily luxurious settings.

This time he was expected and Laincourt was immediately conducted to the terrace, where a square table had been set beneath a white cloth canopy embroidered with gold thread. There, madame de Chevreuse, looking radiant and serene, was chatting with a young girl and an older woman who, like her, was sipping raspberry water that had been cooled at outrageous expense with snow preserved from the previous winter. The young girl was very pretty, lively, and very daintily attired. In contrast, the woman was grey-haired and unassuming, with a dull look in her eye.

Upon seeing her visitor, the duchesse greeted Laincourt with a bright smile and, without rising, signalled him to approach.

"Monsieur de Laincourt! Join us, please."

He obeyed, saluting the mistress of the house first and then her guests, finding himself introduced to Aude de Saint-Avold and her aunt, madame de Jarville. Aude, who was a relative of the duc de Chevreuse, had arrived from Lorraine to be presented at the French court. Her aunt was acting as her chaperone.

"But now that I think of it," remarked the duchesse, "you also come from Lorraine, monsieur de Laincourt."

"Madame, I must disabuse you of this notion. I was born in Nancy, it is true. But I am French."

"Really? How is that possible?"

Laincourt, as was often the case when speaking of himself, became evasive.

"One of those accidents of life, madame."

"We were speaking of the court at Nancy. Don't you think it is so much more appealing and gay than the French court?"

"I am forced to admit that it is, madame."

The court of Charles IV in fact surpassed that of Louis XIII by far. In Nancy, at the ducal palace, the revels were almost unceasing and often licentious, whereas it was easy to grow bored at the Louvre with its austere and timid king who hated to appear in public. The duchesse thus retained an excellent memory of her stay in Nancy, where the duc had welcomed her with great pomp. Laincourt supposed she had made the acquaintance of Aude de Saint-Avold during her time there.

Aude de Saint-Avold.

As he engaged in the conversation, he had trouble taking his eyes off this young woman. She not only pleased him, she also intrigued him. She had a very charming face, with silky light-brown hair, lively green eyes, and full, luscious lips. Who could fail to find her ravishing? She did not even suffer from comparison with the splendid madame de Chevreuse. In her fashion, she was less beautiful but prettier than the duchèsse, less seductive but more moving. And if the duchèsse's confidence added a touch of triumphant arrogance to her beauty, young Aude had preserved something fragile from her adolescence, somehow both sad and carefree.

However, other than the fact that it was lovely, Aude's face attracted Laincourt's eye because he seemed to recognise it. Had he met her in Nancy? Perhaps. But her name meant nothing to him. Could the duchesse have brought Aude to Paris under a borrowed identity?

Ably solicited by madame de Chevreuse, who had no equal when it came to drawing the best out of men, Laincourt surprised himself by sparkling in conversation. He proved himself gallant, witty, and humorous, finding particular pleasure in entertaining Aude de Saint-Avold, whose sincere laughter enthralled him. And so their conversation had been following a most pleasant course for more than an hour when the maître d'hôtel brought a note to the duchesse. She read it without blinking, excused herself, rose, promised to return soon, and took her leave.

Laincourt's gaze followed her and he caught a glimpse of a man in a black cap and black robes who was waiting for her inside the mansion.

"Who is he?" he asked.

"He is the duchesse's master of magic, I believe," Aude replied. "But I have not been introduced to him yet."

Without the duchesse, the conversation lagged a little and they could not count on madame de Jarville to remedy matters: made sleepy by the heat, she drowsed in her chair. The two young people perceived this at the same time, exchanged an amused glance, and stifled mocking laughs. Madame de Chevreuse soon rejoined them, but only to say that she was going to be detained elsewhere and was entrusting Aude to Laincourt's care.

"Be good," she said as she left them.

Which was a little like the devil warning them not to sin.

"What if we escaped?" Aude de Saint-Avold suggested with a rebellious gleam in her eye.

"I beg your pardon, madame?"

"Abduct me. Madame de Chevreuse has placed a coach at my disposal. Let's take it. And go to . . . Let's go to Le Cours!"

"To Le Cours?"

"What? Isn't that what it's called?"

"Indeed. But . . ."

Le Cours, located near the Saint-Antoine gate, was one of the most popular places for Parisians wishing to take a stroll. Rich or poor, aristocrat or commoner, all went there to promenade, seek distractions, or display themselves in public. People chatted, joked, or courted one another. They played hide-and-seek or skittles or pall-mall. On fine days, especially, the place was very popular. The young woman's idea was thus by no means a bad one. But Le Cours was never so crowded as on a Sunday, as Laincourt explained to her.

"Oh . . . You see how ignorant I am of all these things. . . . It will take a long time to make a Parisienne of me, won't it?"

Aude's disappointment saddened Laincourt, who felt a compelling need to console her.

"But we could go to the garden at Les Tuileries," he heard himself propose.

"Really?"

"Yes! We should definitely go, now that it's been said!"

"But . . . What about madame de Jarville?" whispered the young woman with the tone of an anxious conspirator.

"Let's leave her to her rest."

The Enclos du Temple was a former residence of the Knights Templar located on the right bank of the Seine, to the north of the Marais neighbourhood. Ceded to the Knights Hospitaller after the dissolution of the Templar Order in 1314, this building was finally sold to the Sisters of Saint Georges during the reign of François I. It still belonged to them in 1633 and was still surrounded by a high, crenelated wall, punctuated by turrets, and defended by a massive donjon flanked by four corner towers: the famous Tour du Temple. Visitors entered the premises by means of a drawbridge and inside one found everything necessary for the life of a religious community: a large church; a cloister; a refectory and dormitories; kitchens; granaries and wine cellars; workshops; stables; gardens, vegetable plots and more extensive fields; and even some houses and a few shops. All of this contained within a medieval compound in Paris, on the rue du Temple, near the gate bearing the same name.

* * *

Having dined at place de Grève, Marciac and Agnès both entered the Enclos, but only the young baronne was admitted to meet the Mother Superior General. They had shared an enjoyable moment together, the Gascon regaling Agnès with comic tales of his trials and tribulations in love. He was aware that she had once been on the point of taking the veil with the Chatelaines, although he didn't know of the circumstances that had prompted her to change paths and later join the Cardinal's Blades. One thing was certain: at present, she no longer held the Sisters of Saint Georges in fond esteem and even seemed to nurture a particular rancour against the current Superior General, the formidable Mère Thérèse de Vaussambre.

While Marciac waited patiently outside, Agnès was conducted to the ancient chapter hall. The room was immense, broad, high-ceilinged, and illuminated by arched windows. At the rear, a long table covered with several white cloths stretched parallel to a wall adorned with a huge medieval tapestry representing Saint Georges slaying the dragon. At the centre of this table, back to the wall, beneath the tapestry, sat the Mother Superior General. Tall, thin, and stiff-looking, she had the same penetrating gaze as her cousin the cardinal. She was not yet fifty years of age, directed the Sisters of Saint Georges with an iron hand, and had made their order more influential than ever before.

"Approach, Marie-Agnès."

Her hat held in one hand and the other resting on the pommel of her sword, Agnès de Vaudreuil advanced, saluted, and said: "It's just Agnès, now, mother."

"Agnès . . . Yes. So it is. You do well to correct me," replied the Superior General in a tone that implied the exact opposite. "I have trouble forgetting the novice that you once were. You had so much promise! And what a louve you would have become . . . !"

Cautious, the young baronne de Vaudreuil waited silently.

"But the day will come when you will realise your destiny . . ." added the nun, as if to her herself.

Then she added in a solemn and imperious tone: "Madame, your services are required at the side of the queen, whose suite you will join as soon as possible. You have been chosen due to your skills, as well as the abilities revealed during the novitiate which you have so unhappily chosen to neglect. However, we know that we can place our trust in you. . . ."

* * *

A short while later, in the courtyard of the Hôtel de Chevreuse, Laincourt was helping a delighted Aude de Saint-Avold to climb into a coach when he felt a glance fall upon the back of his neck.

He turned around but only had time to see, at a window on the first storey of the mansion's main building, a curtain falling back into place before a thin, pallid face.

The Alchemist released the curtain and turned away from the window just as the duchesse came into his office.

"You will meet her this evening," she promised him. "But for now, without further delay, I can give you some excellent news: our protégée will soon be joining the queen's suite."

"What? So quickly . . . ? How have you managed this?"

"Providence, monsieur Mauduit. Providence. . . . Today, as a favour, someone asked me to—"

"'Someone'?"

"Cardinal Richelieu, through an intermediary. . . . In short, the cardinal asked me to favour a distant relative of his with an introduction into the queen's entourage."

"The king is free to appoint whomever he pleases to the queen's household. And similarly, to expel anyone he dislikes."

"Yes, and the queen is free to turn a cold shoulder to anyone whose presence is forced upon her. And it is just such treatment that the cardinal wishes to avoid for this relative, by asking me to intercede in her favour. I believe it is also the cardinal's way of measuring my goodwill with respect to him."

"So you accepted."

"Of course. But, at the same time, I requested that one of my own protégées be admitted to the queen's entourage. After all, I am the duchesse de Chevreuse. It would be uncharacteristic of me to give without receiving anything in return."

"My congratulations."

"Thank you, monsieur. And on your side?"

"All is ready. However—"

"What?"

"This relative of the cardinal, who is she?"

"How should I know?"

"A spy?"

"Without a doubt, since such manoeuvres are very much in the manner of the king, who may not love the queen but still wishes to know her every deed and gesture. No doubt to make sure she is unhappy. . . ."

The duchesse's expression grew hard: she hated the king.

"This spy could do us mischief," said the master of magic.

"In the little time between now and the ball? Come now . . . When the moment arrives, we only need to keep her apart from our . . . arrangements."

The Alchemist, still looking concerned, fell silent.

Mirebeau did not return until the end of the afternoon.

He had left on horseback three hours previously without saying where he was going or proposing that Leprat should accompany him. The musketeer had waited in the house at Ivry with Bertrand, the chevalier's very dour-looking valet, and a translation of *The Decameron* as his sole company. He was at liberty to move about, but he preferred not to stray beyond the garden. He was perhaps being watched and did not wish to raise any alarms.

Hearing horses approaching, Leprat rose from his bed, where he had been reading, and went to look out the window of his first-storey bedchamber. He took up his rapier as he passed, placed himself to one side so he would not easily be seen, and gently pushed open a window frame that was already ajar, just as two riders drew up.

One of them, still elegantly dressed in beige, was Mirebeau. He jumped down from his mount and, calling out for Bertrand, disappeared into the house. The other man had the look of a mercenary, wearing boots, thick breeches, a leather doublet, a sword at his side, and an old battered hat. Leprat guessed he must be this Rauvin of whom Mirebeau had spoken, the same man who had knocked him out by surprise in the courtyard of the Bronze Glaive. The man with the unnatural sense of wariness, as the gentleman had put it. And therefore someone of whom he should be particularly wary himself.

Very much at ease in his saddle, Rauvin—if it was indeed him—removed his hat long enough to wipe his brow with the back of a sleeve. Leprat caught a glimpse of a bladelike face and a balding crown wreathed by long black hair, belonging to a thirty-year-old man. The man took a jew's harp from his pocket, raised it to his mouth, and made the metal strip vibrate to produce a strange melody.

As he played, he calmly lifted his eyes to the window where the musketeer stood watching him, as if to signify that he had known Leprat was there all along and could not have cared less.

Their gazes met for a long while and Leprat was filled with an absolute certainty that Rauvin represented a deadly threat to him.

"Guéret!" Mirebeau called from the stairway. "Guéret!"

The false agent of the queen mother turned away from the window just as Mirebeau entered.

"Please get ready," requested the gentleman in the beige doublet. "We're leaving."

"We?"

"You, me, and Rauvin, who is waiting for us below."

"Where are we going?"

"To a place near Neuilly."

"And what will we do there?"

"So full of questions!" exclaimed Mirebeau in a jovial manner. "Come now, monsieur. Make haste. Bertrand is already saddling a horse for you."

3

U pon their return to the Hôtel de l'Épervier, Agnès and Marciac waited for La Fargue, who, barely a quarter of an hour later, returned with Almades from the Palais-Cardinal.

"I know," he said, seeing Agnès looking both angry and worried. "The cardinal just informed me of your . . . mission."

"Damn it, captain! What is going on? Did you agree to this!?"

"Hold your horses, Agnès. I did not agree to anything at all. As I just told you, I was summoned to the Palais-Cardinal to have this *fait accompli* presented to me."

They were in the fencing room, where the young woman was pacing up and down.

"And you accepted this?" she asked angrily, as if La Fargue had betrayed her.

"Yes," he said. "Because we are the Cardinal's Blades. Not La Fargue's Blades. And even less, de Vaudreuil's Blades. . . . His Eminence gives the orders. And we obey them. . . ."

With a resigned air, Agnès let herself fall into an armchair.

"*Merde!*" she exclaimed.

"You will only be joining the queen's suite temporarily," the old gentleman explained in a patient tone. "Your sole mission will be to keep your eyes and ears wide open. It's not so terrible. . . ."

"But this is simply a manoeuvre, captain. A manoeuvre!"

"That's quite possible."

"It's damn certain, you mean! Just think for a minute! One evening I go to meet the former Mother Superior General about an affair that might very well prove embarrassing to the Chatelaines, and the very next morning I find myself summoned by the current Superior General. And given an assignment where I will be unable to upset anyone. Come now! You may fool others, but not me!"

La Fargue nodded.

"It may well be true that Mère de Vaussambre wants to keep you away from certain matters. But she did not hesitate in calling upon the cardinal in order to achieve her aims: the threat against the queen could very well be real. . . ."

"I don't believe that for a second."

"But what if La Donna's plot was directed at the queen rather than the king?" interjected Marciac.

Agnès shrugged.

"The duchesse de Chevreuse? Scheming against the queen . . . ? It's impossible."

"As far as I can recall," said Almades, who spoke so rarely that everyone pricked up their ears when he did, "La Donna always referred to a plot 'against the throne.' She never said anything about a plot 'against the king.' We were the ones who concluded that the person of the king was under threat. . . ."

"Nevertheless," insisted the young baronne de Vaudreuil. "La Chevreuse and the queen are sincere friends. Whenever the duchesse has been involved in a scheme, it has been against the king or the cardinal. Never against the queen."

In this, Agnès was right.

"Be that as it may," said La Fargue after a silence, "there is nothing we can do. I'm sorry, Agnès, but if the Superior General wanted you out of the way, then she has succeeded."

"We'll see about that," declared Agnès before turning round and striding away.

"Where are you going?" La Fargue called after her.

"To find a dressmaker who can work miracles, by God! I'm going to need something decent to wear at court. . . ."

After their stroll in the Tuileries gardens, Laincourt and Aude de Saint-Avold returned looking pleased with themselves and with one another, sharing a sense of being guilty of a delicious prank. They were still laughing as they descended from the coach in the courtyard of the Hôtel de Chevreuse, simply two carefree young people on a fine summer day in June. For the space of a few sunny hours, Laincourt had forgotten his mission. He had forgotten about the perils that weighed upon France, the Alchemist's plot, madame de Chevreuse's intrigues, and the war being prepared against Lorraine. He had forgotten his hated profession as a spy and felt like a schoolboy.

Indeed, hadn't they just been playing truant? It was not a serious misdemeanour and the duchesse, who had boldly committed so many of her own, would no doubt forgive them. She might even be amused by their escapade, given her own fondness for the pleasures of life. As for madame de Jarville, the aunt they had been so careful not to wake, she would have to accept matters. It must be said that Laincourt had behaved like the perfect attending gentleman. Thoughtful and courteous, he had offered his arm as they strolled along the crowded lanes of the great park. Then, growing worried about the heat from the blazing sun above, he had insisted on purchasing a parasol for Aude from a hawker. The parasol turned out to be cheap rubbish and broke the moment it was opened, but the young girl laughed and held onto it as a keepsake. Finally, they drank fresh orange juice at a stand, near the pit where they saw the sleeping hydras that the queen mother had presented to the king a few years previously.

And that was all that had occurred, apart from the glances and smiles. . . .

Aude de Saint-Avold was pretty, agreeable, witty, and cultivated. Moreover, she was quick to wield irony with such an innocent air that she caught Laincourt by surprise several times. But above all, there was something luminous and happy about her, like a live flame, transmitted by her eyes and her smile.

Gallant to the end, Laincourt accompanied Aude from the coach to the splendid front hall of the Hôtel de Chevreuse, where the maître d'hôtel informed her that madame la duchesse was waiting for her. Laincourt then wanted to withdraw but the young woman from Lorraine implored him to stay.

"Oh no, monsieur! Don't abandon me!"

"Abandon you, madame?"

"I'm sure to be scolded for our stroll," explained Aude, half seriously. "I shall tell them you abducted me and you must confirm it!"

"Madame!" exclaimed Laincourt, pretending to be worried. "Me? Accuse myself of abducting you? I'll be thrown directly into prison."

"Never fear. I shall arrange for your escape," the girl whispered in a conspiratorial tone.

"Well, in that case . . ."

Thus it was on Laincourt's arm that Aude de Saint-Avold entered the salon where madame de Chevreuse was idly perusing a book on astrology. And he learned at the same time as Aude that she had been admitted to the queen's household as a maiden-of-honour. The distinction was both immense and unexpected. In the heat of her emotion, Aude forgot all about proper form and threw herself at the duchesse's feet, kissing her hands and calling her "benefactress." The duchesse, laughing, asked her to rise and when she was not obeyed, begged Laincourt to intervene. He helped Aude take a seat in an armchair and held her hand.

She cried, but her tears were those of joy.

"Will you visit me, monsieur?" she asked.

Arnaud de Laincourt smiled.

Maidens-of-honour were all of noble birth, lived under the watchful eye of a governess, and did not appear in public except to accompany the queen on grand occasions. As for approaching them . . .

"Madame," he said in a quiet voice, "for that, I would have to be admitted to the queen's entourage as well. . . ."

Before Aude could even begin to express her regret, the duchesse de Chevreuse announced in a playful tone: "Bah! Consider it done, monsieur."

Dusk was falling as the three riders came in sight of the inn. They had not exchanged so much as three words since leaving Ivry. Mirebeau, who led the way, did not seem to be in a talkative mood. As for Rauvin, he expressed his suspicious nature through silence and long stares which Leprat pretended to ignore. But the truth was that the man's hostility weighed on him. Constant and insidious, it seemed designed to play on his nerves and trip him up, and thereby provoke a confrontation. Since Mirebeau acted as if nothing was going on, the musketeer was forced to put up with it. The worst part, however, was that Rauvin—deliberately—rode last. It was his way of saying that he was keeping his eye on Leprat. And he was not the kind of man who anyone wanted to have at their back.

The riders stopped for a moment upon a hill.

The inn was still some distance away. Isolated, it was a former farm whose thick-walled buildings surrounded a courtyard defended by a massive gate. Right now, the two great doors remained open and there was movement in the lantern-lit courtyard. Most of the windows were brightly lit and festive sounds rose into the night: laughter, shouts, music, and singing.

"Is that where we're going?" asked Leprat.

"Yes," replied Mirebeau, urging his horse forward.

They reached the inn at a fast trot, dismounted after passing through the carriage gate, and walked to the stable leading their horses by the bridle. Tables had been set up in the courtyard, along with a stage where musicians were playing. People were dancing. At the tables, the refrains were taken up in chorus, hands were clapped in time with the beat, and glasses were raised only to be swiftly drained. Most of those present were soldiers, enjoying a last night of debauchery before rejoining their regiments, and here they found everything they desired: wine, drinking companions, and women. There were not very many of the latter, but they did not mind being shared. Bawdy and drunk, they went from arm to arm, dancing a turn with every man, sitting on every knee, willingly allowing themselves to be rudely handled, laughing when a hand grasped their waist or a face plunged into their bosom. Anything more than that had to be paid for, however, and couples went off, out of sight from the lanterns and voyeurs, for brief fumbling embraces.

Mirebeau knew the place and was known here. Summoning the stable boy, who responded with the promptness reserved for good customers, he asked that their horses be tended to but not unsaddled.

"Keep them ready for us," he said, giving the boy a generous tip. "We won't be here for long."

"Very good, monsieur."

"This way," he then indicated to Leprat.

"No," Rauvin intervened. "He stays here."

He and Mirebeau stared at one another for a moment and then the gentleman gave in.

"All right." And turning to Leprat, he said, "Wait for us here, please. We'll be back soon."

The musketeer nodded.

He had resolved to appear docile, if only to avoid giving Rauvin any opportunity to tell him to shut up and obey. He wondered whether the man was once again demonstrating his excessive sense of wariness or was simply seeking to humiliate him. But he said nothing and, from the stable's threshold, watched the two men cross the courtyard and enter the big house that constituted the inn's main building.

He thus stood waiting, pretending to watch the dancers and to be enjoying the music, while he discreetly observed the courtyard and kept track of comings and goings without anything seeming out of the ordinary . . .

. . . at least, not until he saw Rauvin come hurtling out of a first-storey window.

That evening, La Fargue, alone in his office, asked for monsieur Guibot to come see him.

"Any news of Leprat?" he asked.

"None, monsieur."

"And of Laincourt?"

"Nothing from him, either."

"Very good. Thank you."

As he was leaving the office, the old porter passed Marciac, who knocked on the open door by way of announcing himself.

"Yes, Marciac?" asked La Fargue.

The Gascon seemed embarrassed. He entered, shut the door behind him, and sat down.

"Captain . . ."

"What is it, Marciac?"

"I have something to tell you. It's about your daughter. . . . I'm not sure of anything, but I think she may be in danger."

Having been thrown, with a tremendous crash, through a first-storey window of the inn, Rauvin landed in the courtyard under the astonished eyes of the dancers, who came to a standstill, and of the musicians on their stage, who stopped playing. He immediately ran off, as a furious-looking comte de Rochefort stuck his head out of the wreckage above.

"STOP!" shouted the cardinal's henchman, before firing his pistol.

But he missed his target and Rauvin disappeared into the darkness.

"AFTER HIM!" Rochefort ordered, and a group of red-caped guards suddenly issued forth from the inn's front door and set off in pursuit of the fugitive.

Out of instinct, Leprat had taken a step backward into the stable, and concealed himself from view.

Evidently Mirebeau and Rauvin had come here for a clandestine meeting, a meeting that Rochefort had gotten wind of and decided to attend, along with a detachment of Richelieu's men. An ambush had been set up. But if Rochefort and the Cardinal's Guards had arrived first to organise this mouse-trap, they must have seen the duchesse de Chevreuse's agents arrive.

Which made Leprat wonder why he had not yet been apprehended himself.

"Don't make a move!" a voice behind him suddenly said. "You are under arrest."

In spite of the pistol whose barrel was now touching the back of his neck, Leprat smiled.

"You are going to be surprised, Biscarat," he replied, extending his arms away from his body and turning around slowly.

After even a few months' service, the King's Musketeers and the Cardinal's Guards all knew one another by sight, if not by name and reputation. Leprat had earned considerable renown when he wore the blue cape, while Biscarat had been a member of the Guards for at least eight years and had achieved some fame of his own by crossing swords with Porthos in a celebrated duel.

The guard's eyes widened upon recognising his prisoner.

"You?"

There was no time for explanations, but this second of astonishment was all that Leprat required. Pushing the pistol to one side, he swiftly kneed Biscarat in the belly and knocked him out with a right hook to the head, catching the man as he fell to prevent any further injury. Then he relieved him of his scarlet cape and put it on before venturing back out of the stable.

He quickly made his way across the courtyard, beneath the lanterns, moving toward the main building of the inn.

Rauvin had fled and, under the cover of night, would no doubt evade capture, but Mirebeau appeared to be trapped. While the fate of the first man was of little concern to him, Leprat could not permit the second to be arrested. The gentleman in the beige doublet was the only means he had of becoming involved in the duchesse de Chevreuse's schemes. Leprat was thus forced to rescue Mirebeau, even if it meant thwarting Rochefort and inflicting some blows and injuries on His Eminence's Guards.

The success of his mission depended on it.

With a resolute step, Leprat approached the row of curious onlookers who had gathered before the door of the main building and, lowering his hat to conceal his eyes, he passed through them with an authoritative air.

"Make way! Make way!"

The red cape was impressive and a passage was cleared for him.

Inside, dozens of torches lit an immense hall that rose to the rafters. Twenty tables were set out on a dirt floor scattered with straw. A gallery ran along the rear wall, with a corridor and several doors on the first storey, which was accessible via two staircases that climbed the walls on either side. The hall was packed and noisy, to the point that it was impossible to be heard without raising one's voice, or to move without sidling and shouldering past people. The crowd here was the same as in the courtyard: soldiers and non-commissioned officers, prostitutes and serving wenches, plus a few debauched gentlemen. Almost everyone was on their feet protesting. The sound of a brawl coming from one of the chambers, followed by that of a breaking window and gunfire, had initially caused confusion. The appearance of the Guards in their capes and the prohibition of anyone entering or leaving the premises had then started to worry some of those present and to anger others.

Rochefort had in fact given orders to seal all the exits from the building.

He was descending one of the stairways from the gallery when Leprat entered, and two guards armed with short muskets immediately took up posts in front of the doors. The musketeer congratulated himself on not having delayed any longer. He didn't know how he was going to get out, but at least he had managed to slip inside without hindrance.

"Place more guards here at the bottom of these stairs!" ordered Rochefort. "And where is Biscarat? Somebody go find Biscarat! There were three of them!"

Merely one more red cape among all the others, Leprat shoved his way through the crowd while keeping his chin down. He chose the stairs opposite those Rochefort had taken, arrived at the bottom of the steps where three guards were standing, and walked brazenly past them, helped by the fact that their eyes were fixed on the angry crowd. The inn was full of soldiers and gentlemen who did not appreciate being locked inside. Emboldened by wine, some were just waiting for a chance to have a go at the cardinal's representatives, who were almost universally detested throughout the kingdom.

With the exception of Rochefort, who followed his progress with a frowning gaze, Leprat reached the gallery without attracting anyone's attention. Then he walked along the corridor where a guard was posted in front of a door.

Why keep watch on a door, unless Mirebeau was being held prisoner behind it?

Still walking with the assured step of someone who knows where he is going and who has every right to be there, while keeping his chin tucked in so that the brim of his hat concealed the top of his face, Leprat was relying on the scarlet cape to work its magic. He advanced and, at the last minute, surprised the guard by brandishing the pistol he had stolen from Biscarat. Then he forced him to turn round and roughly pushed him against the wall.

"Open the door," he demanded.

"Impossible."

"Where's the key?"

"Rochefort."

Leprat cursed but did take long to reach a decision. He knocked out the guard with a blow from his pistol and then kicked open the door with his heel.

"It's me," he announced to Mirebeau, who stood at the rear of the small room in which he had been imprisoned, blinking in the sudden light.

"Guéret?"

"Yes. Hurry up!"

Waving Mirebeau forward, Leprat glanced toward the end of the corridor.

"Good Lord! I thought you had fled—"

"I'm not Rauvin. Come on!"

The gentleman in the beige doublet was coming out just as Rochefort arrived, intrigued by this guard he had seen coming up the stairs, perhaps a little too hastily.

"GUARDS! TO ME!" he shouted as soon as he came onto the gallery. "UP HERE!"

Leprat fired his pistol in Rochefort's direction, taking care as he did to aim high. The pistol ball lodged itself in a beam, but caused the cardinal's henchman to retreat, which was all the musketeer had wanted. With Mirebeau on his heels, he entered the nearest chamber and the two men pushed the bed against the door before Leprat went to take a look through the window. It opened onto a section of roof by means of which the fugitives made their escape as the guards attempted to force their way into the room.

"To the stable!" Leprat cried. "We need horses; it's our only chance!"

Mirebeau nodded.

A few seconds later, just as Rochefort ran into the courtyard with several guards, and still more were cautiously exploring the rooftops, Leprat and Mirebeau burst out of the stable at a gallop, having first liberated all the horses they found there. Spurring their own mounts and yelling like demons, they provoked a stampede, aggravated by the muskets fired at them on Rochefort's order, the furious shouts from the soldiers who saw their horses dispersing into the darkness, and, finally, by the anger of those inside the inn jostling with the guards who were still trying to prevent them from leaving. Leprat and Mirebeau, moreover, decided to take the shortest route away from the scene. Charging straight at the gate, they jumped their horses over the musicians' stage, and in doing so, carried away with them the strings of hanging lanterns. The little oil lamps broke as they fell. Trailing behind the pair of riders, they formed blazing splatters pointing in the direction of the exit, completing the panic of the other horses that had been set free. The two fugitives made good their escape, galloping flat out into the night and leaving a veritable state of chaos in their wake, as men and beasts alike ran among the scattered flames.

4

Having been warned by Marciac that Rochefort—which amounted to saying Cardinal Richelieu—was seeking to lay hands on his daughter, La Fargue had kept his fear firmly in check. But once night had fallen he retired to his bedchamber, carefully locked his door, and used the flame he had brought to light some candles, filling the room with a red and amber glow.

He took out a small key which he always kept on his person and used it to open a case tucked away among his clothing, removing a silver mirror which he placed on a table in front of him. That done, he gathered his spirit, keeping eyes closed, and in a low voice uttered ancient words in a language that had not been invented by men.

The surface of the precious mirror rippled, like a pool of mercury stirred by a breeze. It ceased to send back the reflection of a tired old gentleman, replacing it with the image of the one answering his call. The mirror did not lie. It revealed the true nature of those who used it and, in this case, revealed the slightly translucent head of a white dragon.

Such was the nature of La Fargue's contact.

But what did the dragon see, when it looked back at La Fargue?

"I need to meet with one of the Seven," said the captain of the Blades.

"Impossible," replied the dragon. "It's too dangerous."

"Do whatever is necessary."

"No."

"No later than three nights from now."

"Or else what?"

"No later than three nights from now. In the usual time and place."

IV

THE DAMPIERRE RITUAL

1

In an antechamber at the Louvre, Captain La Fargue stood looking out the window while Almades maintained a discreet guard at the door. They were waiting for Agnès, who had joined the queen's household three days previously and had not communicated with the Blades since.

Attached to the household of Anne d'Autriche, Agnès now lived in the palace and was no longer free to dispose of her time. Moreover, she knew she was being closely observed, the public manner of her arrival having aroused both curiosity and envy among her new peers. Although of the noblest breeding, she was nevertheless practically unknown and her sudden ascension had surprised the entire court. For two whole days, no one had spoken of anything else. It was rumoured she had been presented to the queen by the duchesse de Chevreuse, which was true. It was also said that the king had admitted her to his wife's entourage in order to initiate a reconciliation with the duchesse, which was false. Agnès's role was to watch over Anne d'Autriche and to protect her if needed—a mission which the Sisters of Saint Georges' Superior General had entrusted to her with Richelieu's assent and which she was now carrying out, albeit under protest.

La Fargue turned around upon hearing the door open and saw Agnès enter. She looked very beautiful, with her hair and dress done in the latest style, her outfit including an elegant red hooped skirt, a square neckline, and short puffed sleeves.

"I only have a little time," she said as she carefully closed the door behind her.

The old gentleman understood.

"Yesterday," he said, "Laincourt supped at the Hôtel de Chevreuse. . . ."

"I'm sure it was more amusing there than it is here."

"No doubt. This supper, in which the marquis de Châteauneuf also took part, was given in honour of a certain Aude de Saint-Avold."

The young baronne nodded.

"She is to be presented at court today, before joining the queen's household tomorrow. As a maiden-of-honour, I believe. . . ."

"She is a distant relative of the duc de Chevreuse. She has arrived in Paris directly from Lorraine, where the duchesse no doubt made her acquaintance during her exile. . . . Coming a few days after your own, this new appointment to the queen's household cannot be a coincidence."

It was only at Cardinal Richelieu's private request that madame de Chevreuse had agreed to introduce Agnès to the queen and to recommend her. Louis XIII alone decided who was to be admitted to his wife's entourage and had occasionally used this privilege to punish her by excluding ladies she liked, claiming they exercised a bad influence over her. Thus Anne d'Autriche had learned to be wary of new faces, for she knew they had been chosen by the king and his chief minister. That was why the cardinal had sought, in this case, the good offices of the duchesse who enjoyed the queen's trust. The problem was that the duchesse had no particular desire to please either the cardinal or the king, and the fate of this little baronne de Vaudreuil was a matter of perfect indifference to her. She thus required some persuasion to become better disposed toward the idea. . . .

"The duchesse," Agnès suggested, "might have agreed to vouch for me with the queen on condition that Aude de Saint-Avold also became a maiden-of-honour."

"Is there anything else that would have induced the king to allow one of La Chevreuse's protégées to join the queen's suite? Especially given that . . ."

La Fargue did not complete his train of thought.

They both knew that the duchesse—who never ceased to plot—was on the point of being arrested as part of a general roundup of suspects which would spare neither the wealthy nor the powerful. The king had decided to strike the day after the great ball the duchesse would be hosting at the Château de Dampierre, so that her fall would come as swiftly as possible after her apparent triumph.

"What do you expect of me, captain?"

"Laincourt assures me that this young Saint-Avold is not mixed up in La Chevreuse's schemes. Nevertheless, keep your eye on her. You never know."

Agnès sighed in resignation.

"All right," she agreed.

"Listen, Agnès, I know you feel you are wasting your time here, but—"

"What could possibly happen to the queen here? The Louvre is swarming with the king's men, including both the Swiss Guards and the Musketeers!"

"There are dangers against which courage and steel alone do not always suffice. And it is those sorts of dangers, with respect to the queen, that worry the cardinal and the Mother Superior General. . . ."

The dangers that La Fargue was referring to were dragons and their spells. And he was not mistaken in his assertion that it required more than good soldiers to combat them. It took counterspells and fearless souls who could wield them. It took the Sisters of Saint Georges, who had been protecting the throne of France for the past three centuries.

But the Chatelaines—entrusted with Anne d'Autriche's security—were now claiming they could no longer carry out their sacred duty.

"What exactly is the problem?" the Blades' captain wanted to know.

And Agnès was regretfully forced to admit: "It is true that the queen does nothing to make the Sisters' task any easier. You might even think she is trying to hamper them—"

"But the queen's dislike for the Sisters of Saint Georges didn't start yesterday."

"Oh, as far as that goes, she spares the unhappy wretches assigned to her protection nothing. She gives them the cold shoulder, openly expresses her scorn, and never misses an opportunity to humiliate them. From what I have been able to learn, there is nothing new there. What has changed, however, is the fact that the queen now avoids them whenever she is permitted to do so. And sometimes more. Last Friday, for example, she forbade them to accompany her to the Val-de-Grâce."

The Val-de-Grâce, on rue Saint-Honoré, was a convent for which Anne d'Autriche had laid the first stone and was one of her favourite retreats.

"That's extremely imprudent," commented La Fargue.

"The queen's resentment toward the White Order seems to have redoubled. . . ."

"Then perhaps you are the best choice, after all. You almost completed your novitiate with the Sisters and came close to taking the veil yourself—"

"That page has been turned, captain," the young woman said brusquely.

"I know, Agnès. I'm only asking you to trust your instincts and act for the best. You are capable of detecting things that escape the rest of us."

Pensive for a moment, Agnès turned toward the window and then asked: "Has Mère Emmanuelle de Cernay tried to contact me?"

Out of affection for Agnès, Emmanuelle de Cernay, formerly Superior General of the Sisters of Saint Georges, had promised to help her uncover what had happened to a certain lieutenant serving in the Black Guards. The young officer was both the son of an old friend of La Fargue and the brother of a Blade who had died in the course of a mission.

"No," the old gentleman admitted.

"Will you let me know right away if—?"

"I promise, Agnès."

"I must go. . . . Any news of Leprat?"

"Nothing from him, either."

"Or of the Alchemist?"

This time, La Fargue remained silent and the young woman judged it best not to press him any further.

She left.

When he arrived that afternoon, Laincourt found the Hôtel de Chevreuse in a state of upheaval. Out in the courtyard, beneath the hot sun, the servants were loading wagons with furniture, boxes, chests, and rolled-up tapestries. The duchesse was not emptying the premises, but she was preparing to live elsewhere for a while. On her estate at the Château de Dampierre, as it happened.

Laincourt joined the duchesse's maître d'hôtel on the front steps, where the head servant was very busy giving orders and supervising the move. As Laincourt was now a familiar figure at the mansion, the young man did not need to present himself but simply asked if he might see madame de Saint-Avold. He was informed that as she was about to go out and she was not receiving visitors. Laincourt insisted: he would wait on the terrace and only desired a short interview with her. The maître d'hôtel finally consented to this request.

"Very well, monsieur."

And with a snap of his fingers, he summoned a lackey whom he charged with delivering the message.

Laincourt waited on the terrace, admiring the magnificent garden that stretched as far as rue Saint-Nicaise.

So, madame de Chevreuse was leaving Paris . . .

She would soon be emulated by others. As wild and welcome as it had been, the nocturnal storm that had been unleashed over the capital had merely offered a brief respite. The hot weather had resumed and, after a few days, had become an ordeal, especially with the disease and foul odours which accompanied the stifling heat. Paris had become a cesspit. Beneath a merciless sun, a nauseating muck polluted the ditches, manure baked at the stable gates, blood simmered on the pavement in front of the butchers' shops, and faecal matter fermented in the latrines. This pestilence caused headaches, nausea, and respiratory disorders in weaker persons and the only effective relief was flight. Soon, as occurred each year at this time, the wealthy would begin to desert the capital. It was the season when loved ones were sent to the country or whole families emigrated, along with their baggage and servants, to some favoured retreat or ancestral castle. The king himself set an example by leaving the Louvre every summer while the palace moats were cleaned. The royal court followed suit, while more ordinary Parisians were forced to shut themselves up in buildings where the atmosphere was scarcely purer than the contaminated air outside and to wait until Sunday when they could go and breathe freely in the countryside.

"I am truly sorry, monsieur. But I can only grant you a few moments. Madame la duchesse is already waiting in her coach, ready to take me to the Louvre, and—"

Laincourt turned round and saw Aude de Saint-Avold, looking more adorable than ever in a dress he hadn't seen before. He thought she was quite ravishing, although he didn't dare say as much. But the expression on his face must have betrayed him, for she stopped speaking, smiled, and blushed, her green eyes sparkling with joy.

They stood joined in silence for an instant and Laincourt resisted the desire to take hold of her hands.

"I know, madame, that you are to be presented at court today. And that you will enter the queen's household as of tomorrow. But before that, I wished to salute you and assure you of my friendship."

"Thank you, monsieur. Thank you with all my heart."

"I also wish to offer you a few words of advice. The royal court of France is not like the court of Lorraine. And your proximity to the queen will earn you enmity in certain quarters. Don't be fooled by false smiles, beware of hypocrites and those who aspire to a higher rank, learn to spot those who act out of self-interest, and, above all, avoid getting caught up in intrigue."

He realised that he had in fact seized her hands and that she had not withdrawn them from his grasp. She was looking at him and listening carefully, convinced and touched by his sincerity.

He stopped speaking, without releasing her hands and without her attempting to remove them.

At least, not until they heard the sound of a throat clearing: the sad-looking madame de Jarville had come in search of her niece.

Full of life and joy, Aude de Saint-Avold then took her leave with a rustling of silk.

"Farewell, monsieur! We'll meet again very soon!"

He did not reply, sure that fate had just separated them for good.

* * *

Coming from Ivry, Leprat and Mirebeau arrived in Paris by way of the faubourg Saint-Marcel. They rode side by side, at a walk, conversing in a friendly fashion.

These past few days spent together at Mirebeau's house had brought them together. On the day after the famous night when Leprat had risked his life to free him, Mirebeau had pledged his friendship, solemnly but sincerely. Leprat had initially been glad to have won the trust of the duchesse de Chevreuse's agent, for the sake of his mission. Later, he had come to like Mirebeau himself. In truth, the two men resembled one another. They were of roughly the same age, both were elder sons from noble families, and both had followed military careers: Leprat with the King's Musketeers and Mirebeau in the company of guards led by monsieur des Essarts. If life had robbed them of many of their illusions, both tried to conduct themselves as gentlemen; and finally, as they learned exchanging confidences one night over a bottle, they had both been unlucky in love and realised, to their regret, that they would no doubt never become fathers.

They smelled the capital well before they actually saw it and were soon sorry they had not chosen another route. To be sure, all of Paris stank beneath the burning sun. But Paris never stank quite so much as in the vicinity of rue Mouffetard, which they rode along with tears in their eyes. Here, the nearby Bièvre—a river that crossed the neighbourhood before plunging into the Seine—attracted various activities such as knackers' yards and tanneries which consumed great quantities of water and polluted both the river and the atmosphere.

It was therefore a relief to pass through the Saint-Marcel gate, despite the odour of a warmed-up old latrine that prevailed within the city walls. Finally able to breathe without keeping a hand over their nose and mouth, Leprat and Mirebeau took rue de la Montagne-Sainte-Geneviève as far as Place Maubert. They crossed the small arm of the Seine by way of the Pont au Double, thus named because use of this bridge entailed a toll of a double denier. Mirebeau paid their fee. They passed before Notre-Dame cathedral, made their way through the maze of medieval streets on the Ile de la Cité, reached the Right Bank by the Pont au Change, and ended up in front of the Grand Châtelet.

Leprat still did not know where they were going.

That morning when, after several days of idleness, Mirebeau had suddenly announced that they needed to be in Paris that afternoon, he had refused to say anything more. But he had refused in a playful manner. It was no longer a matter of distrusting Leprat, but of offering him a surprise.

A pleasant surprise.

Going along with the game, the musketeer had cherished the hope that they might be going to the Hôtel de Chevreuse to meet the duchesse. But he was forced to abandon this notion once they continued beyond Le Châtelet. Instead of going west along the quays or following rue Saint-Honoré to rue Saint-Thomas-du-Louvre, they first took rue Saint-Denis northward, turning off once they reached the Saints-Innocents cemetery, then passed Les Halles, and, keeping the Saint-Eustache church on their right, entered rue Traînée.

Mirebeau smiled as he watched Leprat out of the corner of his eye. In fact, the former musketeer had no idea of their destination until the last moment.

And it was only when they were in front of the monumental gate that he understood.

"The Hôtel de Châteauneuf?" exclaimed Marciac.

He turned to La Fargue and then looked again at Leprat, who confirmed the information: "To the home of the marquis de Châteauneuf, yes."

They were meeting this evening in rue Cocatrix, on the Ile de la Cité.

The place didn't look like much: a rented bedchamber beneath the rafters with cracked walls and a rough wooden floor, containing a bed without a canopy or a curtain, a clothing chest, a small dressing table, a chair in considerable need of being restuffed, a stained mirror, and a crucifix. It was fairly wretched, but a musketeer's pay did not allow for anything better. However, the landlord was friendly, the neighbours were discreet, and the street was quiet.

And Leprat felt more at home here than anywhere else.

"The truth," he explained, "is that Mirebeau does not belong to madame de Chevreuse or even to her husband. He belongs to Châteauneuf, who has placed him at the duchesse's disposal for her . . . affairs."

Although night had not yet fallen, the three men had already lit a candle so they could see one another within the dark bedchamber. Leprat was sitting on his chest, La Fargue was straddling the chair backward, and Marciac was leaning against the wall with his arms crossed, next to a crookedly hung crucifix.

"Châteauneuf and La Chevreuse are lovers, as practically everyone knows," observed the captain of the Blades. "But what you have discovered, Leprat, is something else again. . . ."

Born of a lineage that had produced several royal councillors and secretaries of state, Charles de l'Aubespine, marquis de Châteauneuf, had been the ambassador of France in Holland, Italy, and England. He was reputed to be subservient to Richelieu, who, in 1630, had rewarded his loyalty and devotion by making him Keeper of the Seals. Now fifty-three years old, he was one of the most important figures in the kingdom. But he was also a somewhat ridiculous old fop who had an eye for the ladies and who, despite his age, persisted in behaving like some young Romeo.

"It would seem that La Chevreuse only likes old codgers," observed Marciac. "The duc de Luynes was already forty when he married her, I believe. The duc de Chevreuse was forty-four. And now Châteauneuf . . ."

"It is one thing for Châteauneuf to make the horns on the duc de Chevreuse's brow grow a little longer," said La Fargue. "He is not the first man to do so and, knowing the duchesse, there will be others after him. But in placing Mirebeau at La Chevreuse's disposal for her schemes, he has made himself her accomplice. And who knows what State secrets he may have let slip during their bedchamber conversations?"

"And all this has been taking place on the eve of a war against Lorraine," added Leprat.

"Yet I thought Châteauneuf was completely devoted to the cardinal," said the Gascon.

"No doubt that ceased to be the case the day he caught sight of the duchesse's beautiful eyes," the captain of the Blades surmised. "God only knows what ideas the she-devil has put in his head. . . . And you may recall the ball where Châteauneuf danced all night while the cardinal lay at death's door."

The musketeer nodded.

"It was shortly after Montmorency's execution. It was said that Châteauneuf could already see himself succeeding his master."

"What a triumph that would have been for La Chevreuse," Marciac noted. "Her worst enemy dies and her lover takes his place as chief minister to the king."

"But the cardinal did not die in the end," said La Fargue.

"Did you actually meet Châteauneuf?" the Gascon asked.

"Yes," replied Leprat. "The marquis has asked me to join the group of gentlemen escorting him to Dampierre, in order to attend the ball being held there by the duchesse. We're leaving tomorrow and, since Mirebeau wanted to spend the night with his mistress, I used the same excuse to get away myself. I thought it would be more prudent if I avoided going to the Hôtel de l'Épervier, and I must confess that I've missed sleeping in my own bed. . . ."

Marciac considered the bed in question, looking deeply perplexed. Even imagining one or two naked beauties lying in it, it still seemed unwelcoming.

A bell tolled.

Realising the time, La Fargue rose from his chair to take his leave.

"You have done very good work, Leprat. My congratulations."

"Thank you, captain."

"Be careful, though."

"I will. . . . By the way, was anyone injured at the Neuilly inn?"

"Among the Guards? Just a few bumps and bruises, as far as I know. But Rochefort is perfectly furious about the whole incident."

"Tell him that I . . . No, on second thought, I shall reserve the pleasure of revealing the truth to him for some other day."

The captain of the Blades smiled. He was not fond of Rochefort, either.

"Understood."

He was the first to depart and descended the stairs while Marciac, on the landing, shook the musketeer's hand.

"Since you are supposedly spending the night with your mistress," he murmured, "what would you say if you and I were to pay a visit to the ladies? I know two sisters who live close by here and—"

"I'm tired, Marciac."

"Tell yourself that it would be for the good of your mission—"

"I'll see you soon, Nicolas."

"All right, as you wish. . . . But where's your sense of duty, Antoine? This is very poor of you. And a disappointment to me!"

"Out!"

Down below, waiting in the shadowy rue Cocatrix, La Fargue found Almades, who had been keeping watch. Marciac had just joined them when the captain of the Blades announced: "I have something else to do. I'll see you both tomorrow."

The two other men exchanged astonished looks. It was not unusual for La Fargue to leave the Gascon behind. But to separate himself from Almades . . .

"Captain . . ." said Marciac, attempting to intervene on the Spanish fencing master's behalf, "Are you quite sure that—?"

"I will see you tomorrow."

And the old gentleman went off alone.

"Let's go after him," suggested the Gascon after a moment.

"No."

"But it's for his own safety!"

"No," repeated an impassive Almades.

"Well, stay then. But as for me—"

"No."

"Since when do you give me orders?"

The Spaniard drew his sword in lieu of a reply.

"You're jesting."

"No, I'm not."

Marciac took a step backward and hunched his shoulders, displaying a look of wounded surprise like some scoundrel whose honesty was being placed in doubt. It suddenly occurred to him that La Fargue might not have left the two of them together in order to go off on his own, but so that Almades could keep an eye on him, Marciac, and make sure he did not try to follow his captain.

"Would you really run me through with your sword?"

"Yes."

Back at home, Laincourt looked out the window without seeing anything.

He was lost in thought and, slowly, the blood-covered face of the hurdy-gurdy player appeared in the reflection from the windowpane, above his right shoulder, as if the old man was approaching him from behind.

You're thinking about that pretty young thing, aren't you, boy?

Her name is Aude.

Well, she certainly seems to be to your liking.

You might say that.

If she matters that much to you, no doubt you did well to warn her of the dangers awaiting her at the court. However . . . However, perhaps you too should be wary, of her. . . .

"Me, wary of her? But why?" Laincourt asked out loud. "On what grounds?"

He turned around without thinking.

And remembered that he was in fact alone.

Midnight.

The night was still warm when La Fargue started to cross the Pont Neuf. Around him, Paris was swallowed up in deep shadows, except for a few scattered lights here and there, fragile and distant. A thick silence reigned. One could just barely hear, rather than see, the low black waters of the Seine lapping beneath the bridge's great stone arches.

As agreed, La Fargue stopped in front of the Bronze Wyvern.

This statue stood at the end of the Ile de la Cité, where the two halves of the Pont Neuf joined at Place Dauphine. It consisted of a wyvern with spread wings, resting on a marble pedestal at the entrance to a balustered promontory that—pointing downstream from the bridge—overlooked the river. Although it was represented saddled and harnessed, the Bronze Wyvern was riderless, among all the other trials and tribulations it had undergone. A gift from the grand duke of Tuscany to Marie de Médicis, following the death of her husband, Henri IV, the statue had sunk off the coast of Sardinia along with the ship transporting it. Fished out of the sea a year later, it had finally been lifted into place by the Pont Neuf in 1614. But in 1633 it had still not been mounted by anyone other than the occasional drunkard or prankster.

La Fargue walked behind the statue.

A gentleman was waiting for him, leaning on the parapet and looking out at the reflections of the moon and the stars that danced upon the inky waters of the Seine. He had a felt hat with a plume on his head and a sword at his hip, and wore a black cloak over a light grey doublet with white slashes and silver thread. He seemed to be about thirty years old, although his hair had already started to grey. He was a tall, slim, and fairly handsome man, whose eyes had pale irises surrounded by a dark rim.

La Fargue halted

"Who are you?" he asked in a suspicious tone.

"I am the one who has been sent to you," the other man replied calmly.

"I don't know you."

"Well you're free to leave."

The old captain thought for a moment and then asked: "Your name?"

"Valombre."

"Do you serve the Seven?"

The gentleman smiled.

"I serve them."

"And are you—"

"—a dragon? Yes, I am. But unless you have a Chatelaine nun hidden up your sleeve, you will have to take my word for it."

The jest did not make La Fargue smile and he stared at this so-called Valombre before finally saying: "I believe you."

"Good for you. And if we get down to business now, monsieur?"

The captain of the Blades nodded.

"I am worried," he confessed. "Rochefort's men are on my daughter's trail. Is she quite safe?"

"I can assure you that she is. Your daughter is doing splendidly and is out of reach of even the best of the cardinal's agents."

"And of the Black Claw?"

"She is out of their reach as well."

"They have immense resources at their disposal."

"Our own are by no means negligible. Do you want to know where your daughter is?"

"No. I would be the first to be interrogated if—"

La Fargue walked several paces, turned around, and raised his eyes toward the Bronze Wyvern.

"In two days' time," he said, "the king will have arrested his Keeper of the Seals, the duchesse de Chevreuse, and all those who, with them, have plotted against the throne. The cardinal has been gathering testimonies and evidence against them for months now. It will cause a great deal of noise, no doubt about it."

"This affair does not concern us."

"Indeed not. . . . But there's something else going on, isn't there? Something important. Something serious."

He lowered his gaze to look at Valombre, who did not answer right away.

"Yes," the dragon admitted at last, without any trace of emotion.

"Is the Alchemist part of it?"

"Possibly."

"Are you not sure? Or don't you want me to know?"

"We're not sure."

The old gentleman frowned.

"What are you hiding from me?" he asked.

"Nothing that the Sisters of Saint Georges don't already know. Perhaps you should take an interest in their secrets."

"They seem to believe that the queen is threatened."

"If it exists, the threat against the queen is only the beginning. But the greater danger that we fear will not spare anyone."

2

In the Chevreuse valley, evening fell across the vast domain of Dampierre, and Leprat watched from the bank of the great pond as the sunset lent its colours to the waters. Turning his back to the castle, he enjoyed a moment of peace, filling his lungs with fresh air.

As they had agreed, he and Mirebeau had followed the marquis de Châteauneuf as part of his escort. It was composed of over thirty gentlemen of noble birth, each of whom attempted to outdo the others in elegance. Their presence was meant to enhance the prestige of monsieur de Châteauneuf as much as to ensure his safety. A great lord never travelled in public on his own and his status was measured by the number and rank of those accompanying him. Charles de l'Aubespine, marquis de Châteauneuf and Keeper of the Seals of the kingdom of France, could hardly ignore convention on this occasion.

The only road from Paris to Dampierre passed through the villages of Vanves, Vélizy, and Saclay. It was a journey of ten leagues, which the marquis wanted to make on horseback, without resting and despite the burning sun, leaving his coach and baggage trailing behind. He was obviously impatient to reach their destination. But he also wished to make a grand entrance at the castle, where madame de Chevreuse was already waiting. So they halted at the gates to the domain for long enough to shake the dust from their clothing, refresh themselves, and brush down their mounts. It was a matter of putting on a proud display. For Leprat, it allowed him to observe that Châteauneuf, despite being in his fifties and having considerable experience when it came to women, seemed as eager and anxious as an adolescent before his first gallant rendezvous. The duchesse had indeed made him lose his head.

They had arrived in the afternoon to find Dampierre swarming with busy servants and craftsmen. The paths were raked clear, the gardens were tidied, the trees were pruned, and the canals were dredged. But at the heart of all this laborious agitation was the castle itself, where preparations for the forthcoming festivities would continue well into the night. The king, the queen, and the entire royal court would be arriving on the morrow, the day of the ball itself. Everything had to be ready to receive them.

"It's beautiful, isn't it?"

Leprat turned his head toward Mirebeau, who had come out to join him, and then looked again at the sunset reflecting off the calm, shining waters.

"Yes," he said. "Very beautiful."

"This domain is one of the most splendid places I know. Whatever the season, it's a veritable feast for the eyes . . ."

He broke off as a deep, mournful trumpeting almost deafened the two men.

"And for the ears!" exclaimed Leprat before they both burst out laughing.

They turned around to watch as a tarasque crossed the terrace separating them from the castle, plodding along at a slow and steady pace. The enormous, shelled reptile was pulling a train of three wagons piled with the pruned trunks of trees that had been cut down to embellish a prospect in the park. Two tarasque drivers were guiding the beast, using both their voices and their pikes. It moved forward with a rattle of the heavy chains linking its six legs to the collar encircling its neck.

Still smiling, Leprat and Mirebeau returned to admiring the view of the pond, without either feeling any need to speak. Since he had discovered that Mirebeau was actually in the service of the marquis de Châteauneuf, Leprat had felt himself drawn even closer to the gentleman in the beige doublet. Now there seemed to be really little difference between them, other than the fact that they served their respective masters with equal loyalty. Life might easily have reversed their roles or allowed Mirebeau to become a member of the Cardinal's Blades. It was perhaps simply a matter of circumstances.

Leprat's gaze was drawn to an island at the far end of the pond, an island upon which he was able to make out some ruins and the silhouettes of men apparently keeping watch over them.

"What is that?" he asked, pointing his finger.

"It's the island of Dampierre. An island which isn't truly an island, since it's connected to the bank by a causeway that you can't see from here. The duc is having some pavilions built there."

The ruins were in fact buildings being constructed.

"According to legend," Mirebeau went on to say, "in the time of Charlemagne there was a lord living in a black tower upon the island. He performed vile rituals there and terrorised the entire region, to the point that some valiant knights came to challenge him. Unfortunately for them, the lord was not only a wicked sorcerer, but also a dragon. . . . There is, in the castle here at Dampierre, a tapestry representing the heroic combat between these knights and the monster."

"Did they defeat the dragon?"

"Don't knights always triumph in tales?"

"And the tower? It looks like there is nothing left of it."

"It was razed to the ground and its stones, reputed to be cursed, were thrown into the pond so that they could never be used again."

"Legends have an answer for everything."

"It seems that these cursed stones also gave rise to the name 'Dampierre,' although I know nothing of Latin. . . ."

As for the musketeer, he possessed only a smattering of church Latin. He pursed his lips and the two men fell silent again.

"Enough lazing about," Mirebeau suddenly declared. "Come with me, we need to go to the Château de Mauvières and make sure that everything is ready there to receive monsieur de Châteauneuf's entourage."

"We're not sleeping at Dampierre?"

"In the castle?" the gentleman asked with amusement. "Tonight, that might be possible. But tomorrow there will be marquises in the servants' quarters, comtesses in the attic, and barons sleeping on straw mattresses. Where do you think they would put us? No, trust me, we shall be better off at Mauvières. And it's close by."

Leprat regretfully dragged his eyes from the pond and its island. He was following Mirebeau, who had set off at a brisk pace, when he heard the sound of a few notes being played on a jew's harp.

He halted, turned around, and saw Rauvin in the shadows.

Mirebeau had told Leprat that the hired swordsman had escaped, but he'd not seen him since the night when Rochefort had laid his trap for them. How long had the other man been standing there, spying on them? And why had he decided to reveal his presence, if not to make Leprat understand that he was still keeping an eye on him?

As he continued plucking notes on his harp, staring directly at the musketeer, Rauvin gave a slow nod of the head.

The barony of Chevreuse had been made a duchy in 1555, as a favour to Cardinal Charles de Lorraine, who had just acquired it as his holding. The seigneurial seat at the time was the Château de la Madeleine, an austere medieval fortress built on a height overlooking Paris and whose only real advantage was its unequalled view of the surrounding countryside. Its lack of comfort displeased the cardinal, who preferred a more elegant manor nestling in the Yvette valley barely a league away from Chevreuse. It had belonged to a royal treasurer who was obliging enough to die quickly, leaving behind him some debts and a widow who posed no objections to selling off the entire domain.

This domain was Dampierre, whose name was perhaps derived from either *domus Petri*—Peter's dwelling in Latin—or from *damnæ petræ*, meaning cursed stones. Its manor became the new ducal residence. The cardinal transformed it into a castle that was later inherited by the youngest son of the duc de Guise, who also came from Lorraine, along with the land and title in 1612. This duc de Chevreuse did not add any great distinction to the name, as opposed to the woman he wed ten years later. The famed and indomitable duchesse loved Dampierre. She stayed there often and, at her urging, her husband enlarged and embellished the property further.

However, if the domain was vast and prosperous in 1633, its castle, despite acquiring a luxurious steam bath and some other interior improvements, still compared poorly with the magnificence of the Hôtel de Chevreuse in Paris. Its roofs were covered with tiles rather than more handsome slate, while the four sides formed by its sandstone towers and pavilions enclosed a rather small courtyard, entered by means of a drawbridge leading from a forecourt lined with the castle's outbuildings.

But the main attractions of Dampierre lay elsewhere.

They included the magnificent forests in the surrounding area; the orchards and splendid flower beds arranged in the Renaissance fashion; the beautiful water-filled moats that encircled the castle and its garden; the canals feeding these moats, lined with leafy walks and bordering the main flower bed; and, finally, the pond where one could take pleasant boat trips out to the island where the new pavilions were being built.

Pavilions which were being guarded for no reason that Leprat could see.

Mirebeau had not lied. The modest Château de Mauvières—sometimes also called Bergerac—was located just beyond the outer wall surrounding the domain of Dampierre. It belonged to a minor nobleman, Abel de Cyrano, whose son Savinien was already beginning to make a name for himself in Paris, both as a man of letters and with his sword.

Leprat waited until nightfall before slipping out of his bedchamber, which was fortunately close by the stables. He saddled a horse, and led it out of the manor before mounting and urging it forward with a dig of his heels. The summer nights were short and he had to be back before dawn.

Who would post a guard over some unfinished pavilions on an island?

Once inside the domain at Dampierre, Leprat stayed away from the paths. He entered the woods, tethered the horse to a tree, and continued onward by foot. Remaining concealed, he soon found a place where he enjoyed a clear view of the island in the middle of the large pond. As he had expected, he saw men with lanterns guarding the causeway that gave access to the building site from the shore furthest away from the castle.

It would be impossible for him to cross over that way.

Leprat stripped down to his breeches and shirt, and swung his baldric round so that his rapier hung down his back. Then he took careful note of the place where he left his belongings, slid into the cold water, and began swimming toward the island and its mysteries.

He had no idea who these men were or what they were doing here. During supper, Mirebeau had also confessed his ignorance but said they did not belong to the marquis de Châteauneuf. Did they serve madame de Chevreuse, then? Perhaps. Or else some third party.

Leprat swam steadily to conserve his strength and to splash as little as possible. He drew close to the island, regained his footing once more, and hurriedly climbed the bank. Then he took up position on a height where, hidden by some thickets, he was able to catch his breath while observing what was going on.

He saw more armed mercenaries guarding the building site itself, which was lit here and there by torches planted in the ground. Five pavilions had started to emerge from the scaffolding and piles of building materials. They surrounded a roof made of wooden planks. Leprat was unable to see what lay concealed beneath it, but there were mounds of earth nearby.

Had the construction project made an unexpected discovery? Or was the building work only a pretext intended to mask other activities? Whatever the case, Leprat intended to get to the bottom of the matter.

He studied the movements of the hired swordsmen before creeping forward. Quickly and silently he entered the site, tiptoed among the shadows, and managed to slip beneath the wooden roof without being spotted. It sheltered a pit into which he could descend via a ramp and several ladders. The excavation of this pit had exposed the ancient foundations of a large circular building which immediately called to mind the black tower of the legend. The same black tower whose cursed stones might have inspired the name Dampierre.

The musketeer leapt into the pit and landed nimbly upon a floor of bare flagstones. There was a gap where some steps descended into the ground.

They led to a very old door made of black wood which appeared to have been blocked up long ago and only recently unsealed. Its relatively well-preserved state was, upon reflection, rather astonishing. As was the ease with which it opened to reveal a spiral staircase lit by candles in a succession of niches. Leprat made his way downward with caution, counting seventy-one stone steps which took him to a level beneath the bottom of the pond. After opening another black door, he found himself in a fairly vast but empty chamber, whose vaulted ceiling was supported by rows of round columns. Here, again, a few candles shone in the darkness. The air felt damp and water dripped from the ceiling into age-old puddles.

More and more intrigued, Leprat continued his exploration. There were several doors—low and again black—on either side of the chamber. But the central aisle between the columns, illuminated by the candles set at regular intervals, seemed to indicate a path leading to an archway at the rear over which a last, solitary candle burned.

But as he stretched out a hand to draw open the purple curtain concealing the archway, he sensed a sudden movement behind him. He spun round, but only had time to see a scaly tail snaking away into the darkness. A syle. Bad news. Sometimes growing as big as cats, the carnivorous salamanders were both extremely swift and voracious. They became frenzied at the scent of blood and, when gathered in numbers, they were capable of attacking a wounded man and devouring him alive. And where there was one, there were usually others. . . .

Pulling himself together, the musketeer lifted the curtain.

Having left the castle in the middle of the night, seven riders trotted forth upon the causeway joining the island to the shore of the pond. At their head was Savelda, the Black Claw's most effective servant when it came to carrying out foul deeds. Behind him rode the Alchemist, the false master of magic using the name of Mauduit and true mastermind of a plot intended to change the destiny of France forever. The third rider was in fact a very beautiful woman: the duchesse de Chevreuse, dressed as a horseman and thrilled at taking part in this nocturnal expedition. The four others were hired swordsmen who, like those guarding the island, had been recruited by Savelda to replace the mercenaries killed in Alsace by the troops serving the Sisters of Saint Georges.

The riders reached the building site and dismounted.

Only Savelda, the Alchemist, and the duchesse, however, passed beneath the roof protecting the pit and disappeared down the spiral staircase. Wearing the silver-studded leather patch over his left eye, the Spaniard led the way again with a confident air. His two companions wished to make sure that everything was ready for the ceremony the following evening. He already knew this to be the case. In preparation for the last-minute inspection, Savelda had even ordered candles to be lit underground. The same candles that were at this very moment aiding Leprat's exploration.

Leprat was a musketeer.

He did not know much about draconic magic, but enough to recognise all the signs indicating a spell chamber. The drapes embroidered with esoteric patterns. The tall black candles waiting to be lit. The small table for ritual items. The lectern to support the heavy grimoire as the incantatory formula were pronounced. The altar, a large platform carved from a single block. And finally, the pentacle engraved on the black stone floor and embossed with scarlet and golden glyphs.

But above all, there was an atmosphere of evil haunting this place. Whatever danger threatened the king, whatever the nature of the plot concocted by the Alchemist, it had something to do with this chamber which now only awaited the arrival of a sorcerer and, perhaps, a victim.

"Damn it!" Leprat muttered.

He started to feel ill.

He was suddenly very hot. His vision blurred. Dizzy, he felt his legs start to give way under him. He did not understand what was happening to him; indeed he had trouble keeping any wits at all. Then the disease eating away at his back awoke. It was as if the patch of ranse had come alive and was biting ever more deeply into his flesh. Leprat grimaced, fighting back moans of pain. In a feverish delirium of confused thoughts, he sensed that he had to leave this cursed chamber. He needed to get back to the surface and away from this place that was increasing tenfold the virulence of the ranse. He clung to this idea, concentrating on its urgency. He tottered back through the curtain. The pain lessened, but the dizziness remained. Gasping, his brow bathed in sweat, he staggered from column to column, moving in the direction of the staircase and the exit. He could barely see the way. His ears were filled with a buzzing sound and he failed to hear the party descending the steps. Sapped of his strength, he continued to stumble toward the door, which Savelda was going to open at any instant . . .

. . . when he felt a pair of arms seize hold of him and haul him away.

A gloved hand blocked his mouth.

"It's me," a familiar voice murmured in his ear.

Saint-Lucq.

Dressed entirely in black, the half-blood with the red spectacles dragged Leprat into a dark corner just before Savelda entered. The Black Claw's agent preceded madame de Chevreuse and her master of magic. He held a lit lantern in his left hand, as the candles burning in the hall of columns did little more than point the way to the spell chamber.

Halfway to the purple curtain, Savelda slowed and then came to a complete halt. His two companions imitated him, looking puzzled. He turned around with the expression of a man who senses he has overlooked something. The leather patch concealing his eye failed to mask the stain of the ranse that spread, starlike, toward his brow, his temple, and his cheekbone. His fist closed about the pommel of his rapier.

"What is it?" asked madame de Chevreuse.

"I thought . . . I thought I heard . . . I don't know. Something."

The gaze of the one-eyed man passed over Leprat and Saint-Lucq without seeing either of them. Saint-Lucq kept hold of the musketeer and had not taken his hand away from the other man's mouth. With a considerable effort, Leprat managed to control the shaking of his legs which risked betraying their presence.

"I didn't hear anything," said the duchesse. "Did you, Mauduit?"

"I heard nothing either, madame."

"It must have been a syle," Savelda conceded.

"Good Lord! There are salamanders down here?"

"This place is safe, madame," said the Spaniard as he reluctantly moved on. "My men have made sure of that. But down in the lower levels . . ."

The two men and the woman soon disappeared behind the curtain.

"You'll see," they heard madame de Chevreuse promising, "everything has been scrupulously arranged according to your instructions."

"Let's get out of here," said Saint-Lucq.

With the half-blood assisting Leprat, they returned to the open air by way of the spiral staircase, climbed out of the pit, slipped past Savelda's men, and found refuge in one of the pavilions under construction. Sitting with his back against a large block of stone, the musketeer took his time to recover, drawing in deep breaths while Saint-Lucq kept watch over their surroundings.

"Have they come back up?" he asked after a moment.

"Not yet."

"The duchesse was there, wasn't she? But who were the other two? I could barely see."

"One of them was Mauduit, the duchesse's master of magic. The other one was Savelda, a Spaniard working for the Black Claw. I almost had a chance to fight him when we prevented the vicomtesse de Malicorne from summoning the soul of an Ancestral Dragon."

"I missed all of that. I was in a gaol cell in the Grand Châtelet that night."

"That's true. . . . But what was wrong with you just now? It looked like you were overcome by a fever or by too much drink. . . ."

Without mentioning the ranse, which he wished to keep secret, Leprat spoke of the spell chamber and the effect that he suspected it had on him.

"I almost fell right into the arms of our enemies. If it hadn't been for you . . ." And when Saint-Lucq did not respond to this, the musketeer prompted him, "What were you doing down there?"

"At the cardinal's request, I have been watching Dampierre for several days now. I was intrigued by the pavilions that they were building here. And you?"

"I entered La Chevreuse's service by passing myself off as an agent of the queen mother. And, like you, I was curious about what this building site might be hiding."

The half-blood nodded.

Leprat crouched and as his wits returned to him along with his strength, he noticed that Saint-Lucq was gloved, booted, and impeccably dressed, as usual.

"You didn't get here by swimming."

"No. I came underground. There is a passage that leads to the old cellars here. No doubt it was once used by the residents of the tower in times of siege. The entrance lies beneath a very big oak tree in the forest, not far from a stone cross that stands where two paths meet. I discovered it when following Savelda's men. Several of them came back wounded and I wanted to know why. As it happens, the tunnel is swarming with enormous syles."

The Alchemist, Savelda, and the duchesse returned to the surface. Leprat and Saint-Lucq watched them depart, along with most of their hired swordsmen. The torches were extinguished. Only a handful of sentries remained.

"I better go back myself before someone notices my absence," said Leprat.

"Well, I'm going back down. I need to see this spell chamber with my own eyes."

"We must also inform La Fargue of our discoveries."

"I'll take care of that. I will be in Paris tomorrow."

"Understood."

"Have you fully recovered?"

"Yes. Don't worry about me."

The half-blood was about to leave when Leprat called him back: "You saved my life, Saint-Lucq. Thank you."

The other Blade gazed back at him from behind his red spectacles. He did not react, no doubt seeking a suitable response, to no avail.

And so he left.

In his turn, the musketeer slipped out of the unfinished pavilion. He tried to ignore the burning pain in his back, forcing himself to focus on the approaching day instead. He had lied to Saint-Lucq. He knew what was happening to him, although it cost him to admit it, even to himself.

The causeway was no longer guarded. Leprat crossed it quickly, then found his clothing and his horse in the forest. He did not spare his mount and arrived at the Château de Mauvières just as the night sky was beginning to grow pale, but before the cock's first crow. He left his horse in the stable and hurried back to his bedchamber.

But someone was watching him.

A new day dawned in Paris and, by midmorning, the air had already grown unpleasantly warm. From all its streets, all its courtyards, all its gutters, and all its ditches, the city's stink rose stronger than ever beneath the relentless sun. The sun's rays, however, did not reach sieur Pierre Teyssier's study. Behind closed shutters, His Eminence's master of magic had fallen asleep at his worktable after a hard night of labour, his head resting on his forearms, snoring loudly and drooling slightly.

He awoke suddenly to what sounded very much like an altercation in the stairway outside, complete with cries and the sound of blows being exchanged. He sat up, with bleary eyes and tousled hair, to gaze with astonishment and then alarm at the individual who had just burst into the room. He was a squat, solidly built man with white hair and a ruddy face. One could tell he was an old soldier from ten leagues off. He shoved his way past the valet who had been trying to deny him entry.

The tall, gangly young magic master rose and looked for a weapon to defend himself. He found nothing but consoled himself with the thought that he would in any case not have known how to use it.

"Monsieur?" he asked, mustering a degree of dignity.

"Please forgive this intrusion, monsieur. But the matter is an important one."

The valet, seeing that a conversation had been engaged, awaited the outcome.

"No doubt. However, I don't believe I know you."

"I am Ballardieu, monsieur. I am in the service of Captain La Fargue."

"In whose service?"

The question surprised Ballardieu. He hesitated, casting a wary glance at the valet before stepping forward, leaning over, clearing his throat, and whispering: "The company of the Cardinal's Blades, monsieur."

Realisation finally dawned upon Teyssier.

"La Fargue! Yes, of course . . ." he sighed with both relief and satisfaction which were readily shared by the old soldier . . .

. . . but which still failed to clarify the situation.

With uncertain smiles on their lips, the two men gazed at one another in silence, each of them expecting the other to speak. The valet also waited with a smile.

Until at last Teyssier enquired: "Well? La Fargue?"

The question woke Ballardieu from his daze. He blinked his eyes and announced: "The captain wishes to meet you."

"Today?"

"Yes."

Although he tended to be taken aback by unforeseen events, Teyssier was a young man of goodwill.

"Very well . . . Uhh . . . In that case . . . In that case, tell him that I shall receive him at a time of his convenience."

"No, monsieur. You need to come with me. The captain is waiting for you."

"Now?"

"Now."

"It's just that I don't go out much."

"Can you ride a horse?"

"Not very well."

"That's too bad."

* * *

An hour later, at the Hôtel de l'Épervier, Teyssier was still trying to convince himself that he had not actually been abducted. Feeling unsteady, he was finishing an ink drawing of the pentacle which Saint-Lucq had reported seeing at Dampierre and had described to him from memory. He found himself in the large fencing room, lit by the sunlight pouring through the three tall windows that looked out on the garden with its weeds, old table, and chestnut tree.

Carefully avoiding the scarlet gaze of the half-blood and his disturbing spectacles, Teyssier concentrated on his sketch, which he corrected and completed in the light of his own knowledge. He could not prevent himself, however, from glancing at La Fargue, who was slowly pacing up and down the room, or looking over at Marciac, who was sipping a glass of wine and daydreaming as he rocked back and forth on a creaking chair. Laincourt remained outside his field of vision, but Teyssier could sense the man behind him, watching over his shoulder as the drawing took shape. Silent and expressionless as ever, Almades guarded the door. As for Ballardieu, he had left the magic master in the front hall.

In fact, as soon as Teyssier had arrived at Hôtel de l'Épervier he had immediately been taken in hand by La Fargue, who explained what was required of him: a drawing of a pentacle based on a verbal description.

"Do you think this is possible, monsieur?"

"Yes. On condition that—"

"Because Laincourt, who knows something about magic, claims that the purpose of a pentacle can be divined from its appearance. Is that true?"

"Certainly, but—"

"Perfect! Then let's get to work, monsieur."

Time was indeed running short. The pentacle in question had probably been traced in preparation for a ritual that would take place that very night, during the ball being given by the duchesse de Chevreuse. And the Blades suspected this ritual of being a means, if not the ultimate end, of the plot against the king.

Teyssier, on the other hand, was growing more and more doubtful that this was the case. . . .

"There was a symbol resembling the letter N, here," Saint-Lucq was saying. "And over here, something that looked rather like the number 7. . . . And that's about all."

The young master of magic had recognised the two draconic glyphs recalled by the half-blood. He copied them onto the paper.

"Nothing else?" he asked.

"I don't think so."

He made a few revisions to his sketch and then turned the sheet of paper around and pushed it across the table toward Saint-Lucq.

"So it looked like this?"

The half-blood studied the drawing carefully and then nodded.

"As far as I can recollect, yes."

La Fargue ceased his pacing. Marciac stopped rocking in his chair. As for Laincourt, he straightened up with a puzzled look and said: "There must be some mistake. . . ."

"The drawing is just like the pentacle I remember," asserted Saint-Lucq crossing his arms.

"What?" asked the old captain. "Why would it be a mistake?"

Teyssier hesitated.

He exchanged a glance with Laincourt that confirmed the doubts and fears of both men. But still he kept silent. It was therefore the cardinal's former spy who announced: "This pentacle is beneficial, captain. It can't harm anyone. Neither the king, nor anyone else."

The king and his court arrived at Dampierre during the afternoon.

Louis XIII and the gentlemen of his suite rode at the head of the procession with panache, followed just behind by a detachment of musketeers. Pulled by a team of six magnificent horses, the king's golden coach followed. Then came that of the queen, and finally those of the great lords and courtiers, in order of their rank and favour. More riders in small groups brought up the rear; others trotted alongside the carriages so that they could converse with the passengers; while the most impetuous urged their mounts to prance and twirl in an effort to please the ladies who watched and laughed, bright-eyed, from behind their delicate fans.

Leaving the baggage train far behind, the parade of coaches was a splendid, joyful sight to behold, sparkling in the sun despite the dust that rose in its passage. It attracted crowds of spectators who gathered at the entrances of villages and along the roads. As it approached Dampierre, heralds spurred their horses forward to announce the coming of the king. While protocol required this, it was an unnecessary precaution. Runners had already cut across the fields to deliver breathless warnings at the castle, alarming those who had not yet finished erecting a platform, painting a fence, or raking a lawn. "The king! The king!" From the kitchens to the attic, and all the way out into the gardens, there was a great flurry of activity, with a final nail being hammered down just before the trumpets sounded.

Everything was ready, however, by the time His Majesty passed through the gates of Dampierre.

Leprat took advantage of this distraction to slip away from Rauvin, who had been breathing down his neck all morning. Although the mercenary was not following him openly, he was always somewhere in the background, no matter where Leprat went or what he did. The musketeer therefore had no choice but to carry out the tasks assigned to him by Mirebeau, who had become strangely distant. This coldness left Leprat perplexed, but he was not inclined to dwell on the matter. After all, Mirebeau must have worries of his own. For his part, Leprat had enough to think about between his mission, the danger posed by Rauvin, the underground spell chamber, and the possible plot against the king. And when he wasn't preoccupied by all that, his ranse—which he knew had taken a sudden turn for the worse—continued to haunt him.

But the king's arrival gave Leprat an opportunity to take a horse and discreetly get away on his own. There were things he needed to do in the woods and, in any case, he was better off avoiding Dampierre now that the castle was swarming with blue capes. Louis XIII never went anywhere without his regiment of musketeers, all of whom knew Leprat by sight and were thus liable to unmask him.

He rode for a quarter of an hour through the underbrush before coming across a path.

What was it Saint-Lucq had told him? *Beneath a very big oak tree in the forest, not far from a stone cross that stands where two paths meet.*

If Leprat wanted to explore the underground tunnels below the ruins of the black tower that once stood in the middle of the Dampierre pond, first he needed to find the entrance to them.

The afternoon was ending when Arnaud de Laincourt crossed the Petit Pont and, with long strides, passed beneath the dark archway of the Petit Châtelet.

His surmises upon seeing the pentacle described by Saint-Lucq had been confirmed by Teyssier, the cardinal's master of magic, who explained that there existed several different kinds of pentacles and, despite possible errors, omissions, and guesswork, the one he had drawn was intended for a beneficial ritual. Certain features of its general design left no room for doubt in the matter.

"I can affirm to you," he had said, "that the person who drew this pentacle did not wish to harm anyone. In fact, in my view, quite the opposite."

But Teyssier had been unable to say which particular type of ceremony the Dampierre pentacle was intended for. Protection, healing, benediction, rejuvenation? The sketch was too imprecise. He would have to compare it with all the others he had recorded in his grimoires and then, after careful cross-referencing, he might be able to reach a conclusion. Hearing that, La Fargue had permitted the magic master to return to his home, accompanied by Ballardieu, who would remain with him until the pentacle had been positively identified.

Laincourt followed the old and very narrow rue de la Bûcherie, toward Place Maubert.

Saint-Lucq had not lingered after Teyssier's departure, saying simply, "I'll see you this evening in Dampierre, no doubt." La Fargue, Marciac, and the cardinal's former spy had continued the discussion in the fencing room at the Hôtel de l'Épervier, while Almades contented himself with listening in. They had traded various hypotheses back and forth, trying to integrate the pentacle into a possible plot by the Alchemist and the duchesse de Chevreuse against the king. None of these speculations led anywhere. They didn't have enough facts and in the end were left with nothing but reasons to worry. Chief among them was the presence of Savelda, the Black Claw's most trusted henchman. The threat was therefore real.

Rather than continue going round in circles, Laincourt had decided to find out more about Mauduit, the duchesse's master of magic. After all, he was directly involved with the pentacle, wasn't he? Laincourt had thus gone to the Hôtel de Chevreuse, which he found almost empty and where he had learned nothing about Mauduit except that he had only recently entered the duchesse's service. The man was troubling and elusive. He was said to be a sorcerer. People tended to avoid having anything to do with him, and even the Swiss guard on duty at the mansion gate did not know his address in Paris.

After rue de la Bûcherie, Laincourt crossed Place Maubert which, at the entrance to rue de la Montagne-Sainte-Geneviève, was one of the five places in the city where prisoners were tortured and executed. Preoccupied by his mission, the young man did not even spare a glance for the gallows or the sinister wheel that was being set up on a new platform.

Upon leaving the Hôtel de Chevreuse, it occurred to him that the duchesse was fond of luxury. She only allowed herself the best, the most beautiful, and the most expensive items available. Her new master of magic was, no doubt, no exception to the rule. Mauduit had probably been recommended to her or was at least fairly renowned in certain circles. The fact that Laincourt didn't recognise his name wasn't significant, since the small world of magic masters was extremely secretive.

But there was someone who was well acquainted with this small world. On rue Perdue, Laincourt entered Bertaud's bookshop.

An hour later, just as night was falling, Laincourt arrived back at the Hôtel de l'Épervier, out of breath. He had hoped to find La Fargue still there, but the captain had already left for Dampierre with Almades and Marciac.

"What about Ballardieu?" he asked Guibot.

"Monsieur Ballardieu has not yet returned," replied the old porter.

"Too bad. Fetch me a horse. Quickly!"

But just then a rider entered the courtyard. It was Ballardieu. He had come from the home of Teyssier, who had finally succeeded in identifying the pentacle described by Saint-Lucq.

"You're not going to believe this!" the old soldier announced as he jumped down from the saddle.

But Laincourt did believe him.

He mounted Ballardieu's horse and left at a gallop.

As evening descended upon Dampierre, raised voices and bursts of laughter resounded in the small castle courtyard. Some Italian actors were performing, by torchlight, a lively farce which had all the guests enthralled. Even the king, who had little taste for bawdiness, appeared to be enjoying the comedy. He guffawed readily enough. Since he was normally of a dismal, brooding nature, his excellent humour astonished those observing him. It should, instead, have alarmed some of them.

La Fargue looked down into the courtyard from a first-storey window. The Italians' pranks did not amuse him. Since arriving at Dampierre he had asked to be received by monsieur de Tréville, captain of the King's Musketeers, and had communicated his suspicions to him: a plot against His Majesty was about to unfold. The two men knew, liked, and respected one another. But without taking La Fargue's warnings lightly, Tréville had assured him that Louis XIII could not be in danger because an elite company of gentlemen was there to protect him. The captain of the Musketeers nevertheless allowed La Fargue to remain, on the condition that he and his Blades would not hinder Tréville's own service. He also required that they stay away from the gardens, particularly once night fell.

"My musketeers don't know you and they have strict orders. They will open fire on your men, if they do not obey these instructions."

In the courtyard, before a painted backdrop, Arlecchino was kicking Matamoros's rear end, for vainly seeking the hand of Colombina in marriage.

In a decidedly joyful mood, Louis XIII was laughing heartily at the grotesque hopping of the actor each time he received a boot to the arse. It made a sharp contrast with the attitude of the queen, seated to the left of her husband, who was forcing herself to smile and, distracted, applauded with a slight delay. She was obviously preoccupied with something. . . .

"It will happen this evening," declared La Fargue in a grave tone. He looked up at the darkening sky where the stars were beginning to come out. "I can feel it. I know it. . . ."

Tréville was reading a note that one of his musketeers had just brought him. He nodded.

"Perfect," he said to the musketeer.

The man withdrew with a martial step and, folding up the piece of paper, the comte de Troisvilles, more commonly called Tréville, approached La Fargue and placed a friendly hand on his shoulder.

"You're obsessed with this Alchemist, my friend."

"No doubt. . . . But he is one of the kingdom's most formidable enemies. And I can sense his presence here."

Tréville shrugged his shoulders

"I can only repeat that all the necessary precautions to ensure His Majesty's safety have been taken."

"They may not be enough."

"I know. There are always unforeseen events."

Both men were haunted by the spectre of Henri IV's assassination. They remained silent for a moment and then La Fargue said: "The queen seems worried about something."

Tréville leaned forward to have a look.

"Indeed she does."

Turning from the window, La Fargue went over to open the door and called in Almades, who was waiting in the antechamber.

"Yes, captain?"

"Go and find Marciac. I want him to ask Agnès if the queen has any legitimate, admissible cause for concern."

"Understood, captain."

The Spaniard immediately complied, descending the stairs to find the Gascon, who was busy trying to work his charm on a very pretty and still very innocent young baronne. If there was little doubt that he wished for her to remain pretty, her innocence, on the other hand, was under serious threat. He was unflustered at seeing Almades, but promised the young woman that he would return, caressing her chin with his index finger and grinning before going over to the austere fencing master.

"I'm listening."

"The queen is preoccupied. Perhaps Agnès knows why."

"All right."

"And who is that you're with?"

"Delicious, isn't she?"

At that very instant, Matamoros finished covering himself in ridicule, the Dottore married Colombina off to Arlecchino, and the play ended to considerable applause.

"Don't delay, Marciac."

The Gascon thus hurried off, repeating his promise to the pretty young baronne as he passed, then seemed to change his mind by turning back and surprising the lady with a kiss on the cheek, before going in search of Agnès.

Thanks to Saint-Lucq's directions, Leprat located the secret passage leading to the black tower.

This edifice had long ago been taken apart stone by stone, before its very foundations were buried, no doubt so that all memory of it would be lost forever. But it had once stood in the middle of the pond at Dampierre, less than a cannon shot from the present castle belonging to the duc de Chevreuse. Legend said that a dragon sorcerer had built it and lived there. Legend also said he had worked terrible, evil magic and added that he had been finally vanquished by valiant knights. The tale might have been mostly invention, but Leprat was convinced the underground vestiges of the cursed tower had not yet given up all of their secrets.

The entrance to the passage lay in the forest, not far from a granite cross that stood where two tracks met. The way had recently been cleared to an old gate set in the brush-covered flank of a mound topped by a large oak tree. Behind the gate were stone steps, the beginnings of a narrow spiral staircase that led down into the darkness.

Leprat tethered his horse a good distance away, where it would not be spotted.

Then he approached the gate cautiously, creeping through the underbrush, his sword in his fist. He had feared that the place might be watched, but there was no one about. However, he did see numerous boot prints scattered across the ground, no doubt left by Savelda's men when they had opened a path to the passage. And close by, at the beginning of one of the tracks, there were traces indicating that horses had been guarded here.

Leprat had brought a lantern. He lit the candle with his tinder lighter and, without resheathing his rapier, started down the stairs.

At the bottom he found a long corridor leading in the direction of the pond, and the island.

In the castle courtyard, the guests had watched the comedy standing behind the royal couple. Still chuckling over the antics of the players, they were slow to disperse, walking toward the salons and stairways, or lingering to converse in the light of the great torches held aloft by lackeys in livery aligned at regular intervals with their backs to the wall, standing as still as Atlases on a palace façade. Supper was due to be served before the costume ball and a fireworks display that promised to be splendid.

With a quick step that betrayed her anxiety, Anne d'Autriche regained the apartments that madame de Chevreuse had assigned to her. Accompanied by the duchesse, she was trailed by the women of her suite, including Agnès de Vaudreuil, who was doing her best to keep up her role as a lady-in-waiting. She tried to be discreet, helpful, and considerate, taking care not to encroach where she was not wanted. With her hair and face prettily made up, this evening she was wearing a magnificent scarlet dress with a plunging neckline trimmed with lace, a starched bodice, and a hooped skirt. She knew she looked beautiful. Nevertheless, she had missed having her rapier these past few days since she had joined the queen's household. The stiletto dagger tucked in her garter was a poor substitute.

One of the last ladies to start up the great stairway, Agnès felt someone take her by the hand . . .

. . . and allowed Marciac to drag her behind a pillar.

"Do you know what's wrong with the queen?" he asked without any preamble.

"No. But she was in a very sombre mood when she woke this morning, and it has only grown worse since. In fact, she has spent most of the day in prayer."

"Try to find out more, all right?"

"All right. Where can I find the captain?"

"He is with Tréville."

"I'll do what I can."

"Say . . ."

"Yes?"

"We've been seen going off together on our own."

"So?"

"Perhaps we should kiss. To keep up appearances, of course."

"Or perhaps I should just slap you and adjust my attire as I leave. To keep up appearances, of course."

With a quirk at the corner of her lips, Agnès climbed the stairs as quickly as her dress and manners allowed. She passed between two halberdiers, opened the door to the queen's apartments, entered an antechamber, and smiled at the duc d'Uzès, who served as knight-of-honour. Proceeding to a second antechamber, she joined madame de Sénécey, a lady-in-waiting, the elderly madame de La Flotte, a royal wardrobe mistress, and several other attending ladies, including two ravishing young women, Louise Angélique de La Fayette and Aude de Saint-Avold. All of them were waiting in the antechamber unsure what to do because, bordering on tears, Anne d'Autriche had just shut herself up in her bedchamber with madame de Chevreuse.

On learning this news, Agnès adopted a suitably serious expression, asked whether there was anything she could do to assist, and upon being told there was not, she withdrew. Then she moved quickly without seeming to be in any great hurry. She smiled again at monsieur d'Uzès, left the apartments, and followed the corridor as far as a small door hidden behind a curtain. She waited until no one was looking at her and then promptly disappeared through this exit. She had discovered it that afternoon, during a discreet examination of the castle's layout.

The queen's bedchamber communicated with the antechamber where the ladies of her suite gathered, but also with another small room where the duchesse would sleep tonight, a bed having been installed there for the occasion. Agnès found this room lying empty. She slipped inside and, on tiptoe, went to press her ear to the door behind which Anne d'Autriche and madame de Chevreuse were alone.

One of them was pacing back and forth.

It was the queen who, in a nervous tone, was explaining that after much reflection and much prayer she no longer wished to go through with a certain project. That it was madness and she should never have agreed to it in the first place. How could she have ever believed in the success of this enterprise? But she saw things more clearly now. Yes, she was going to renounce the whole thing.

"Madame," the duchesse replied calmly, "there is still time to back out. Everything will be done according to your wishes. You only need to give the order."

"Very well. Then I am giving the order."

"What could be accomplished this evening may never be possible again. The stars are not—"

"I don't care about the stars!"

"Are you certain you have thought this through, madame? Your Majesty's duties—"

"My duties forbid me to betray the king! As for the rest, I must place myself in the hands of divine Providence. One day my prayers shall be heard."

"Has it occurred to you that if you renounce this project, you will still have to confess everything to the king? For the secret will come out, madame. Believe me, secrets always come out in the end. The cardinal's men are everywhere."

"I shall beg for the king's pardon."

"And for those who have lent you their assistance?"

"I will not allow you to be persecuted, Marie."

"I was not thinking of myself, but of all the others."

"How can one reproach them for having obeyed their queen?"

"Richelieu can, and he will."

There was a silence.

Then Agnès heard madame de Chevreuse rise and take a few steps. . . . A drawer was opened and closed. . . . Then her steps returned. . . . And the duchesse said: "I had hoped to spare you this ordeal, madame. I'd hoped that . . . Well, look at this."

"What is it?"

"I beg you, madame, read. And see what they have been hiding from you."

There was a rustling of heavy silk fabric: Anne d'Autriche had just sat down. The two women remained silent, until the queen asked in a strangled voice: "All this . . . Is it true?"

"I believe so. I fear so."

"The king really intends to repud—"

"Yes, madame."

The queen began to sob.

It might have been a spectral rider passing in the night.

But in fact it was a dust-covered Laincourt who was galloping on an ashen horse. He had been riding since Paris at a speed that risked killing his mount. He charged through villages, cut across fields and farmyards whenever possible, leapt over hedges, ditches, and streams, taking all manner of risks. He now knew the purpose of the pentacle. And thanks to his friend the bookseller, he also knew that the master of magic serving the duchesse de Chevreuse was not who he claimed to be.

Faster, boy! Faster!

Laincourt would arrive at the Château de Dampierre within the hour. But would he be in time?

At Dampierre, supper was being served, the queen having reappeared before anyone began to wonder about her absence.

Three tables had been set up in the castle's great hall. The high table was at the rear. The two others, much longer, faced one another and were perpendicular to the first. At these tables, the guests were seated on only one side, with their backs to the wall, while the servants waited on them from the space in the middle. Helped along by wine, the proceedings were very merry. Men and women ate with their fingers, exchanging anecdotes and jests, making fun of one another and laughing. Toasts were made, where a glass was passed from hand to hand, each person taking a small sip, until it reached the person to whom the toast was addressed. The recipient had no choice but to finish off the drink and, accompanied by cheers, eat the *tostée*, the piece of toasted bread that lay soaking at the bottom of the glass. These toasts went back and forth along the tables like playful challenges and provided an excellent pretext to become drunk. The selection of a new victim was greeted with expectant joy by all present, and of course no one dreamed of declining.

Naturally the king and queen sat at the high table, in the company of the duc de Chevreuse, the duchesse, and a few privileged individuals such as monsieur de Tréville and the marquis de Châteauneuf, the kingdom's Keeper of the Seals. The atmosphere was a little more formal than at the longer tables, although Louis XIII did honour to all the dishes—as was usual for him, since he had the same solid appetite as his father, Henri IV. Still looking pale, Anne d'Autriche only picked at her plate. Her eyes were a little red, causing madame de Chevreuse to worry aloud, as if on cue. The queen explained that she was suffering irritation from the heavy fragrance of a bouquet of flowers in her bedchamber. Did this little comedy fool anyone? It made the king smile, at any rate.

Retained by her duties as a lady-in-waiting, Agnès was unable to escape until halfway through the meal. Slipping out of the hall, she found La Fargue and Marciac in the dimness of an out-of-the-way antechamber. Almades closed the door behind her as soon as she arrived.

"Well?" demanded the Gascon.

Agnès recounted the conversation she had overheard between the queen and madame de Chevreuse.

"So La Chevreuse has indeed hatched a plot against the king," concluded La Fargue. "A plot that will unfold tonight. And the queen is an accomplice. . . ."

"But what exactly is it all about?" asked Marciac. "Are they going to make an attempt on His Majesty's life?"

"I don't know," Agnès admitted.

"Was there any mention of the Alchemist?"

"No. But I think I know the queen's motives. . . . After she and the duchesse left, I slipped into her bedchamber to look for whatever the duchesse gave her to read in order to persuade her. And I found it. It was the pamphlet that the queen mother's emissary was carrying hidden in the lining of his doublet."

"The pamphlet that accuses the king of planning to repudiate the queen because she has not borne him an heir?" asked La Fargue.

"And claims that the king has begun negotiations with the pope on the subject, yes."

"So the queen has become involved in a plot against the king because she fears repudiation. . . ."

"Well, yes . . ."

"But the king will never repudiate her!" exclaimed Marciac. "Anne is the sister of the king of Spain. It would be an insult! It would mean war!"

"It is enough that the queen believes it to be true," Agnès pointed out. "Or rather, it is enough that the duchesse has persuaded her that it is so. . . ."

The captain of the Blades nodded.

"Very well," he said. "I must speak to Tréville. Agnès, you must return to the queen and try not to let her out of your sight. The ball will begin soon."

Leprat ran through a syle as it tried to scurry between his legs and, on the point of his sword, held it up to the light from his lantern. With thick red arabesque patterns running down its black back, the salamander was as long and as heavy as a fair-sized rat. It squirmed on the sharp steel that was tormenting it, spitting and seeking to bite and claw at him rather than to work itself free.

Filthy creature, thought Leprat as he cleared his blade with a quick flick that sent the reptile flying.

The syle crashed into a wall, then fell to the ground with a soft thump. It was still alive, however. In the dark, forked tongues hissed. The sound preceded the massed rush that the musketeer was expecting. With claws clattering and bellies scraping against the stone, syles closed in from all directions to devour the injured member of their own kind. The excitement of combat and the scent of blood soon produced a predictable effect. The reptiles' scaly backs began to glow and their furious melee, invisible up until now, became wreathed in a faint halo. The sacrificed syle was not the only victim of this savage frenzy. Others, wounded in turn, were attacked and eaten by bigger and more ferocious individuals.

Leprat turned away from the carnage.

Sword in hand, he continued his exploration of the underground chambers of the black tower, chambers whose scale he was still attempting to grasp. They were vast, perhaps immense, in any case far bigger than the two or three cellars he had imagined he would find beneath the ruins of a medieval donjon. Most of the rooms had flagstone floors with short round pillars supporting low, vaulted ceilings. Standing empty and bare, haunted only by the furtive movements of the syles guarding them, and dotted with puddles that the musketeer disturbed with his tread, these chambers had survived the passing centuries down here in a dark, abysmal silence.

La Fargue managed to send a note to Tréville and met him privately after the banquet. He informed him of the conversation Agnès had overheard between the queen and the duchesse de Chevreuse, affirmed that there was no longer any doubt that a plot was about to be sprung and insisted that the king's security be reinforced until morning.

In vain.

"I will not increase the patrols or the number of sentries," replied the captain of the Musketeers.

"The king's safety is under threat, monsieur."

"Perhaps. But I cannot go against the will of His Majesty, who has demanded that my musketeers be as little visible as possible, in order to display his lack of concern over sleeping within these walls—"

"—and thereby further relax the vigilance of those he will have arrested tomorrow," deduced La Fargue.

"Precisely. On the other hand, if the castle, for whatever reason, should suddenly be swarming with blue capes . . ."

The old gentleman nodded in resignation.

His left hand on the pommel of the old Pappenheimer in his scabbard, the other hand gripping the loop of his heavy belt, he turned to the window and lifted his eyes to the night sky.

"Besides," added Tréville, "the ball is about to begin. The king will open it with the queen and then, as he said he would, he will retire for the night, on the pretext that he needs his rest before the hunt the duc de Chevreuse has organised for him in the morning. . . . So the king will soon be in his apartments, with musketeers at his door and even in his antechamber."

A musketeer entered and announced to his captain: "A rider has just arrived. He claims to have urgent information concerning the safety of the king."

"His name?"

"Laincourt. A former member of the Cardinal's Guards."

La Fargue spun round.

After the ordeal of his long ride, Laincourt was trying to make himself presentable when Marciac found him in the stable courtyard. In his shirt sleeves, he was washing his face and neck with water from a bucket. Upon seeing the Gascon, he quickly dried himself with a towel and pulled on the freshly brushed doublet held out to him by a servant.

"I must speak to the captain," he declared, giving a coin to the servant and accepting his hat in return.

"I will take you to him," replied Marciac.

"Good."

Grabbing his sword as he passed, Laincourt matched his stride to that of the Gascon, who asked him: "Any news from Teyssier?"

"Yes. He finally recognised the pentacle."

"So?"

"It is a pentacle of fecundity, employed in a ritual intended to make a barren womb fertile."

"Are you sure of that?"

"No. But according to Ballardieu, His Eminence's magic master was positive. That's enough for me."

They crossed the small drawbridge just as the first notes of music from the ball sounded within the castle.

As he continued exploring the ancient underground spaces beneath the black tower, sword in one hand and his lantern in the other, Leprat wondered who had built them and to what end.

They called to mind a sanctuary or refuge that might have once sheltered a community of sorcerers, or members of a heretical sect, or dragons. Who could say? The only thing for certain was that this place was no longer—if it had ever been—a peaceful haven. It was as if its walls were impregnated with an evil that weighed upon the soul. Its silence seemed haunted by painful echoes and its shadows hid lurking nightmares. And the air he breathed had . . .

Leprat suddenly realised his mind was starting to wander.

He shook his head and shoulders in an effort to gather his wits.

He could not allow these sinister chambers to take control of his thoughts. No doubt he had been wandering down here for too long. How long had it been, in fact? No matter. The musketeer deemed that he had seen enough. Besides, he noticed that the syles were starting to become dangerously bold and, to make matters worse, the flame in his lantern was showing signs of weakness.

Rather than retrace his steps, Leprat looked for stairs leading upward. But it was, instead, a door that caught his eye: a large, black double door whose stone lintel was decorated with entwined draconic motifs. Intrigued, he approached cautiously. He listened closely and heard nothing within, then drew in a breath before pushing one half of the door open . . .

. . . to find himself in a circular room beneath an onyx dome.

Vast but empty, it was plunged in a dim amber light, coming from the glowing golden veins in the black marble that lined the floor and ran around the room in a frieze where the dome rose from the wall. The room had a large well at its centre. And four identical doors—including the one by which Leprat had entered—which faced one another in pairs as if marking the cardinal points of a compass.

The musketeer set down his now useless lantern and stepped forward, keeping his rapier unsheathed. He became filled with the conviction that the black tower had once risen directly above this dome which he examined with an attentive eye. But his thoughts were interrupted by a sound that made him turn round.

Mirebeau was aiming a cocked pistol at him.

"A fertility ritual," repeated La Fargue after listening to Laincourt's report.

"That's what Teyssier claims. And we already knew that this pentacle was not harmful in purpose. . . ."

They were in a small room adjoining Tréville's bedchamber. The captain of the Musketeers had allowed the Blades to meet here while he watched over the opening of the ball. The orchestra was playing at the other end of the castle. They could hear the music rising through the open windows into the warm night.

"Might the pentacle be for the duchesse de Chevreuse?" suggested Marciac. "After all, we're here in her home and it is her master of magic who—"

"She has already had six children," Laincourt pointed out.

"No," said La Fargue. "The ritual is intended for the queen. She has not yet provided an heir to the throne and we know she now fears being repudiated."

"We do?"

"This evening Agnès overheard a conversation between the queen and the duchesse," the Gascon explained to the cardinal's former spy. "Very upset, the queen said that she wanted to renounce . . . we don't quite know what. In order to overcome her misgivings, the duchesse gave her the pamphlet that the queen mother's secret emissary had on his person. You recall it?"

"Yes. Claiming the king intends to repudiate the queen."

"We believed this prospect was enough to convince the queen to participate in the final act of a plot against the king. An act that would take place this evening or later in the night."

"It seems we were wrong," concluded La Fargue.

His eyes became absorbed in thought.

Anne d'Autriche was desperate to become a mother. But the years had passed leaving her prayers unanswered and now, in addition to suffering from the king's estrangement and attacks from within his court, she faced the despicable threat of repudiation. . . .

"So the queen has decided to resort to magic in order to become fertile," Marciac reflected out loud. "As for the duchesse de Chevreuse, she has taken it upon herself to arrange the whole matter with the aid of her new master of magic. And all this is taking place in utmost secrecy, as one might imagine. For if it were discovered that a queen of France—"

"A queen of Spanish origin, moreover," added Laincourt.

"—was subjecting herself to a draconic ritual . . ."

The Gascon judged that there was no need to finish his sentence.

"Whatever the queen's motives," said Laincourt, "the king will not pardon her. In addition to other considerations, he has despised all magical arts ever since La Galigai was beheaded for bewitching his mother."

"Not to mention the fact that an heir born in such circumstances could only be—"

Once again, Marciac did not complete his sentence, but this time because Almades had knocked on the door and entered.

La Fargue shot him a questioning look.

"Their Majesties have just opened the ball," the Spaniard reassured him. "All is well."

"And Agnès?"

"I saw her and she saw me. She did not seem alarmed."

"Very well. Thank you."

Almades nodded and returned to keeping track of the comings and goings in the castle.

"The king must be warned about what is afoot," said Marciac after a moment of silence. "But there is no plot. Only a desperate queen."

"You're forgetting a little quickly that the Alchemist and the Black Claw are also mixed up in this," replied the old captain. "Last night, Saint-Lucq formally recognised Savelda in the company of the duchesse and Mauduit."

"True, at least as far as Savelda and the Black Claw are concerned. But as for the Alchemist, we only have La Donna's word that—"

"What does it matter?" asked La Fargue, raising his voice. "Why would the Black Claw want to help the queen have a child? Why would it favour the birth of a royal heir and thereby put an end to the divisions weakening the kingdom? And why the devil would it seek to prevent a repudiation of the queen which, if it were merely hinted at by the king, would be enough to provoke a war between France and Spain . . . ? Do you even have the beginning of an answer to any of these questions?"

"No," admitted Marciac, lowering his eyes.

"There is a plot!" declared the captain of the Blades between clenched jaws. "There is a plot, and the Alchemist is at its head!"

The Gascon did not reply, but turned his head away.

"Captain," ventured Laincourt.

"What?"

"It's about Mauduit. I'm not sure, but . . . well, here's the thing. One of my friends is a bookseller and I was able to consult a very rare work that he has in his shop, of which Mauduit is the author. There was a portrait at the front of the book and . . . I know these engravings can often be misleading, captain. But this picture looked nothing at all like the man serving the duchesse de Chevreuse as her magic master."

For a long moment La Fargue remained immobile, silent, and expressionless. Could Mauduit be the Alchemist? The conviction slowly took shape in his mind, and at last he began to grasp the nature of the plot against which La Donna had warned them.

"The Alchemist," he said in a grave voice, "plans to abduct the queen."

* * *

His pistol aimed at Leprat, Mirebeau crossed the threshold of the circular room but did not come any closer. Perhaps he feared to advance any further beneath the rock dome. Perhaps he was reluctant to step on the slabs of black marble with their strangely glowing golden veins. Perhaps he preferred to keep his distance from the man who, sword in hand, was looking him straight in the eye without blinking.

They stood about seven metres apart. The musketeer had his back to the well, the other man had the dark cellars of the black tower behind him.

"What is this room?" asked Leprat. "What is its purpose?"

"I don't know. Just as I didn't know of the existence of these underground chambers until I followed you. Indeed, one might be surprised to find you of all people down here. . . ."

Leprat did not reply.

"But considering that I am the one holding the pistol," Mirebeau continued, "let us agree that I shall be the one who asks the questions. All right? Good. Who are you, monsieur?"

"My name will tell you nothing."

"Nevertheless, please satisfy my curiosity."

"I am Antoine Leprat, chevalier d'Orgueil."

"A musketeer?"

"Yes."

"Nothing else?"

"No."

"A spy, then."

"I obey the cardinal's orders in the service of the king."

"A musketeer who obeys the cardinal? Is that possible?"

"It is in my case."

"And the real Guéret?"

"Dead."

"Killed by your hand?"

"No."

"On that point, I'll have to take your word, won't I? Since you are a gentleman, I won't ask you to relinquish your sword. But please return it to its scabbard. . . ."

Leprat honoured his request.

Mirebeau looked at him sadly. He was slightly more relaxed but still had not lowered his weapon.

"What am I to do with you, monsieur le chevalier d'Orgueil?"

"As you said: you are the one holding the pistol."

"I offered you my friendship. I offered you my friendship and you accepted it."

"Yes."

"You betrayed my trust."

"I know."

"Don't misunderstand me. I don't blame you. It was me. I made a mistake. Why didn't I listen to Rauvin's initial warnings? Unlike me, he saw right through you from the beginning. Did you know I took your side this morning when Rauvin claimed to see you returning on horseback before dawn from some mysterious errand? I thought he was slandering you out of jealousy, that he had not forgiven you for behaving better than he did on that famous night when the comte de Rochefort arrested me. After all, he fled while you stayed behind to free me. But I imagine that was just to safeguard your mission, wasn't it? And to win my trust."

When Leprat failed, again, to reply, Mirebeau let out a desolate sigh.

"Fortunately, the friendship that I felt for you did not completely blind me. And that brings us to this. . . . What am I to do with you, monsieur le chevalier d'Orgueil? Rauvin would shoot you down."

"You won't do that. You're a gentleman."

"So are you. Let us settle this affair as gentlemen, then."

The musketeer shook his head.

"I feel both friendship and esteem for you, Mirebeau. Don't make me cross swords with you. . . . Besides, it would be futile."

"Futile?"

"Tomorrow, at the break of dawn, the marquis de Châteauneuf will be arrested for treason, among other things. So will the duchesse de Chevreuse and all those who have plotted the downfall of the cardinal, or against the king. Everything is ready. The orders have already been signed and Tréville's musketeers are masters of Dampierre. His Majesty has already won the match. But you are guilty of nothing but loyally serving a master who proved unworthy."

"What do you know about that?"

"I know you to be a man of honour, Mirebeau. Nothing obliges you to pay the price for the crimes of Châteauneuf. Nothing."

"One is not always free to choose."

"Châteauneuf fancied that he might one day replace the cardinal. Forgetting all that he owed Richelieu, he schemed against him. His ambition has made him lose everything. Don't accompany him in his downfall."

Mirebeau hesitated.

"It's . . . It's too late," he finally said.

"No!"

Leprat felt that he could persuade—and save—this gentleman.

"Leave," he said. "This very night. Take a horse and go without further delay. Don't let the king's justice catch up with you. And before long you'll be forgotten. . . ."

Mirebeau reflected for a moment. The arm holding the pistol was no longer quite as steady as before when the point of a blade suddenly punched through his chest. He stiffened and gazed down with eyes widened in shock at the length of bloody steel which then vanished almost as quickly as it had appeared. He hiccupped, coughed up blood, and gave Leprat a last incredulous look before falling to his knees, then facedown against the hard marble floor.

Rapier in his fist, Rauvin stepped over the dead body and advanced, followed by five hired swordsmen.

"I do believe he would have accepted your offer," he said, "but I grew tired of waiting. . . ."

Having opened the ball with the queen and paid her a much remarked-upon compliment, the king retired to his apartments. He had announced his intention to make the most of the game-filled forests of the Chevreuse valley, and go hunting early the following morning. He had promised, however, to watch the fireworks display that would be the high point of the evening from his window. The gentlemen who were his closest attendants, including the comte de Tréville, had followed him. And since the castle could not be taken by assault, the musketeers now reduced their watch over the area outside to mount an extremely vigilant guard at the doors, along the corridors, and in the antechambers.

Arnaud de Laincourt discreetly stole a mask that he saw lying on a bench, put it on, and began to mingle with the courtiers who chattered, drank, and nibbled as they watched the dancers—two by two—execute a graceful choreography to the sound of the music played by the orchestra. Everyone had disguised the upper portion of their face behind a mask. But if those worn by the men were relatively sober, those of the women—matching their dresses—boasted a profusion of gold and silver brocade, plumes and ribbons, pearls and jewels. Wearing their finest attire, the royal court provided a superb spectacle that evening, beneath the gilt of Dampierre. In their display of elegant luxury and playful insouciance, the courtiers seemed completely unaware of the danger threatening them.

Laincourt tried to find Agnès.

He caught sight of her near the dais reserved for Their Majesties. Now only the queen occupied her armchair. It was impossible to approach her. She was surrounded by madame de Chevreuse and by her ladies-in-waiting, who were seated according to their rank on chairs, stools, or cushions. They gossiped and laughed behind their fans, the youngest and least dignified among them pointing out the gentlemen they liked best. Among the dancers, the marquis de Châteauneuf in particular attracted much commentary, although most of it was not in praise. Watching out of the corner of his eye to see if the duchesse de Chevreuse was glancing in his direction, he exerted himself with each movement to adopt the most advantageous poses. But his age of over fifty rendered all these efforts somewhat ridiculous.

Spotting Laincourt, Agnès joined him by a window overlooking the moat and the great Renaissance flower beds among which couples strolled in search of a quiet corner.

"Did La Fargue let you know?" asked the young man.

"Yes."

"It's now more important than ever that you remain with the queen."

"I know."

It was a trap.

The fertility ritual which the queen was supposed to undergo was nothing but a trap intended to lure her away, with her own consent, from the guards who watched over her. The Chatelaines' Superior General had been right: there was a plot threatening the queen. A plot in which madame de Chevreuse was a participant, acting in the belief that she was serving Anne d'Autriche's interests. A plot hatched by the Black Claw and the Alchemist, who had usurped the place of the duchesse's master of magic. A plot, finally, whose object was to abduct the queen.

But after that?

"It will happen tonight," said Laincourt. "And it cannot be done without the complicity of others. That of the duchesse, certainly. But also that of most of the ladies in her entourage, whom the queen has probably won over to her cause. . . . Since you are not a part of the plan, they will try to divert you at the crucial moment. Keep your eye out. And be careful."

"Don't worry."

"Marciac was looking for you a short while ago and could not find you."

The baronne de Vaudreuil reflected for an instant.

"Yes. It must have been when I went to fetch the queen's jewel box. Her pearl necklace broke just after the king retired to his quarters."

"And the queen? Where was she?"

"She was waiting in the antechamber for me to return so that we could change her finery."

Laincourt nodded distractedly as his gaze slowly swept over the queen and her entourage.

Then he frowned.

"I don't see Aude de Saint-Avold," he said.

Agnès turned toward the group formed by the maidens-of-honour and their governess, at the foot of the royal dais.

"You're right," she replied.

"Do you know where she is?"

"No."

The cardinal's former spy became worried. If Agnès—because she was a newcomer to the queen's suite—could be diverted when it came time to execute the plot, Aude was a different matter.

Like everyone else, the queen was wearing a mask.

Without meaning to, Laincourt caught her eye . . .

. . . and suddenly recognised—now looking alarmed as she realised she had been found out—the face of Aude de Saint-Avold.

"They've already abducted the queen!" he shouted as he left Agnès standing there.

Unlike Mirebeau, Rauvin had not ventured alone into the underground chambers. He was accompanied by five mercenaries whom he immediately ordered to attack Leprat.

That's one, counted the musketeer as he ran his sword through the first man to come within reach.

He freed his blade, dodged an attack, parried another, and forced his opponents to retreat with a few furious moulinets.

He then returned to the *en garde* position and waited with his back to the well which, beneath the dome, marked the centre of the circular room. The four mercenaries supposed that he was allowing them the initiative in making the next assault. They started to deploy in an arc. If the man before them was foolish enough to let them organise themselves, they would take advantage of the fact. . . .

But in fact he wanted them to spread out in a row.

And to gain confidence.

So that they would lower their guard slightly.

Leprat suddenly attacked with a great shout. He deflected one mercenary's sword, stunned another with a blow of his fist to the chin, spun around as he raised his blade to shoulder height, and carried through his motion by slitting the throat of the freebooter who was about to strike him from behind.

That's two.

The man staggered backward, choking, his right hand trying desperately to staunch the wound from which blood was flowing freely, while his left hand flailed in the air, seeking a shoulder, a support, help of any kind. He finally fell backward and lay still.

Leprat gave himself space to face a renewed attack. It was led by two mercenaries who knew how to fight a lone opponent without hindering one another. Taking a step back, and then another, the musketeer had to defend himself against two men and two sets of skills. Against two blades which he finally managed, with a single slash of his own weapon, to force away from his own body and downward to the ground. His move unbalanced both his adversaries and made one of them particularly vulnerable. Leprat delivered a blow with his fist that caused the man to stumble forward, right into the waiting knee that lifted his chin sharply and broke his neck with a sinister crack.

Three down.

Only two mercenaries remained.

Parrying a high sword stroke from one man, Leprat pushed the other back with a violent kick to the stomach. Then he surprised the first by elbowing him in his Adam's apple and finished him off by head-butting him right in the face. His nose and mouth covered in blood, the man crumpled to the black marble floor.

Four.

The last mercenary was already charging him from behind.

Leprat spun and riposted in a single movement of lethal fluidity. He was still only halfway round and bending his knees when he blocked a vicious cut. Then he rose, letting the other man's blade slide down his own until it reached the hilt. Finally, he completed his turn by plunging a dagger he had snatched from the belt of his previous opponent into the mercenary's belly. The unfortunate wretch froze, dropping his blade and fumbling at the dagger's hilt. He collapsed after managing a few erratic steps.

And that makes five.

Out of breath, his brow shining with sweat and his eyes blazing, Leprat turned toward Rauvin and once again placed himself *en garde*.

"My congratulations," said the hired killer as he drew his sword. "Now it's just the two of us."

He slashed at the air with his blade and the duel commenced.

At Dampierre, three silhouettes were crossing the duchesse de Chevreuse's private garden. Closed to guests on a false pretext, this little park adjoining the castle was now standing empty except for shadows. The trio, all wearing dark cloaks, were obviously in a hurry. They turned back several times toward the windows as if they feared being seen and hid themselves whenever the moon peeped out from between the clouds.

The one who claimed to be Mauduit, master of magic, was leading them.

"This way, madame."

Anne d'Autriche followed him, unaware that she was placing her fate in the hands of the Black Claw's most formidable agent. She was accompanied by a chambermaid who, when the moment came, she believed, would help her to disrobe and put on the ritual garment before the ceremony that would at last let her become a mother. The young servant girl was trembling and casting frightened looks all around, but was ready to do anything in the service of her queen. Both of them were wearing black velvet masks beneath their large hoods.

At the rear of the garden, they came to a gate set in the wall.

"Be brave, madame," murmured the Alchemist. "The hardest part is over. Once we reach the cover of the trees, we can no longer be seen from the castle."

He opened the gate with a key the duchesse de Chevreuse had given him and then held his hand out to the queen to assist her passage over a small wooden bridge, a sort of covered walkway that allowed strollers to cross the moat and enter the orchard.

There were armed men waiting on the other side, beneath the trees, some of them carrying dark lanterns.

"Who are these men?" asked the queen in a worried voice, but stopping herself from retreating.

"Your escort, madame. Don't be afraid."

Anxious but still resolved to see the matter through, Anne d'Autriche nodded. She drew closer to her servant, however, and took her hand while the Alchemist exchanged a few words in a low voice with a one-eyed man whose face was visibly marked by the ranse. With an olive complexion and craggy features, the man was wearing a black leather patch adorned by silver studs over his missing eye. It was Savelda, although the queen remained ignorant of his name. Just as she was unaware that he was the henchman most valued by the masters of the Black Claw.

He finally nodded in agreement, and the false magic master returned to the two women.

"All is well, madame," he affirmed. "However, we must hurry because it will soon be midnight. The coach that will take us to the place of the ceremony is waiting at the gate to this orchard."

But Savelda, who was about to take the lead, suddenly froze, with the absent gaze and slightly tilted head of someone listening very intently.

"What is it now?" asked the Alchemist in an irritated tone.

Without turning round, the Black Claw's envoy lifted an imperious index finger: he demanded silence. After which, he called out softly to the three men he had left as sentries in the orchard.

There was no answer.

Savelda snapped his fingers, and two of the hired swordsmen accompanying him approached.

"Go and have a look," he said with a strong Spanish accent that drew the queen's attention.

The two men unsheathed their swords and ventured out cautiously. One of them held a lantern in his left hand and a pistol in his right.

They had not taken ten steps when they came across a dead body, while an individual emerged from the shadows beneath the fruit trees. The proud, elegant assurance of the stranger worried them only slightly less than the faint smile they detected on his lips. He was dressed entirely in black, except for the slender feather decorating his hat: it was scarlet, as were the round spectacles hiding his eyes. His left hand rested nonchalantly on the pommel of his rapier in its scabbard.

The two hired swordsmen placed themselves *en garde*. The one with the pistol aimed it at Saint-Lucq, but as he continued to advance they slowly retreated until they had rejoined Savelda and the others.

The half-blood halted and brandished a pistol of his own in his right hand. In response, three more pistols pointed at him and blades were unsheathed. The queen and her chambermaid jumped, stifling startled cries. Saint-Lucq did not even blink.

"You will go nowhere with the queen," he said in an even tone.

"Do you intend to stop us on your own?" asked Savelda with a sneer.

"I've already started to."

"Give it up. The numbers are in our favour."

Saint-Lucq conspicuously pointed his pistol at the one-eyed man's brow.

"If I fire, or you do, the place will be swarming with musketeers. Is that really what you want?"

"Monsieur, tell me what is going on?" the queen asked the Alchemist. "Who is this man and why is he trying . . ."

She trailed off, shocked at finding herself ignored by the master of magic, who instead stepped forward among the swordsmen to address the half-blood: "Then why don't you shoot? Are you afraid of wounding Her Majesty?"

"My pistol ball will not miss its target."

"To be sure, but after that? You are familiar with the hazards of battle, aren't you?"

"I am also familiar with them," said a voice that no one had expected to hear.

Flanked by Marciac and Laincourt to his left and right, La Fargue had entered the orchard. They had arrived from the garden, their blades already pointed in the direction of their enemies.

"And I tell you that if you harm the queen in any way," the captain of the Blades added, "your death will owe nothing to the hazards of battle."

Defended by steep moats, the Château de Dampierre had only two exits: its guarded drawbridge and the small gate at the rear of the deserted garden. Thus the Blades had no difficulty in guessing which way Anne d'Autriche had been taken. Leaving Almades behind to gain access to the king's apartments and alert Tréville as quickly as possible, La Fargue had decided to go in pursuit of the queen without delay.

And in pursuit of the Alchemist of the Shadows.

The Alchemist now turned to the old gentleman. He recognised him and gave a twisted smile.

"La Fargue? Is that you?"

"It's me, Alchemist. Or whatever your real name is."

"We meet at last! We almost met at La Rochelle, but . . . Ah! We both know what happened there, don't we?"

Savelda and his swordsmen had clustered round the Alchemist and the two women. Calm and resolute, they placed themselves on guard against attack from either direction. Rapiers in their hands, some of them also had pistols aimed at Saint-Lucq, on one side, or at La Fargue, Laincourt, and Marciac, on the other. They waited for an order, conscious of the fact that the first pistol to be fired would raise an alarm. The music coming from the castle would not be loud enough to cover the sound of shots. It merely drifted hauntingly through the otherwise silent orchard.

Anne d'Autriche and her chambermaid were clinging to one another in fright.

"This man has abused your trust, madame," said the captain of the Blades. "He is in the service of the Black Claw and is conspiring to bring about Your Majesty's ruin."

The queen turned her worried but furious eyes to the Alchemist.

"What do you have to say, monsieur? Will you deny it?"

He shrugged.

"What good would it do?" he replied before coughing, short of breath, into his handkerchief. "It would seem the play is over, is it not?"

La Fargue frowned.

There were four Blades. Savelda and his men numbered ten in all and they were in possession of a most precious hostage. Taking that into consideration, the Alchemist's defeatism was troubling, to say the least.

It proved unbearable to Savelda.

"Enough!" he spat.

The queen's attendant screamed and promptly fainted when the one-eyed man seized her by the wrist and roughly threw her aside. Before anyone else could react, the Spaniard was clutching Anne d'Autriche against his body, threatening to slit her throat with a dagger.

The same exclamation escaped from the lips of both La Fargue and the Alchemist.

"No!"

"I won't hesitate!" Savelda promised.

"You fool!" the Alchemist swore at him.

"I won't surrender!"

"Don't you understand? We just need to wait!"

"Wait for what?"

In the castle, the musicians ceased playing.

The silence became immense.

"Oh, Lord!" murmured Marciac as realisation dawned on him.

There was a whistling noise . . .

. . . and the first rocket exploded in the night sky.

The Spaniard's men immediately fired their pistols. The detonations cracked and balls whizzed past the ears of the Blades as they charged forward.

One of them struck Laincourt in the shoulder, halting him in his tracks. A chaotic battle broke out beneath the boughs of the trees in the orchard.

In the underground chambers of the black tower, under the dome of the room paved with golden-veined black marble, Leprat was engaged in a duel to the death with Rauvin.

And he was losing.

It had not taken him long to realise that his opponent was of a different calibre to the mercenaries whose bodies lay scattered across the luminescent floor. Like them, Rauvin had experience. But he also had talent. His strokes were quick, precise, and powerful. Although driven by a ferocious hatred of the musketeer, he kept his calm.

Surprised by a thrust, Leprat was forced to step back and parry several times as Rauvin launched a series of attacks, high and low, in rapid succession. Their blades ended up crossed near the hilts and the two men circled before shoving one another away roughly, both of them nearly stumbling.

Leprat moved back, seeking room to manoeuvre.

No longer able to conceal the fact that he was struggling, he feared Rauvin would try to wear him down. His combat with the freebooters had drained him and he sensed that he had still not recovered from the worsening of the ranse that had struck him the previous day. Indeed, he wondered if he would ever truly recover. He was also wielding a rapier made of ordinary steel, which demanded far more of his wrist than the elegant ivory blade to which he was accustomed.

All things considered, the only point in his favour was the fact that he was left-handed.

It was not much of an advantage.

Rauvin attacked, obliging Leprat to step back again. But with a wide swing of his blade, the musketeer forced the other man to expose himself and landed a nasty right hook with his fist. The hired swordsman staggered. Emboldened by this success, Leprat seized the upper hand and made his opponent retreat. Rauvin quickly pulled himself together, however, feinting and slashing at face height. That stopped Leprat's momentum as he had to duck in order to avoid being disfigured.

Rauvin managed to disengage and quickly discarded his doublet which was making him uncomfortably hot.

For his part, Leprat caught his breath.

He had lost a lot of energy in this last assault and his wrist was hurting him more and more. Sweat was making his hair stick to his brow and his eyes sting.

"It looks like you're having a hard time," observed Rauvin ironically. "Age, no doubt. . . ."

Leprat, who was approaching forty, displayed a weary smile.

"I . . . I still have some resources left. . . ."

"Really? And for how much longer?"

Both remained *en garde*, circling and giving each other a measuring stare.

Rauvin suddenly delivered a cut, which Leprat parried and then riposted. After that, there was a whole series of parries and ripostes, one man retreating while the other advanced, and then vice versa as the advantage switched direction. Their soles slipped on the dark marble and the heels of their boots clattered beneath the great dome. Their blades clashed with a clear ringing sound. Their features tightened and their gaze became fixed with the strain of their efforts.

Leprat was weakening.

He wanted to put an end to matters and delivered a false attack. It fooled the hired swordsman who was expecting a flurry of strikes and had modified his guard position accordingly, exposing himself to a thrust which he saw coming too late. The musketeer lunged and scored a hit. Unfortunately he lacked reach and could not press the blow hard enough. Nevertheless, Rauvin took an inch of steel in his left shoulder. His surprise and pain made him cry out. He stepped back in a panic, pressed one hand to his wound, and watched the blood trickling down over it with astonishment.

"Hurts, doesn't it?" said Leprat.

Humiliated and furious, Rauvin launched an assault so vigorous that the musketeer could only defend himself, parrying, dodging, and retreating, again and again. For too many long seconds, Leprat had to mobilise all of his strength and attention for the sole purpose of surviving, blocking, and deflecting attacks that became increasingly sly and dangerous. He was being overpowered. Which was as good as saying that he was vanquished in the long run, because eventually he would make a mistake.

So he was already seeking some way out when the course of the fight took a disastrous turn for the worse.

His rapier broke.

The steel snapped cleanly and most of the blade bounced on the marble floor with a clang. It was a moment of amazement for Rauvin, and absolute horror for Leprat . . .

. . . after which the hired swordsman smiled and resumed his attack with even greater energy than before.

Leprat leapt backward to avoid a cut, quickly stepped aside to stay clear of a thrust, and parried another with the remaining stub of his sword. Other desperate manoeuvres permitted him to stave off the inevitable. But he finally lost his balance and only managed to avoid falling thanks to his right hand, which reached out and grabbed the blade of his enemy. In spite of his glove, the steel cut viciously into the palm of his hand. The musketeer screamed in pain before retreating from Rauvin, who stalked toward him, jabbing with his rapier, his arm outstretched. Leprat reeled like a drunkard, unable to take his eyes off the metal point threatening him. Finally, he felt his calves bump against the rim of the central well and almost fell backward into it, in danger of being swallowed up by the shadowy void.

It was here that all strength abandoned him.

He fell to his knees and, with a confused gaze, watched Rauvin looming over him.

The mercenary was cold-bloodedly preparing to deliver the fatal blow.

So this is how it ends, Leprat thought to himself.

"Any last words?" asked Rauvin.

The musketeer somehow found the force to utter a painful snort and, in defiance, spat out some bloody phlegm.

"No? As you wish," said the hired swordsman. "Goodbye."

He lifted his arms up high, both hands gripping the pommel of his rapier, holding the weapon point downward, ready to plunge it into Leprat's unprotected chest . . .

. . . when someone said: "Just a moment."

Rauvin halted his gesture to glance over his shoulder . . . and saw Mirebeau.

Stunned by this development, he turned around.

It was indeed the gentleman in the beige doublet who had somehow risen from among the dead and, pale and bloody, approached with a stiff, hesitant step, his left arm held against his body and his right straining to lift his sword.

Leprat struggled to stand, leaning on the rim of the well.

"I wanted . . ." Mirebeau said to Rauvin. "I wanted . . ."

"What?"

"I wanted you to know who was going to kill you."

The mercenary sneered at this: Mirebeau was unable to even hold his rapier up, much less fight with it. . . . But the sneer vanished when Rauvin saw the gentleman suddenly lift the pistol held in his left hand.

The gun fired.

The ball hit Rauvin in the middle of his forehead and he fell over backward, arms extended, as Mirebeau sank to the floor in exhaustion.

Having made sure that the mercenary was quite dead, Leprat hurried over to the dying gentleman. He gently lifted his head. The other man could barely open his eyes.

The musketeer didn't know what to say. He could not utter any words at all, with his throat constricted and tears welling in his eyes.

"Th . . . thank you," he finally managed to croak.

Mirebeau nodded very faintly.

"A . . . A favour . . ." he murmured. "For me . . ."

"Ask it . . ."

"I do not . . . I do not . . . want . . . to die here . . . Please . . . Not here . . ."

Beneath the trees of the orchard at Dampierre a bitter fight had ensued during the fireworks display. The Blades and Savelda's mercenaries engaged one another while dazzling flashes accompanied by loud bangs lit up the foliage before gradually fading into flickers. The changing light sculpted their faces and silhouettes as the steel of their rapiers reflected back the same light as the blood of their wounds and the feverish gleam in their eyes.

A nasty kick and a two-handed blow with the pommel of his sword delivered between the shoulder blades allowed La Fargue to eliminate his first opponent. At last enjoying a moment's respite, he looked around him at the scene revealed by a crackling bouquet that illuminated the whole sky and dispersed into thousands of multicoloured sparkles.

Saint-Lucq, having coolly shot down, at close range, one of the three mercenaries who had rushed him at the beginning of the assault, was now battling the other two with his rapier, holding his pistol by the barrel in his left hand as a parrying weapon. He did not seem to be in any difficulty, in contrast to Laincourt, who, having received a pistol ball in the right shoulder, was backed up against a tree and defending himself as best he could. Fortunately Marciac had come to his aid and was fending off three men with his sword and dagger, despite a wound to the arm. The Alchemist had disappeared. But where was the queen?

La Fargue saw her.

Savelda was carrying her off toward the wooden walkway that crossed over the moat. Was the Black Claw's agent intending to reach the garden and then seek refuge in the castle? It would be like throwing himself into the wolf's jaws, but there was no time to ponder the matter.

"The queen!" La Fargue yelled, just before another mercenary engaged him in a duel. "Savelda has the queen!"

Only a short distance away in the orchard, Saint-Lucq heard his captain's call over the explosions of the fireworks. But he also heard an order to surrender. He had just eliminated a second opponent and, keeping the point of his elegant rapier pressed to the throat of the third, he glanced over his shoulder. Some musketeers were taking aim at him. . . .

Alerted by the sound of shots being fired, members of the King's Musketeers patrolling in the domain had rushed to the orchard.

"IN THE NAME OF THE KING, CEASE FIGHTING!"

La Fargue froze, having planted his sword to the hilt in the belly of a freebooter who now clung to him in a close embrace, glassy-eyed, and had started to drool a reddish foam. He allowed the dying man to sink to the ground as he freed his blade with a flick of his wrist and then looked around him.

The musketeers had already surrounded the site and, acting on the commands of their ensign, tightened their ring. They obviously intended to push everyone out from beneath the cover of the trees.

Savelda and the queen were almost at the small wooden bridge.

"THROW DOWN YOUR SWORDS AND SURRENDER!" the ensign ordered.

The fight had come to a halt but everyone present still hesitated. The threat of being shot down on the spot, however, overcame any inclination on the part of the Black Claw's mercenaries to resist further. Weakened by his wound, Laincourt was only too happy to slide down to the foot of the tree he had been leaning against . . . and then he passed out. Cautiously, La Fargue and Marciac resheathed their swords and slowly backed away from the musketeers, their arms extended from their bodies.

"IN THE SERVICE OF THE CARDINAL!" called the old gentleman, between two pyrotechnical explosions. "DON'T SHOOT!"

"WHO'S SPEAKING?" demanded the ensign, keeping his distance.

"CAPTAIN ÉTIENNE-LOUIS DE LA FARGUE."

"NEVER HEARD OF YOU!"

"MONSIEUR DE TRÉVILLE KNOWS ME."

But something else drew the young officer's attention.

"WHAT THE . . . YOU! HALT! DON'T MOVE!"

La Fargue was horrified to see several muskets turn away from Marciac and him to point instead at Savelda and the queen by the bridge. Anne d'Autriche seemed more dead than alive in the arms of the one-eyed man with the ranse.

"No!" exclaimed the captain of the Blades. "YOU RISK KILLING THE QUEEN!"

"YOU SHOULD LISTEN TO HIM!" cried Savelda as he retreated up the few short steps leading to the walkway.

The fireworks' grand finale was now bursting overhead. The rockets' explosions sounded like cannon fire and, in the deafening din, no one could be certain of being heard.

"HALT, OR WE'LL SHOOT!" warned the ensign.

"IT'S THE QUEEN!" La Fargue screamed. "BY ALL THE SAINTS, LISTEN TO ME! IT'S THE QUEEN!"

He tried to take a step forward to explain. Three muskets immediately took aim at his chest and forced him to stop.

Savelda and the queen were now crossing the bridge. They would soon be out of sight.

"MUSKETEERS, ON MY COMMAND!" ordered the young officer raising his hand.

"NO!" yelled La Fargue at the top of his lungs.

But the order he dreaded so much never came.

Bringing the fireworks to a culmination, two immense gold and blue comets exploded at the same time as dozens of more ephemeral stars. The lights dazzled everyone except Savelda, who had his back to the spectacle. The others averted their eyes, squinting or protecting them with their forearms.

It was the moment the Black Claw agent had been waiting for.

Pushing Anne d'Autriche over the railing on the left, he leapt over the one on the right. The two bodies splashed into the moat's deep waters only a second apart. That of the unconscious queen immediately began to sink.

Marciac was the first to react.

He took off running, making himself the target of a volley of musket fire, the balls buzzing past him as he dove into the moat. He vanished without it being clear whether or not he had been hit. Everyone present—La Fargue and the ensign leading the way—rushed to the edge of the steep ditch. The incandescent remains of the fireworks falling back to earth were reflected in the black waters while, at the other end of the castle, the duchesse's guests applauded the end of the display.

Unbearable seconds passed by as they all waited . . .

. . . until Marciac finally resurfaced holding the queen, who was coughing.

And therefore alive.

"Her Majesty is safe," the Gascon announced to the dumbfounded musketeers. "Could you lend me a hand? If you please?"

They hurried to assist him just as Almades and Tréville arrived from the garden along with more men in blue capes, the captain of the Musketeers quickly taking charge of the situation.

Unnoticed by anyone, La Fargue stood apart from the others and looked out at the orchard for a long while, hands on his hips. The queen had been saved and that was the main thing, but the Alchemist had once again escaped. . . .

Then he heard that two musketeers had been found unconscious among the fruit trees and, noticing that Saint-Lucq had also vanished, he smiled.

Saint-Lucq moved through the forest skirted by the road upon which the Alchemist's coach was travelling. He had heard the horse-drawn carriage leaving by way of the gate to the orchard and since then he had been following its progress by sound, pushing aside the low branches and eating up the distance with his steady, powerful strides. Thanks to the days spent watching the Dampierre domain, he knew which route the coach would be forced to use. Right now, the road curved around the woods while the half-blood was able to take a shortcut. The vehicle would have to slow down as it approached a small bridge, and that was where Saint-Lucq hoped to intercept it.

The trees became more spaced out as the noise of the carriage came closer. Saint-Lucq realised that he was in danger of arriving too late. He picked up his pace, plunging through the underbrush, and emerged from the forest, his face covered in scratches, only to see the coach disappearing over the bridge.

He'd missed it!

But the Alchemist was escorted by several riders, including one straggler who was only now arriving.

Saint-Lucq seized this last chance available to him. He did not slow down but instead adjusted his trajectory and gathered his momentum to take a flying leap from a mound close to the road. The rider never saw him coming. The horse whinnied and crashed to the earth in a great cloud of dust . . .

. . . and stood back up, full of fright, but now mounted by the half-blood who urged it to a gallop.

Inside the coach, instinct warned the Alchemist that he was in danger. Leaning his head out the passenger door, he looked back and saw Saint-Lucq hot on his trail.

"BACK THERE!" he alerted his escort, yelling to be heard over the thunderous hoofbeats and the creaking of the axles. "A RIDER! STOP HIM!"

Then he sat back and rapidly came to a decision.

Leaning forward, he opened a compartment beneath the bench opposite him and took out a case which he placed on his knees before opening its inlaid lid. Inside was a flask containing the liqueur of golden henbane.

He would have to transform himself.

His last metamorphosis, in Alsace, had exhausted him to the point that he was still unable to regain his primal form, but even an intermediate stage might be enough to save him now. He removed the stopper from the flask and greedily emptied its contents before he was overcome by a fit of coughing, shortly followed by violent pains.

Three riders on horseback were escorting the coach, one before and two behind. Warned by the Alchemist, those two slowed down to detain Saint-Lucq, who had already caught up with them. Shots were exchanged, using pistols that had been tucked into the saddle holsters. The half-blood came under fire first and responded in kind. He hit one of the mercenaries, who toppled out of his saddle. His companion fired at the half-blood in turn. The ball narrowly missed Saint-Lucq, who drew closer still. The other man then took hold of his second pistol and turned to shoot, but the Blade was quicker and succeeded in lodging a ball in the middle of his brow. The mercenary fell forward and was carried off into the distance by his mount.

Seeing the turn that events were taking, the coachman screamed and was heard by the rider galloping in front. The latter drew aside from the road and, hidden behind a thicket, allowed himself to be passed by. Saint-Lucq remained unaware of this trickery. He drew abreast of the horse belonging to the first mercenary he had shot and only had eyes for the pistol remaining in its saddle holster. He grabbed the weapon as he went by and tucked it into his belt, then spurred his own mount forward.

He caught up with the coach in the long dusty cloud raised by the hooves of the horses and the iron-rimmed wheels. He drew as close as possible, reached out his arm, found a handhold, and clambered onto the narrow platform used by the footman. He thought he could then catch his breath, but a detonation sounded and a ball smashed into the coach next to his head. Still hanging on, he turned to see the last escort rider coming up the road at breakneck speed, already brandishing his second pistol. The shot, luckily, misfired, the powder burning without exploding and the weapon only spitting out a jet of flame. The mercenary threw it away and drew his sword. Saint-Lucq did the same. A fight commenced between the two men. The half-blood only had the one handhold and one foot on the platform, and he found himself hanging halfway out over open space, at the rear of the coach whose jolting caused him to sway back and forth, thumping violently against the cabin. As for the rider, he was making wild slashes with his sword which Saint-Lucq sometimes parried and sometimes evaded by swinging a quarter turn to the left or right. But finally the half-blood struck back. Reaching out as far as he could, he planted the point of his blade into the mercenary's flank, who hiccupped and dropped his weapon in order to hold his belly with both hands. His horse slowed to a trot and then a walk, before coming to a halt as the coach vanished into the night.

Saint-Lucq replaced his rapier in its scabbard and took three deep breaths. He now needed to eliminate the coachman or at least force him to bring the carriage to a halt. Gripping the edge with both hands, he climbed up to the roof of the cabin and crawled over it facedown. Unable to leave his station, the coachman tried to drive him away him with blows from his whip. Saint-Lucq protected himself with his forearm before managing to seize the leather cord and pull the whip toward him. The coachman gave it up, too busy trying to negotiate a curve which the vehicle was approaching at excessive speed. It leaned dangerously and the two wheels that lifted off the ground on one side fell back with a thump that shook both the axles and Saint-Lucq. Sliding across the roof, the half-blood caught hold at the last second and found himself once again hanging from the rear of the coach.

There were a series of thuds coming from inside the cabin and a scaly fist punched through the roof once, twice, three times, until it shattered the wood completely. Then a creature, combining the features of both a man and a dragon, emerged from the cabin, forcing a passage with the help of its muscular shoulders. More than two metres in height, it stood up straight, screaming to the sky as it unfurled huge membranous wings. Stricken with panic by the sight, the coachman jumped from the vehicle. As for Saint-Lucq, he kept his wits. He understood that he was dealing with the product of an intermediate metamorphosis. The Alchemist was truly a dragon. It remained to be seen whether it was capable of regaining its primal form. For Saint-Lucq's sake, it would be better if it couldn't.

The creature looked down at the half-blood. If its features still evoked those of the Alchemist, the reptilian eyes blazed with a primitive, bestial fire.

It roared and abruptly took flight.

A riderless horse was still galloping alongside the coach. Saint-Lucq leapt toward it, managed to grab the pommel of the saddle with both hands, hit the ground with both feet together, and bounced back up to straddle the animal, which he promptly urged off the road in pursuit of the draconic creature. Seconds later, the runaway coach tipped over as it came to a bend in the road and broke apart with a crash, the team of horses whinnying as they fled.

Saint-Lucq's horse jumped a ditch, then a fence, and galloped through the fields. He kept his eyes on the creature whose scales glittered beneath the moon and the stars. He feared that he would soon be outdistanced. His horse was tired, not to mention the obstacles he was encountering on the ground. But he still had a pistol, the one he had snatched from the saddle holster as he passed and tucked into his belt.

Which meant he had one shot left.

One last hope.

Sensing it was being chased, the creature turned back and as if suspended in midair, it lingered for a moment, beating its wings and considering this miserable mortal determined to hunt it down. It hesitated. But a proud and ferocious instinct had already taken control of its mind, banishing all intelligent thought. It let out a great warlike scream and then dove toward the rider.

The creature and Saint-Lucq rushed at one another. The hybrid being came from above with great flaps of its wings, displaying vicious fangs and extended claws. The Blade was riding flat out, controlling his mount with his knees in order to hold the pistol with both hands. Neither of them was willing to turn aside. The creature gave another menacing scream. Saint-Lucq took careful aim. He needed to hold on until the last moment before firing.

To wait, hoping that his horse would not suddenly veer off . . .

To wait, just a little longer . . .

One shot. One hope.

Now!

Saint-Lucq pulled the trigger. For an awful instant, he was convinced it had misfired, but the gun went off just before the hybrid collided with him.

The impact was tremendous. It threw the half-blood out of his saddle and he rolled across the ground as the creature crashed a short distance away, and his horse continued its mad gallop.

Nothing moved and the nocturnal silence returned, disturbed only by the fading hoofbeats of the fleeing steed.

* * *

Saint-Lucq opened his eyes, spitting out blood and dirt, and stood up painfully on trembling legs. Drawing his sword, he turned around seeking any sign of danger and almost tripped over.

He saw the form lying on the ground and limped over to take a closer look.

It was the creature who, unconscious and bleeding from a pistol ball in the shoulder, was recovering a more human appearance. As Saint-Lucq watched, its size diminished, its wings atrophied, the scales were absorbed into smooth skin, and its features once again became those of the Alchemist.

The latter came to his senses and saw Saint-Lucq standing over him with a sword at his throat.

Bare-headed, Saint-Lucq was covered in dust and blood. A long lock of hair hung down before his bruised face. One of the lenses of his spectacles was missing, revealing a bloodshot draconic eye. He was struggling to remain on his feet and kept his left elbow tucked against his side to protect his damaged shoulder.

But his determination was made of the same steel as the blade of his elegant rapier.

"It's over," he said.

With Leprat supporting Mirebeau's weight, the two men returned to the surface by way of the foundations of the ancient tower. They emerged from the covered pit and remained for a moment, tottering but nevertheless standing, beneath the great starry sky, enjoying the cool air and the quiet of the night. Then Mirebeau, who was having more and more difficulty breathing, coughing up the blood filling his lungs, pointed to the outer wall of one of the pavilions under construction.

"Over there," he said. "That would be . . . good."

Leprat helped the gentleman walk to the spot he had chosen. He installed him against the wall, facing east, and sat down next to him.

"And now," said Mirebeau. "We only need . . . We only need to wait for the sun . . ."

He died a short while later.

Leprat still hadn't moved when dawn broke.

3

Afew days passed before La Fargue, for the second time in less than a fortnight, paid a visit to the Grand Châtelet. Accompanied by Almades, as always, he arrived by way of the Pont au Change, whose houses aligned on either side completely hid the Seine from view and gave one the impression of travelling down an ordinary street. The two men rode at a walk, side by side, in silence. It was late morning, on a sunny day, and Paris stank more than ever.

Nothing had filtered out concerning the plot that the Blades had thwarted and—it was hoped—nothing ever would. The scandal would be enormous. Although she had obviously been unaware that she was delivering herself into the hands of the Black Claw, Anne d'Autriche was nonetheless guilty of having wanted to subject herself, unbeknownst to the king and contrary to the laws of the kingdom, to a ritual involving draconic magic. Besides, like the duchesse de Chevreuse, most of those implicated in this affair believed they were doing no evil, having persuaded themselves—out of loyalty, affection, or naïvety—that they were secretly helping an unhappy and humiliated sovereign conceive an heir to the throne. Within the queen's entourage, no one knew what would have really happened if the queen had been successfully abducted by the Alchemist. . . .

La Fargue and Almades exchanged a look before they passed through Le Châtelet's dark archway. La Fargue guessed what the Spaniard was thinking and waited for him to say it out loud.

Although planned for some time, the wave of arrests ordered by the king on the day following that famous night had very opportunely dominated public attention ever since. The gazettes and the gossipmongers had discussed nothing else, in Paris, in France, and in the other princely courts throughout Europe.

The arrest that caused the most astonishment was that of the marquis de Châteauneuf, who was third personage of the State in his role as Keeper of the Seals. He was reproached for being too eager to succeed Richelieu in the post of chief minister to His Majesty, which was often the first step on the path leading to treasonous plots. But more to the point, he was accused of confiding State secrets to his mistress, the highly suspect duchesse de Chevreuse.

Some of those secrets concerned the citadels France was occupying in Lorraine. And there was also the matter of a French officer, an intimate friend of the marquis, who had been arrested recently, just before he could divulge information about the army the king was presently mustering. Thanks to the confessions of this officer, a trap had been set at an inn near Neuilly, but unfortunately it had not led to the arrest of any accomplices. Châteauneuf's guilt, however, had clearly been brought to light. He had been thrown into a prison from which he would not emerge for a long time, while others were also being dealt with by the king's justice. Convicted of having communicated State secrets, confided to her by the besotted marquis, to the duc de Lorraine, the duchesse de Chevreuse was of course one of them. But her rank still seemed to protect her, even if in truth she was skillfully negotiating the terms of her silence about what threatened to become the affair of the Dampierre ritual.

The two Blades dismounted in the courtyard of Le Châtelet and again La Fargue's eye met Almades's. This time, however, the fencing master asked: "What do you expect from this meeting, captain?"

"I don't know," the old gentleman admitted. "Answers, I think."

"Answers to which questions?"

He fell silent and the two men let themselves be led into the imposing tower that housed the prison.

Even if the duchesse managed to evade the full severity of the punishment she deserved in the Châteauneuf affair, La Fargue deemed that the greatest dangers of the Dampierre case had been averted. The queen was safe and the Black Claw mercenaries who had not been killed would never again see the light of day. To be sure, Savelda had escaped and could not be found. But the Alchemist was behind bars. As for the Blades, they had come out of the whole matter quite well. They had even acquired a new member, Laincourt, whose shoulder wound had not proved serious. Also slightly injured, Marciac was torn between two sentiments: joy at having held a queen of France in his arms and frustration at not being able to boast about it. Saint-Lucq had disappeared again and Agnès was occupied elsewhere after receiving a letter from the former Superior General of the Sisters of Saint-Georges. In the end, the captain was only worried about Leprat, who had returned from his mission looking much the worse for wear. Physically, but also mentally speaking.

At Le Châtelet, a gaoler opened a door on the level containing individual cells and stepped aside to allow La Fargue and Almades to enter. The room was cool, quite dark, and sparsely furnished with a table, a stool, and a bed. They found the Alchemist there, looking through an arched window defended by thick bars. As solemn and sinister as ever, he was dressed in grey, with a bandaged shoulder and his wrists bound by shackles made of a steel alloy containing draconite, the alchemical stone that inhibited the power of dragons.

The Alchemist's thin, scarlike mouth twisted into a strange smile as he turned toward his visitors.

"How kind of you to accept my invitation, captain."

The first person to raise an alarm was a ditch digger who, looking up at the sky, could not at first believe his eyes, but then ran to the nearest village. He arrived frightened and out of breath, hammered at the door of the presbytery, and then had trouble making himself understood by the parish priest. The latter also had difficulty believing the news. The man's eyes had played a trick on him. Or he had been drinking. But other witnesses arrived soon afterward.

They had also seen it.

They were also afraid.

The priest decided to ring the church bells.

Looking out the window of his private office, the comte de Tréville looked out over the courtyard of his mansion in the rue du Vieux-Colombier for a long while. Then he turned away and asked Leprat: "Have you truly made up your mind?"

"Yes, monsieur."

The captain of the King's Musketeers seated himself at his desk and granted himself a few more moments of reflection. He used this time to examine Leprat, who stood at attention without blinking, with his ivory rapier at his side and his right hand wrapped in a bandage.

"Don't misunderstand me," Tréville said at last. "I ask for nothing more than to see you wear the blue cape once again. Indeed, no one is more worthy of wearing it. . . ."

"Thank you, monsieur."

"But I know what the Blades represent in your eyes. And I also know the respect and the friendship you have for monsieur La Fargue. . . . Have you told him of your decision?"

"I shall tell him this evening, along with the other Blades."

"It won't be easy."

"I know."

At the Hôtel de Chevreuse, Arnaud de Laincourt joined the duchesse on the large terrace. Still looking pale, he had his arm in a sling. As for the duchesse, she was no less beautiful or less elegant than usual, but she was alone and wore a grave expression on her face. She stood beneath a canopy that shaded chairs and a table bearing untouched delicacies: crackers, cakes, marzipans, fruit jellies, preserves, and syrups. In her hand she had a liqueur glass filled with golden henbane and, from the gleam in her eye, Laincourt guessed she had already been partaking of it immoderately.

She held out her hand to be kissed and then said: "So, you never stopped being an agent of the cardinal, monsieur de Laincourt. . . ."

"No, madame."

"Well, it's only fair, I suppose. . . . In contrast to the marquis de Châteauneuf, who wanted to recruit you, monsieur de Mirebeau never believed it would be possible to win you over to our cause. He said the cardinal is a master one never ceases to serve."

"No doubt he's right."

"Do you know what became of him? Was he arrested?"

"Mirebeau? No. He's dead, madame."

"Oh! That's a pity, isn't it?" said madame de Chevreuse in the same tone she might have employed to regret the loss of beautiful rosebushes killed by frost.

Laincourt did not reply and together they turned toward the magnificent garden.

"I must thank you for agreeing to visit me, monsieur. No one knocks at my door anymore, you know? All those fine people who danced at my ball and applauded my fireworks now avoid me as if I had the ranse. . . . But I've long been accustomed to changes in fortune at court and I wait patiently to learn the fate in store for me. It will be exile, won't it?"

"Probably, yes."

"And what about poor old Châteauneuf?"

"I doubt he will ever emerge from His Majesty's prisons."

"Exile . . ." sighed the duchesse, her eyes lost in contemplation.

A lackey brought, upon a tray, a box covered with a piece of cloth. He stood there waiting patiently for his mistress to notice him.

"Ah!" she said at last. "This is why I asked you to come see me. Take it, monsieur. It's for you."

Intrigued, Laincourt picked up the box, but waited until the lackey turned away before opening it. It contained a letter—which was addressed to him—and a small painted portrait.

"The letter," indicated madame de Chevreuse, "is from madame de Saint-Avold, who, for reasons you must be aware of, has been obliged to return to her native Lorraine with all due haste."

The portrait was also of Aude de Saint-Avold. The same one the duchesse had commissioned in order to show her master of magic how much, if the upper part of her face were masked, the beautiful Aude resembled the queen: they had the same eyes, the same mouth, the same chin, the same throat.

"Please accept this gift from me, monsieur. For if I have many faults, above all I suffer from that of loving love."

Laincourt accepted it, feeling moved.

Bells were ringing in the distance and the sound seemed to be drawing closer, but the Blade and the duchesse paid it no heed.

"Goodbye, monsieur de Laincourt. I doubt that we will meet again for a long time."

"Goodbye, madame. But—"

"Yes, monsieur?"

"Would you agree to answer a question?"

"Is it a question the cardinal is asking through you?"

"No, madame."

"Then I will answer."

Laincourt took a breath and then asked: "Why, madame? Why did you wish to help the queen to conceive a child? Your hatred of the cardinal is a secret to no one. And, for reasons that are strictly yours, you do not seem to like our king at all. And a throne without an heir means no end of pretenders and opportunists willing to scheme and rise up against your enemies. By favouring the birth of an heir apparent, you would have strengthened the throne and consolidated Louis' reign."

The duchesse smiled.

"You forget, monsieur, the affection I have for the queen, and how painful it is for me to see her so unhappy and so often humiliated. . . . And then there was that night when, as a game, I encouraged her to run through the Grande Salle at the Louvre. If not for me, she would not have tripped against the platform. If not for me, she would not have fallen. And if not for me, three days later she would not have lost the child she was carrying. A boy, apparently. . . . And while the queen forgave me, I never could forgive myself. . . . So, when the man I believed to be a wise master of magic confided to me that he could . . ."

Overcome by emotion, she could not finish.

Then she exclaimed: "Those bells are going to drive us all mad!"

To the bells ringing in the faubourgs, were now added several more in the neighbourhood of Saint-Thomas-du-Louvre.

It was both unusual and disquieting.

Laincourt lifted his eyes to the sky just as a great shadow passed overhead.

Leprat descended the great staircase in the Hôtel de Tréville when he suffered an attack. He was suddenly very hot, his vision blurred, and, realising what was happening, he murmured: "Oh, Lord! Not here . . ."

In a sweat, staggering, he bumped into a musketeer who was coming up the stairway, tried to grab hold of another, and only managed to tear the man's sleeve as his legs gave way beneath him.

He tumbled to the bottom of the steps and lay there, convulsing.

A crowd gathered round him. A few men seized hold of his limbs to restrain them. They also attempted to slide a belt between his jaws to save his tongue.

"A doctor. Someone fetch a doctor!"

And while he arched his back, moaning, a black bile began to flow from between his grimacing lips.

"It's the ranse!" one man exclaimed. "He's been stricken by the Great ranse."

"The poor wretch . . ."

"Do you hear that?" said another. "It sounds like the tocsin."

Close by, the bells of the Saint-Germain-des-Prés abbey were pealing.

An immense, terrifying, winged shadow settled upon the prison at Le Châtelet. In the Alchemist's cell the light suddenly dimmed, while a booming roar shook the walls. Outside, all the bells in Paris were ringing.

La Fargue turned toward the darkened window . . .

. . . and saw the great black dragon that faced him, opening its menacing jaws ready to breath fire. . . .

He faced it, frozen in awe.

4

The young Chatelaine who, torch in hand, was the first to enter the dark corridor was both worried and in a hurry. Behind her, Agnès de Vaudreuil seemed more assured, although all her senses were on edge too.

In coming this far, she had scrupulously respected the warnings to be cautious addressed to her by Emmanuelle de Cernay, the former Superior General of the Sisters of Saint Georges. In a letter that Agnès had found upon her return from Dampierre, Mère Emmanuelle informed her that she had been unable to discover what had become of the chevalier Reynault d'Ombreuse, the son of the gentleman who had asked the Blades for help. On the other hand, she had uncovered the identity of the sister Reynault and a detachment of Black Guards had accompanied to Alsace on their secret mission: Sœur Béatrice d'Aussaint. As well as where she could now be found. She and the baronne de Vaudreuil had undergone their novitiates together. They were friends, or they had been. Strangely, Sœur Béatrice was now being held in isolation, like a prisoner, on the orders of the current Superior General, the formidable Mère Thérèse de Vaussambre.

Advancing along the corridor on tiptoe, Agnès was led to a door. The Chatelaine guiding her looked furtively to the left and right before pushing it open and then moving aside.

"Be quick," she murmured. "They could discover that I took the keys at any moment."

Agnès nodded and entered.

It was an ordinary convent cell, austere and lacking in any comforts. She saw Sœur Béatrice lying on the narrow bed. Pale and with drawn features, she remained beautiful but seemed worn out. She was a mere shadow of the superb, proud Chatelaine who, early one morning in a corner of Alsace, had stood alone against a great dragon with a draconite blade in her hand and an incantation on her lips.

She was asleep.

Agnès removed the great black cloak with a hood that had hidden her head, then sat by the sleeping woman and touched her hand.

The sister opened blind eyes, filled with a glassy whiteness.

"Agnès? Is that you, Agnès?"

"Yes, Béatrice. It's me."

"Lord be praised! My prayers are answered at last!"

"My God, Béatrice, your eyes! What happened to you?"

"It's nothing. Nothing but the price of . . . It won't last, I believe."

"The price of what?"

"You need to know, Agnès. You need to see what I have seen!" said the Chatelaine in an anguished voice.

She wanted to sit up in her bed. Agnès gently held her down and said: "Calm yourself, Béatrice. You need to rest. I'll come back later."

"No!" cried out the other woman. "Now! It can't wait . . . ! Give me your hands, Agnès." The young baronne obeyed. "And now, see . . . See," she repeated in a weaker tone. "You need . . . to see."

Her white eyes darkened as if injected with a black liquid.

An abyss was born into which Agnès's awareness suddenly plunged.

And she *saw*.

She saw what the Chatelaine had seen that morning in Alsace when she looked into the mind of the dragon.

She saw glimpses of a future that was both terrifying and close at hand.

It was night. Panicked crowds were running through streets lit by crackling flames. Fire was raining from the sky. It was being belched by a black dragon. Or by several. Fiery blasts were striking the rooftops; dazzling columns provoked explosions of tiles; red-hot sprays fell back in incandescent particles. Screaming, terrorised people were jostling, fighting, and trampling one another in their desire to flee. Some soldiers were firing their muskets futilely into the air. Human torches wriggled and thrashed horribly. The blazes consumed entire neighbourhoods and the immense conflagration was reflected in the dark waters of a river.

A river that ran past the Louvre, which had also been set alight.

Trembling, her eyes full of tears, Agnès watched Paris burn.

ABOUT THE AUTHOR

PIERRE PEVEL, born in 1968, is one of the foremost writers of French fantasy today. The author of seven novels, he was awarded the Grand Prix de l'Imaginaire in 2002 and the Prix Imiginales in 2005, both for best novel.